This Eternity

Richard Wilks Taylor

First published in Great Britain in 2016 by Jojosala Publishing Ltd.

Copyright © 2016 by Richard Wilks Taylor

Cover illustrations by Ivan Zanchetta
www.ivanzanchetta.com

Interior illustration of the boys by Cody Kuehl
www.facebook.com/cody.kuehl.9

Cover illustration Includes modified stock imagery copyright
GaryCantrell,Village near Kontum, 1 January 1971,
https://flic.kr/p/nPTnnf available to share without fee under
license from creativecommons.org

Embedded correspondence by Richard Wilks Taylor

Richard Wilks Taylor has asserted his moral right to be identified as the
author of this work.

A CIP catalogue record of this book is available from the British Library.

ISBN: 978-0-9576996-8-7 (Paperback)
ISBN: 978-0-9576996-9-4 (EPub Edition)

First Edition

For Mary,

My friend and lover, who puts up with me

Beyond the Epilogue, interested readers will find:

THESE SOULS — short biographical sketches of the villagers

THOSE OTHERS — a list of characters and their relationships

THESE WORDS — a glossary that includes military jargon

THESE THANKS — I could not have done this alone

Richard W. Taylor

10 August 2015

Contents

THIS PROLOGUE

When the prison doors are opened, the real dragon will fly out.

—Hồ Chí Minh

27 May 2000

Vietnam War Memorial, Washington, DC

"Smells brings it back for me. I 'member my niece born. I 'member 'Bye, Bye, American Pie' blarin' on the AM in my '71 Vega up to Bradenton. Grandma in Bradenton."

He looked around. "Anyone listenin'? Rest of the time my brain's all wrapped up with other shit, all muddled up, like that first cat tongue lick on the cheek. Shit like that sardine stink. Every time I think of that stink, I 'member the time I tried to hide 'em under the tablecloth. Make a big greasy spot. Hope she don't notice. Prob'ly still there. Fuckin' Grandma. One of the best things growin' up is you don't have to eat no fuckin' sardines."

He chuckled again, to himself this time. He disappeared deep inside as the smile washed from his face. A tear formed at the corner of his eye.

He closed his eyes and drifted away. A minute passed. He was a greasy, grimy, disheveled mime, vertical like a statue—asleep on his feet. Then, like a toy with a switch, he came to life again. He took a step toward the marble and pointed as if speaking to an engraved name. "Smells brings it back. Fuckin sardines. Fuckin Blue said it smelt like tuna fish. Not to me. Fuckin' sardines."

He scanned for onlookers, then raised his voice. "Sometimes when I stomp on a juicy fat palmetto bug—you know, roach—that smell. I'm gonna puke right now. Fuckin' Nam. Not the killing or the other shit, the fuckin' smells. Next time you stomp on a fat roach, pick that mutha up and bring it real close to your nose." He pantomimed with his right hand. "That yellow stuff, roach guts I guess. Smell all its own."

As if on a soapbox with a willing audience, he raised his arms to the sky, drawing them in. Names on black granite. "If you do that, I guarantee you the rest of time when you get that whiff of fuckin' stomped roach, you gonna fuckin' 'member when you put that baby up to your nose and took a whiff. And you smell your fingers right then and you swear you can still smell that fucker. Nothin' else like it. Well, almost nothing."

Aqualung was sitting dead center on the gray granite chunks of the walkway in front of the memorial—right where the names go from right-justified to left-justified. He cracked a smile. "Fuck outta my way, dude. I never put one of those bugs at my nose, but you didn't have to in Nam. Ever drive in that monsoon? Remember them fuckin' rice beetles? After rains, the streets was covered in them giant fuckin' rice beetles. Giant fuckin' rice roaches!"

The man saw Aqualung in his peripheral vision, the only audience he could discern. But he wasn't looking for an audience. He was inside himself. Him and black stone. He paused for a minute, lost in a passing thought. It was a rant. It was a ramble. It was under his breath. A mumble really. And barely audible.

"Fuckin' A right! Yum! Right? Rice beetles are them Godzilla fuckin' roaches with claws like tiny lobsters. Live in paddies I s'pose, so I don't get why they come out in floods. That monsoon. When them Jeep tires squash them rice beetles they have that same yellow guts you can only find in good old American roaches. Florida roaches. The best are them palmetto bugs all over Okeechobee. So when I get a whiff to this day, right fuckin' now, *bam!* There's Nam. And up comes a little puke right here in my throat." He gagged while putting two dirty fingers into the back of his mouth.

"And it brings up some wicked memories. Like when fuckin' Mesner got hit in the head by that big chunk of Mister Land Mine. Some kind of slow motion silent movie. I swear I could see this big chunk of steel come sailing at his head right when he was turning to yell something. *Bam!* This big chunk sailed right into the back of fuckin' Mesner's head. Missed his steel pot. Didn't miss his head."

He teared up again. He spread his hands on the wall over a half dozen names. "I shit you not—he was looking right at me. Really fuckin' surprised. And the thought I had right then was the stupidest fuckin' thing. And every time I think of that motherfuckin' Mesner losing the top of his head, I think of that same thing. I think I'm that Secret Service motherfucker diving to catch that chunk of Kennedy's head when it sails off the trunk of that convertible. I get Mesner's head all mixed up with that fuckin' Zapruder film. And it really pisses me off, because I should be able to just 'member Mesner, not JFK. But I didn't dive for that piece of Mesner's head, because I was starting to feel weak. Weak in the knees. Collapse like."

Two vets nearby turned their heads when the quiet ranting stopped. The man wandered off again, a wind-up toy out of juice, lost in a meandering train of disjointed thoughts and unintelligible drivel. Then, as if waking up from a bad dream, he shook his head and spewed another stream of regurgitated memories. The two vets stepped around Aqualung and gave the wild man space.

"Least it wasn't fuckin' roach guts. Those motherfuckin' slopes did that. It's the smells brings it back. When Mesner got scalped, I was fuckin' wearing his head. I was wearing the inside of his motherfuckin' head. Little bits of bone all mixed up with blood like a ski mask all over my face, my hair. And this jelly stuff. Brains, I guess. And I was screaming, so it was all in my mouth. And kind of like when you take a sip of milk just when someone cracks something funny in the mess hall and you get it up your nose. I got Mesner's blood and brains and maybe some of his snot up my nose. Never gonna forget that smell."

He looked around. "Go ahead, smell your fingers. See if you can conjure up that juicy roach. Don't need no roach smell for me to remember Nam. Me? I've got Mesner's brain in my nose for fuckin' ever."

He wiped away tears. Turning to his left, he was surprised to find Aqualung staring. He said, "Fuck you lookin' at? Go ahead, smell your fingers. See if you can conjure up that juicy roach. I got Mesner in my nose for fuckin' ever. That's what brings back Nam for me. And you know what that smells like? Not fuckin' Nam, but that jelly they used to call Mesner's head. Sort of like a dumpster behind that hamburger stand. Like that. Like that, just after they empty that fuckin' dumpster on a hot day. And its leakin' shit, kinda brown liquid milky sort of shit. There's lots of dumpsters around and lotsa hot summer days. So I get to remember Nam a lot."

Looking at no one in particular, he added, "Right? Am I right? Fuckin' Nam. Fuckin' dinks."

He turned and almost tripped and fell over someone. Like when a kid gets in your personal space, but you don't see him, and you have to hold him up while you fight to keep your balance. But this was no kid. It was a short man. He might have been Filipino.

"Fuck outta my way dude," he said to the little man.

The man ignored him and instead held up a hand as if he was stopping traffic. He said, "I know who you are and I know what you did."

"I'm only gonna say this one more time. Fuck outta my way, 'cause I don't know who the fuck you are. And I don't give a fuck what you did."

"I know who *you* are. I know what you did."

"Fuck outta my way, flip."

28 May 2000
Somewhere near Washington, DC

The last thing he remembered was sitting on a brass-clad stool in an upscale Georgetown bar. A fan of craft beer, he was nursing his third or fourth. He'd been laughing out loud with a newfound acquaintance, a DC lawyer dressed to the nines in an Italian-tailored suit. It made him think of high-powered lobbyists—suits that fit. In fact, as he looked around the bar he guessed he had about a four out of five shot of talking to a lawyer, male or female. He felt out of place in his cowboy boots, but the beer was fine and the scenery was great. He could see his hog through the picture window safely parked perpendicular to the curb.

He and his new friend were exchanging inebriation-fueled snickers over the sight of a beautiful woman. She was not only a little drunk but evidently fond of the young buck sitting by her side. A betting man would have placed a wager on full-blown public sex, but for now she was enjoying herself with a few discreet grinds on the leather-covered cushion of the bar stool. She was unaware of the spectacle she was making or the audience enjoying life at her expense.

In those few seconds it was great looking back. And he might have even enjoyed it under different circumstances. But these were tough times. He had a bad feeling about his current condition. With more time to think he could have made some guesses about how he'd gotten here. As it was, he was utterly terror-stricken.

He had awakened lying on his back in a locker room with a

rifle barrel down his throat. He'd known where he was even before he'd opened his eyes—he played football in high school, and he recognized the smell of Bengay and a coach's stale cigar. He cracked his eyes, and in the edge of his vision he could just make out green vinyl. He was on a trainer's table. He couldn't make out more of the room because of the light in his eyes--a clamp-on job, like the light he used when he worked on his bike after dusk began to settle outside his garage.

He couldn't hold back a terrible gag reflex. It was like when he was a kid. His mother had always made him eat Brussels sprouts at Thanksgiving. Less eating and more retching. And he had always been able to get a free trip to the school nurse by putting a finger down his throat. So the metal thing forced deep into his esophagus was causing him some serious issues. He had a flash of some poor soul waking in the operating room with tubes stuck in every orifice. But this was no operating room. People could die here. He could die here.

He looked behind, since that was the only direction available —stretched back, neck tendons bulging, duct tape over his forehead pulling his head secure to the table legs. It was futile; he couldn't get a good look at his assailant. All he could make out was a tripod rigged with a "C" clamp that held the butt end of a rifle. Small caliber. It was adjusted so that with his head contorted back as far as it would go while lying on his back, the rifle was parallel to the ground and the trainer's table. For an instant he thought he might be able to scoot forward enough, scrunch his butt just enough, to get the barrel out of his throat. But he was tightly secured to the table and could move no more than a half inch, not nearly enough to work free of the length of steel down his throat.

This all went through his mind in fewer than five seconds of situational assessment. Then he was the personification of panic. His eyes bugged out in a sort of mock hyperthyroidism; they were the only parts of his body not held tight.

He screamed. He screamed bloody murder, a response that was appropriate considering the circumstances. But all that came out was a retch, the sound of puking. He wanted to puke, but in his position, it just wasn't possible. Good thing. He might have drowned.

Time passed. He cried. He sobbed, complete with quivering chin.

Time passed. He had to get rid of a couple of beers.

Time passed and he heard nothing. Nothing.

He discovered he could doze off. So he did.

He awoke to the sound of soft soles on what must be a concrete floor. That was when the real terror began.

He could see a leather jacket, and a single hand clad in a black leather glove. In the hand was a magazine, but because of the bright light he couldn't make out the photo. A second gloved hand adjusted the light to remove the glare.

It was a faded but still slick magazine cover. A single finger pointed at it. He looked, and he knew his wild eyes betrayed his fear and recognition.

He prayed he'd die of fright.

When the assailant pulled the trigger, he was surprised to

feel only the sensation of indigestion, acid reflux. That was the last thing. The last.

THIS BAD AND THAT GOOD

*If time is not real,
then the dividing line between this world and eternity,
between suffering and bliss,
between good and evil,
is also an illusion.*
—Herman Hesse

*History will have to record that the greatest tragedy
of this period of social transition
was not the strident clamor of the bad people,
but the appalling silence of the good people.*
—Martin Luther King, Jr.

CHAPTER 1

22 June 1950

DeSoto County Courthouse, Arcadia, Florida

Juvenile Court Judge Andrew Miller walked in through a side door into a room reserved for these cases. No one stood. No bailiff announced the judge's presence. No *All Rise*, just a somber start to a sad proceeding. After shuffling some papers he'd taken from a red cardboard accordion file, Judge Miller glanced down his nose over his reading glasses and said to no one in particular, "What's going on?"

Attorney Robert Hagen had been representing young men and women before the juvenile court in DeSoto County for the five years since the war ended. Judge Miller knew full well he was the advocate, but the formality was important to create a complete and accurate court record.

"Your Honor, Robert Hagen, present to advocate for this delinquent, though I really think *advocate* is the wrong word since I have never seen anything so disgusting in my eleven years before the bench."

Judge Miller removed his glasses. "Bob, did you really just

say that? JoEllen, don't record that response. Just make it right for the record."

Mr. Hagen replied, "Apologies, Your Honor. JoEllen, off the record please. This kid is the Prince of Evil."

Judge Miller panned over to the young man and then looked the boy's mother up and down. Turning back to the defendant, he said, "Lionel, what are you doing back here? I told you if you came back it was not going to be a picnic."

Lionel Rook shifted in his chair but did not straighten up. He mumbled something unintelligible.

His mother pulled him up by his collar and necktie. She slapped him on the back of the head, spit into her hand, and while trying to smooth a cowlick on Lionel's fire-red hair, said, "You best be respectful of His Honor or he's gonna throw the book at you." Her smile told Lionel she didn't mean it.

Judge Miller asked, "Lionel, how old are you?"

Lionel raised his head only enough to look at the bench, not at the judge. "Thirteen."

"Thirteen what?" the judge asked.

"Just thirteen."

"Lionel, remind me. When you were here last," the judge shuffled through some papers, "on March twelfth, didn't we have a discussion about how to address this court?"

Lionel wasn't interested. "I don't remember."

Judge Miller glared. "It's 'Thirteen, *Your Honor.*' I'll even settle for 'Thirteen, *sir.*' Do you understand, Lionel?"

"I guess so, sir."

Judge Miller then turned to Mr. Hagen. "Bob, let's go ahead and summarize the case for the record."

"Yes, Your Honor." Mr. Hagen opened a red legal-sized folder filled with an inch and a half of paper all bound at the top with a two-hole metal clasp. He flipped to the second or third page.

"Last Saturday, on the seventeenth of June, Your Honor, Mrs. Sadler—"

The judge interrupted. "Mildred Sadler?"

"Yes, Your Honor. Mrs. Mildred Sadler was looking for her dog, that little white Pomeranian she's always walking around town."

"I love that little dog," the judge said. "She always has that red leash and collar with all the rhinestones."

Mr. Hagen looked up. "Off the record JoEllen—Your Honor, I'm afraid you're going to have to visit him in the pet cemetery. Lionel killed him."

Judge Miller knew the case from the brief, so he was nonplussed. "Go on, but while you're at it, let's all try to remember you're the advocate."

"Apologies for showing my disgust, Your Honor." Mr. Hagen returned to his notes. "As I said, Mrs. Sadler was looking for her dog. It had been yapping in the back yard, and then everything got quiet. He was gone. Mrs. Sadler stepped out to find him. She was walking down Seminole Street next to the orange grove, the one by the Texaco station, and saw one Lionel Rook kneeling between the road and the first row of trees. She called out to him, 'Have you seen my dog?' Lionel looked up. He had blood on his hands and lap. Hidden behind his thigh and bent knee was Mrs. Sadler's dog.

Thankfully, it was dead, Your Honor, probably bled to death. Lionel had a pair of pruning shears in his bloody hands. One by one, he had cut all the dog's feet off."

The judge looked over his reading glasses and glared at Lionel.

"He was trying to run away!" Lionel said, as if in his warped sense of reality cutting a dog's feet off to keep them close was a normal practice.

Although the judge had read the brief, this was the first time that JoEllen, the court stenographer, had heard any of the details. She asked Judge Miller if they could stop for a minute. Even blood made her feel faint, but this… She turned her head to the side and worked to hold back a little nausea. Tears ran down her cheeks.

What's the big fuckin' deal? It's a fuckin' dog. Got caught. Big deal. Shoulda gone off in the grove. Little dogs is strong. Shit, that one almost got away. Tie him up next time. Like them Okeechobee rodeo cowboys. Sling that twine around the legs. Hang 'em up. 'Bout had it up to here with Hagen. His rug rat in second grade over there at Millwood. Could cut his feet off. Need something better'n snips. Pickers left that rusty saw in the grove. That'd work. Have to tie him up.

Lionel glanced over at the bailiff. *'Bailiff', what kinda word is that? 'Nother name for nigger? That nigger better not touch me again. Needs some bare wires on his privates. Fuckin' dog. Who gives a shit? Fuckin' judge. He don't give a good goddamn, just his job. Guess it's against the law or some such.*

The judge tossed Lionel a disgusted look. "Are you ready to continue, JoEllen?"

"Yes, Your Honor," she sobbed, her chin quivering.

In Judge Miller's court, which was not long on burden of proof, Lionel's statement constituted admission of guilt. The judge scowled at Lionel. "To echo the words of your advocate, I must agree, son, this is one of the most disgusting acts that has ever come into my courtroom. What in the tarnation were you thinking?"

"I guess I'm supposed to be sorry, Your Honor, but he was running away." Lionel cocked his head a little and produced a smirk.

Judge Miller said, "It's a little late for 'sorry,' son. Mrs. Sadler has to live the rest of her life thinking about how you tortured her puppy. I don't even want to think about what happened after you took the first foot off."

Fuck's the matter with this guy? It's a dog.

"It's a small dog, Your Honor. He don't move much when you hold him tight." He lifted his right leg. "Gotta get your leg over like this—"

"Shut up, Lionel," the judge said.

"Okay."

"Okay what?"

"Okay, I'll shut up."

JoEllen's chin quivered, big shakes now. She released an audible moan. And the judge followed suit with his own moan, but for a different reason.

For more than a minute the judge stared silently through the half-open venetian blinds out into the sunlit park next to the courthouse. "What grade are you in, Lionel?" the judge asked at last.

For the first time, Lionel got the idea that this might not

turn out as it had last March. Everyone knew about Chad Peterson, who had died in reform school somewhere upstate. "I just got done with seventh grade." Lionel's eyes glassed over, fixed on the specks in the linoleum. "Uh, sorry. I just finished the seventh grade, Your Honor."

Fuckin' Hagen. Fuckin' Hagen. What's fucking Hagen got against me? Dogs and cats all over the grove. Gone missin'. No one gives a shit. Why the judge give a shit? Fuck that. Shoulda looked all over the groves. Stopped burying them. Why do these fuckers care? No summer? Whaddya mean no summer? School? Mom, stop spittin' on my head. That disgustin'.

In the back of the chamber, sitting by himself, was Mr. James Armstrong, the County Truancy Officer. The judge looked over to him. "Jim, what can you tell me about Master Rook's record of school attendance?"

Mr. Armstrong spoke up. "Your Honor, for a boy so young, Lionel Rook is one of the worst offenders in the county."

The bailiff interrupted. "Please step before the bench when you address the judge."

Mr. Armstrong knew better. He walked up the center aisle and through the swinging wooden gates. "His mother don't have no home phone, so the principal out at Arcadia Junior High would have to send a runner to the house to learn of Lionel's whereabouts. One time he was actually out sick, but…" Mr. Armstrong looked at the clipboard he was holding and flipped a few pages up. "But only that once. I have twenty-six unexplained absences from school during seventh grade alone."

"Is that a lot?" the judge asked, knowing the answer.

"Your Honor, school is only in session a hundred and eighty days a year, so, yes, that's a lot. On three occasions I found him out walking around town. Your Honor, I have his elementary school record here as well."

Saw that motherfucker drive by a hundred times. He never saw me in the grove. Indigo snake. Man, that was a beauty.

The judge waved him off. "That won't be necessary." He turned his gaze back to the boy. "Lionel, it's good you completed your first year of junior high, but I talked to your teachers. You barely made it without flunking. Maybe if you hadn't been absent so much, you'd have done better."

The judge flipped through the file from front to back. That took about five minutes while everyone maintained their positions, Mr. Armstrong standing next to Bob Hagen.

Finally the judge looked up. "Lionel, for eighth grade I am going to send you to a different school where it will be a little harder to skip. In fact, you're going to start in the summer session. This week."

Lionel perked up, but he still had no idea what was coming. "It's summer vacation. No one's at school just now. I can wait till it starts back up in September."

The Judge didn't respond. Instead he looked at Lionel's mother. He expected some emotion from her, but he was met with a bewildered stare. "Mrs. Rook, this court orders your son, Lionel Bodean Rook, to spend a minimum of one year at the Florida Industrial School for Boys in Marianna. One year from today you will return to this court. We will then discuss Lionel's record at the school, and I will make a determination as to whether he can return to Arcadia."

It was a little late, but a tear formed in Mrs. Rook's eye. "Is that far away, Your Honor? Will I be able to visit?"

"It is far away, Mrs. Rook—up by Tallahassee. As far as visiting, you'll have to take that up with school officials. Lionel is remanded to custody of the state of Florida. We will transport him to the school before the end of the week."

Mrs. Rook, now crying, said, "Can I go with him?"

The judge replied, "Mr. Hagen can give you all the details. If you choose to make the trip to Marianna, you will do so at your own expense. But you may decide it's not much worth it because you'll only be able to say goodbye to him when he gets off the state bus, before he enters school grounds. I suggest you make your goodbyes now."

What're they talkin' about? Goodbye? I ain't goin' nowhere. Summer school? Fuck that.

It was clear that neither Lionel nor his mother had had any idea that this might be the result of this court appearance. Mrs. Rook was still crying, but she managed to hit Lionel on the back of the head one last time. "You idiot!" Then she turned to the bench. "Your Honor, is this *reform school?*"

"It is, Mrs. Rook, and God help us that it reforms your son." Judge Miller pursed his lips, paused a moment and declared with a bang of the gavel, "Juvenile Court is dismissed."

24 June 1950
Florida Industrial School for Boys, Marianna, Jackson County, Florida

Still don't know if my mama is comin' up. Never been away from my mama. Don't cry. That bus driver'll think you're a fairy. Hot as shit in here. What kind of bus is this anyway? Bars on the windows? Some kinda rolling jail. Reform school? Can't be. Chad Peterson. Pissed on me once in the john. Said I was looking at him. Asshole. He deserved to die. Reform school? Pissed on someone in reform school maybe. They killed him. Brother's still cryin'. Fairy. Seats too short to sleep. Floor smells like piss. Gotta piss. Crack by the 'mergency door. It'll flow out there.

"Don't you dare!"

It was the first time Lionel had any idea the bus driver even knew he was there.

"If you take a leak in this bus, I will make you lick it up with your tongue."

"I gotta use the bathroom, mister."

"I do not give a shit. Hold it. We'll be stopping in a half hour or so. You can go then."

Four hundred miles in a school bus would wear anyone out. Lionel Rook was no exception. Just Lionel, the driver, and a white, locked bus. They stopped in Perry, Florida to pick up a fifteen-year-old boy who Lionel learned was Nathan Belford. Nathan was going to repeat ninth grade for the third time in Marianna. He had stolen a can of Hershey's syrup from the local grocery store. On the surface, a tiny infraction, but for his father it must have been the last straw, because he asked the County Juvenile Court to send Nathan to reform school. The judge complied. Nathan would be home for next year's summer vacation if he behaved himself.

It was not quite dusk when Nathan and Lionel stepped off the bus. Even with the barred windows down, it was a hundred degrees and a hundred percent humidity—a Florida oven. They were glad for a little fresh air. A swarm of interested mosquitos found the two in short order. While they were slapping left and right, a red-faced, heavy old man stepped out of a reception building. Corralling the boys with a hand lightly on their backs, he said, "Gentlemen, welcome! Welcome to the Florida Industrial School for Boys!"

The bus pulled away, leaving the boys choking and the man shielding his eyes from the cloud of dust kicked up from the dirt road. "How was the trip, boys? Comfortable, I hope." The man sounded as though he was reading from a script, not interested in the least.

Lionel replied, "Nope. It was bumpy as all get out. I need to use the restroom."

The man ignored the request and increased his volume. "This used to be called the Florida State *Reform School!* Have you heard of reform school, you fucking maggots? We are here to *reform* you! How fucking lucky can you get?" He chortled with phlegm-filled laughter before clearing his throat and letting a large green hocker fly to the other side of the road. He spun around, spreading his arms wide to show the expanse in front of them. "Look at this place! It's paradise! A resort! You are going to fucking love it here, getting a good dose of Florida Industrial… whatever the fuck that is."

Lionel couldn't hold back a chuckle. Except for his father, whom he had not seen in years, he had never heard so much profanity from anyone. Ever.

"What the fuck are you laughing at, you pile of shit?"

"That's for me to know and you to find out," Lionel answered.

"Who the fuck said you could talk?"

An instant later, Lionel found himself lying on the ground in dust the consistency of baby powder. He hadn't been fast enough to avoid a wicked slap to his head and face. It was the kind his mother gave him a half a dozen times per day, but this one was ten times as hard.

"Do you know who the fuck I am, you fucking pipsqueak?"

Lionel stood up and brushed himself off. "Nope."

"I am the fucking school principal. You will call me Mr. Fucking Sherman! Do you understand that? Sir, or Mr. Sherman! Got it?"

Lionel said, "Yep."

Nathan was a little faster on the uptake. "Yes, sir."

Mr. Sherman sized the two boys up for about thirty seconds. "Which one of you killed the dog?"

Nathan looked puzzled. Lionel looked at his dusty shoes.

Mr. Sherman looked at Lionel, "Red, did you kill the fucking dog?"

Lionel looked up, rubbed the tingling on the side of his

head, and began to cry.

"Red, if you start fucking crying, I am going to give you something to fucking cry about. Do you understand me?"

"Yes, sir."

"Fuckin'-A right, yes sir! I am very sorry to tell you that I am a dog lover, Red. We dog lovers on staff will deal with you later, but right now let's get on with the orientation."

Mr. Sherman led them both through the front gate. "Fuck happen to your face?" he said to Lionel. "You got enough freckles to have named constellations."

Lionel didn't know what that meant, but he rubbed at his face hoping he could get whatever was on it off.

The sun was beginning to speed its descent into the western sky, but there was still plenty of light to see. The last of the afternoon thunderstorms were dissipating. None had touched the school, but a thick cirrus cloud deck loomed high overhead, the remnants of storms to the south and west.

Mr. Sherman went back to his script. "The Florida Industrial School for Boys is a school, a ranch, a farm, and your home away from home. Now, see those buildings over there?" He pointed toward the horizon. "That's the Jackson County Jail. Stay away from there. Those guys will hurt you." He emphasized *will*.

Lionel and Nathan took stock of their surroundings. *Place is a resort*, Lionel thought. *Looks like that Bradenton country club up by Grandma's house. They call this a reform school? More like fuckin' vacation. Shit, must be swimmin' pools and everything. This is gonna be a walk in the park.*

It did look like a resort to the two of them. All the buildings were freshly painted, the lawns were mowed to perfection, and there were trimmed hedges surrounding the grounds and around every building. Even the live oak trees seemed to be perfect: trimmed branches, no Spanish moss, nothing to rake. And the place was huge. Simple but tidy cinderblock cottages were situated on the other side of a large field.

It didn't occur to either Nathan or Lionel how it happened that the grounds were so well manicured. *Must be a lot of work for someone*, Lionel thought.

"Look around you, gentlemen," Mr. Sherman continued. "Notice that there are no fences. You can walk away from here any time you want. There will be no one stopping you. However, before you think that's a good idea, you need to think about the staff and faculty who will go out and find you. Be sure to ask some of your bunkmates whether leaving is a good idea."

Lionel had already been thinking about just walking away. Perhaps he should give that idea a second thought. Fuck's 'faculty'?

"Boys, we are on the south side of the school grounds: Number One. We're Number One. When you hear 'Number One,' you know where you belong. You belong on Number One, because you are white boys." Mr. Sherman pointed. "Over there is the north side. The north side is Number Two. Number Two is for the colored boys."

For the first time since getting off the bus, Nathan spoke up. "There's colored here? My papa won't let me consort with colored folk."

Mr. Sherman leaned over and got his face right in Nathan's. Nathan tried to turn away, but Mr. Sherman lifted up a fat hand with fat fingers and pulled the boy's chin around.

"You fucking cracker. Your papa has no say at this school. I do not, *we* do not, give a good shit what your papa thinks. And where did you learn a word like 'consort' anyway?" Mr. Sherman stepped back, smiled, and added in a normal tone of voice, "Am I clear? You *will* be 'consorting' with the colored. Get fucking used to it."

"Yes, sir," the boys answered in unison.

When Mr. Sherman turned around to continue the tour, Lionel and Nathan looked at each other with a wide-eyed, puzzled look that said, *Who has ever heard of something so stupid?*

At the center of the school grounds were four large two-story houses, red brick with green slate roofs and bright green canvas awnings, each with a large screened porch. There were no fences. Another dozen one-story, open-bay cinderblock cottages were surrounded by trimmed hedges, pine trees, and live oaks just about everywhere. Mr. Sherman walked them by the swimming pool, and they peeked through the six-foot clapboard fence that surrounded it. There was a church, too. The whole place was just beautiful. Nathan and Lionel commented that they'd seen postcards in the Rexall Drugs that didn't look as good as this place.

"What the heck," Nathan whispered. "How bad can this be?"

As Mr. Sherman led them toward the dining hall, Lionel said, "Mr. Sherman, sir, can I ask a question?"

"Sounds like you already have."

Lionel pointed to a spot near the school chapel. "Is that some old cemetery?"

"Been here since the school was built fifty years ago. That's where we bury the dead boys." Irony was lost on Mr. Sherman.

Nathan had a startled look on his face. "Dead boys?"

"You got that right." Mr. Sherman stopped, looked back at them, and smiled. "Some boys don't make it." He must have read Lionel's mind. "This is no walk in the fucking park. Fun begins now. Go get some fucking chow."

June 1950 – June 1951
Florida Industrial School for Boys, Jackson County, Marianna, Florida

Beatings were a daily occurrence. For killing a dog, Lionel drew the immediate attention of the "dog lovers," and he spent the majority of his first week in the school hospital recovering from a concussion and deep gashes on his buttocks.

On day three, Nathan tried to help his only friend and got a broken left arm for his trouble. The nurse was practiced at setting bones and crafting plaster casts; she had experience. Nate was not the only boy with a cast. Everyone signed it. Nate thought it might get him out of work detail. He was wrong.

Nathan was a good-looking kid. One of the staff, Mr. Wilding, thought he looked like the actor Tim Holt, who had played the character "Curtin" in *Treasure of the Sierra Madre* with Humphrey Bogart. So Mr. Wilding took to calling Nate, Curtin"

Mr. Wilding was only twenty years old or so, but the boys all had to call him "Mister." It was unbelievable to them, but Mr. Wilding had once been one of the boys at the Institute. He came back a few years later to be on the staff. He told people he missed the place. Almost everyone figured this was where he'd turned queer.

Fuckin' Wildman. Fairy. Place is bad 'nuff. Why's Nate gotta deal with fuckin' Wildman? Curtain. Calls him "Curtain." What the fuck does that mean? Touch Nate again and I will hurt you. I am not kidding.

The rumors were flying around that Mr. Wilding took Nate behind the *curtain* more than once and had his way. There was nothing anyone could do about it. Lionel felt sorry for him, and once he got off a perfect punch into Mr. Wilding's solar plexus. The room was pitch black when he did it, so no one ever knew it was him, and everyone was punished. It was worth it to Lionel, and Nate was appreciative.

But Nate had to get out of there. And on his third escape attempt he was put in solitary in "the White House." He was visited in his cell once a day visited for a sound beating or to spend some personal time with Mr. Wilding. No one was sure what exactly happened then, but one boy who was on the White House cleaning detail said Nate killed himself. He saw him half sitting, half slouching, held by the neck from a belt hooked to a doorknob in his cell.

That wasn't the only reason everyone was scared to death of

the White House. The kids who would not follow the rules, and those who were violent, were put in there for "special treatment." Built of concrete blocks with a flat, gravel-topped roof, the one-story, nine-room building was painted sparkling white like the cottages. From a center hallway, colored boys turned left into one of four cells. White boys turned right to their own set of cells. There was no heat in the winter, and in the panhandle of Florida there are frigid days and colder nights. No one who went into those cells came out in good shape.

Mr. Bidwell was the "owner" of the White House. He was the most feared man at the entire school. The boys thought he must have lost his left arm in the war, but no one was certain. Lionel once asked Mr. Bidwell if he had learned his torture skills in a Jap prisoner of war camp. That got him a night in the White House and his worst beating since the week he arrived.

But as bad as it was for the south side—Number One—there was not a single boy who would trade a minute with the colored boys up over on the north.

Hate this fuckin' place. Resort, my ass. Queers, niggers, screamers, assholes, one-armed motherfuckers. How'd I get myself in this mess? Nate. Not gonna cry over Nate. Should never've let that motherfucker suck him off. Shoulda bit his dick off. Hungry. So hungry. Never thought I'd eat that shit. Starvin'. Dead boys. Dead niggers. Diggin' holes out there. Stay away from that place. Look at that cemetery, someone's gonna drop the evil eye on me. End up in the ground. Sherman. Tidwell. Wildman motherfucker. Come back and kill 'em? No fuckin' way. Never coming back to this place. Never. Get me the fuck outta here. Fuckin' Miller. Fuckin' Hagen. Cut their dogs up? No. Go after their kids? No fuckin' way. Not gonna come back here. Gonna tell 'em about this place. Some kinda fucked-up, this place.

Once a bunch of boys hid outside an open window and listened while the staff entertained a group of inspectors from the state capital. The boys had spent three weeks making the place look spic 'n' span—perfect, not a blade of grass out of place. Fourteen-hour days in ninety degree heat. They heard Mr. Sherman telling the visitors about corporal punishment, whatever that was. "Sometimes we have to spank the boys, or use a paddle," he said.

Lionel scanned the boys, wide-eyed, incredulous, and whispered, "What a fucking lie."

Yes, what a lie. There was no spanking going on in the White House. What happened in there was called whipping, or flogging—like a sailor on a pirate ship who had disobeyed an order and was tied to the mizzenmast and beaten to within an inch of his life. Mr. Bidwell's favorite tool was a heavy leather strap tied to a wooden handle. Brutal. The staff would turn on a big industrial fan in the front room to drown out the screaming. It didn't help much. From inside the front room they couldn't hear anything but the fan, but step outside and they couldn't hear the fan at all, only the boys. Screaming boys. Those boys would come back to the dorm needing help pulling bits of their cotton underpants from the bleeding wounds on their butts. The school called this "Final Disciplinary Action," which was the exact right term if you were Nathan Belford hanging by the neck from a doorknob.

On the bright side, once you had survived a stint in the White House you were able to carry the title "White House Boy," a badge of honor, but it was not a distinction many wanted to earn.

One of the punishments that most boys kept silent about was homesickness. Lionel's mother and little brother visited the week before Christmas, but other than that, he never saw anyone else he knew. He spent every night at the school sobbing into his pillow. To add insult to injury, he failed eighth grade and had to repeat it in Arcadia. Looking back, and he did look back, it was the worst year of his life.

But that year in Marianna was also a university education in sadism. Lionel was able to make friends with Jerry Caudle, another like-minded sadistic kid two years older than him. Jerry had been at the school since Thanksgiving the previous year. He had stolen a cooked turkey for his family from a soup kitchen in Orlando. Of course, he'd gotten caught, and the judge hadn't been too concerned about how little food his family had to eat over the holidays.

Over the next few months, Jerry and Lionel taught each other the finer points of animal torture. Lionel had the goods on skinning rabbits alive and then having them hop around skinless with lit cherry bombs in their mouths. Jerry had a foolproof method for tying the tails of cats together and then tossing them over a power line so it was easier to watch the show. "Fences are too low," he said.

By the time Lionel Bodean Rook left the Institute, he was not reformed, but he certainly vowed to never get caught again. He was not going back.

18 May 1953

DeSoto County Courthouse, Arcadia, Florida

Lionel Rook would be seventeen years old in just a few weeks. In some ways he was acting his age, and in other ways he was twelve going on thirty. A sick, misguided, sociopathic kid who had no place in functioning society.

"Your Honor, permission to approach the bench."

Juvenile Court Judge Andrew Miller waved him up without a word. In a déjà vu moment, Attorney Bob Hagen stepped forward and began whispering in earnest; the sort of whisper you want to be a scream, but you don't want others to hear. "I don't want this case. I hate this fucking kid. We need a trap door in front of the bench that leads to a bottomless pit."

"Let's stop the profanity right now," the judge replied.

Still whispering, but with spittle flicking onto the bench, Hagen said, "Screw you, Andy. Find someone else who might actually give a shit. How can I advocate for this worthless piece of crap when I don't give a shit in a hat if he lives or dies, right now, at this moment?"

"Sit down and keep your opinions to yourself," Judge Miller replied. "Let's get on with this."

Hagen returned to stand beside his client while the judge looked at the top pages of a file three inches thick on the bench before him. Finally the judge turned to face the boy. "Lionel, what are you doing back here?"

"Don't know, Judge, guess the counselor at school don't like me."

"Did you know the person who arrested you in school was an actual police officer? Why in tarnation would you take a swing at him?"

"Judge, I ain't gonna apologize for anything. That colored boy hit my brother Bobby. I know you agree with me, no nigger is gonna hit my brother and get away with it."

"Lionel, for the record, I do not agree with you. That boy is in the hospital. How's your brother?"

"He's okay. Got a bruise on his arm, but shit, I got a career slugging Bobby on the arm. He's gonna be just fine."

"So, Willie Johnson is in the hospital and Bobby Rook has a bruise on his arm. Do you see any disparity in that?"

"I don't know what that means."

Mr. Hagen reached up and pulled Lionel's ear. "I've been counting," he said. "If you don't say 'Judge or Your Honor,' I promise you, you are going to jail to think about it."

"I don't know what it means, Your Honor," Lionel said.

"It means you overreacted, Lionel. You can't beat someone to a pulp just because they hit your brother." The judge lifted a paper while taking his glasses off. "Did Willie even hit your brother?"

"Dave Jensen said he did."

Judge Miller shook his head and let out an exasperated sigh. "What am I going to do with you?"

"Don't know, Your Honor. I'm good if you don't do nothin'."

"It was a rhetorical question."

"I don't know what that word means." Then, remembering, he added: "Your Honor."

"Lionel, how did you like Marianna?"

"Fucking hated it, Your Honor."

"If you resort to the use of profanity again, Lionel, this is going to be a short hearing."

"That's good, Your Honor, I got stuff I need to take care of."

Judge Miller took off his glasses again and stared down at Lionel Rook in disbelief. "You just do not get it, do you?"

"Get what?"

"Never mind." It took Judge Miller five minutes to flip through Lionel's case file before looking up again.

Jesus, these motherfuckers take everything too seriously. It's just animals. Who cares? Just a little wailing. Just a little caterwauling. Just some entertainment for everyone's benefit. Beating a few kids up. So what. Part of life. Don't hit my brother unless you want a beating. Don't hit my brother anyway.

"Says here that last year, before school one day, you tied the tails of two cats together in some kind of slip noose and tossed them over a power line in the assembly area." Without waiting for Lionel to answer, the judge looked at Robert Hagen. "Why didn't I know about this sooner?"

"Your Honor, we just found out. Jim Rattray is one of the school guidance counselors. He came forward after this most recent fighting incident."

"Why did it take him so long?"

"Says Lionel threatened to kill him if he spoke up about the cats." This was followed by another pregnant pause of astonishment from every person in the courtroom—except Lionel's mother.

"That's a lie, Your Honor," she said. "Plus, it was a telephone line. No power in it."

The judge stared at her. Everything he needed to know about heredity and the genetics of stupidity was standing right here in front of him. "Sit down, Mrs. Rook. Here's what we're going to do." He took his glasses off and rubbed his forehead. "Lionel has a choice. I will either remand this case to criminal court, where Lionel will be tried as an adult twice. First we'll throw the book at him for assault and battery against that kid. Then we'll get him again for cruelty to animals. I will make sure his juvenile record is admissible. Or… there is another way. Hear me out. Lionel will enlist in one of the armed services, the first one that'll take him. God help our country."

Mr. Hagen stood. "Your Honor, I'd ask you to recall the Williams case from two weeks ago. The fighting in Korea is coming to a close. They're winding down. None of the militaries are taking new recruits."

Judge Miller looked up one last time, forgetting his glasses were in his hand. His expression and smirk said, Give me a break. "I think we have three armed forces recruiters in the county. Give them a call and tell them to visit me in chambers."

CHAPTER 2

14 November 1960

Near Ri'Ga Village, Hien District, Quảng Nam Province, South Vietnam

Tigers were such a rare sight, they still elicited celebration when seen. Kiep sat still and quiet, as small as he could, to observe without becoming prey. He saw the tiger and recognized the omen.

There is no decision to be made. I am compelled to name my son in honor. I will make the beast a spirit-member of the village. This will bring safety from attack. There is no doubt of that.

The tiger knew Kiep's son was hours old. Kiep took the namesake honor to use for himself. He came to believe the tiger had no need to threaten the family or Ri'Ga. Sustenance was plentiful in the jungle. So was danger.

Today was a day to rejoice. Kiep left Thia with the village women. They would take care of her and their newborn. He sat on a moss-covered, fallen tree behind the cover of some elephant-ear ficus and steadied his gaze.

It is a beautiful beast. More beautiful than the others in this jungle. He's a fitting namesake.

Kiep noticed and pondered an anomaly in the otherwise bookend pattern of the striping on the tiger's head between his eyes and ears. Over his left eye was a near-perfect circle.

How interesting. The fur pattern almost forms the image of a third eye.

Kiep averted his gaze. His father had taught him well never to sustain eye contact. And despite his attempt to remain hidden, to get small, the tiger seems to know exactly where he was. The beast stared back with curious intent.

He hears my call to his spirit. He knows I will name my newborn in his honor. He will be Tsov. The beast will protect Tsov. The beast will safeguard Tsov's people. The beast will shield our village from harm.

The tiger registered the mental call and was honored. He pivoted on a rock outcropping and gave Kiep a final nod of thanks while sweeping his tail and ambling off into the bush.

Kiep wondered aloud, "Will I see this majestic animal again?"

He turned his thoughts to the coming feast. This would not be a day of celebration for one of the nearby herds of boar that spent their days and nights avoiding the tiger. Kiep's trap was tried and true. He had improved on his father's methods, and through them he provided a steady supply of meat to Ri'Ga, thereby saving the water buffalo for when significant sacrifice was called for. Kiep had developed a reputation as a compassionate hunter who also understood the wide-ranging needs of his village.

The boars were vicious, but not smart. Time and time again, Kiep was able to rig his traps along the low, canopied wildlife paths. His spots were village-owned and *toring*-protected. There was no worry of theft.

As memorials, Kiep let stand the remnants of traps his
father had once used to teach Kiep—traps he had employed to keep
the families of his *toring*, his clan, alive so many years ago. And Kiep
recognized, and used as markers in the jungle, long-abandoned
termite mounds the only remaining evidence of his grandfather's
traps, which had taught his father to provide, one generation to
another. Kiep looked forward to the day when he would teach Tsov
to trap, to hunt, to gather.

Two boars, two traps. Success is paramount. Today I need to make way
to my most reliable spots.

The major improvement Kiep had made to his father's
methods was to construct his traps as collapsible boxes. His panel
design had proven successful time and again. Kiep went to his knees
and raised the sides against the support of a natural tunnel in the tall
grass. Two short, wide "ladders" connected with heavy bottom
rungs flush to the ground. The back of the contraption was
narrower, but as tall. Once raised, a rectangular box began to take
shape with overlapping rungs interlacing at the corners. Then, on
the exterior, a stack of vertical L-shaped cross-members formed and
permitted easy lashing with woven jute and leather straps. On the
interior, these bindings were inaccessible to an angry animal. The
finishing touch was the entrance. It was raised, lapped, and lashed
like the end, but it included a swinging door hinged at the top. An
unlucky boar would enter, trip the door, and find itself trapped
pondering its future, left only to commune with jungle spirits.

From time to time Kiep found evidence that other animals

using the canopied paths had been trapped in his tiny corral. But with no top, they were able to escape without difficulty. His father had once pointed out evidence of cat claws. Not a tiger, but rather a leopard that had left angry scratches on the logs before uncoiling his lithe body and springing from the trap. Boars were not intelligent or agile enough to make that jump—but they were skilled in rooting around to get under the box. For this reason, years of trial and error had dictated that bamboo was too light to keep the animals contained. Straight wooden branches, chopped to matching lengths, proved the best and most reliable construction materials. And the heaviest pieces, the largest logs, were reserved for the lowest level to thwart escape attempts.

Kiep took his steel hammer from the bag on his hip and drove bamboo stakes into the ground at the corners of the trap. Boars couldn't jump, but on open terrain they were powerful enough to move a trap hundreds of meters. The final step was rigging the trigger, an ingenious method that responded to an angry boar by releasing a stay that enabled the door in the rear to swing closed, slide vertically, and lock into a slot.

Kiep's second trap went in just as easily on the other side of the brook. He inspected his handiwork with a sigh of satisfaction. At worst he'd have one hog for the feast to celebrate the birth of his son. At best there would be two, enabling an invite to Thia's *toring* and Xa Ruh Village in the valley over the ridge line.

By dint of habit, Kiep pulled his long pipe from his loincloth, packed the bowl full from his tobacco pouch, and reached to light it. It was mindless activity that his limbs performed automatically. The absence of a source of fire stopped him in his tracks. He remembered leaving his smoking materials behind in the longhouse. But it was all well and good. Nothing, he knew, would alert the jungle spirits faster and for a greater distance than men wafting smoke. He knew better and chided himself as he slid the pipe with its well-packed bowl back into the material around his waist.

Kiep packed his tools, extra rope, leather straps, and an odd metal bottle that looked similar to a flattened teapot with corks and a leather strap. It was a soldier's canteen, passed down from his father and the French soldiers who had been his friends. Then Kiep began the hour-long trek back to Ri'Ga.

The rain ended early in the morning, but it left a heavy mist hanging thick below the triple canopy above. Insects roared. Untold birds shared mating calls. Kiep heard a family of monkeys in the distance. He reached the path and gathered up a handful of porcupine quills, spent in earnest, perhaps the night before. He hiked with a spring in his step back along well-worn trails, contemplating how his son's birth had changed his life forever. Rumbling booms from over the distant horizon reminded him of other dangers lurking in this land.

Hiking off the ridge line into the mist-filled valley, Kiep could hear Tsov's crying from a distance. Pride. A son. Honor. He saw the top of the Guol, then the roofline of the longhouse. He reached for his pipe and placed it in the right side of his mouth.

Kiep stepped through the door of his own longhouse. He smiled to himself and chuckled. He stepped to the hearth, took a shoot of elephant grass, and used it to light his clay pipe. Twenty-five centimeters long, the pipe was a work of art, curving in a smooth but shallow arc down to a tiny bowl.

The crying from one of the back rooms went on. He was still not permitted to lay eyes on his new son, or his wife Thia. She had returned from her ten-day stint in the jungle where only her sister had assisted in bringing Tsov into the world. After ten sunrises, he had proven he was strong and viable, worthy of joining the *toring*.

Now that Thia and Tsov were permitted back into the longhouse, Kiep's job was to prepare for the celebration and to bring one, perhaps two, boar from the hills to the village. For now, he had done what he could do. A return to the traps the following morning was next. So he strolled around the longhouse, restless with anticipation, for his third-born was finally a boy, and he was anxious to see him. Carrying the family name, Tsov continued to cry in back, with *toring* women attending to the needs of both mother and son.

A shrine of sorts hung on the wall of the longhouse common area. Kiep moved to commune with this, a single framed black and white photo, the only image of his father. Tears welled in his eyes as he thought of how he'd like to share this moment, this son, this legacy with his father. He touched his index finger to his lips, then to a tear on his cheek, and then to his father's face in the photo. His father, a legend, a memory in the center, surrounded by twelve French soldiers. All smiles. And handwritten in black fading ink: *Tu es un vrai ami, comme un membre de la famille. Nous ne t'oublierons jamais.*

Kiep had no idea what the symbols meant, but he knew his father had loved these men as family. They were honorary members of the *toring*, those few who might still be alive. They were forever welcome in the longhouse. Even in death, the spirit of his father was ever-present in the entire village. They would never forget him.

Kiep would honor his father for the respect he had brought to the tiny village of Ri'Ga, but he would not go with those men, or any of their ilk, if they returned. He would not leave his family, his *toring*, his village. Part of him harbored anger toward his father for splitting loyalties away from the community, away from family. His father's reward for doing so was death. Why else, after years, had he not returned? Kiep had abandoned faith in ever seeing his father again. *One day we will be rejoined in the spirit world.*

Kiep saw his own faded reflection in the glass covering the photo. He imagined it was his father's spirit. "I love you, Papa," he said. "You have a grandson. His name is Tsov. Remember the day we saw the tigers fighting in the jungle? How could we forget? One returned. I am certain it was one of them. Or was it you, Papa? Did you come to me as that tiger? Yes? I saw you today. I saw your eyes. You stared me down. You congratulated me on the birth of my son. I love you, Papa."

Kiep gazed at the image some more. "Papa, if you *are* the tiger, then please protect my family. Protect your granddaughters, your daughter Thia, and protect, most of all, your grandson."

The photo was symbolic for Kiep—the beginning of the end for his father. He repeated a vow to himself to never leave his family behind no matter the danger from armed men in and around the jungle. Already there were rumors of white-skinned men returning to the mountains.

He thought back again and remembered the day everything changed. Kiep was nine. His bunny had died in a bamboo rabbit trap a short distance from the village—an omen for the death of his father. Kiep's Uncle Vak, his father's brother, had come into the Ri'Ga with two tall white men and another with darker skin who lacked the Polynesian features of the DeGa, but was Asian like those others his father and grandfather despised. He later learned the white men were from a faraway country called "France."

The dark-skinned Vietnamese man could not only speak the language of the white men, but he spoke enough of the basic DeGa language that Kiep could almost understand what he was saying— although many of the words and tones didn't sound right. It reminded Kiep of a feast after the monsoons, when a family from a distant *toring* attended and spoke with an accent and many different words, but most of all, different tones. This foreigner seemed to know many of the words of the tribal language, but he placed he emphasis on the wrong words and the wrong parts of words, changing their meaning. Like one of his aunts who, when singing, sent people to the far end of the village, there was just something wrong.

Kiep had heard his father and uncles talking about these white men traveling the country, fighting some unseen common enemy. But hill people stayed to themselves and had little engagement with anyone farther away than a few valleys. Kiep had never seen a white man before then.

He listened and watched from the deep roots of a nearby tree. The men wore the oddest clothing: heavy shirts and trousers that looked like they had been stained crisscross with green and brown dye. Kiep could not imagine why someone would want to appear so ridiculous. The shirts and pants had bulging pockets and metal buttons, and they had colorful embroidery on their chests, which looked like a diamond with cross stripes. The men carried what looked like cooking pots, and Kiep was surprised to see one of the men place his pot on his head while talking to Uncle Vak and his father, as if it belonged there.

"Hlong," began Uncle Vak, "I want to introduce you to two military men…"

Uncle Vak used a word that sounded military-like, but Kiep didn't know what it meant. The white men each reached out a hand to Kiep's father, which caused him to take a step back.

The men talked to Uncle Vak and Kiep's father. "… friends … fighting … independence … enemies … the north … China … the sea … the mountains … government … communists." Few of the words made any sense to Kiep, but from the tone and his father's expression, Kiep knew his father was both alarmed and transfixed by the conversation. Kiep was more interested in the rudeness of these white men. Over and over they attempted to touch, to place hands on Uncle Vak and other villagers. And they looked straight at his father while talking. How impolite!

They talked for hours, ate with villagers in the Guol, and slept in it overnight. Kiep could only grasp bits and pieces of the adult conversation because of all the unusual language. But what he never forgot was his father sitting him down the following morning and telling Kiep that he would be gone for a time. Kiep, as the eldest, was to take care of his mother and brothers, to "be a man." Kiep was nine. He didn't feel like a man. And he acted like a child when tears welled up in his eyes.

Now he stepped away from the photo, his eyes tearing once again. He honored his father. He wanted to remember the good, not the bad.

Not the abandonment.

Kiep snapped out of his trance and daydreams of the past when he heard the pitter-patter of tiny feet running down the hallway into the meeting room.

"Papa, Papa! Papa, Papa! Where have you been, Papa? Mama has a baby. It's a boy, Papa!" Mai, now three years old, was the first of Kiep's children, a daughter, but he was proud of her nonetheless.

Kiep swept Mai off the floor and into his arms. "And how is your mother, Mai? How is the boy?"

"Papa, Paj and I helped. Mama was screaming. Grandmother

and the aunts took her into the jungle. They came back with a baby. Papa, they found a baby in the jungle!"

On Mai's heels but with shorter legs and a little slower was Kiep's second daughter, Paj. Paj, just two last month, was a gleam in Kiep's eye. A sweetheart from the day of birth, she seemed to be content to be a member of the village from day one. Hardly a whimper, never a complaint. Paj was not as precocious as Mai, but still she was tugging at her father's loincloth in excitement over the new member of the family.

"What is the baby's name?" Kiep asked the girls, knowing it was a question they would not be able to answer.

Mai scrunched her face into a wrinkled look of pure confusion. "I don't know, Papa. We need to go down the hall and ask Mama right now." She began pushing against Kiep's chest to drop to the floor.

Kiep smiled. "Mai, your papa is not yet permitted to visit the boy, but he does know the boy's name. I have not spoken to your mother yet to tell her what it is."

Paj was picking up on the conversation; "Baby… name," she said in a voice you'd expect from a two-year-old.

Kiep picked up Paj and held one daughter on each hip. "Can you girls guess what your father saw in the jungle today?"

Holding one finger up in front of her face and cocking her head to the side as if the most fascinating idea had just occurred to her, Mai widened her eyes and replied, "Mama's baby?"

"That was a good guess, but no, I didn't see Mama's baby."

Mai thought some more. "A tiger?"

Kiep was so surprised by her response he almost dropped her. "How did you guess a tiger? You have never seen a tiger, have you?"

"No Papa, but I heard the old men talking about tigers. There is tiger fur in Grandfather's house." For a few seconds Mai looked into her father's eyes, and then she looked right through them... off into an inexplicable distance, transported to another place. Then she came back and said, "Papa, I had a dream about a tiger last night."

Kiep felt a spirit dancing in the room with him. "Mai, tell Papa the truth. Did you really dream about a tiger last night? Was it a bad dream?"

"I really did, Papa. It wasn't really a bad dream, but not really a good dream either. In the end, the tiger lived."

Then Mai went again to that other place for an instant. When she came back, she stared into her father's eyes. Her eyes welled up, but without shedding a tear. "I told a lie, Papa. It was a bad dream."

Vietnam's Central Highlands are a wide expanse of mountains separating Laos (to the west) from Vietnam (to the east), along what geologists have named the Annam Cordillera. Located on the western end of the Quảng Nam Province in the Hien District, neither Ri'Ga nor Xa Ruh show on maps, but both are situated within two kilometers of the Sông Cả River. A location closer to the valley would mean frequent flooding during monsoon. Three kilometers separated Kiep's and Thia's villages, but both were situated in protected mountain copses, offshoots of the cordillera just five kilometers east of the Laotian border and one hundred kilometers west of the South China Sea at Da Nang. They are as remote as remote can be, and a villager could live an entire life without ever seeing a marginally more civilized existence at the larger villages of Ta Ko or Rah just kilometers away. The nearest improved road was cut through the heavy mountainous forest and jungle twenty kilometers to the east. On rare occasion the villages would see aircraft that had taken off from A'Ro to the south.

Movement was by foot or with the aid of beasts of burden. Water buffalo could pull wheeled wagons in the valleys and in the widened trails cut around rice paddies, but once one stepped foot onto a ridge line, transportation was relegated to feet, and portage to gui baskets of varying sizes carried on the back with shoulder straps. Human power did all the work as it had done for centuries.

Across the valley to the east, along the unmarked border with Laos, was a trail system well known to every village in the area. It brought a steady stream of visitors from the north and south and extended as far north as China. No one in Ri'Ga or Xa Ruh could imagine how far that was, though the village was replete with mythology about soldiers and foreigners in close proximity. During the coming war, this trail would come to be known as the Hồ Chí Minh trail. Too close for comfort.

Kiep set his daughters back down on the floor of the longhouse. On this wondrous day of the birth of his son, he was horrified to think of the mountain spirit that had put this image of a tiger in the head of his elder daughter. Part of him wanted to query her further on the dream so that he might better understand its significance, but he knew dreams were built from fleeting images. What the spirit had wanted Kiep to know it had released from Mai's mouth: "In the end the tiger lived."

When he thought of this single phrase, uttered by his daughter, the hair stood up on the back of his neck. The sign he was implored to recognize was the implication in her words that when something lived in a dream, something or someone else died.

Kiep walked to a longhouse window that faced the plaza and the Guol across the way. He studied the jungle beyond, wondered whether his traps were doing their work, and knew he had to rid his mind of negative thoughts on this day of joy. To belabor the spirit dreams of his daughter would be to place evil in the longhouse, and it could then penetrate the hallways and rooms where his son lay.

The first night with a new son was longer than most, but Kiep knew Tsov was going to be a good baby. Kiep rolled on the floor mat toward Thia. Tsov was suckling. Paj and Mai breathed deep in sound sleep on the other side of the room. They were not bothered by Tsov's intermittent wailing.

"How are you this morning, my love?" Kiep rested a hand on Thia's hip and snuggled closer.

"Tsov will be different from your daughters, Kiep. Is it

possible he already has a tooth? This one learned fast how to get his next meal. My breasts are already sore." She caressed baby Tsov's dark hair and said, "The good milk will come soon, my son. Be patient."

Day was breaking. One of Thia's sisters was busy in the hearth room preparing a meal for Kiep's family. In Co-Tu tradition, Thia's sisters would take over the wife's chores until mother and baby bonded, until he was feeding, until his eyes could fix on his father's face.

There was commotion in the plaza outside the longhouse, unusual activity for this time of the morning. Kiep thought he could hear someone barking orders, high-pitched voices yelling.

Kiep's cousin, Baap'Can, a couple of years older than Kiep, climbed the steps to the longhouse. He called for Kiep even as he entered the hallway and walked toward Kiep's family sleeping space.

"Kiep! Kiep! There are soldiers in the square. They are speaking Vietnamese and demand to talk to the village elders." Baap'Can looked nervous.

Kiep responded, "Did you wake your father?"

"I did, but you speak Vietnamese better than anyone else in the village. We need you to come now." Though Kiep was younger than Baap'Can, and younger than many of the others in his village, he had proven himself to be a fierce warrior, hunter, and reliable village provider. He had also learned some Vietnamese during his hunting excursions throughout the Highlands. The language ability and hunting prowess had garnered him village status beyond his years.

Kiep gathered his things, adjusted his loincloth, and pulled on a hemp wrap. He stepped out of the longhouse into the square and saw his Uncle Vak appearing from one of the surrounding houses.

In the plaza Kiep found four Vietnamese soldiers yelling orders and working to establish their authority over every living being they encountered. Kiep smiled to himself as he watched the villagers ignore the newcomers as if they didn't even exist. An onlooker would have wondered if the soldiers were invisible and inaudible. This refusal to acknowledge their presence caused enormous frustration among the soldiers, who were apparently accustomed to being listened to. They apparently had no understanding of the DeGa culture which didn't permit contact of any sort with outsiders unless village elders gave permission.

How long will this take? Kiep wondered. *I have to check my traps.*

"Good morning, soldiers. Welcome to Ri'Ga village." Kiep said it without meaning it.

Judging by the way three of the men were kowtowing to the fourth, there was one clear leader among the soldiers. On Kiep's greeting he turned and scowled and in Vietnamese barked, "You *moi* dogs! Don't your people know they are in the presence of the People's Army?"

"*Moi*" was a highly derogatory Vietnamese term that loosely meant "savage." There was no word in either Co-Tu or Vietnamese that was more offensive.

Kiep looked around at doorways of homes, the Guol, and the longhouse. He was on display; the entire village was craning their necks from every available opening. Then he turned to stare at this person, this People's Army soldier, for an uncomfortable moment. He repeated, as if he had not heard the insult, "Good morning, soldiers. Welcome to Ri'Ga village."

Kiep had long since gotten over being intimidated by the military, having grown up with all manner of visits from the French, South Vietnamese soldiers, and civilian members of the Liberation Front. The DeGa were known to disparage outsiders, but they held a particular disgust for anyone in uniform and anyone from the government. Such men had discriminated against the mountain people for time immemorial.

With his hands on his hips and his chest puffed out, the lead soldier said, "I am Captain Nguyễn Hữu Thảo. I am commander of a logistics and engineering company from Hà Nội. We represent Group 559."

Kiep placed his hand up in the universal sign to cease, stopping him there. "Captain Nguyễn, I am Kiep Dool. I will act as interpreter for you, but I am not the village elder, so I am not permitted to speak for the village."

"Well get him out here now—we do not have much time!"

With an idea to antagonize the insolent interloper, Kiep said, "If you don't have much time, I suggest you be on your way. We don't have time for you either."

The captain turned a shade of red in his already dark face. A head taller than Kiep, he marched toward him, puffed his chest out again, and just fell short of touching his nose to Kiep's. Angry. Hot.

"Watch yourself, *moi*. Watch yourself."

Kiep smiled. "Do you think the four of you can escape this village before we return you to the spirit of the Earth?"

Captain Nguyễn drew his sidearm and placed it on Kiep's forehead. From the corner of his eye, Kiep could see his Uncle Vak approaching.

"What can I do for you gentlemen?" Vak asked in a calm tone. "There is no need for anger. We are a simple village with simple people and simple needs."

The captain did not understand the Co-Tu language, but he took the pistol away from Kiep's head and brandished it in all directions before finally holstering it. "If you keep up this kind of behavior, you will be a village of dead people," he said to Kiep.

Vak responded to this affront by miming a sign to calm down with his hands.

"I told your *moi* dog here that we are from the north," the captain said, with Kiep translating. "The army from Hàroội to the north. We are an engineering company charged with improving the road to your west."

"The trail?" Vak asked.

"Your trail, I suppose, but soon it will be large enough to support motorcycles and small trucks. That is why we are here. Your village will be assisting in the work."

At that, Vak took two steps back from the captain. By this time a crowd of villagers had gathered to observe the interaction— mostly men, standing on the periphery of the village square. "Captain Nguyễn, I want to be clear. I will speak slowly so that my nephew Kiep can translate well. I am not the village elder, but I am one, and I have the authority to speak for this village."

Nguyễn took a step toward Vak as if he was following him in a fighter's stance.

Vak continued. "Ri'Ga Village has been here as long as time. And for that time, for eternity, we have never assisted any soldiers, any government, any village, any people who are not our people, who are not Co-Tu. Years ago my brother Hlong left Ri'Ga Village with some French soldiers. He never returned. Our help to soldiers began and ended there."

Captain Nguyễn held up the back of his hand as if he was ready to swat something. "Your brother never returned because he is a *moi* dog burning in hell for helping the French."

It was all Vak could do to contain himself. His stance stiffened, his face reddened, his fists curled at his side. But if Vak was upset, Kiep was near exploding. He could barely remember his father, but an insult like this was unconscionable. Yet for the moment he was outmatched. Captain Nguyễn was not a stupid man; he could read body language. He placed his hand on top of his holster and unsnapped it, placing his pistol at the ready.

Vak raised his voice a little, but remained calm. "I will continue, and I will ask my fellow villagers not to kill you on this spot. On this plaza. Captain, do you know the Co-Tu are famous? For generations we hunted men and kept their skulls as trophies. I can show them to you if you like. If you retain this attitude, if you continue talking to me as if I am a dog, or worse, a savage, then we will collect the heads of you and your men at this moment."

The three soldiers had taken positions in the shape of a

triangle, back to back, rifles pointed at the ground. They were now looking out on some thirty Co-Tu with spears and crossbows. No gun, no rifle would save them if the sign was given.

The captain remained indignant, pure bluster, perhaps to show his men who, in his mind, was in charge.

Then, in a measured monotone without raising his voice, Vak said, "You will leave our village now. You will never return." Vak surveyed the other soldiers. One of the junior men was in a state of panic, judging by the look on his face. "Captain, have I spoken enough?" Vak said. "Have I spoken clearly enough? Was my nephew Kiep able to translate my words so that you are able to understand me?" Vak looked at the officer in the eyes and held his gaze. "Now. Depart this instant."

Captain Nguyễn had the temerity to laugh: an awkward, affected belly laugh as if he had just heard something hilarious. "We will leave," he chortled, "but we will return and burn this village—"

Vak didn't wait for Kiep's translation; he'd had enough of this captain's attitude, his lack of respect, his insolence. He raised a hand and pointed one finger to the sky. The surrounding warriors reacted without hesitation. Well-aimed spears and arrows flew. Four North Vietnamese regulars were dead in an instant.

Vak shouted orders, pointing at warriors in groups. "Patrol the area *now*! Find those who may have been observing. These men will be missed. We must return to normalcy as if they never arrived." He spun on a foot in a full circle. "There was no visit! There were no soldiers! You, you, you, and you," he said, pointing, "take these bodies to the jungle spirits now. Make them part of the land, never to be seen again."

Even as he spoke, groups were forming to carry the lifeless soldiers into the triple canopy. "Collect their weapons and place them in the cache under the longhouse!"

Baap'Can and Kiep followed the jungle trails with a little more care than they had taken in the past. There were others now. There was worry. The two were separated by the length of a four-meter sturdy bamboo pole held between them on their shoulders.

"That added some excitement to the day," Baap'Can commented in a sarcastic, understated way.

Kiep replied, "In all my years with your father, I had no idea of his mean streak, but I know he did the right thing. If he had let those soldiers return, it would be the end of life as we know it."

"They won't be the last," said Baap'Can.

"Did you hear that officer talking about making the north-south trail into a road? I have been as far north as anyone in our collective Co-Tu community. There is nothing there, no equipment to move. What could he have been thinking about? Trucks? Motorcycles? It's impossible."

They arrived at Kiep's first trap. A tired but still angry wild boar was corralled there. Kiep pulled a knife from his loincloth, and in a fluid motion he reached into the cage from behind, grabbed the boar by one tusk, and slipped the knife into the soft spot behind its left eye. The animal dropped to the ground like a stone. Baap'Can helped Kiep dismantle the trap over the boar and returned it to its hiding spot.

Baap'Can then fixed a loop with three quick spins over the boar's hind legs. He tossed the other end over a tree limb, pulled the boar off the ground, and slit its throat. Blood drained in a pool on the ground.

"I put the other trap up the trail, hidden in the grass of a tiny clearing. Perhaps we were twice lucky," Kiep said.

And in fact, there it was, a second boar, perhaps related to the first. Baap'Can wondered aloud, "Do we need two? What is your plan for the feast?"

"The women are in charge," Kiep smiled, "but now in addition to the banquet for my son's birth, your father will want to celebrate clearing our village of four enemies. And we will get a large crowd from Thia's village." He thought for a moment, did some mindless counting on his fingertips, and said, "Yes, let's take this one too. It's a long way back—can we carry them both on the one pole?"

"My brother," Baap'Can laughed, "I am a man. I can carry these two boar by myself, but since you are feeble, I will accept your assistance if you think you are capable."

Kiep laughed out loud and faked a punch to Baap'Can's stomach. The two embraced. "Let's get going."

CHAPTER 3

17 February 1962
Lufkin, Angelina County, Texas

Saturday noon there was always a rush at Francisco's Drive-In. Bill Wolusky, the weekend manager, leaned his head out the screen door. "Darren, it's your mother on the phone."

Darren looked up from the order he was putting together. "Mr. Ski, can you tell her I'll call her back?" But even as he said it, he realized that his mother had never before called him at work. Not once. He had to take it. "Hang on, Mr. Wolusky, I'll be right there."

Darren ran the tray of burgers, fries, and shakes out to the curb, where a nice older couple was waiting in a red Ford convertible. On two slots, the tray was secured to the open driver's window. Darren replaced their speaker/microphone box on the rack next to the lighted menu, trotted back inside, and grabbed the phone sitting on Mr. Wolusky's tiny desk. "Yes, Mom."

"You have some mail here, Darren. Department of the Army. I thought you'd want to know."

Darren stood straight and moved the phone from his left to his right ear. "Can you tell if it's from ROTC or somewhere else?"

He had already gotten notification of his full ride to Texas A&M, an army ROTC scholarship and the chance to serve in the "Corps of Cadets," like his father, his two uncles, and his grandfather before him—but he still had high hopes for something he considered an even better deal.

"I can't tell," his mother answered. "It's a big, thick manila envelope that has a return address in Washington, DC."

Darren was too excited. He couldn't wait to know. "Open it, Mom."

Darren heard a rustling of paper through the phone, and then his mother read aloud, "Dear Mr. Bross, the United States Army is happy to inform you that you have been selected for a Congressional appointment to the United States Military Academy at West Point, New York."

Darren bellowed out a "Yes!" and followed up with fist pumps. Everyone in the kitchen turned around in interest.

His mother went on, "Your high academic standing at Lufkin High School, combined with your demonstrated leadership in sports and extracurricular activities, has convinced the army that you are the kind of young man who has the potential to lead…"

Darren was no longer listening. He was whooping and caterwauling. He unwrapped a stick of Clark's Teaberry gum, folded it between his teeth, and on the way out with his next order, he broke into the Teaberry Shuffle, the music from the TV commercial playing in his head. Mr. Wolusky looked up, laughed, and twirled the cuckoo sign with his finger.

Darren said, "West Point, Mister Ski! I got into West Point!"

24 February 1962

Lufkin, Angelina County, Texas

Christy was sobbing. She had been in bitter cold Chicago at her grandmother's funeral when Darren got news of his acceptance to West Point. Now she was back, and upset. "I don't want you to go," she said. "The only reason I'm going to A&M is because you were going to be in the Corps. We were supposed to be there together."

Darren was sympathetic. He and Christy had been a steady item since the summer between ninth and tenth grades. They were the clichéd high school couple, him captain of the football team, her head of the cheerleaders. The senior yearbook had just come out, and everyone was asking for them both to inscribe a personal note on the page for "Mister and Miss LHS."

For Darren, the big downside of heading off to West Point was knowing he would be leaving Christy behind. He held her hand and looked into her eyes. "I'm not leaving forever. In fact, I'll be here with you every day from now until after graduation. Let's make every day count."

Christy took a handkerchief from Darren's back pocket and wiped her nose. "I know, but I still don't want you to go."

Darren said, "When Eric Snedeker went, he got to come back to Texas and spend most of the summer in training at Fort Hood over near Waco. I'll be able to do stuff like that, and you can come visit. And my dad will want to go to the Army-Navy game, I guarantee it. It's in Philadelphia. You can come along."

Darren gazed out the windshield overlooking the construction of the new McGee Bend Dam. This whole area would be under water soon. It looked to Darren like they would be ready to start filling the reservoir any day now.

"Christy," he said, "I hear you. I love you. You know that. But you also know that going to West Point has been my dream since I was a kid. I want to be a part of that. I've been studying like mad. I took all those jobs in school clubs so I could make my application stronger. I had no idea I'd get to be captain of the football team, or class vice president, but all that stuff helped. I'm as surprised as you that I was picked. But now that I've made it, I have to go."

Christy wiped away more tears. "I found a book at the library on West Point. Can we get married at the Cadet Chapel? There's a picture of a beautiful wedding."

Darren pulled Christy close and held her tight. "If you'll have me."

22 May 1962
Lufkin, Angelina County, Texas

"Darren, take a look at this, you're going to love it. General MacArthur was accepting some kind of award at West Point." Alex Bross began combing the media for snippets on the Academy as if he'd been associated with the institution all his life. He was a proud father and felt, by association, that he had the right to be familiar. He handed Darren the Sunday *Daily News*. The commentary included excerpts from MacArthur's May twelfth speech on the West Point motto.

"Duty, Honor, Country. Those three hallowed words reverently dictate what you ought to be, what you can be, what you will be. They are your rallying points: to build courage when courage seems to fail; to regain faith when there seems to be little cause for faith; to create hope when hope becomes forlorn.... They give you a temperate will, a quality of imagination, a vigor of the emotions, a freshness of the deep springs of life, a temperamental predominance of courage over timidity, an appetite for adventure over love of ease. They create in your heart the sense of wonder, the unfailing hope of what comes next, and the joy and inspiration of life. They teach you in this way to be an officer and a gentleman."

After reading, Darren held the paper in his hands and looked up. "Dad, that's it. That's what I've been talking about. I know you understand, but I'm having a problem getting Christy on board."

He walked to the kitchen, took scissors from a drawer, and while cutting the words from the printed page he remarked, "I have to find the rest of this speech." He folded the clipping and put it in his wallet right next to another clipping, one where President Kennedy asked him what he could do for his country.

Mr. Bross did understand. When he thought about his son's accomplishments already at this young age, his heart filled with pride.

7 June 1962

Lufkin High School, Lufkin, Angelina County, Texas

"Though we gotta say goodbye for the summer, baby, I promise you this. I'll send you all my love, every day in a letter, sealed with a kiss…" Darren Bross daydreamed while driving and singing along with the radio. "God, I love that song! It's my song to you, Christy. You know that, right? The singer must have known I'd be leaving. I remember, he called me on the phone and asked me when the best time to release it was." Darren chuckled.

Christy laughed too. "Who is that?"

"I think it's the same guy who did 'Itsy Bitsy Teenie Weenie Yellow Polkadot Bikini'—Brian something or other. He was on *American Bandstand* last Saturday."

"You sound just like him when you sing. Where did you learn to sing like that?" Christy asked. "That guy has a voice. I think you're related."

Darren reached across the bench seat of his parents' 1958 Chevy Impala and took Christy's hand in his. "Sixth grade choir, St. Cyprian's. Mrs. Case taught me everything I know."

He went on, but not singing, "This is it, baby. This is the end of the beginning and the beginning of the something new."

"What do you mean by that?" Christy asked.

"I just mean that with graduation today, we're ending this part of our lives. From today on, we'll only look back on our time in high school."

"Well, we had a great time together. At least it will all be happy memories. But I hope we don't have to remember that silly number three on your mortarboard."

For all his work in school, trying every day to be good enough to beat out other students in the Seventh District for Congressman Polk's West Point appointment, Darren had maintained an underlying dream to graduate as valedictorian—or at least salutatorian. But in the end he would have to settle for being ranked third in his class. *Not bad*, he thought, *when you consider I was up against three hundred and twenty-five others*. To mark his achievement, he had cut out a large gold #3 in poster paper and pasted it to the top of his purple mortarboard, school colors and all. His plan was to walk across the stage, accept his diploma, and bow to the class revealing the #3.

"Oh, I'm pretty sure it's going to show up somewhere. Too late for the yearbook, but if that photographer from the *Daily News* is paying attention, he'll snap a shot."

Christy reached across the seat, grabbed his hand, and said, "You're crazy, Darren Bross. Crazy."

CHAPTER 4

1960 through 1964
Ri'Ga, Xa Ruh, and neighboring Co-Tu villages
Hien District, Quảng Nam Province, South Vietnam

Captain Nguyễn Hữu Thảo and the three soldiers under his command learned a lesson in the worst possible way that the DeGa people of the Central Mountains of Vietnam, the Co-Tu in specific, were not to be trifled with. Since being pushed from coastal regions to the mountains in times gone by, they had a thousand-year history of resisting any and all pressure from governments. Even in the early 1960s, when much of the rest of the world was entering the "Space Age," the Co-Tu were simple people who just wanted to be left alone.

But they were also in an unfortunate position with respect to geography, and times had changed. A stone's throw away, the countries around them were preparing for a war that never seemed to end. Ri'Ga, Xa Ruh, and the neighboring Co-Tu villages had remained neutral for decades. While some individuals joined the French in a struggle against the government the Co-Tu so hated, most chose the path of staying out of any and all contact with the outside. Villages were small, and when a warrior was lost—like Hlong Dool, Kiep's father—the impact was felt for a generation. All hands were needed to maintain and sustain the villages.

The word for the tribes in the white man's jungle was "Montagnard," a French word meaning "mountain people." The French established and forever changed the relationship between the residents of the Annam Cordillera and the modern world. Before the French arrived, contact had died down, had nearly come to a stop. Many villagers had never seen a Caucasian. But those times were coming to an end. War was back. For the DeGa, an accident of geography made an almost impassable mountain range in Asia a strategic, if improbable, supply route for war.

The DeGa people recognized the threat. The Co-Tu worked to ignore it. And they were successful for years. In the spring of 1961, Co-Tu villages were visited by like-minded members of other mountain tribes. Self-appointed leaders had worked to organize them into a cooperative resistance group—resistance against all interlopers. The loosely aligned organization was given the moniker "BAJARAKA"—a word formed by combining the first two letters of the names of four of the largest DeGa tribes. When formed, the BAJARAKA were not interested in the North or the South, in communism or democracy. The rallying cry was simple: they wished to rid themselves of all things Vietnamese.

A subset of BAJARAKA was a military contingent of DeGa warriors formed under the French title "FULRO," the United Front for the Liberation of Oppressed Races. FULRO's objective was to build a united force of fighters, an army, to force the larger governments to agree to autonomy for all DeGa tribes. Vietnam, France, the United States, it didn't much matter to the DeGa. All outsiders were the enemy. FULRO fought the good fight for thirty years.

It was not lost on Vak and his elder cousins—the few who could read and write—that the group's name did not include the letters "CO" from Co-Tu. Nevertheless, they had some interest, if only because the message and impetus to join ranks was in an effort to unite all tribes against the Vietnamese. But they maintained their *toring* commitment to non-intervention.

Vak rose to prominence as the leader of Ri'Ga, and with countless ties to Xa Ruh and other surrounding villages, he was looked to as a sage of wisdom and counsel. The Co-Tu in the few villages surrounding Ri'Ga were approached, over and over, by members of the larger DeGa community, and urged to join the fight. But under Vak's leadership they refused and became an alliance only unto themselves.

By 1964 the United States was involved, recognizing that this group of people could serve as a back country resistance. A new organization, the Central Highlands Liberation Front, worked incessantly to co-opt support from the Co-Tu. With no luck. The Co-Tu admitted to sharing a common hatred of all things outside their conclave, but not to the extent that they would join other mountain tribes in resistance.

The BAJARAKA, the FULRO, and later the Liberation Front employed low-pressure tactics to encourage Co-Tu participation. Government representatives visited the villages—

soldiers, but not uniformed. After suffering countless inexplicable disappearances, the North Vietnamese regular army grew wary of approaching the Co-Tu for assistance. The Co-Tu were already considered the most primitive of the primitive—true *moi*—but their reputation for being headhunters spread like wildfire on the strength of one incident where a squad of headless NVA was found in the jungle. In reality, a South Vietnamese Army platoon had done the deed, but they knew in advance that a nearby DeGa group would take the blame—or the credit. In any case, it was a good reason to avoid these jungle phantoms. No one wanted to be the subject of a human sacrifice.

A second, less formal group had more success, in part because they looked less like government and more like friends. The Viet Cong worked hard to warm up to the Co-Tu and other DeGa tribes to reduce their level of resistance. To say that their supply lines were remote was a gross understatement. Any assistance or comfort they could receive from local villages would make the isolation more bearable. But that support was hard-won.

The Co-Tu existence was a hard life of subsistence. They leveraged the growing season to maximum benefit for the primary purpose of staving off starvation. Weeks were spent clearing mountain locations that had the potential for planting, and on roughly a ten-year cycle, the Co-Tu were practiced at slash-and-burn agriculture. Using well-controlled fires, axes, and machetes, they would cleared large swaths, plant seeds, and harvest crops. Mountain slopes were scraped clear for terraced rice paddies, and the Co-Tu would plant, harvest, and thresh, one stalk at a time. Wood was cut and collected. Nothing was wasted. One village elder would keep an eye on overuse to ensure that weak pastures, meadows, and paddies were left to go fallow after every season. And the Co-Tu were ranchers as well, practitioners of primitive techniques of animal husbandry in the raising of water buffalo, domestic pigs, chickens, and dogs.

A typical day was backbreaking for nearly every adult in Ri'Ga and Xa Ruh villages. Men hunted or trapped wild boar, cleared land, fished, and with the help of adolescents, gathered boong'boong fruit from secret trees. The location of boong'boong was one piece of jungle intelligence not shared with other villages; the fruit was rare, delectable, and jealously guarded. Women planted, harvested, milled grain, threshed rice, ported water, cared for children, had babies, fermented rice and cane wine, and in their spare time wove baskets, wove hemp and jute cloth, made handicrafts, sewed clothing, and prepared meals.

From the youngest age, Tsov accompanied Kiep on every excursion, first in a special sling designed for long-term carry, then in carts, then on foot. Tsov became a relative genius among his peers. He could wield an accurate tiny crossbow against the rare striped rabbit, clear brush with a machete like a professional, build a wild boar trap, and even weave small baskets with his mother. On occasion his father would let him practice marksmanship with a crossbow, but he was physically unable to cock it without help. Tsov and Kiep were inseparable. A boy beyond his years; a father like no other.

7 June 1966
Sông Cả River Canyon, Hien District, Quảng Nam Province

The monsoon phenomenon occurs in subtropical regions the world over. The difference is magnitude. In the simplest terms, after the spring equinox Earth's northern hemisphere begins tilting toward the sun, and the sun heats the landmasses north of the equator. Over the land, hot air rises while cooler air fills the void from below. In the case of Vietnam, the cooler air comes from the south and southeast and picks up moisture as it crosses the South China Sea. The result is rain—and lots of it. In the Central Highlands monsoon effects are magnified. Air rising over the mountains cools and condenses, resulting in extended periods of torrential steady rain accented by occasional embedded thunderstorms. The Co-Tu had lived for centuries in the midst of the annual monsoon. They knew it well. From April until October they expected and received daily downpours. It was part of life.

Uncle Vak reminded Kiep of his father, although his father was a fading memory, having now been gone over thirteen years. Kiep had forgotten, or perhaps never knew, that Vak and his father Hlong were twins. There were no other twins in any of the surrounding villages, so the Co-Tu word for a twin didn't translate well, especially when there were no examples to illustrate the phenomenon. When they were younger, villagers could tell Hlong and Vak apart only by a tiny mole underneath Vak's left eye.

After his father was killed, Kiep always thought of Uncle

Vak as a father figure, and Vak thought of Kiep as a son. Vak had one living son of his own, two years older than Kiep, Cousin Baap'Can. And Tsov had a playmate and idol in Vak's eight-year-old grandson, Siu.

Tsov was just five years old, but well on the way to building skills in the responsibilities he would need to reach manhood. And today was the first time Tsov was invited to fish with the menfolk. They would hike a few kilometers to the Sông Cả River, then upstream, following steep trails to reach hidden canyon spots. Uncle Vak knew of some secluded pools where the delicacy *cá mrớng*— mountain trout—could be found. The rising sun was their signal to move, though today the group would have to settle for breaking dawn through the clouds above.

Village weavers, men and women who were experts in their craft, provided Kiep, Vak, and Baap'Can two *tian* fishing basket traps. Shaped like a wine glass from the top of the stem up, the *tian* baskets were open-weave cages of bamboo in strips radiating from the bottom to top. These strips were spaced closely enough to prevent fish from escaping. The business end was a large opening a meter across. On the other end was a small opening wide enough for an arm to reach in. Inverted, the *tian* was raised at an angle and walked into the sun to prevent casting of shadows, toward a basking fish in a shallow pool. The large end was then quickly jabbed into the pool, over and around the fish, in hopes of trapping it. A caged fish could then be speared from the top and retrieved by hand to be placed into a *gui* basket for transport back to the village.

Detachment 19, 30th Weather Squadron

Da Nang Air Base, Quảng Nam Province, South Vietnam

FORECAST DISCUSSION: 1200Z06JUN66 THRU 1200Z07JUN66. HAPPY 22ND ANNIVERSARY OF THE D-DAY LANDING, THE WEATHER FORECAST WAS VITAL TO OPERATIONAL SUCCESS ON THAT FATEFUL DAY. HERE'S TO HOPING THIS FORECAST WILL ASSIST YOU AND YOURS IN SUCCEEDING AGAINST THE ENEMY. STATIONARY UPPER AIR HIGH PRESSURE COMBINED WITH LIGHT WINDS PERSISTS OVER THE REGION. ATMOSPHERIC MID LEVELS CONTINUE HIGHER THAN NORMAL MOISTURE. RELATIVE HUMIDITIES FROM THE SURFACE TO 500MB HAVE INCREASED OVER THE PRIOR FORECAST PERIOD FROM 58 PERCENT TO 82 PERCENT WITH AN ASSOCIATED PERCENTAGE RISE IN PRECIPITABLE WATER. RIDING THE INTERTROPICAL CONVERGENCE ZONE, A HEAVY BLANKET OF CLOUDS AND MODERATE TO SEVERE RAINFALL WILL ENVELOP THE FORECAST REGION WITH CEILINGS BELOW LANDING MINIMA FOR ALL COALITION AIRCRAFT. LIFTED INDICES REMAIN NEAR ZERO INDICATING CONDITIONAL INSTABILITY ACROSS THE REGION. THUNDERSTORMS ARE LIKELY IN COASTAL AREAS AND A HIGH PROBABILITY IN THE CENTRAL HIGHLANDS. A WEAK EAST TO WEST ORIENTED COOL FRONT WILL

PASS THROUGH THE AREA IN THE MIDDLE OF THE
PERIOD TURNING SURFACE WINDS FROM THE
SOUTHWEST TO THE EAST AND NORTHEAST
RESULTING IN SIGNIFICANT MOISTURE AND POSITIVE
VORTICITY ADVECTION OVER THE REGION. SURFACE
TEMPERATURES WILL REMAIN IN THE HIGH 80S AFTER
NIGHTFALL AND THE HIGH 90S DURING DAYLIGHT
HOURS. UPSLOPE FLOW AND RESULTANT OROGRAPHIC
LIFTING AGAINST THE NORTH-SOUTH ORIENTED
RANGES IN THE CENTRAL HIGHLANDS ALONG THE
ANNAM CORDILLERA WILL ENHANCE INSTABILITY
AND RESULT IN POTENTIALLY SEVERE STATIONARY
THUNDERSTORMS IN THE LATE AFTERNOON. LOCAL
AREAS OF FLOODING IN MOUNTAIN VALLEYS IS
FORECAST. TAKE NECESSARY PRECAUTIONS. CLIMB TO
SAFEY. VRT SENDS

Headwaters of the Sông Cả River Canyon
Hien District, Quảng Nam Province

The rain hadn't stopped since daybreak, but it was cool and
provided some respite from the sweltering heat. The DeGa lived
with rain as they lived with air. Six months per year a village could
count on rain, rain, and more rain. Because the cloud cover was
traditionally so thick, there was little opportunity for sun to bake the
ground to begin the formation of thunderstorms.

Today the wind was from the east. Uncle Vak knew from experience that this wind, blowing in their faces while looking up the canyon, was a recipe for something different. With enough fish to feed the entire village for the coming two days, a nearby flash of lightning and a bleat of thunder gave the group a pressing invite to move on.

Uncle Vak departed from his traditional unflappable bearing. Looking uphill into the canyon, he read the weather, cursed himself for his greed against the Fish Spirit, and knew they had waited too long. "Leave the *tians* behind," he said. "Baap'Can, you're stronger than the rest. Take the *gui* from Kiep." A woven, open backpack. It was full to the brim with live fish flapping on top in an effort to escape.

The group heard the urgency in Vak's voice. They knew the stories of others who had been caught in a canyon, whose spirits never left it, who shared space with the river and fish spirits for eternity.

"Hustle. Move it! Now! Kiep, pick Tsov up. He cannot move fast enough. Siu, take my hand and run with me." Vak knew it was going to be bad, but he didn't know just how bad. At the top of the canyon and extending three kilometers in either direction was a massive storm building to eighteen kilometers tall. The thunderstorms were self-feeding monsters growing to the stratosphere before flattening into anvil clouds. Easterly winds up the canyon would turn to the sky to be blocked by high pressure to the west and north. The storm would grow in the vertical until it could grow no more, and then it would begin collapsing, then grow again, then collapse again. It could not move, this self-generating engine, an intractable and powerful force of nature. Every mountain creek that fed the Sông Cả would fill simultaneously, meet in the center, and then fill again.

Kiep, Uncle Vak, Baap'Can, Siu, and Tsov were running as fast as they could on the narrow path beside the stream. Already the water was rising and covering parts of the trail. To their left was a steep embankment, to the right the rushing Sông Cả in its canyon spirit, flowing with reckless abandon, carrying rocks, rotten logs, and small trees through rapids. Steep rapids.

The water rose faster than Vak had ever seen. Too fast. He knew what to do, but he was not quite quick enough to scream instructions to the group. Baap'Can, with the *gui* full of fish, thought he could outrun the flow. "I'm off!" he shouted as he sprinted ahead. "I'll meet the rest of you below where the canyon widens!"

Before Vak could scream *"No!"* Baap'Can was gone, adroit and sure-footed. And for a short moment it looked like he might make it. But lightning and thunder were already upon them. Rain was coming down in sheets so thick it became difficult to breathe. Rain so hard it was an endless tiger's roar. A scream came out as unintelligible and inaudible.

"Up! Up!" Vak shouted. "Climb! Kiep, climb now! Siu, stay with me, climb."

"Uncle Vak, it's too steep," Kiep said. "I can't do this with Tsov in my arms."

"You have no choice. Find a root, a limb, a rock—find

anything. We have to climb up the canyon. It is impossible to outrun this water."

They did as Vak instructed, and it was working. Slowly the group was able to get above the flow of the water. Kiep's lungs were screaming with exertion. Tsov's tears added a little to the flow. Siu was proving himself a worthy warrior. Not content to hold on to his grandfather's hand, he was getting ahead and reaching back for the others. A helping hand.

Rest at last. The four found a ledge about eight meters above the fast-flowing water. Two sturdy pine trees occupied the outcropping, two trees that knew this river spirit and had survived over the decades again and again. Two trees bent so far off the rock face, it was impossible to know how they held on to what looked to be feeble roots. But hold on they did.

Vak thought they had reached safety, but then he pondered the trees. *They have seen the river spirit at this level. They know.*

It was too late. It happened. They could all hear it coming. The river spirit was now a monster ready to swallow them. So thick was the rain they never saw it, but a ten-meter barrage of water came down the canyon like a rock wall itself, proving to the canyon it was the stronger.

"Hold the trees!" Vak cried. "Do not let go of these trees! Hold!"

Siu saw Kiep struggling to set Tsov against the tree trunk. He released his own hold for an instant and reached out to help secure a foot or an arm. But water pushed at his back and over his head so hard, he had to fight for breath. No one really knew what happened, but when they looked up, he was gone, Siu was gone, taken by the river spirit in an instant.

"*NO!*" Kiep cried out, but his howl was drowned out by the storm. With no thought and no hesitation, Kiep struggled against the tree, pulled Uncle Vak toward him and wrapped Vak and Tsov together as best he could. Then he dove after Siu. If you could call it a dive; it was more of a headfirst slip into a cauldron, leaving Vak and Tsov on the precipitous ledge above.

"Siu! Hang on!" But he knew the boy was swept away. Gone. Rescue was futile.

Kiep had no sense of direction. No up. No down. His thought was only on simple survival as he was roiled in the flow. But it did begin to wane. Pushed and held to the bottom, he struggled to get his face to the surface to gasp for air. Now moving again with the speed of the water, he found some stability and frog-kicked to the surface. And then he saw the boy—Siu was ahead to the right, lying on his back, hugging a log wedged crossways between rocks, blocking the flow. Water poured over and under the log, and Siu could just hold on, but he was pinned in place by the weight of the water.

Kiep swam to his right with all the power he could muster. He reached the log and held on. "Let go, Siu!" he screamed. "Let go, I can see ahead there is safety."

"I can't!" the boy said. "My foot is wedged—rocks—"He gasped for breath, the water pouring over him, around him. "—roots. If I let go, my head will go under!"

Again, without contemplating for a second, Kiep pushed

against the log with his left hand and arm and sank beneath the flow. He reached for Siu's legs, his feet. He was lucky. He found Siu's stuck foot, and on the strength of the single breath he had taken before going under, he was able to pull it forward enough to release it. By the time he bobbed to the surface, pinned now between the log and the flow, Siu was gone again. Kiep took three deep breaths and followed, diving once again below the surface.

The canyon widened. The flow decreased. And this river, normally a few tens of meters wide, now stretched side to side more than a kilometer. Even flowing fast, that made it shallow enough that they could stand against the current.

Kiep stood, looked ahead, and saw Siu standing just downstream with his arms raised and his smile wide.

"You saved my life, Uncle Kiep. You saved me from the angry river spirit!"

The two embraced and laughed—a natural release from the tension of near-death.

The trail was gone, deep under water and washed away, but both Siu and Kiep turned their gazes upstream through relentless rain. Kiep wiped the water from his eyes. He had complete confidence that his Uncle Vak was protecting Tsov.

Baap'Can was gone. The trout-filled *gui* was gone. Vak and Siu were joined by a dozen villagers. They searched far and wide for two days before succumbing to the reality that Baap'Can had been swallowed by the river. It was a noble death, but not one they would wish on each other.

They would never know that, despite all their searching, Baap'Can had slipped just a few meters from where he had made the fateful decision to run. His corpse was hidden from view, the empty *gui* still attached to his back, wedged under large boulders and the steady flow. They had not searched the area so far upstream, thinking it too improbable that they would find him there.

Word spread as Uncle Vak told the story over and over about the brave warrior Kiep who had risked his own life for Siu's. Vak gave Kiep a water buffalo in reward, a lavish offering that no one in the village had ever witnessed.

Kiep was appreciative. He hugged Thia, Tsov's arms around his thighs, the boy's feet on Kiep's own, as he stood before the village and announced, "I am no hero. Any one of you would have done the same."

Music began. There was no fish tonight, but a roasted boar was ready to be feasted upon.

Vak stood. He quieted the crowd's caterwauling and shouts of adoration for Kiep. He raised a bamboo cup of rice wine and toasted, "To Kiep. To Baap'Can." The villagers responded in kind.

Tsov looked up into his father's eyes. "Papa. You are a hero to me. You will always be a hero to me."

Kiep called his daughters over. Paj and Mai joined in. With Thia and Tsov they became a huddle of manifest love. Kiep hugged them all and thought how lucky he was, not just for this family, but for the chance to live another day.

CHAPTER 5

8 June 1966, the fortieth Wednesday after Labor Day
Michie Stadium, United States Military Academy, West Point,
New York

Graduation was a double-edged sword. It made Darren
think about the cycles of life—at least the repeating cycle from the
bottom to the top. He remembered junior high, where he had been
a snot-nosed kid in seventh grade, but by the end of eighth he was
"Big Man on Campus." That same cycle started over in high school.
To the freshmen, the seniors looked like men. Then Plebe to the
cushy life of a First Classman. Then lazy Firsty, to scum of the Earth
at Ranger School. Now 2nd Lieutenant to what? What was next? As
an Army "butter bar" Darren would out-rank something like 80%
of the Army, but he would be stupider than 99%. It was an exciting
time, but a scary time. The world was changing.

Five years ago President Kennedy had spoken to Darren,
asking not what his country could do for him, but what Darren
could do for America. That was Darren's junior year at Lufkin High,
and it seemed like an eon ago, but he had taken those words to
heart, carried them in his wallet alongside General MacArthur's

thoughts on Duty, Honor, and Country. He was comfortable knowing he had been serving his country until now, but the real test was yet to come.

Here on the field in Michie Stadium, 575 first classmen sat in folding chairs. *Right now, every one of us has a class rank,* Darren mused, *but in ten minutes we will all be the same: second lieutenants.* From the Cadet Corps Commander, the biggest man on campus, to "the Goat," the bottom-ranked man in the class, everyone would toss his cadet hat high into the air and be commissioned a second lieutenant in the regular army. A new cycle would start.

The graduation speaker, Vice President Hubert Humphrey, droned on in a strange voice, un-inspirational to Darren, who was daydreaming. He smiled thinking of that bucket at out-processing where everyone tossed in a dollar for "the Goat." Popular culture dictated that General Patton was the Goat of his class, but Darren didn't know if that was true.

Then at last the moment came when hats went high in the air among whoops and hollers. It was over. The cycle started anew.

Darren's and Christy's parents had arrived the night before for the ten a.m. event and a vacation of sorts before the wedding on Sunday. They joined in the rousing applause then stepped out of the stands to meet out front at a predetermined spot. Brand-new lieutenant Bross had a plan. He would run back to his room to get out of his cadet uniform, don his "greens," and meet the family and his history professor, Major Ted Ferriter, out at Trophy Point. There in front of Battle Monument overlooking the Hudson River, they would share in a private ceremony to pin on his gold bars and re-

recite the oath of office. A race was on since Darren was one of about a hundred cadets who had the same idea.

Darren and Christy were married at the West Point Cadet Chapel on Sunday, June 12. Like the line of new lieutenants waiting over the Hudson for their gold bars, cadet weddings were a production during "June Week," after graduation. Darren's and Christy's Episcopal priest, Father LaBarre, was given special permission to conduct the ceremony, but the highlight for the families was the Arch of Sabers ceremony outside the chapel as the bride and groom exited. Five of Darren's ushers were brand new lieutenants. A sixth was a new West Point firsty, one of Darren's teammates on the lacrosse team. The six formed two lines, two paces apart, facing each other. Rob Batchelder from Madison, Wisconsin was best man. His position was last on the left as the couple emerged.

One usher in front welcomed the couple to the army. Then Lieutenant and Mrs. Darren Bross approached the arch and stopped. Batchelder began barking orders to the formation. By the look of things, they had practiced. "Left face! Right face! Present sabers! Arch sabers!" Darren and Christy walked beneath the arch until they reached the final two ushers, who brought their sabers to waist level, blocking passage forward. To continue, the couple was required to kiss. They did, and the sabers went back up; the couple was permitted to pass. As they did, the usher closest to Christy lowered his saber and, with its flat side, gave her a slap on her butt. "Welcome to the army, Mrs. Bross," he said.

Christy knew the tradition. She had been a bridesmaid in

three weddings that week, but it was the first time her family had witnessed this "rite of passage" into a brand new culture, a culture that would drive Christy nearly insane with new spousal rules, both written and unwritten. They laughed. Her mother blushed. It was memorable, and best of all, the photographer was Johnny-on-the-spot in the creation of a black-and-white album of memories that captured every seminal moment, including a sword, the sun glinting off it artistically, against Christy's posterior.

June – July 1966
West Point, New York; Oahu, Hawaii; Lufkin, Texas

During his four years at West Point Darren never thought much about money. The army paid cadets the base pay rate of a buck sergeant, and with no real outlets for spending it, aside from a monthly allowance, that salary built up in a mandatory savings account. Cadets could use the funds to purchase items from the Post Exchange, the PX. But the options were limited. They could buy uniform needs from the military clothing sales store, along with shoes, ball caps, and gym gear. For four years Darren's family members received some unusual Christmas gifts from him, not knowing that he was merely selecting from what he was permitted to purchase with money "on account." The West Point bookstore had worked a deal with the army to debit the cadets' balances, so T-shirts, hats, and heavy sweats seemed like free stuff to Darren, who never saw any cash in the transaction; he just had to sign a receipt.

But as he neared graduation, his biggest expenses had been the cost of a closet-full of uniforms (museum pieces now, since they could not be used in the active army) and a few other necessary items such as the obligatory class ring. And thus there remained a sizable pot of money in his account. A majority of cadets spent that money during spring break in the first class year on a new car. Cars had been prohibited on campus for the better part of four years— cadets couldn't even own a car in their hometowns—so this week was one of the most anticipated weeks of the two hundred they would spend in four years at the academy.

Darren was caught up in the hoopla. A class committee formed to work with local dealerships in order to secure a solid package deal. The dealerships were quickly on board, recognizing the windfall that comes with selling over five hundred vehicles in a single week.

And it was in the fall of 1964 that Ford unveiled its new Mustang. That's what Christy wanted Darren to get: a 1966 convertible. Seventy-four firsties agreed with Christy and became Ford Mustang owners. Everyone had kept and studied months of car magazines. There were "secret" photos of a new model from Chevrolet, the Camaro, but it was not ready in time for the Class of '66. But this was no real matter to Darren since, like many cadets, he had his heart set on a Corvette. He had dreamed of it since plebe summer when he saw brand new lieutenants driving them around Grant Barracks looking like Tod Stiles and Buz Murdock on *Route 66*, a popular TV show he tried to catch when he could during his last two years of high school. He even wrote a letter to CBS once asking them to air the series any night other than Friday—since Friday meant high school football, and in that conflict, *Route 66* lost out. He never got a response from the network. During plebe year, even with reruns, he was only able to catch three episodes while home on vacation, and the series had run its course by the time he graduated and had permanent TV viewing rights as a lieutenant. But he could not get the perceived freedom out of his mind, that dream of the open road and adventure.

Darren was also in love with Pontiac's GTO, but after a lot of deliberation he decided on a brand new 1966 Corvette convertible, a 427 cubic inch, 425 horsepower L72 model. In "mosport green," it had a black and beige soft top, green and black interior, posi-traction, and what seemed to be every other option available—except that he stuck with a four-speed manual close-ratio transmission. A Chevy dealer in Fort Montgomery, New York had been supplying Chevrolets to cadets since the mid-1930s, and the class of 1966 placed an advance block order for eighty-one Corvettes to be delivered in March. While they got a better deal than anyone walking in off the street could get, Darren, with all the bells and whistles, found himself with one of the most expensive cars in his class. To make up the shortfall from his cadet account, the local credit union helped out with a low-interest loan. He drove it off the lot for $4,673.84, an unheard of sum for transportation. Darren never once considered where he would later stash luggage as he and Christy drove away from New York as newlyweds. It was impracticality at its best.

Years in the future, on May 23, 2009, after spending two days detailing that Corvette—complete with three coats of carnauba wax—Darren Alexander Bross III was permitted to take the car from his grandmother's garage to the Lufkin High School prom. Darren was named after his grandfather. But in eighth grade the best-looking girl in school told him that his name, Darren, was the name of a dork—so he made an on-the-spot decision to go by "Ren" from then on. Naturally all his friends dubbed him "Stimpy," a nickname that stuck with him the rest of his life. In 2015, he married Lindy Warren, the very same best-looking girl from his eighth grade class, and every class from then on for that matter. In fifty years of marriage she called him only Darren, but she frequently reminded him that he was, and would forever be, a dork.

On prom night, in the warm late east Texas spring over forty years after the Corvette had rolled out of a New York lot, a classmate of Ren's pulled up next to him in a 3-Series BMW coupe at a stoplight on the Lufkin "Miracle Mile," and with a flick of his left index finger signaled a drag race. There was no contest. With exceptional clutch and shifting technique, Ren hadn't even gotten out of third gear yet when he lost sight of the Bimmer in his rearview mirror.

On Saturday June 6, Ren entered his grandfather's Corvette in a Dallas show. In a collector's world of "known vehicles," onlookers were seeing *this* car for the first time. One hundred percent original except for the tires, it seldom left the garage—and since 1995, his grandmother had had it sealed in some sort of inflatable climate-controlled plastic bag to keep out the Texas climate. It had just 43,119 miles and was in showroom condition. One man spent three hours, off and on, marveling at the machine, then offered Ren $85,000 cash on the spot. When Ren said it was not for sale, the man upped the ante without blinking to $100,000. Still no sale.

In 2016, retired lieutenant colonel Paul Gibson reached out to the family for permission to show the car as a static display at the fifty-year reunion for the West Point Class of '66. Gibson was the very kid, so many years ago, who had been in charge of arranging the Chevrolet package deal. Air Force Captain and now fighter pilot Ren Bross agreed, and the class paid for white-glove shipping to West Point. With permission, the Chevy dealer at Fort Montgomery gave the car a free two-week custom mechanical overhaul. They replaced some ancient parts, but agreed to clean and keep all the originals for shipping back to Lufkin. The overhaul was supervised by the very same mechanic who had changed the oil at 418 miles in May 1966 (the dealer found the original record): sixty-nine-year-old Chuck Young. He felt young again as he traveled back in time in this labor of love. The dealer verified that Darren's car had, in fact, been the most expensive Chevrolet in the class. On that day in 2016 it was priceless. Three hundred and nineteen classmates made it to the reunion. Everyone remembered the Corvette; fewer the owner.

In comparison to the last time Darren had earned a paycheck—running food out to patrons at the drive-in—he felt like a rich man. The army paid in chunks and categories depending on rank, living situation, married status, and such. With a monthly base pay of $325, combined with a quarter's allowance for married lieutenants of $109 per month and a stipend for food called a "subsistence allowance," Darren and Christy felt downright wealthy. What would they do with all this money?

Both sets of parents kicked in for a two-week honeymoon in Hawaii. On Oahu, they were able to secure an amazing oceanside cabin at an army recreation facility outside Waianae on the leeward side of the island. They enjoyed the beach and the island, and saved money by taking advantage of bus transportation to and from Honolulu—but most of their time was spent indoors. They were no different from a thousand other newlyweds in Hawaii in June 1966.

Darren spent the rest of his thirty days of post-graduation leave in Lufkin. He got Christy situated in a one-bedroom apartment just a couple of miles from her parents, helped his dad with a bunch of projects, and found time to paint the trim on Christy's parents' house as well. He also spent about an hour every day teaching Christy to drive the Corvette, which was so powerful it would have been comfortable as a pace car in the Daytona 500. Christy was adept with a stick shift and manual transmission—she had driven a Volkswagen beetle since the age of sixteen—but the clutch in the Corvette gave her fits. She could depress it well enough, but releasing it smoothly was a challenge. She tried again and again, but just didn't have the leg strength. She never got the hang of it. So when Darren returned from Fort Benning and took off for Vietnam, her dad gave her the VW back, and Christy parked the Corvette in their one-car garage.

Darren's orders to Fort Benning had originally been to attend the Infantry Officer's Basic Course, but army brass considered it superfluous for West Point graduates, and the week prior to Darren's scheduled start, the army made the decision to cancel the course altogether. General Ralph Haines had run a study to devise ways to more rapidly make new army officers ready for combat. Army Chief of Staff General Harold Johnson began implementing Haines's recommendations on the spot, and chief among them was Ranger School for everyone.

Lucky Darren.

19 July 1966
Fort Benning, Columbus, Georgia

It seemed like old-home week at Fort Benning. Nearly every member of the West Point class of 1966 ended up there on the way to follow-on assignments—on the way to war. Second Lieutenant

Bross's original set of orders had him serving in South Korea, but he volunteered to go to Vietnam, and, even though he didn't have a choice, he had a fervent desire to become a member of the "Ranger Club," those officers and NCOs who wear the coveted Ranger tab on the upper left shoulder of every uniform combination.

When Darren arrived in Georgia in mid-July he discovered that he was slated to begin Army Course 7-D-F4, Ranger Class 2 in September. Arriving so early to Benning saved him some leave, but put him on "casual status." And it was then he learned a new military term: "snowbirding." Snowbirds were people who were required to be at a certain location but couldn't yet begin their assignments—and so were usually kept busy with menial work. Darren was no exception. He was required to check in with Headquarters Company at 0730 every morning for tasks, and he spent the next two months in mundane busy work that included moving the post library (all its books and shelving) to a new building, auditing infantry platoon leader lectures at the Officer Candidate School, and trying to pick up some Vietnamese language skills in self-study with army manuals. During the first week he stopped by Ranger Joe's, an iconic shopping experience off post. There he talked to some old heads who helped him make some small purchases—webbing, fire starter, knives, and higher quality boots—to make his Ranger School experience "easier." He lived in Bachelor's Officer Quarters, the BOQ, and shared an adjoining bathroom with a classmate he'd never met.

But mostly, he was bored out of his skull.

On the first and second of August, Christy drove her

parents' Plymouth seven hundred miles from Lufkin to spend a week with Darren. It was her first taste—a bad taste—of future army life. A week later, after spending her visit sick as a dog, she contacted Darren from Lufkin to let him know she was pregnant. They laughed on the phone and thought back to their idyllic time in Hawaii. Her due date fell on "the Ides of March." Darren said if it was a boy, they'd name him Caesar. They both laughed and wondered who would get the joke.

Two weeks into Ranger School, during a difficult land navigation problem, Lieutenant Bross had some time to think back to a professor at West Point who had led a discussion on the concept of hell. Those who were religious were convinced the Bible contained detailed descriptions of the place, but they were wrong. The professor convinced everyone that western civilization's concept of hell had come from Durante degli Alighieri—more commonly known as simply "Dante." Dante published his *Divine Comedy* around 1300, forever sealing in the minds of men every facet and detail of "Dante's Inferno"—hell embodied. *Fun comedy*, Darren thought. When he got back to Fort Benning he would do some research to see if Dante had been a student at Ranger School.

The Ranger School experience could be summed up in a few words that included hunger, pain, exhaustion, humiliation, and pain. And then there was pain. Oh yes, and fear. But Darren was disappointed to find that the nine weeks were more of a fraternity hazing, a rite of passage, than they were true preparation for combat. He wondered what value sleep deprivation practice was supposed to provide a soldier. He was so tired in the Georgia mountains outside Dahlonega that he and his squadmates tied parachute cord to the front sights of their M-16s, and then to their TA-50 web gear suspenders, to prevent losing the weapon while walking in what they recalled as deep sleep. Losing a weapon was the ultimate Ranger School sin. Months later, while sleeping in the jungles and mountains of Vietnam, Darren would wake up from a Ranger School nightmare terrified that he'd lost his rifle or sidearm.

At one point off the Gulf Coast, near the fighter bombing range at Eglin Air Force Base, he came as close to death as is possible when while exfiltrating the beach in an LFRB: a "Little Fucking Rubber Boat." He almost drowned when he fell asleep trying to climb into a Coast Guard cutter about a mile off shore. He hit his head on the steel hull and, in the dark, might have fallen to his death—except that an NCO who was a fraction more alert than he was saved his life by reaching into the darkness and pulling him out of the water. It was the first time he seriously considered quitting the program. But a horror greater than anything he experienced during Ranger School was the fear of recycling: of having to start over at square one in the next nine-week class. For this reason, when he took a broken branch through his jungle fatigues into his left thigh after slipping in up to his neck in a Florida swamp, he didn't tell anyone.

Reconnaissance, land navigation, tracking, survival, teamwork, leadership, prisoner of war techniques, weapons search, clearing villages, and dealing with booby traps. It was all a blur while he nursed an infected wound that could have killed him. But in his warped sense of reality he deemed that starting over was a thing worse than death. While he could remain vertical, he would stand. While he could stand, he would walk.

And so on December 3, 1966, thirty pounds lighter than he had been on day one—and hypothermic and nauseated to boot—he walked across a portable stage on the grounds of Harmony Church to accept his Ranger tab from the school commander. He shook hands and traded salutes with his lead officer and lead NCO instructor, took a half dozen steps, and, without ceremony, fell down the stage stairs, unconscious.

He woke up two days later in the post hospital with an IV bag attached to his right hand. Christy and his father had just arrived and were standing by his bedside. To add to his problems, he had broken his collarbone in the fall.

It turned out that an untreated abscess in the leg, accompanied by extensive necrotic muscle tissue and osteomyelitis, took some time to cure and rehabilitate. So Darren spent Christmas 1966 in the post hospital. After the New Year he was permitted to move to Fort Hood, outside Killeen, Texas. There he could be closer to family as army doctors worked magic with experimental antibiotics to save his leg. He'd have a scar-filled hole in his left thigh for the rest of his life.

CHAPTER 6

1 October 1966

Ri'Ga Village, Quảng Nam Province, South Vietnam

The first removal of errant soldiers from the north had begun in Ri'Ga in 1960 with Uncle Vak's dispatch of Captain Nguyễn Hữu Thảo and his tiny group far from home. The killing went on as Group 559 continued construction on the Hồ Chí Minh Trail over the subsequent six years, although the display of guerrilla power was less brazen. Like a wild animal who has found a competitor wandering in its territory, the DeGa did what was needed to rid their homelands of outsiders.

The disappearances might have caused an overwhelming response from the north—in sheer numbers the murders, with no remaining evidence of bodies, could be counted in the high hundreds—but by 1965 the outsiders had grown from a trickle to thousands, so the disappearances were still a sufficiently low percentage of the total. And the Co-Tu were careful to keep that ratio reasonable—just enough to maintain resolute fear of the jungle in the minds of the North Vietnamese, and just little enough to prevent retaliation.

The Co-Tu were also careful to ensure that the missing were gone in ones and twos. They collected a head here and there to punctuate a story to be shared in the Guol. For all anyone knew they could have been taken by the odd tiger or leopard. But it was enough: both the North Vietnamese regulars and the Viet Cong gave the Co-Tu villages wide berth, even while other DeGa, outside the Co-Tu, were for all intents and purposes forced into slave labor to build a dirt highway through one of the densest jungles on Earth.

The VC were up against skilled jungle warriors, a fact they did not take lightly in the preservation of their own skins. Avoidance of the locals flew in the face of standard practice, since the Viet Cong were so far from supply lines that they had to rely on local villages for cover and sustenance. Their dilemma lay in how to befriend a village in this Godforsaken territory when everything around them was foreign.

Viet Cong is a contraction of Việt Nam Cộng-sản— essentially, Viet communist, the National Liberation Front for South Vietnam. And Nguyễn was a name like Smith in America. The local company commander of the Viet Cong was Captain Nguyễn Văn Trà. In the search for equality among the masses, the captain was referred to by his superiors and subordinates alike by the common nickname *Nhung*. Unfortunately, since it was a common name, if someone called "Nhung" in a crowd, a dozen heads turned.

For the Viet Cong, subsistence was often as important as

participating in the fight. This meant foraging, befriending villages, and, today, fishing.

"Nhung! Over here. Look over here." One of the captain's minions had located a dead body in the mountain stream. Wedged between two large boulders were the bony remains of a human. Any other time the discovery would have not drawn a sideways glance, but in the highlands the sight was rare, especially when it was a local. No one in the squad had ever seen a dead DeGa.

The captain approached, working his way around to the pool where his soldiers were fishing. He recognized the style of clothing —a loincloth had survived, as well as a colorful, patterned vest.

"*Moi,*" the captain said. "He's *moi.* Get him out of there."

"But Nhung, what do we want with a dead body?"

In the leader's mind the concept of equality didn't extend beyond the use of familiar names, and Captain Nguyễn was not in the mood for insolence, nor questioning of orders. He was close enough to the soldier to backhand him across the side of his head. "Don't question me. Get that *moi* out of there, bundle him up, and get him ready for transport."

The captain saw what his troops did not—a potential entry into a village. He knew the patterns on the clothing were specific to individual villages. This was someone's relative who had drowned in the stream. They would want him back, to return him to his spirit world. "Wherever that is," the captain said aloud.

It took some confusing discussion and yelling orders until the men in the squad realized that they were going to be tasked with wrapping the body in available cloth and building a travois to drag him around from village to village. Their first mistake was heading north. The DeGa at the first village they encountered might well have dispatched the group immediately, but luckily for the Viet Cong, the DeGa realized that these men were trying to do them a favor. One village elder recognized the pattern on the corpse's vest and, through gestures, indicated that it had originated in a *toring* on the other side of the Sông Cả, the south side. So the soldiers took turns dragging the travois south, from village to village, fearing for their lives. Village "greeters" carried spears, crossbows, and machetes.

Finally, at Xa Ruh, Thia's village, an elder directed them to Ri'Ga. "You are transporting Baap'Can," said Thia's uncle, in a language the Viet Cong could not hope to decipher. But the captain knew he was on to something when Keip's Uncle Thi agreed to lead them over the ridge line to Baap'Can's home.

The group approached Ri'Ga from the south, where the nadir of the ellipse that formed the central village plaza was located. Tsov and some of his playmates saw them coming and sounded the alarm.

Several of the most senior elders were absent, off on various tasks, but Vak was available. When he saw Thi, he relaxed his warlike stance against the outsiders. Thi explained what he could about the entourage. "I think they have Baap'Can secured in that triangular frame over there." Thi pointed to the soldier who had the current travois duty.

"How can that be?" Vak asked.

"They must have found him in a spot where you didn't

look."

Vak held up his hand in a gesture that said, "Let's wait." He sent Tsov after Kiep, the only member of the village who knew enough of the outsiders' language to make sense of this. For any other group, Ri'Ga would offer a welcome, something to drink, and a spot to sit in the shade while the guests waited. But not the Viet Cong. Vak stood stoically, leaving the squad in the plaza to bake in the sun for over an hour. This could be a ruse, after all.

Although Baap'Can's body was wrapped in a cloth, it was not lost on anyone present that there was something ripe on the travois. Walking through the triple canopy had left most of the stench behind them, but now, standing in the hot sun in the Ri'Ga square, it was back, and it invited a swarm of flies. Failing to find purchase through the wrapping, the flies took to biting the bystanders—specifically, the Viet Cong bystanders. The flies had standards to uphold, and they kept their activity to the more delectable of those present—the more recently bathed. The DeGa had not bathed in months.

To Captain Nguyễn the wait was interminable. But Vak didn't move a muscle; he stood like a French-taught mime in white makeup on a Saigon street. And Captain Nguyễn had learned enough of the DeGa to understand that trying their patience would not clear a route to their hearts—and might result in an even less-appealing outcome—so he waited quietly, despite the heat, the flies, and his irritation.

The captain spent the time observing the village. Two dogs, which looked to be feral, barked at the soldiers in a way that only

yapping dogs can. Never-ending. Annoying. They showed their teeth
and raised their hackles until an adolescent girl attached a single
leash with two identical loops around their necks and pulled them
away. Children played a game of marbles in the shade of the Guol.
Two little girls fought over a doll made from bamboo; the doll's hair
appeared to have been shaved from bamboo a strand at a time, and
it looked real. Men and women squatted on their haunches in lines
trading all manner of pipes full of fresh burning tobacco. The
village seemed like it was inhabited by normal people, and the
captain questioned whether the villagers were fairly called savages—
or whether they were just human beings trying to eke out a living in
an inhospitable land.

For the most part, the villagers kept their distance, but one
infant, who couldn't have been walking for more than a few months,
persisted in approaching the soldiers, grabbing their legs, tugging on
their holsters, and generally irritating them. The child's parents were
nowhere to be seen, and no one corrected the tiny boy. In fact, the
villagers seemed amused by him. Even this distraction was an
entertaining departure from an otherwise humdrum life. One soldier
smiled at the child, knelt, and patted him on the head.

At last Kiep appeared between two homes on stilts. He
sauntered forth in the deliberate countenance of a man who had
better things to do and so was in no hurry. Later he would tell the
elders that Tsov had located him in minutes, but that Kiep had made
a quick decision to have the squad wait in the sun while he went
about his other tasks. He regretted making Uncle Vak stand there as
well, but he knew the tactic to establish dominance would be

congratulated in the end.

Kiep walked toward the group without any display of welcome. He sidled up to Uncle Vak to learn what had transpired thus far. In front of the soldiers they traded whispers in each other's ears, knowing full well the soldiers would have no idea what they were saying even if they screamed.

Thi had been waiting in the main room of the longhouse. When Kiep arrived, he emerged and joined in a threesome with Vak and Kiep to huddle over possibilities. They could not display any emotion or interest, but they were excited by the possibility that the soldiers might have found Baap'Can.

In the end, they accepted Baap'Can's body from the soldiers. And in return, they welcomed the soldiers as guests for their roles in enabling Baap'Can to return to the spirit world. The Ri'Ga prepared a feast—it took some time, since they were not ready—and invited the soldiers to take part. Though lavish by DeGa standards, the proportions barely filled the soldiers' stomachs. However, *ta vak* and *manioc* wine were not in short supply, so everyone was able to forget their hunger. Kiep spoke for Uncle Vak and, according to custom, reluctantly told the soldiers they were forever members of the Ri'Ga village and were welcome to return at any time. Captain Nguyễn would later receive a medal from his commanding officer for facilitating the first known successful infiltration of a Co-Tu village in this section of the Central Highlands.

As an important member of Group 559, the captain had access to all things dealing with peasant logistics, except for food. He snapped his fingers at a soldier who was on guard duty at the entrance of the Guol. The man produced a neat stack of black clothing items. Brand new, they would offer the Ri'Ga villagers warmth and protection from the elements for the coming monsoon. There were not enough outfits for everyone, but Vak permitted individuals to accept the clothing from the captain, who dug though the bundle for a suitable size to fit each person who approached. Most popular were the tailored lightweight black quilted jackets that not only provided warmth, but added protection from jungle vegetation on the trails. Ri'Ga would never know that accepting these VC uniforms was a fateful decision that would make all the difference to their future.

From time to time over the coming months, Captain Nguyễn and some of his men would return to Ri'Ga for the odd meal, but the frequency of these visits waned as he realized that the villagers had even less food than the Viet Cong themselves. It was a fool's errand to try to take something from nothing.

CHAPTER 7

9 October 1966

Near Rah, Quảng Nam Province, South Vietnam

U.S. ARMY FIELD MESSAGE Ø9163ØZ OCT66

FM: 제 7 임시 보병 중대

TO: 대대본부

REFERENCE: 사전 교신

SUBJECT: 지원 요청

NARRATIVE: 오늘은 한글날입니다. 저희 중대와 함께 이 날을 기렸으면 하는 마음에 이렇게 글을 올립니다. 한글은 제가 지금 이 전문에 사용하고 있는 언어로써 제 상관들께서 이 글을 받으셨으면 하는 마음에 한글로 글을 올립니다. 다른 방법으로 이 글을 전달하려 시도했었지만 제대로 전달되지 않아 병사를 통해 전달합니다. 간간히 미군과의 라디오 교신도 실패하곤 합니다. 우리가 잊혀지지 않았다는 것을 알지만, 우리 중대가 하는 임무의 중요성을 재확인 하고 싶습니다. 우리 중대는 이제 4개월 째 야전에서 임무를 수행하고 있으며, 하루 빨리 우리를 대체할 중대를 고대하고 있습니다.

BZX99842 중대장 육군 대위 박훈세

U.S. ARMY FIELD MESSAGE Ø9163ØZOCT66
FM: 7TH INFANTRY COMPANY PROVISIONAL
TO: BATTALION HQ PROVISIONAL
REFERENCE: PRIOR COMMUNICATIONS
SUBJECT: REQUEST FOR SUPPORT
NARRATIVE: SIR, TODAY IS HANGUL DAY. JOIN MY
COMPANY IN THE CELEBRATION OF OUR WRITTEN
LANGUAGE. THIS IS A LANGUAGE I WRITE TODAY,
ON THIS MESSAGE, IN THE HOPE THAT MY
SUPERIORS WILL RECEIVE IT. THIS COMES BY
RUNNERS SINCE OTHER FORMS OF
COMMUNICATION HAVE FAILED. INTERMITTENT
RADIO CONTACT WITH THE AMERICANS FAILS. WE
KNOW THAT WE ARE NOT FORGOTTEN, BUT SEEK
SOME ASSURANCE THAT THE IMPORTANCE OF OUR
MISSION CONTINUES. WE BEGIN OUR FOURTH
MONTH IN THE WILD AND SEEK A REPLACEMENT
COMPANY.
AUTHENTICATION: BZX99842 -- CAPTAIN PARK HUN
SAE COMMANDING

Captain Park read it over one last time then folded the
message, wrapped it in aluminum foil, and rolled it into oiled paper.
He handed it to Corporal Byung. "You and Private Lee will find

Lieutenant Colonel Song at Battalion and deliver him this message. You may be ordered to return, but if not, remain at headquarters until you see us again. Do you understand?"

"Yes, sir, I understand. What is not clear to me is how I will find Battalion."

"I chose you, Corporal, because you are my best land navigator. My pressing concern is how *we* will find Battalion without *you*." The captain smiled, stood, and held out his hand for a departure shake. Corporal Byung shook, then snapped to attention and rendered a salute.

"We will not fail you, sir."

"I know you will not."

CHAPTER 8

18 December 1966

**East of Ri'Ga Village, southeast of Rah, Quảng Nam
Province, South Vietnam**

Kiep, his family, and all the other villagers were accustomed
to the sound of distant explosions to the east. They knew war was
on their doorstep, though they were precious little concerned with
what to do about it. They were to receive Captain Nguyễn and his
men, but to deal brutally with any other soldiers who made the
tragic mistake of coming too near Ri'Ga.

It was on a three-day solo hunting expedition over the range
to the east that he heard his first evidence of war too close for
comfort. This was as far to the east as he had been in years. He had
no actual traps set this far out; it was more of an escape than a true
hunting trip—a reason to get away. But he set snares on the way, and
he knew from the evidence of droppings along the trail that his trip
back would be rewarded with ten or more jungle fowl, they
themselves fattening up for the cooler weather to come.

When he heard the explosions, he made a snap decision to
investigate. He had originally planned to return home the next day,

and this detour might result in another night out, but no matter; he had not promised an early return, and the village knew there was no better man in the jungle than Kiep. Thia, the girls, and Tsov would not worry.

After a night of uninterrupted sleep in the cradle of banyan tree roots, he awoke, took care of some personal hygiene matters off the game trail, and began his trek in the direction of the sound he'd heard before sunset the day before. He wasn't certain how he'd find the spot, but he continued walking in the direction he'd marked in his mind. Distance and sound traveled on strange spirit-driven tracks in the jungle. He knew that. But his attention was drawn to birds soaring, scavengers. And he knew from their call that it was buzzards on carrion. With olfactory organs that could smell death from great distances, buzzards were often the first to find a waiting meal—the fresher the better. He followed in their direction.

As he drew closer he witnessed their competitive activity, working to fight one another off while diving back in to rip free a piece of flesh for themselves. The black ones were a common buzzard, well known to Kiep and all mountain people. Their name for the bird was something roughly equivalent to "large black scrounger." But the lighter one with the red wings was new to Kiep. He had no way of knowing it was a "rufous-winged buzzard," nor could he know that months from now an American soldier would watch this very bird through his binoculars, setting them down and raising them up over and over while sketching an image in a book filled with unlined white paper.

Kiep shooed the birds off. They reacted at first and flew

upward, but then they came to think of Kiep as competition and returned. He swung a broken branch to hit one square in the breastbone, and after that they kept a respectable distance. Fast learners.

On the ground before him was the clear recipient of the damage caused by the explosion that had disturbed the tranquility of the jungle. Kiep had no special love for animals, but when he saw this sight his chest filled with emotion. He let out an anguished cry and fell to his knees. His torment began with dry sobbing, followed by tears that flowed down his cheeks in rivulets. It might as well have been a dead relative, for in one sense at least, it was kin he would never forget.

It was a tiger. Over its left eye, disturbing the symmetry of the pattern of his fur, was a near-perfect circle of black fur centered with lighter colored gold. *It could be a third eye*, he thought—the same thought he'd had on the day when he celebrated the birth of his son, six years ago. This *tsov*, this tiger, was *his* tiger—the namesake of his son. And here he lay dead, mutilated almost beyond recognition.

The beast was lying on his right side, probably thrown to this spot, and his left eye stared upward from beneath the circular patch of black fur. And in that eye Kiep saw a plea for dignity. *How am I, great tiger, dead so young? Who will care for my young, for my mate, for my den?* In that eye, Kiep saw sadness. The jungle spirit had not cared well for this magnificent beast.

Kiep surveyed the scene and thought back to the premonition Mai had related so many years ago: "Papa, in the end, the tiger lived." But that turned out to be false. Something massive had lifted this regal jungle cat off its feet while taking out its tail, most of its hindquarters, and its spine. What was left was a mass of red mush. The buzzards could make easy work of a dead animal like this, but not in the few hours since the explosion.

Kiep searched the jungle before him. He saw small trees that had been sheared in two. In the trunks of larger ones he found tiny metal balls. A mixture of wooden and bamboo stakes were hammered into the ground here and there. He found a remnant of a handcrafted twine braided from the finest possible splitting of elephant grass. He held the string up to the sunlight and wondered who would have spent so much time to kill a tiger. He was flummoxed. His nearly complete lack of exposure to the outside world left him without the knowledge to be able to draw even one reasonable explanation. Instead he looked to his right and left and behind him out of habit to make sure no one was eavesdropping— then he sat on his haunches and cried.

Why would the jungle spirits take their king? No, not spirits. No. No. This is the work of men. There is evil here, but it is not spirits, it is men. Do spirits bring men to this jungle? It is possible spirits bring men to this jungle to hunt the tiger, to kill the king. He wiped tears from his face. *Who would want this beast dead? Did he harm men? Did he kill men? Where are the men? I see no men. I see no signs of men. It is a mystery. How is it possible? Why would spirits of the jungle permit this tiger to suffer this fate?* Kiep stood, but he continued to weep as he paced in small circles, trying to make sense of how something like this could happen. *Is this senseless death my omen? Is this senseless loss a message to me? To my family? Did the jungle spirit focus the sound of the blast in my direction so that I would come to witness this death, so that I would see the premonition of my family's future, of my son? My son Tsov?*

He snapped out of his grief and formulated a plan.

It would be two days on foot at a fast pace to learn whether his son had suffered the fate of his namesake. But first Kiep would respond to the tiger's plea for dignity, and he knew just the right way. He would hang what he could salvage of the pelt in a place of honor in the village. He would tell Tsov the story of his birth, of Kiep's friend in the jungle, of the origin of his name. This tiger would join other revered relics.

As he knelt to begin the task of skinning the carcass, he noticed that the tiger's eyelids had closed shut. He took the sign as an offer of thanks. He said a few ritual words to help the tiger's spirit soar, batted off another buzzard, and made a clean straight incision from the center of the tiger's lower lip to his neck. He would take maximum effort to retain the symmetry that defined the animal; the symmetry that was its soul. That would be preserved.

CHAPTER 9

23 June 1967

Travis Air Force Base, Vacaville, California

For some reason—one that may have had something to do with Charles Darwin and Darren's personal failure to evolve—Darren couldn't wrap his head around calculating the time consequence of crossing the International Date Line. What he did know was that it was the twenty-third of June at Travis Air Force Base, and he was boarding a DC-8 for Vietnam. A contract carrier, the plane was going to be jammed with over 150 soldiers, all uniformed and nervously resigned to their future of war in a far-off land.

Darren looked down at his collar rank. It was the first time he'd worn the uniform since departing Fort Hood and starting leave in Lufkin. First lieutenant. No pomp, no ceremony, just a set of orders. First Lieutenant Darren Bross, 8 June 1967. The year since graduation had passed in a flash.

He was one of only ten officers on the flight. Before general boarding was announced, they called one bird colonel, a couple of majors, one captain, and five lieutenants, including him, by name.

Their seating was up front—a nice gesture, but they were still packed in as tightly as every other soldier behind them. There was no first class section on this "silver bird." Darren was surprised to see the colonel on this flight; he'd had an idea that the higher-ranking officers would get special treatment. Apparently "front row, aisle" was about as special as it got.

The jet smelled to high heaven, as his mother always said. Not quite like a locker room, but like a crowd of sweaty teenagers, salty and tangy and stale. Darren knew, from discussions in the terminal waiting area, that the plane had just made a return trip, carrying one hundred fifty or more soldiers who had survived a year and stepped directly from combat in half a day to California—with dirt, grime, blood, sweat, and tears aplenty.

The colonel found his seat beside Darren, pulled a pillow from the overhead rack, and untied his shoes. "Where you headed, son?" he asked Darren, with a big smile on his face.

"You're kidding, right sir?"

"Hell no. Shit, you might be getting off along the way." The colonel laughed out loud.

"No sir, Vietnam sir, like all the other poor suckers on this flight."

The colonel gave a nod of agreement and said, "Best seats in the house." He looked over at Darren's name tape and added, "Bross."

"Yes, sir, at least we have a little leg room."

"Screw leg room." The colonel pointed with his index finger like a pistol toward the cabin door, still open as soldiers filed on.

"Right there. See those folded seats?"

"Yes, sir."

"That's where the stewardesses sit. Right there." He smiled big. "Legs, my man. Legs. If they fall asleep you might get an even better look."

Am I destined to become a pervert? I might have a different perspective on the way home, but I have other stuff to worry about right now.

And Darren *was* worried. In fact, though he couldn't tip his hand, he was about as scared as a person could be. He knew full well that in short order he was going to have the lives of men in his hands. He was already homesick. He began to daydream even as the colonel droned on.

"Vietnam it is." The colonel paused for a second. "I'd tell you it's a vacation spot, but that would be a lie. You know what?" A pause. "Bross, snap out of it. You know what?"

"What's that, sir?"

"My parents actually did go to Vietnam on vacation years ago. R&R. My dad was in the navy. We lived on Subic in the PI. Vacation. French Indochina. Imagine that."

"Do you think it'll be everything we fear?" Darren asked.

"Nah, don't sweat it. This is my second tour. My vacation was on the army staff at the five-sided wind tunnel."

"Not familiar with that, sir."

"The Pentagon, five sides. Get it."

"Ah. Sorry sir, I can be pretty stupid."

"Yeah, I had a little cross training with the ACSI," the colonel said.

"Ack Sea, sir?"

"Sorry son. Can't expect you to know that one yet. Army Chief of Staff for Intelligence. I was XO for the Deputy Chief, Herb Taylor. But enough about me. What's up with you, Lieutenant?"

It was a mentoring session for Darren, but his mind wandered. As soldier after soldier stepped through the cabin door, he felt their fear meld with his own. They were wide-eyed, and to a man, they carried with them the body odor that comes with anxiety and distress. He'd heard a couple in the terminal comment that they had never even been on a plane before. *Poor saps. Looks like they're skipping school. That kid can't be old enough to drive.*

The colonel knew his stuff, and when Darren managed to listen, he soaked it in. The colonel had been a successful battalion commander on his last tour and was slated to take a regiment this time around. His orders said he'd be assigned to Fourth Infantry Division regiment, but "everything can change," so he was not "counting his chickens."

Early in the flight—though midnight according to Darren's watch, which he had not reset—he realized he wasn't going to be able to sleep. So he stepped around the colonel's feet and made the ten-foot trip to the tiny airline latrine. And when he stepped back out of the folding doors, he looked down the fuselage at the plane full of men. About 90 percent of the overhead lights were still on. *They can't sleep either. They're as scared as I am. Jesus, why in God's name are we involved in this nightmare? How many of them will die? How many will come home in pieces?*

As if they were all waiting for permission from the front row, the soldiers began taking the lieutenant's lead and making their way to the tiny latrine up front. And while sitting up front had at first seemed like a great perk—and one stewardess in particular made Darren pine for Christy—he and the other officers soon learned that they would spend much of the flight with soldiers standing next to them in the aisle, their butts right at eye level. With the cabin altitude adjusted to around 8,000 feet, combined with nervous bowels, the cabin smell went from stale, acrid sweat to methane gas mixed with the chemical aroma of airline blue water. And when someone wasn't farting in their faces, they were all startled by the occasional sound of a rectal explosion in the head and the follow-on sigh of relief.

At one point one young man unfolded the doors, stuck just his head out, and said, "Can you find a stewardess?" The theme of the response from those nearby started with: "Trying to join the mile-high club?" Laughter and such while everyone breathed through their noses. "Fuck you, asshole. I'm outta toilet paper."

Now that would be a disaster. Darren scooped up the napkin that had fallen from his cup of coke, found two others on the floor, and stuffed them in his pocket.

The colonel showed his smarts once again. He tapped on the knee of a major to Darren's right, in the window seat, and said, "Major, I'll bet you want the aisle seat." Without a sound, the major gathered his things and made the swap.

Darren noticed the major had deep elliptical sweat stains from his armpits to his belt line. *Everyone, including this guy, gets twelve hours to think about dying, over and over, second by second. My God, this flight is never going to end.* The major's fear seeped across the armrest, amplifying Darren's own, until, like a song you can't get out of your head, Darren found himself running implausible scenarios of death through his mind, over and over. He got some fitful sleep, but he repeatedly awoke in terror and night sweats when, in his dreams, one soldier or another was killed in front of him. Viet Cong charged him. He froze and couldn't move an eyelid as bullets flew and an angry Vietnamese army officer stabbed him over and over with a bayonet.

There was one stop at Andersen Air Force Base on the island of Guam. The colonel took the handheld microphone from the stewardess, announced he was "troop commander," and said everyone could get off the plane to stretch their legs. The airline captain thanked him, saying it was smarter and safer to refuel an empty jet.

Darren took the opportunity to stroll around Base Operations. He ended up in the weather shop and cajoled some poor staff sergeant forecaster into letting him use the military Autovon telephone system to place a call back to the States. He wanted to talk to Christy one last time. The Andersen operator connected him on a morale call with an operator at England Air Force Base in Alexandria, Louisiana. But that operator wouldn't transfer the call to Lufkin because that would be a long-distance call and was not official business. So the operator did some sweet-talking with the Guam operator and tried again through Fort Hood. Still no luck. And a final try with the operator at Carswell Air Force Base in Fort Worth also struck out. Darren was disappointed, but at least the process killed some time.

Somehow on takeoff, one private first class was nowhere to be found, although his things were left behind in row 41. This could not be easily explained since there was no apparent exit from the passenger terminal and Base Operations. The aircraft captain came back to talk to the colonel after takeoff and climb-out. Word spread to the first few rows. Eventually they found the guy in one of the heads back in Guam, standing on the toilet seat so that his feet weren't visible from below. That stunt saved him a day in Nam, but he'd arrive in country without his belongings, while standing in front of some captain's desk at attention accepting non-judicial punishment under the Uniform Code of Military Justice (UCMJ).

25 June 1967
Tan Son Nhut Air Base, Sài Gòn, South Vietnam

Darren was dozing when the captain announced over the aircraft PA that Vietnam was about an hour out. The flight crew served breakfast. They had departed Travis at around midnight and even after a brief stop in Guam were arriving in Vietnam in the early morning after twenty-five hours of travel.

When the jet was taxiing in, he was astonished to see the size of the facility. He could just as well have been at a large air force base in the States. The DC-8 braked and came to a full stop on the tarmac. One of the blond stewardesses opened the main cabin door, and everything changed. Darren would spend a few moments of every day in Vietnam imagining the comforting sight of a blond stewardess closing the hatch on Vietnam as the "big iron bird" took them all back home. It was a common daydream among every American in country.

It was a bright, sunny day. Cool air from the fuselage met the dead middle of Vietnam summer. A fog formed in the first few rows of the cabin, warm and moist air condensing in the cold. One hundred degrees on the ramp, 100 percent humidity. And the smell. Darren couldn't place the smell. It was just different. An affront to his nostrils. Fetid. Sort of rotten, like there was an all-encompassing stench in the air—at least at the airport. Near civilization. Near people. Near humanity. It was a Vietnamese staple, this smell. It stayed with returning US military men and women throughout their lives. A whiff of this scent found some neurons in the brain and could take you back to Vietnam in an instant.

The tarmac was pandemonium. Hand-pushed luggage carts were headed under the wings of the jet toward the rear. A green air force fuel truck loaded with JP-4 spewed diesel fumes over the departing troops as it got into place to turn the DC-8 for its return trip. It wasn't the crew in a hurry, since they'd have to get some rest in country; rather it was a nervous corporate leadership concerned about losing a jetliner to a rocket attack. Most noteworthy was the line of ragged-looking soldiers, airmen, and marines standing on the tarmac with rucksacks and bags pulled together out of ponchos. More than a few were carrying boxes labeled as stereo equipment. Lieutenant Bross had heard there were good deals through the Post Exchange, the PX in-country.

Walking side by side, the line of fresh faces, clean fatigues and wide eyes passed just feet from the ragtag line of those departing to go home. Like a winning football team lining up to congratulate the losers after the game. Darren Bross could not help smiling. The winners were leaving; the losers arriving.

Someone from the line called out, "Hey, LT, it's good to see a smile, but you guys are so short we can barely see you. Only three hundred and sixty-five days to go before you're standing where we are." Several others chimed in, "Short timers! Time flies when you're having fun—and there's no greater fun than killing dinks!" There was lots of laughter in the departure queue. Less from the arrival group.

A master sergeant with spic 'n' span boots and a new starched uniform was the sum total of the welcome party. He saluted the colonel. "Sir, welcome back to Vietnam. Request you take a seat in that jeep over there. General Wilson wants to see you first thing. I'll be right behind you."

The colonel returned the salute. "Thank you, Sergeant."

Then, at the top of his lungs, the sergeant bellowed, "The rest of you greenhorns, load the buses!"

Sitting behind Darren on the blue military school bus was a second-tour buck sergeant. He saw the lieutenant touching the heavy metal screening over the windows. "Stops Charlie from

tossing shit into the bus, sir. Some of that shit can blow up."
Lieutenant Bross turned around, smiled, and gave the sergeant a
thumbs-up in understanding.

The "distribution center" was a hodgepodge of tents and
wood stitched together into the semblance of a building. It
accommodated the twice-per-week planeload to Tan Son Nhut Air
Base in an auditorium of sorts outfitted with folding chairs. A
private first class was handing out papers to the end of each row of
chairs.

A sergeant first class took a spot in front of the group. "Fill
out the in-processing form. Most important, we need to know your
service number, where you came from, your MOS, and where you
think you're headed."

Darren mused for a second. Landing at Tan Son Nhut was a
sure sign he'd be assigned somewhere in the southern half of South
Vietnam. Classmates had clued him in. Turned out he was wrong.

The clerk went on, "When you came in the center, you
passed by a bulletin board under that little pitched cover outside.
Come back around ten hundred tomorrow to find out where you're
headed. Then grab noon chow early at eleven hundred hours. The
mess hall is right next door. Common in-country training starts right
after chow at noon. If you've been to Vietnam before, come see me
after we break. I am not talking about vacations. Vacations don't
count."

Everyone laughed.

"Just curious. Anyone been here on vacation? No one?
There were big game tours in the fifties. Maybe one of you was on a

big game tour."

Everyone laughed again. No one raised a hand.

Darren was exhausted, but his biological clock was all out of whack with night-day and day-night. He found a Military Affiliate Radio System (MARS) station in a wooden company HQ building marked with signal corps flags. It was getting dark, but he did manage to place an awkward three-minute call to Christy back in Lufkin.

"I made it just fine, over."

"Darren, I can't hear you."

"I made it, over."

"What?"

"I made it, I love you, over."

Christy heard that and offered a quick, "I love you too. Lex is thriving," in return. The connecting operator tried to explain the characteristics of a one-way line and the need to employ radio discipline to ensure everyone had a chance to speak, but it was too much. Christy ignored the advice and waited for Darren to speak. And just when he did, she spoke and messed up the entire transmission.

But Darren heard the sentiment. It was all he wanted to hear. *Lex is thriving.*

Their son had been born on March 17—Saint Patrick's Day —and they had decided to make him a "junior." Darren didn't mind either way, but it was important to Christy; her dad was a junior, and it was a family tradition on her side. Except they didn't actually make Lex a junior, but rather, "the second." Darren Alexander Bross II.

And they called him "Lex."

Had Darren not gotten injured at Ranger School, he would never have even met Lex before being shipped off. As it was, the few months he had with his son passed by too fast. He carried photos of mom and son in his wallet and gazed at them often.

He got a few hours of sleep that night, but it was agitated, in part because his internal clock thought it was daytime and in part because of his restless anticipation of his assignment and future.

Shouldn't have, as an officer, but he sat on the dusty ground in the shade of one of the buildings in sight of the notice board next to the center entrance. Around 0945 a kid in starched fatigues who looked to be about twelve years old shuffled some papers and began stapling them to the corkboard. Darren hadn't anticipated that the entire planeload would also be keeping an eye out. In seconds, the notice board was surrounded by a crowd jockeying for position.

Darren squeezed his way into the mix and located his name. It was easy to spot—he had the good fortune of being near the top of the alphabet. In addition, they listed the officers first on a sheet of their own, so Darren was upper left corner, second name from the top. *Co. B/2ndBn/18th Inf/12th Inf Bde.* Not what he expected. He'd be headed up north to join Bravo Company of the Second Infantry Battalion, Nineteenth Infantry, Twelfth Infantry Brigade, Task Force Oregon—a task force that would become the Americal

Division before Darren returned home.

That's about as far north as you can get, he thought. *I-Corps*.

The remainder of the day was set aside for budget and finance. Most married guys set up their pay to go direct to their bank back at home—that way their wives had something to live on. This worked well for Darren and Christy. He kept the credit union account he'd had since plebe year with a small allotment to himself of one hundred dollars per month. Christy needed a local Lufkin bank since no one would take out-of-state checks even in a small town where everyone knew Darren was off to war. The rest of his money, including a few extra bucks for combat pay and a small "separation allowance," went to that account.

The final payment step was to turn in all US greenbacks in exchange for military payment certificates: MPC, or, more commonly, "scrip." The system was designed to reduce the strength of the black market outside the compounds, where the locals were supposed to deal only in the currency of piasters. But in practice, they would only take scrip—and if you had kept some dollars, you could get a better deal on anything. Darren had been warned about that, so, against official direction, he was careful not to turn in all his US currency. He had some fives and tens stashed in his ruck.

For the purposes of dreaming, the PX had four or five stands set up where soldiers, sailors, airmen, and marines could buy duty-free goods from PACEX, the Pacific Exchange catalog. Darren took about thirty minutes flipping through the color catalog, thinking of Sears and Roebuck, dreaming about what he would order before returning home. The most popular item lined up with

Darren's desires: Japanese stereo gear. A four-track reel-to-reel, amplifier, receiver, speakers. He looked both ways to make sure he wasn't being watched, then he ripped out the catalog pages with "his stuff." He folded them in quarters and filled a top pocket of his fatigues.

28 June 1967
Chu Lai, Núi Thành District, Quảng Nam Province, South Vietnam

After a couple of days of in-country acclimation, culture, weapons, and tactics training, the trip to Chu Lai from Tan Son Nhut was in a C-130 Hercules turboprop cargo plane with canvas sling seats. It reminded him of jump school at Benning during his third class summer. The canvas bench was aligned parallel to the fuselage in case anyone wanted to pretend they were "Airborne," except that the rucksack wasn't a good substitute for a parachute. Darren guessed there were a couple of soldiers on the flight who would jump given the choice when they imagined what they might be facing.

If Tan Son Nhut had reminded him of an air force base in the States, Chu Lai was a little more primitive, as were the other two Marine Corps bases he had seen, but as the location for the army's Task Force Oregon Headquarters with a two-star general in charge, the post got more resources than many other remote marine locations. In less than a month he'd be looking back on Chu Lai as *civilization*. Hot food. Hot showers. Clean sheets.

When they landed in Chu Lai, a line of two-and-a-half-ton trucks, "deuce and a halfs," picked up everyone from the tarmac, sorted by battalion. Darren watched the prop wash cut the humidity into swirling vortices, helical vapor trails formed from the high level of moisture in the air and in the spreading stains under his armpits. Engines running, the C-130 was back in the air before they finished loading the trucks.

First stop was the chow hall for what the two-timers, those on their second tour, called "the Last Supper." It took Darren about a week to understand how right they were.

The place was a standard mess hall. Darren marveled at how close it resembled both the smell and the food choices back home—that is, not good and not much. But he was happy. Food had never been a big priority for him, at least not up until then.

On the wall just to the left of the entrance—a spot that every soldier would have to pass—was a twenty-four-inch framed poster. It read:

THE CG's TENETS OF COMBAT:

Mandatory Reading.

1. **FRIENDLY FIRE IS NOT**
2. **NEVER FORGET THAT YOUR WEAPON WAS MANUFACTURED BY THE LOWEST BIDDER**
3. **THE ENEMY ATTACKS ON TWO OCCASIONS: WHEN THEY'RE READY AND WHEN YOU'RE NOT**

4. INCOMING FIRE HAS THE RIGHT OF WAY
5. IF THE ENEMY IS IN RANGE, SO ARE WE
6. ANYTHING YOU CAN DO CAN GET YOU KILLED. THAT INCLUDES NOTHING
7. IF IT'S TOO HARD FOR CHARLIE TO GET IN, IT'S TOO HARD FOR US TO GET OUT
8. TRACERS WORK BOTH WAYS
9. IF YOU CAN'T REMEMBER, THE CLAYMORE IS POINTED TOWARD YOU
10. MINES ARE EQUAL-OPPORTUNITY WEAPONS
11. WHEN IN DOUBT, EMPTY YOUR MAGAZINE
12. EVERY COMMAND WHICH CAN BE MISUNDERSTOOD, WILL BE
13. IF YOU ARE READY FOR THE ENEMY, HE WON'T SHOW UP

Darren smiled and read the list over a few times, not because he thought the commanding general had made it mandatory—he had—but because he simplicity and truth of the thirteen statements was undeniable. In the coming months, Darren and his men would prove many of them time and time again.

He turned back toward the chow line as soldiers passed on his right. And there he was, four places ahead in line, towering over just about everyone else in the place: Roger Staubach.

Back at Tan Son Nhut he had run into a West Point classmate who told him that Roger Staubach was stationed at Chu Lai and that Darren should try to look him up. Fat chance. When Darren was a plebe and third classman at West Point, Navy had shellacked Army at the Municipal Stadium in Philadelphia. A win in 1962 would have meant special plebe favors throughout Grant Barracks, from the time the game clock ran out in November through to Christmas leave: no squaring corners, no square meals. Then in 1963 Staubach started his powerhouse run toward the Heisman Trophy, which he later won in 1964. Darren remembered being ecstatic when, in November 1964, Army somehow beat Staubach and Navy. But the man was still picked in the NFL draft. Why in the world would any self-respecting West Pointer want to meet Roger Staubach?

But now here he was. And he had on the strangest-looking uniform. Jungle fatigues were just beginning to replace regular olive drab green cotton fatigues in Nam. They were coveted; cotton duck in a loose fit that was cooler than the old style of wrinkle-prone heavier material. The chest pockets were angled to make them easier to access. The pant legs had drawstrings and cargo pockets on the thighs. This was a true utility uniform, suitable for the Vietnamese climate—if anything could be said to be "suitable." Every army soldier and marine Darren saw wore their fatigues, jungle or not, with sleeves rolled above the elbow. At a distance you could separate a marine from a soldier by the way this was done. Marines rolled inside out, soldiers right-side out. But instead of adopting that convention, and even though he was Navy, Staubach wore short-sleeved jungle fatigues. *How weird*, Darren thought. He had never seen such a thing. He later learned if you were never headed into Indian Country, you could get by with short sleeves. He would come to despise these kinds of guys.

Lieutenant Bross was on his way to the Second Infantry Battalion, set up as a temporary, becoming permanent, location out on Route 14 near the village of Dai Loc. The deuce and a half dropped him, eleven NCOs, and a few other enlisted men at a US flag on a pole in front of what was marked by a sign as *2nd Battalion, 18th Infantry.*

He had never seen so many sandbags in one place. The battalion headquarters building—a one-story structure with a low door and shallow pitched roof—was sunk a little into the ground and appeared almost to have been constructed entirely of sandbags. They were stacked four feet high around the perimeter. Darren had taken mechanical engineering at West Point, and he wondered in passing how the roof could take the weight. He had some criticism already. *They should be overlapped like bricks,* he thought, *not stacked in columns side by side.* And, *if you want to protect your headquarters from rocket and mortar attacks, why do you mark the target with the only US flag in fifty klicks?*

A screen door held closed by a long skinny spring creaked open on cheap hinges and slapped shut on the other side of a tunnel of sandbags, and a lieutenant colonel and a captain stepped out.

"Lieutenant Bross, welcome to the Second: *second to none.*"

Darren popped a salute and screwed up his face a little. "Sir? Second to none? I spent some time with the Second Infantry

Division one summer. Sounds familiar."

"Yeah, we know it's the Second ID motto, but we decided to plagiarize it. Oregon brass has no beef."

The colonel returned Bross's salute and extended his hand. "I'm Lieutenant Colonel Jim Long. Are you lovin' Vietnam yet?" Colonel Long wore a combat infantryman's badge with a star fixed in the center of the joined wreath. *He must have served at least one combat tour in the Korean War. The star is probably his second award for Vietnam.*

"Yes, sir." Darren chuckled and then said, "It's everything it was promised to be."

The colonel reached an arm around the captain, pulled the man forward a bit, and said, "Say hello to Captain Mark Evans. You're going to get to know Mark well. He's Bravo Company commander. We haven't figured out where you're gonna go yet, but it's no secret you're going to be out there humping it through the elephant grass and leeches as a platoon leader."

"That's what I expected, sir. I think I'm ready."

"No, you're not ready. You won't be ready until you live through this nightmare for a month or so, but OJT is the order of the day."

"Got it, sir!"

"Get to know Evans here. He's going to be your lifeblood until he thinks you have your shit together." The colonel spun on his heel and headed back into the bunker of sandbags. But before he was out of sight, he turned back and showed a mouth full of teeth. "Come to think of it, he'll be your lifeblood even *after* you get your shit together."

"Yes, sir." The lieutenant held his salute, but it was not returned.

"No saluting here at Battalion, Bross," Evans said. "Makes the old man a target." The captain reached out his right hand for a firm shake. "Mark Evans, class of '62. We didn't overlap. My June week ended a couple of weeks before you started Beast Barracks."

Darren sized up his company commander's uniform. Standard-issue green fatigues, white name tape "EVANS," green US Army tape, division soldier patch, combat infantryman's badge CIB sewn on. This guy had already lived it.

"Let's go get some coffee," Evans said.

Captain Evans and Lieutenant Bross stepped off alongside each other with Bross on the right. Darren quickly took a back step and moved to the captain's left. "Can't walk on your right, sir."

"Cut out that protocol shit, Bross. You're gonna get me killed. There's a sniper out there somewhere who's trying to figure out who you are and who's the boss. You're making it too easy."

"Sir, I doubt the Vietnamese share many of our military customs."

"Bullshit! The traditions of damn near every army in the world are based on Napoleon's ideas. Let's not take any chances."

Darren was thinking *Prussian ideas*, but oh well. West Point training and traditions die hard, but Darren took the hint. "Got it, sir. Won't happen again."

Battalion HQ was set up in a loose square of high-wire fences, concertina wire, short corner guard towers and GP Large tents on wooden floors set up on either side of "roads" crossing perpendicularly. They passed by one of the tents with a plywood entryway. There Out front was a white painted plywood sign on four-by-four posts. It read, "Bravo Company, 2nd BN, Commander:" A spot for a hanging board naming the commander was empty. *"More operations security,"* Darren thought.

Evans saw Darren craning his neck back and pointed over his shoulder with his thumb. "Company HQ," he said. "We'll stop by after chow."

The mess hall was a low-slung, more permanent building. Long, L-shaped, concrete blocks about a meter up, clapboard above that ending in a corrugated tin pitched and gabled roof. Windows were screened, but open air, with plenty of overhang to the eaves to roll off all but the fiercest rainfall. The mess hall entrance was appointed with a flowerbed outlined in a short, lightweight white picket fence.

Someone has too much time on their hands, Darren thought.

He wondered why the mess hall had no sandbags like the battalion and company structures. It was a central gathering spot three or four times per day, but it was located deeper within the compound, so maybe it was better protected than he thought. *It doesn't take much time to start getting in the combat state of mind.* That mindset would soon come even faster than he knew.

In the days and weeks to come, Bross would think back on

this meal with Mark Evans and envision how he could get a "cushy" job back at Battalion Headquarters. He imagined that, as it had for Evans, it would take at least a second tour in Nam and a CIB on his chest. That was way too far out to think about now.

Hot chow. Darren sat down with a couple of burgers, ketchup, mustard, lettuce and tomato, and chips. It came with a bottled Coke to wash it all down. As a kid, Darren had started a collection of Coca-Cola bottles. The bottom of each one told where it originated. He took the last swig, and by force of habit turned it over and read "JOHNSON CITY, TENN." That was one he didn't have. For a brief moment he thought about how he might add this to his collection. That, just before tossing the green tinted glass into the trash.

Captain Evans began, "Bross, here's the deal. Colonel Long is short. He only has something like twenty-something days left in country. As one of his last official acts, he slated you to take Second Platoon. Bobby Jacobs has it now. He arrived in country about seven months ago out of OCS and some infantry school. He's done a pretty good job, so he's being rewarded. He's going to be my company XO. We're going to give you a chance to get your feet on the ground, but that's going to go fast."

Darren was nodding his head and taking it all in. "How long do you think it will take, sir?"

"Kinda depends on you, but I will say when guys find out they're coming back to civilization—and we consider Battalion to be civilization—they start getting really nervous and superstitious. I know, I was out there twice as a platoon leader hoping I'd live long enough to make it back to HQ. Not trying to flip you out, but the gig is getting back home alive. Killing Charlie and getting the fuck back on that freedom bird."

"How's the platoon doing?"

"Bunch of fuckups." Evans laughed to himself. "We're all a bunch of fuckups. Actually they're doing great, but taking their share of the casualties, WIA… and KIA. We just had a seasoned sergeant first class arrive last week. He's out in the field with first platoon getting reacclimatized. Crusty fuck. Old as fucking dirt, but it's his second tour. He volunteered to come back. You're lucky, really lucky. That motherfucker will keep you safe. Keep you alive."

Well that's a relief. I can relax a little. An older platoon sergeant on his second tour. Yes. At least I don't have to worry about getting a brand new twenty-year-old squad leader brought up in the field. Fist pump later. First stroke of luck.

"Good stuff, Captain. I can use all the help I can get," Darren said.

"No shit." Evans smiled.

Lieutenant Bross ducked his head and ran with two other PFCs to the UH-1 Huey helicopter waiting at the Battalion helipad. There was no way his head could hit the spinning rotors, but he wasn't going to take any chances. He was carrying less weight than he thought he would be. That morning Captain Evans went through all his TA-50, all his gear and rucksack, and made three piles.

"This pile is the shit you need. That pile is the shit you may need. The other pile is the shit you will never need. Air mattress? Are you fucking kidding me? If you show up in the shit with an air mattress people are going to die laughing. We can't afford any more casualties."

Darren held it up. "Why do they issue these things?"

"Because the wimp motherfuckers back at garrison use 'em. Might as well bring a twin bed on your back with you. Supply sergeants have a motive. They don't know where you're going and they don't care. What they do care about is moving inventory."

Darren saw his flak jacket in the second pile. "*Might* need a flak jacket? *Might?* Sir, I notice you don't wear it here at Battalion, but don't you recommend a flak jacket out there?"

"Flak jacket is up to you. Lots of guys wear them, lots of guys don't. Right here in our brigade there's a battalion commander who orders everyone to wear it. You want to piss guys off? Order them to wear this short piece of chain mail."

Darren smiled—and almost laughed.

"If it was chain mail," Evans continued, "it would at least let a breeze in. Wearing this thing around is like carrying your own steam bath. But there's no way I'm going to keep you from making your own decision on this one. It has a long history of keeping people alive."

Darren picked it up and tossed it in the pile of "shit you need." "I'm gonna start out with it at least."

"As I said, your call."

Once Darren had his combat gear winnowed and organized,

Captain Evans told him he was headed out to be temporarily attached to First Platoon out at LZ Regulator. "Ten days or so, to get your feet on the ground." That turned out to be the biggest understatement Darren had ever heard. "I'll be out there with the rest of the company day after tomorrow. See you then."

The flight out to the LZ surrounding Bravo was uneventful. The chopper wasn't armed with rockets and grenade launchers like others Darren had seen on the ramp in Chu Lai, but there were two door gunners—strapped in since this chopper had no doors. They were wielding M-60 machine guns to return fire in case someone out there on the ground got ambitious. Darren looked out the door, cooler wind blowing. *Abject poverty. Christ, what if an army was occupying Lufkin? These poor people. They've been dealing with stuff like this for their entire lives. Looks like that cart has wheels that were just invented. Here we are in a chopper. Do they think we're protecting them? Are we the help, or the problem? Damn, it's gonna be a long year.*

Nap of the earth, the Huey flying low to keep snipers at bay, Darren looked down on dusty villes, wooden shacks topped with corrugated steel or thatch, humanity walking, carrying improbable loads, leading water buffalo, slinging water, waving at the chopper and Darren waving back. A subsistence culture wallowing in a filthy, humid, pitiful existence overlaid with war and pestilence. *Every complaining American should spend just one day in some shoes over here to know how good they have it.* He smiled and shook his head. *These people don't even have shoes.*

Pointing down in an exaggerated motion with his left arm and hand, he screamed to the door gunner, "Is that Route 14?" The gunner gave him a thumbs-up. Below them was a patchwork quilt of dirt, mortar craters, concrete patches, rickety bridges, and asphalt. A ribbon of arterial blood from the coast west and then southwest to the central mountains.

They took no ground fire on that trip, but Darren learned not to take the relative safety of a quick ride in a *slick* for granted. Hidden VC were paid more than a year's wage for shooting a chopper down. A single shot had as much chance of making the kill as winning the lottery, but the payback to one sniper was in lottery proportions, and that, in itself, caused constant airborne danger. Darren noticed that the door gunners had extra flak jackets secured to the chopper floor near their feet. Rounds from below. From experience, don't take chances. There were lots of extra flak jackets around, it turned out.

Landing Zone, or "LZ," Regulator was the Bravo Company firebase twenty-five klicks almost due west of Battalion HQ, just north of Route 14 outside the little village of Thuong Duc. It bordered a northwest-to-southeast *ca*, a stream that flowed from the northwest through An Diem. Put two football fields alongside each other, run a stream along one edge, install a boatload of heavy wire fence and concertina, add a few hills for terrain relief, and you've got LZ Regulator. A patch of dirt. Simple. A patch of mud much of the year. Still simple. A sign near the makeshift flagpole next to the helipad named it. Someone had done an excellent job painting a facsimile of an old Regulator school clock. Beneath the clock in block letters it read, "LZ Regulator, Your Time in Vietnam."

To Darren, it seemed like First Platoon was undermanned with thirty-eight soldiers, half with over six months in country, the other half with less. He later found out that thirty-eight guys was more than a full contingent in Nam—"fat" by any measure. The platoon leader, Chad Elbert, was a second lieutenant who had graduated from OCS just before Christmas while Darren was on a pain drip in the Fort Benning hospital. Thirty-two days after graduation Chad was named platoon leader in Nam. That wasn't much time to get acclimated, but Darren soon figured out this guy had his ducks in a row. Either Chad was a quick study, or the six months in country had seasoned him well beyond his years. Darren guessed the latter.

"Two things to remember," Chad said. "If you can make it two weeks, you double your chances of making it two months. If you can make it two months, you quadruple your chances of making it to the end. I spent my first month thinking there was a bullet out there with my name on it. My platoon sergeant told me something that changed it all: 'Don't worry about the one with your name on it. Keep an eye out for the one that says *To Whom It May Concern.*'"

Darren might have chuckled if the lesson hadn't hit home, and if it hadn't been the tenth time he'd heard the aphorism. Nevertheless, he would think back on those words in the weeks to come.

There were four platoons. Bravo Company shared the real estate somewhat equally. An 81mm mortar platoon was centered on

Hill 901, charged with setting up fires to protect the LZ. Although "Hill 901" was not much of a *hill*—it was more like a bump in the middle of the LZ. From the perspective of the guys, the LZ was sort of a mini-firebase with effective fire support out to about five kilometers. They were ready if and when one of the rifle platoons needed help.

Army Field Manual FM 7-15 covered some outdated tactics that had a mortar platoon humping it out there in the bush with the rifle platoons, but those methods were written back when 60mm mortars were the order of the day and the US Army was in Germany preparing for an invasion through the Fulda Gap. You'd kill a mortar platoon in Nam from heat exhaustion asking them to drag weapons like that through the jungle. The weapons platoon had a good number of four-deuce, 4.2 inch mortars for illumination, firebase defense, and heavy, longer-range fires, but no one was asking them to expend manpower moving them around.

Lieutenant Elbert explained to Darren that First, Second, and Third Platoons shared short-range patrol missions, mostly daytime. "Close with and destroy the enemy you encounter. Stay away from booby traps. Keep this piece of ground. Keep your guys alive. Fight the boredom when there's nothing else to do."

Darren took a look at Chad's jungle fatigues. Standardization was an issue here. He'd been lucky enough to pick up a set of the new issue, similar to the ones he'd seen Roger Staubach wearing, but his name tape and US Army tape were sewn horizontal to the ground. Chad's lined up along the angle of his pockets.

Chad saw him looking at the CIB. He touched his left breast

with his right hand. "The MACV requirement is thirty days in active close combat. There's probably an army reg out there that says something different, but who has time for that shit? You started yesterday at Battalion. If you make it thirty days, just plan on sewing it or pinning it on. The adjutant will get to the paperwork later."

Darren was lost in thought for a moment, a pause that went on just too long for a normal response. He considered the possibility that he would not last thirty days, then he dismissed that thought and said, "Not that big a deal to me," trying to sound uninterested, when he was secretly counting the days on the calendar until his CIB award.

"Fuck that," Chad replied. "It makes a difference to the guys out here. First lieutenant with a CIB, when the new guys show up, they just assume you've lived through it and will bring them out alive. One thing you're going to figure out quick is that about one in twenty of the zillion troops over here is actually in contact with the enemy. The rest are assholes back in the rear letting us do all the dirty work, rear area motherfuckers. I shit you not, every week you are going to get a request from some dipshit in the rear who wants to attach to your platoon for thirty days so he can get the CIB."

"You gotta be kidding me!" Darren said.

"Oh yes. I promise you, you are going to zip more than one of them up in a body bag. Once in a blue moon someone shows up who actually helps the cause, but not often enough."

4 July 1967

Landing Zone Regulator, Near Thuong Duc, Quảng Nam Province, South Vietnam

Bross's first mission into the bush was an exercise in army standardization. Lieutenant Elbert was under scrutiny from Captain Evans to get it right, to show Bross that an OCS "ninety-day wonder" could be every bit as sharp as a four-year West Pointer. Bross had classmates who spent too much effort deriding OCS as worthless; Darren had little time for those kinds of unhelpful comparisons. History was replete with exceptional officers who had earned their commissions through OCS. And he had no idea why they were called "ninety-day wonders" since OCS covered more than five months, with as much tactical training as he had gotten at West Point, perhaps more. He learned later in an O Club discussion that the air force school was ninety days. "Now those motherfuckers *are* worthless," his tablemate said.

Darren made a personal vow to avoid the "West Point Protective Association," an ad hoc system more than an organization, whereby the ring-knocking brass would look out for the more recent graduates. There was documented evidence of preferential treatment. Darren wanted no part of it, but out of habit, he felt for the class ring on his right hand, remembering it was secure in Christy's jewelry box alongside his wedding band.

Darren stepped into Elbert's tent and noted two carved wooden plaques from a lieutenant who took them seriously. One sported the unofficial Fort Benning motto: "If You Ain't Infantry,

You Ain't Shit!" The second was less a bumper sticker, more a poem of sorts. It started out, "Far across the Chattahoochee..." Darren was just getting to "For we are Infantry" when Chad said, "OCS motto. You can get anything you want carved in the ville outside Battalion Headquarters. I'll bet they have a lot of practice with 'Duty, Honor, Country.'" He shot Darren a derisive grin. "Let's get to work."

"Trust me on this Chad," Darren said, "I don't have anything against OCS. The top grad in our Ranger class made the rest of us look like amateurs. Twenty-three of us had just graduated. We had no hope of keeping up with that guy. He was OCS in a sea of West Pointers."

"Thanks," Chad said. "Inferiority complex I guess. I worked my ass off to make it to one of the service academies, but I couldn't figure out how to break the code to get a political appointment. And I wasn't a jock. Sometimes it'd be nice to be a member of the club.

"Well, let's get to it." Lieutenant Elbert leaned over a table with a large, taped-together grid map of the area surrounding LZ Regulator and extending to the west. "Battalion transmits the orders direct from S3 and copies Bravo. I suppose Evans could get a veto, but I think Battalion gets their taskings from on high somewhere, MACV, or maybe even the Pentagon."

"So what's the plan?"

"Short story, we wake up at dawn, if a rocket attack doesn't wake us up earlier. Everyone gets chow, brushes their teeth, takes a dump, packs up their shit, and test fires their weapons."

Elbert paused as his platoon sergeant, Sergeant First Class

Major, stepped through the slapping screen door. Before Elbert could make introductions, Darren offered, "Sergeant Major and I met in the chow line yesterday." He reached out his hand to shake. "I didn't think about it until I said it aloud, but your name must confuse the hell out of the brass, Sergeant Major."

"Yes, sir, my plan is to one day be Sergeant Major Major." Major laughed to himself. Not the first time he'd used that line.

Lieutenant Elbert continued. "The thirty-eight of us leave the LZ, walk around in an organized fashion, find and disarm booby traps, detonate enemy mines, and engage Charlie when we find him."

"Ambushes?" Darren asked.

"Sending or receiving?" Elbert answered.

"Both, I guess."

"If we get a bead on NVA or VC we're authorized to set up an ambush, but we've only done it four times since I've been in command."

"Why so few?"

Sergeant Major answered, "Nobody to kill, sir. They should give us authorization to get fast and agile, go out farther and find those fucking zipperheads. Rumor is that new tactics are coming, searching villes and setting up traps on the expected escape routes. We know Charlie is in the villages. Storm in, watch the cockroaches scatter, lay in wait for the ones along the best path out of town."

Darren wondered if he was going to be able to retain the promise to himself to treat the Vietnamese people as people. Maybe he'd be calling them zipperheads after a few of his guys were killed, but for now, it just didn't sound right.

"The tactics you learned at the academy and in Ranger school would tell you that our platoon attacks as part of a coordinated company action. We'd maneuver under cover of fire support to assault the enemy."

"And?" Darren asked.

"Not so here."

Darren thought back to the non-combat lessons he'd learned as a Ranger. "I guess that makes sense if there's no massed enemy to attack."

"That's right. It's guerrilla warfare. We have to sneak around, find them, and zap them. Even so, with freedom of action as an autonomous platoon, I still want to keep the guys alive. So far I haven't come up with anything better than army tactics formulated over two hundred years of fighting."

"So you organize your squads for standard maneuver?"

"Exactly. Well, not exactly, but not far off."

"How long are we out there?"

"Depends on what Battalion orders, but we're on a platoon rotation with the second and third, so a week is normally about the max. There are rumors floating around that we're going to be extended to two weeks to get all the way up to the Laos border, but that hasn't happened yet. Two weeks of C-rations would be heavy as shit."

Darren was impressed. Lieutenant Elbert and Sergeant Major were consummate professionals. Step by step, using the map as a reference, they outlined scenario after scenario with detailed discussions on supporting fires, effective jungle combat formations, keeping fire teams intact, closing with the enemy as a coordinated effort of squads and teams, and keeping some support in reserve. A true leader of his platoon, Elbert walked through continuity of operations—that is, when Sergeant Major takes lead, when a squad leader takes the platoon sergeant role, who takes the squad, and a backup plan for the radio-telephone operator, the RTO. When the RTO went down, it was imperative the position be filled immediately with someone who could haul the extra twenty-five pounds and knew how to operate the equipment and run the ciphers on a whizz wheel without missing a beat, zero hesitation.

By hour two, the night before the July 5 mission, they were planning the time of attack, regrouping, assembly areas, proper attack positions, lines of departure, mission boundaries, and known trail systems to exploit.

The platoon sergeant outlined who would be best on point and on slack to spot mines and booby traps. "They're the most dangerous jobs, Lieutenant Bross, but if you have the wrong guys doing it, you can get in deep shit fast."

Lieutenant Bross pencil-marked every village in the operating area and added a red "X" where VC were suspected. There was no plan to destroy villages—the plan was to gauge the locals for potential offensive activity.

The planning session was exhaustive. Darren was mentally spent when they wrapped it up. He took the lesson from this night as his own model of professionalism.

Darren sat in his bunker quarters as the sun went down on

this 191st Independence Day and wondered whether Lufkin would hold fireworks at the high-school stadium. Or had they already? He still wasn't exactly sure if the clock in Texas was ahead of him or behind him.

After just a few days on LZ Regulator, Darren knew the night belonged to the enemy. You could let your guard down all day on the LZ, but night was different. Eleven hours of biting your fingernails, pretending you weren't scared shitless, and trying to get some sleep. Hoping your LZ wasn't chosen for an NVA overrun. Sunset tonight was at 1842. The setting sun was an important time in Vietnam.

Darren looked at his watch, relaxed as some stars broke through the dissipating thunderstorms, and began nodding off as the sun dipped below the mountains to his west into a beautiful orange sunset. The sky was on fire with wispy high clouds looking like fingers of flames.

He dozed for about forty-five minutes. When he awoke, he took a look at his GI issue watch and noticed he had 17 minutes before his duty rotation at 2000. Every line officer and platoon sergeant on Regulator shared the task of walking the perimeter fence, on the inside, to check on defenses, talk soldiers out of their sleepiness, and to show some command presence. Still groggy, he was startled by *whumpf, whumpf, WHUMPF, bloop-whumpf*. Weapons platoon was lighting off mortars, 60mm and 81mm. The four-deuces might as well have been 105mm howitzers. The night sky filled with tracer and illumination rounds, Willy Pete on parachutes. Whooping and hollering from all over the LZ. Fifty other soldiers were shooting their M-16s with tracer rounds and M-203 grenade launchers indiscriminately into the sky. Someone played the national anthem just loud enough so Darren could hear it. He looked around. Against custom, no one was standing. The enemy and every village within miles could see the spectacle. Other LZs on the horizon joined in. Some lone mortar unit high up in the mountains added to the celebration. Fireworks, expensive fireworks, Vietnam-style. The entire countryside lit, shadows cast in all directions. "Amazing!" Darren mumbled to himself. "Happy Fourth of July."

CHAPTER 10

4 July 1967

Ridge line above Ri'Ga Village, Hien District, Quảng Nam Province, South Vietnam

A clear, bright, beautiful evening was rare in the Central Highlands summer. But since stars had been showing themselves the night before, Kiep took it as a sign to take the family on an outing to see the sunset. The ridge line between the neighboring villages was an easy hike. Mai had just turned nine, Paj was almost eight, and Tsov, at six—going on twelve—could climb like a monkey. A well-worn trail led from Ri'Ga to the ridge, then along its backbone to a small rocky peak above. It was a location known well to them all.

Thia carried a full family meal in a *gui* on her back. Kiep wielded a spear and used it mostly as a walking stick. Their family dog doubled or tripled their walking distance by running back and forth along the trail ahead and behind. He'd stop and point from time to time, then unleash a growl and an angry bout of barking at any of the hundreds of creatures present near dusk on this day.

This ridge was safe sanctuary when we were children. Just wildlife trails. Now I see human activity. The condition of the paths reminds me of searching for the brass casings. Soldiers are too close. Kiep had walked the route the day before to ensure his family would not suffer the fate of the tiger he had found cut in half—or the fate of a number of neighbors. *My tiger was first. My neighbors have suffered death. The tiger's prophecy. I do not offend the tiger spirit. My father did not teach me. I must speak with the elders. They worship the pelt, stroking its fur. I walked this jungle for years with no fear. I do not fear the animals of their kingdom. I do not fear the dark or the unknown. Should I fear man? Should I fear the soldiers? These weapons have no call to return my friends, my relatives, my neighbors to the spirit world.* This, he reckoned, was all the more reason to brutalize the soldiers who dared to enter Co-Tu lands. They were to blame. *We do the work the spirits command. We rid the jungle of this scourge.*

In a three-canopy forest a panoramic view of the sky was rare. Even less common was a simultaneous look at both the eastern and western horizons. That's what made this a special spot. Kiep pushed forward, reaching back to help his family, one at a time, navigate and scramble over steep sections of rock and loose taluses. A final squeeze through a seam in the stone got them to the top.

They stood on a circular pad of concrete with a diameter three or four times the distance Kiep could stretch his hands. This provided the perfect spot for the five of them to spread out and look in all directions. Kiep reminded the girls to be careful of the short jagged pieces of rusted iron that were evenly spaced in a circle around the concrete. Tsov was beyond taking advice; he was already working to sharpen one with the help of a handy rock.

There had been a large gun up here when Kiep was Tsov's

age—a monster spitting flame and angry roars. Strange men, like those who took his father, would come and go along the ridge, bringing the monster to life from time to time.

Kiep looked down upon his land, his earth, and lamented the change growing closer every day. War was back. He knew it would reach Ri'Ga sooner than he liked. Perhaps some soldiers would return to this spot and bring the fire-breathing dragon back, a resurrected beast.

Thia removed long bamboo containers, deep and narrow "cups," from the *gui* and handed one each to Kiep, Tsov, and the girls. They each settled in and took to the task of removing rice, bean shoots, and chicken meat. The business of eating resulted in a moment of quiet serenity. Kiep reflected. Thia held his hand and snuggled close. These were times they would remember, times to reflect on the value of family and the luck they received day by day from the spirits that inhabited their world.

The sunset to the west was spectacular. But in the coming weeks, when Thia and Kiep would think back to this idyllic evening, they would view the sky full of orange fire as an omen from the spirits.

After abandoning it for more than a decade since his youth, Kiep had come to this spot many times over the past two years, but the sky was rarely this clear, this cloud-free. More typical after the summer equinox was a low cloud bank, sometimes laid out like an even layer of smoke beneath him, filling the valleys and extending out as far to the east as the eye could see. He looked forward to the occasional clear evening to survey the activity of the soldiers, helicopters, other airplanes, and the larger equipment he could discern below. Sometimes he was successful.

While the children kept themselves busy in the deepening gloom of night, father and mother kept them on the concrete pad. The dog was down the hill, barking at something in the trees. Kiep and Thia watched the last flicker of sunlight dip below the western horizon and began picking up their belongings to make the trip back. To the east they could make out the lights of distant villages, and brighter locations that must be occupied by soldiers. Kiep had experienced electric lighting in his travels, but Thia and the children had, at most, put their hands on a flashlight.

Their tranquility, combined with the mindless task of packing up, was interrupted by sudden flashes of light appearing in the sky, dotting the eastern horizon. Burning lights high in the air descended like leaves to the ground. The activity looked to be far enough away, to Kiep, that he would not need the family to take cover. So they sat and marveled at this display of lights, listening to the distant booms from their lofty perch. They could not hope to understand the meaning of all this, but they decided between them that the fiery sunset was the work of spirits, and the display of lights below them to the horizon was the work of men. They discussed which to be more fearful of, but could not arrive at a conclusion.

CHAPTER 11

5 July 1967

Landing Zone Regulator, Near Thuong Duc, Quảng Nam Province, South Vietnam

Lieutenant Bross still had a hard time comprehending the fact that twelve thousand miles away from home, in a corner of Earth so remote he could never have imagined being there, in a little screened-in mess hall, a cook in a chef's hat would ask him what he wanted in his omelet.

Omelet. Made to order. Amazing. He stood in line and shook his head. Today was his first day in the bush: "Indian Country." He was filled with nerves and butterflies. Sleeping was not an option. He wasn't sure how early chow started, so he was outside the bunker before 0500.

Bench seats. Sort of picnic table style. Darren wondered if he was supposed to be starting this morning with his adopted platoon. He looked up from his bacon, eggs, toast, and orange juice to a giant of a man holding a tray across the table.

"Mind if I join you, sir?"

"Of course, take a seat, soldier," Darren responded, looking at what appeared to be a National Football League lineman in the flesh here in Vietnam. *Wonder if he knows Staubach is in Chu Lai?*

A hand the size of a dinner plate reached across the table in an exaggerated extension of a shake, angling in over the top.

"Sir, Corporal Clayton Kuykendahl. Pleased to meet you."

Darren returned the shake, feeling like a six year-old shaking hands with an unknown uncle, a used car salesman ready to make the pitch. "Lieutenant Bross."

"I think I know you sir, or at least I know of you. Rumor has it you're taking Second Platoon."

"That's what they tell me."

"I'll be your RTO, sir. Pleasure's mine."

"Really? In the second or for the patrol today?"

"In the second, sir. Lieutenant Jacobs has done a helluva job. He deserves to get some REMF time."

"REMF?"

"I'll try to keep you straight, sir." Kuykendahl smiled. "Rear Echelon Mother Fucker."

Darren thought back to his conversation with Evans. "He's going to be the company XO, not really rear echelon."

"The rear is all relative, sir. To us, company is the rear; to company, battalion is the rear; to battalion, brigade is the rear. It goes like that. But the XO draw is the safest in the company. While the CO is out there traveling between platoons, hanging his butt out there, the XO gets to sit back at the LZ and coordinate with HQ." He smiled. "Your goal, sir, is to land the XO job as fast as possible."

Corporal Kuykendahl saw the lieutenant looking at his name

tape. "Call me Kook, sir. Kook."

"So where are the REMF jobs for guys like you, Kook?"

Referring to the military operational specialty code for rifleman, Kook said, "Sir, for eleven bravos, there's nothing in the rear, unless you get hurt or grow a reputation as a slacker. The LTs like you might spend five months in the bush, maybe six. I could be humping a radio-telephone in Indian Country every day for twelve months."

Lieutenant Bross was nodding his head in understanding while Kook talked. "Where are you from, Kook? How'd you find yourself in this man's army? You should be playing for the Cowboys."

"Jets, sir, AFL. Joe Namath! Who in their right mind would want to play for the Cowboys?" Kuykendahl chuckled. "I don't play football, sir. Never have, but that hasn't kept every coach I've ever run across from trying to strike up a conversation with me. Born and raised in Franklin Park, New Jersey. Drafted. My student deferment ran out."

"Where'd you go to school?"

"Little school near home. Princeton."

Lieutenant Bross put his fork down on his plate and looked up. "You went to Princeton?"

"Yes, sir."

"And now you're dragging a radio around in the jungles of Vietnam."

"Yes, sir, not much I can do about that."

"You look a little older than the other guys. How close did

you get to graduating?"

"Oh, I graduated, sir. Three times. Got my doctorate in history a year ago June."

Darren pushed his tray back a little. "Let me get this straight, just so I don't screw it up. My soon-to-be RTO has a PhD in history from Princeton and is a corporal?" Lieutenant Bross's brow was creased and his mouth was hanging open in disbelief.

"That's right, sir."

"Why didn't you get commissioned? Go to OCS?"

"Long boring story sir, but to keep it short let's say I wanted to experience war first-hand as a grunt. Fancy degrees do not a leader make. Trust me on this one, I'm a lot better off following you around with a bitch box."

"Why RTO? Why didn't you at least go for intelligence or something that could use your mind?"

"Never had any plan to be an RTO. Ten minutes into the bush on my first outing, one Corporal Lance Oberle took a sniper bullet through his bush hat." Kook paused for a minute in reflection as if he was remembering the day. "We all wondered if the outcome would have been different if he'd been wearing a steel pot. Lieutenant Jacobs asked who knew how to use the radio. I didn't have a clue, but I was the guy who had the extra mass required to haul that beast around. Everyone knows it's a target."

Corporal Kuykendahl mopped up his chipped beef on toast by swabbing the plate with the last piece. "Where are you from, sir?"

"Lufkin, Texas. I graduated from a boy's school on the Hudson in upstate New York."

Kuykendahl let out a guffaw, pretending it was the first time he'd ever heard that characterization. "Think I've heard of that one, sir. Did my dissertation on one of your more famous alumni."

Lieutenant Bross looked up. "And?"

"General of the army Douglas NMN MacArthur."

"NMN?"

"No middle name, sir. The Big Chief himself."

"One of my personal heroes. Truman screwed him."

"We could debate that, sir."

"S'pose we could. My minor at West Point was history. What do you know about Nam?"

"I am embarrassed to say, not much, sir. No more than any other grunt out here."

"Maybe once in while we could discuss our observations about where they need to get to and how to get there."

"I'd love that, sir, but one thing. I don't share much with the other guys about my college time. It doesn't do me much good to get called 'college boy' all the time. I shucked that after basic at Fort Jackson."

"Got it." Lieutenant Bross saw Lieutenant Elbert and Sergeant Major step into the mess hall. He swung his head and eyes in their direction for Corporal Kuykendahl's benefit. "Gotta go."

5 through 9 July 1967

Lampshade Valley, near Thuong Duc, Quảng Nam Province, South Vietnam

At first, no one knew for sure why they called it Lampshade Valley. But it was not a name the locals came up with. They didn't have lamps, let alone lampshades. Best guess was that every square inch that could be converted to rice paddies had been transfigured about a hundred years ago. It was a bizarre, unimaginable sensation. Here was a country at war. Shadowed ragged lines of American soldiers, thirty deep, were crisscrossing the landscape without much concern for the local workers—but there *were* locals, and plenty of them. In fact, if you didn't know better, you would wonder if this place was at war at all. By the hundreds, the thousands, the average young, old, and female Vietnamese citizen seemed to continue on with everyday life as if they had no clue a war was going on around them. As you walked to the west from LZ Regulator, in every direction you would see workers in the paddies, all wearing "lampshades." That was Darren's assessment of the moniker.

He wanted to respect these people, and he did, but he couldn't hold back a smile. His mind raced back to his youth when he snuck under a carnival tent and watched a vaudeville routine where a woman on stage, wearing nothing but pasties and long tassels, put a lampshade on her head and asked passing men to "turn her on." Roars of laughter from the crowd, confusion for a kid. Darren hadn't thought of it in years, but only just now got the joke. A smile, not even a chuckle.

Chad Elbert told him that this "lampshade" was a type of conical palm frond, a grass hat, called *nón lá* by the Vietnamese. He'd sent a few home as souvenirs to his family. Americans call it a leaf hat, or a grass hat, but not a coolie hat. The local population had learned that "coolie" was a disparaging term and wanted no part of it.

Lieutenant Bross learned a lot during that three-night orientation visit with First Platoon—both good and bad. Lessons for his command. Vietnam is hot. Vietnam is humid. It's beautiful and breathtaking if you can take a moment to give up worrying about being shot, getting malaria from chopper-sized bugs, stepping on nasty things, wondering if your feet will ever be dry again, surviving the nights, and all manner of other worries. And the people are crafty. He had learned about booby traps at Ranger School, and he'd done some animal trapping in east Texas as a teenager, but Bross marveled at the ingenuity demonstrated in some of the Vietnamese designs. Anything with gunpowder or C4 plastique explosive could be modified to make a remote killing machine. But there were some clues to watch out for: errant uniform items left strewn on the trail, tufts of grass bundled by wire, spindly trees unnaturally bent, empty C-ration cans.

The bush was quiet for his three-day stint. No snipers, no KIA, no WIA, no enemy. And Darren was impressed by Elbert. Darren had learned a lot about being a leader by his fifth year wearing a uniform, but Chad Elbert was leadership personified. He was crafting leaders, professional leaders, with every decision and every example he set. PFCs were future squad leaders. Squad leaders were future platoon sergeants. Platoon sergeants were future company first sergeants. This platoon was bonded with glue reinforced by daily doses of adrenaline. Those who survived would be friends long after their time in Nam was a distant memory. Those who died would never be forgotten. No one would forget Chad Elbert or Sergeant Major.

Darren also learned some lessons in humanity from Elbert, who admonished his troops for any acts with the local population that could be considered inhumane.

"Unless you know they're the enemy, don't shoot. Do you fucking get it?" This, when one FNG—fucking new guy—starting using a distant paddy-stricken water buffalo for target practice. A field worker, who must have owned the beast, was apoplectic, and moved toward the gunshots to protect his animal, slogging through thigh-deep mud. "It's probably a year's wages for that man!" Elbert said. "Do you want me to garnish your fucking paycheck for a year's pay?"

"No, sir."

"Then cut that shit out right now!" The platoon sergeant pulled him aside and told the kid next time he'd get rewarded with mouse duty. That is, walking point, looking for mousetraps.

Darren observed how, in front of the troops, the platoon sergeant projected complete respect for his platoon leader. He set the example for the squad leaders, and by empowering them to act on their own, he created a cascade of respect from the lieutenant to the platoon sergeant to the squad leaders to the soldiers. It worked both directions, and it worked well. And although racial tension was a well-known issue in Vietnam, it was not evident in this platoon. The lieutenant and the platoon sergeant treated everyone as equals. It didn't matter to anyone who was colored or Latino. One Korean-

American corporal on his second tour said he'd felt guilty shooting his own kind, but he got over that in his first firefight when he came around to thinking of himself first as an American soldier and not Oriental. They all laughed when he self-deprecated by screaming out, "These slopes are trying to kill me!" Then there was more laughter when a colored sergeant responded just as loud, "Never heard no Oriental calling his kinfolk slopes like we call each other niggas."

It wasn't all rosy. Lieutenant Bross picked up an unreasonable, but perhaps justified, fear of the dark from the thirty-eight men around him, including Elbert. It was justified, he discovered, because it seemed like the enemy, the NVA, the VC— they all had night vision. How was there a daily casualty or two in Bravo from a booby trap or sniper's bullet when they couldn't even see an enemy? How did that enemy avoid tripwires in the night? Magic. "Foxtrot Mike," one of his squad leaders would later say, invoking the phonetic alphabet. "It's fucking magic."

Bross expected that, like when you come across a wild animal in the woods back home, he's just as scared as you are. But that didn't help much. He couldn't shake the feeling that this danger might not be worth the risk. How would he, when put in charge, keep three dozen men alive? It was a rhetorical thought, one pondered while trying to make the night pass faster than it possibly could. *Einstein had it right. Time is relative*, he thought to himself.

He took his mind off the long night by digging into a pile of letters from Christy.

2, 1967

My dearest Darren,
    This letter will be a little
longer. I miss you so much. Our
little Lex is changing so fast. He's
starting to sit up by himself. He
rolls across the living room floor
to get to poor Race, who just
lays there contently and lets Lex
pull on his ears, hair and tail.
Race has become protective of us
since you left. He barks like
crazy every time Mr. Shaw puts
the mail in the slot. That dog used
to love the mailman! Speaking of
mail, I love getting your letters.
They usually show up eight or
nine at a time, every couple of
weeks. I try to read them in order
if I can. It made me so sad when
you said you thought about Lex
being four months old, because it
made me realize again how long
you've been gone.
    To answer your question about
him knowing who you are when
you get back -- probably not, baby
But don't worry, he'll be your little
sidekick in no time. He loves
visiting Nana and Pop and he

loves my Mother too, but Daddy makes him cry for some reason. It's actually pretty funny. Lex and I went to lunch with my folks after church last Sunday, at Francisco's. Mr. Wolusky asked about you. He said Lex has your eyes. I think so too. Your parents are good about making us get out of the house. Most days, I just want to stay home because that's where I feel closest to you. I know you can't call home, but I worry that if I leave it would be the one time you figure it out and do call. Or heaven forbid, what if something happened to you and I wasn't home to find out? Every time I go to the grocery store or to play cards with the girls, I hold my breath when I turn down our street to come home, half expecting to see a military police vehicle in our driveway. I don't know Darren, I just can't shake this feeling in my stomach. It's like love, and sickness and exhaustion and hope and anger and sadness all mixed together. Sometimes I just cry for no reason. I'm just tired & doing this alone. Sex is cutting his first tooth and wakes up several times a night. Going to bed is my least favorite part of the day. It's quiet, but I can't sleep. I still haven't washed the shirt you wore the night before you deployed. It still smells like you and I sleep with it every night. I try to lay there and close my eyes and imagine what you are doing right at that moment. I think about the palm trees and the rain you described in one of your letters. I wonder why a war is more important than our family. But then I make myself snap out of it. I know you are serving our country with pride, and it's a noble sacrifice for us all. Sex will be so proud of his daddy one day. I know I am. Please do everything in your power to come home to us. Please Darren. I don't know what I would do without you. There's a long, wet kiss waiting for you in Lufkin.

All my love,
Christy.

14 July 1967

Landing Zone Regulator, near Thuong Duc, Quảng Nam Province, South Vietnam

Sitting in the hooch space Elbert had set aside for him, Darren worked to finish letters to both his parents and the most recent from Christy. It was a daily ritual, trying to write a letter per day to Christy while also keeping his parents' worries at bay. Take some time, record the thoughts you can jot down without ticking off some censor who might happen to read your mail, and tell your family every day that you're still okay and that you love them.

Even while surrounded by more than two hundred men in the LZ, Vietnam, it turned out, was a lonely place—and mail call brought with it a slice of home. A little touch of reality from The World. Today, for the first time, he'd gotten a care package from his parents. Thomas's English muffins, which he relished. He'd never have thought to ask for them. He wondered how he'd get one of the cooks at the LZ to set aside a tray full of toast while he asked for butter in his "nooks and crannies." He dug deeper in the box. Postage stamps: kind of worthless. His parents didn't yet know that letters home were mailed free of charge. Heavy woolen socks—an amusing thought for comfort, but useless in this environment. Some Old Spice Lime aftershave. He laughed out loud remembering the ad: "Things happen when you give Old Spice Lime." Just the thing he needed when he needed things to happen. He chuckled some more, thinking how much Charlie would love this. They'd be able to pick him out in the dead of night by scent alone. More important than anything else in the box was a fifteen-pack of Clark's Teaberry gum, his hands-down favorite. And in the bottom of the box he found about three dozen chocolate chip cookies individually wrapped in aluminum foil.

Darren took the cookies outside the bunker hooch, scanned the area to make sure no one was looking, folded a stick of Teaberry into his mouth, and to the sound of the jingle in his head, he "Teaberry shuffled" as the screen door slapped closed behind him.

With a half dozen cookies in tow, he expected some "friends" to join him. He sat on a three-legged stool and watched a shirtless soldier on the helipad tossing a Frisbee to a feral dog. Darren remembered them being called "Pluto Platters" when he was a kid. He picked up on a bond between this dog and that man; the dog wanted to please, and relished the simple pleasure of catching a sailing plastic disc.

As he'd expected, a couple of soldiers joined him in front of the hooch when they realized cookies were in the offing. But just as he offered them each a stick of gum, they all turned their heads to the sky. The distant sound of helicopter rotors approached.

Elbert's hooch was a GP small tent dug into a dirt encasement lined with plywood and supported by rough-hewn beams. Marsden matting, the heavy stuff used to create runways over dirt, was laid over the ceiling beams, then plywood, and then sandbags on top. The size of most bunkers and hatches was determined by the length of the Marsden matting. Ten feet long and just fifteen inches wide, a steel section was heavy. And because of the ten-foot dimension, most of the hooches on LZ Regulator were that same width or length. Elbert's had ten strips interlocked, making his hooch 150 inches deep, just over twelve feet. Ten by twelve, it was tiny, but secure, in a relative sense.

There were five identical bunkers lined up in a row. Originally it had been "Officers' Row," until someone figured out that concentrating all the leadership in one area was a bad idea. They were rectangular beehive-looking structures. Some had a concrete floor, thanks to a Navy Sea Bee construction battalion visit the year prior. Most had stacked bunks, plywood walls, and sandbags everywhere. Some had electricity, but most did not. A few had tar spread on the wood beneath the matting, stolen in the spring in a raid on the combat engineer compound in Chu Lai. A common feature to all of them was the horizontal slits on all sides: firing ports in case NVA sappers, bad guys in the night, attempted an overrun of the LZ.

Lieutenant Bross opened the canvas flap, put the box of cookies inside, and peered back out just in time to see Lieutenant Colonel Long, the battalion commander, step off the arriving chopper. Unlike most Hueys he'd seen, this one was armed with rockets and M-79 grenade launchers in addition to door gunners.

Captain Evans, already on the LZ, quick-stepped from behind the mess hall, jogged to the idling chopper, and in a command voice loud enough to overcome the rotor noise said,

"Welcome to LZ Regulator, sir."

"Thanks, Mark, did you give Bross the news?"

"No sir, not yet, I was waiting for your arrival."

"Have someone go tell Jacobs to pack his stuff. I'm going to give him a taste of R&R back at my place. Then I think he's off to real R&R in The World."

Lieutenant Bross heard his name and double-timed it to the boss. He stood like a West Point plebe at a near brace, popped a salute, and said, "Good to see you, sir!"

"Didn't someone tell you this was a no-salute zone, Bross?"

"My apologies, sir. Old habits die hard."

"Understood, but let's not let your old habits die hard while they're killing the both of us. I'm too short to go down now."

"Yes, sir, got it." Darren wondered if the presence of the first armored chopper he'd seen at the LZ would alert the enemy to important visitors more than a demonstration of respect, but the feeling wore off fast. "How short, sir?"

"Shortness is not something you talk about with your guys. Tell your squad leaders that too. But since you asked: four days and a wakeup. I'm so short I can walk under your LZ sign without touching a hair on my head." He laughed to himself. Everyone else envied him. "Let's get to the company TOC. I'm here to tell you to remember this date. Today you are a US Army platoon leader. It's a date you'll never forget. Elbert and Evans tell me you're ready. You get the second."

"I'm honored, sir. My plan is to make you and Captain Evans proud."

"Fuck that, Bross, just keep your soldiers alive while making the other guys dead." He tossed that out while giving a hand-wave toward the horizon, no place in particular.

"Got it, sir."

Colonel Long arrived with the battalion first sergeant, Master Sergeant Wayne Blocker. They walked as a group to the company headquarters. From the corner of his eye Lieutenant Bross could see a couple of other senior soldiers joining him. One was an E-7 he recognized from the mess hall. Master Sergeant Blocker placed his hand on the SFC's shoulder and pulled him front and center.

"Lieutenant Bross, let me introduce you to your platoon sergeant, Sergeant First Class Lionel Rook."

The E-7 reached out his hand for the greeting. "Just Rook." *Just Rook,* Darren noted. This was the first time he had heard an NCO fail to add "sir" since he'd been in Nam. He held out his hand and shook.

CHAPTER *12*

THE CURIOUS CASE OF LIONEL BODEAN ROOK
SERGEANT FIRST CLASS, SFC, UNITED STATES ARMY

To the military outsider, it is difficult to explain how a sociopath can serve a career in what is ostensibly the defense of his nation. But it happens. It happened with Lionel Bodean Rook, who, for reasons having to do with the failure of leadership and lack of adequate record-keeping, managed for years to navigate a complex bureaucracy to his own benefit and to the detriment of nearly every person he touched and every unit he served.

Lionel Rook took the oath of office at the Military Entrance Processing Station (MEPS) in Jacksonville, Florida on Tuesday, the eighth of September, 1953. This was normally a Monday event, but the seventh was Labor Day, so in-processing was delayed. Lionel was just seventeen years old, and was therefore on an age waiver signed by his mother, and for reasons not well understood by his DeSoto County army recruiter, his uncle had also signed. The recruiter thought it best to keep the court order to enlist out of the mix. "Don't wanna affect Lionel's career from the get-go. It's all copacetic."

For any normal enlistee, the oath of office was something you did as they lined you up like cattle and moved you through every imaginable irritant from tongue depressors to immunizations to ID card photos. But for Lionel it was the start of a planned subterfuge. One word in the oath caught his eye: "domestic." Something about defending the Constitution against enemies foreign and domestic. From that moment forward, Lionel would decide which "domestic" enemies needed to be defended against. The foreign enemies could wait for an uncertain future, although he surely hoped he could deal with some of them too. He would.

By the time Lionel Rook departed from Clark Air Force Base in the Philippines on a C-47 in the late fall of 1965, he had managed to work the system for twelve years. On the paper available in his official records, he had the makings of an experienced NCO. And he *was* experienced, but from the outside looking in, a keen observer would have questioned whether Rook's experience was suited to helping solve any problem in Vietnam—or any problem anywhere, for that matter.

Lionel's un-recorded record was replete with examples of egregious behavior that should have got him booted out of the army a dozen times over. But in the 1950s and 1960s the military in general, and the army in particular, was a place a mentally deranged person could hide. Supervisors and commanders could ease the overwhelming task of unit leadership by moving problems to other units, and the military assignment system—that is, moving between posts—served to facilitate the expunging of bad behavior. For example, when then-PFC Rook traveled from Germany to Fort

Hood, Texas, the official record of his beating a German teenage girl stayed in Germany. The poor young girls in Killeen, Texas had no idea what was headed their way. And neither did the company first sergeant, nor the commander.

Following Basic Training at Fort Jackson, South Carolina, Private Rook's first assignment was as an "eleven bravo, or 11B, a military specialty code he would carry throughout his career, meaning infantry rifleman. He was assigned to a US Army training area at Hohenfels, Germany, where he got some early attention from his battalion commander in the mess hall. Everyone knew the boss ate in the enlisted mess hall from time to time. It was a way for him to stay connected to the troops. And during one breakfast meal, Private Rook looked up to find a lieutenant colonel standing next to his table. The colonel looked at Rook. "May I join you, soldier?"

Lionel did not stand for the colonel. The colonel said nothing at the time, but Rook's behavior would be corrected later, loudly, in front of the facility by the battalion first sergeant. "But he's colored," Rook would reply. "You expect me to stand for a colored?"

Yet as the colonel stood next to the table, Rook gestured with a hand holding a fork loaded with two sausage links. "Sure, have a seat."

The subsequent discussion was what you would expect. "Where are you from? What's your MOS? What's your job here in Hohenfels? Sisters? Brothers?" The fact is, most unit commanders are genuinely interested in their soldiers.

The colonel waded through the initial questions before

changing the subject. He had noticed that Private Rook was wearing a combat infantryman's badge on his uniform. Hohenfels was crawling with CIB-wearing soldiers who had returned from the Korean War, but it was rare to see someone as junior as a private who had earned one and had not yet been promoted to at least PFC, or more likely corporal.

The colonel asked, "Where'd you serve in Korea?"

Private Rook was ready for this question because he had spent weeks fabricating a plausible story. He had never even set foot in Korea, of course. He had purchased the CIB from the military clothing store and had drastically underestimated how much attention wearing it would generate. It had required some research in the post library, but Lionel was an intelligent, if misdirected, young man, and he had prepared a speech that included a detailed and convincing account of the battle of Kumsong. He had memorized units, leadership, and seminal moments in the battle. He was a crafty storyteller, and careful to use the third person, thereby allowing the listener to draw the conclusion that Lionel himself had been there. No matter that the battle had ended on the twenty-seventh of July, six weeks before Rook enlisted in the army.

"Thank you for your service, soldier. How is it that you have not been promoted?"

"Oh, I was promoted," Lionel lied with a straight face. "My commander took a stripe last month when I was caught sleeping on duty." He had an answer for everything. He'd told this story dozens of times. This was a piece of cake. He was practiced.

The phrase "badge of honor" is overused in the English

lexicon. We have largely forgotten its meaning, but if there are truly badges of honor, then the CIB hovers near the top of any US military list. It is awarded to infantrymen—and Rook at least qualified on that count—who were engaged in active and close combat with the enemy. It is not taken lightly by the army. Earning the badge alone can be a discriminator for promotion, particularly in a negative sense when a soldier held an infantry MOS for the duration of a conflict but did not earn a CIB. An officer is likely to look at such a soldier and wonder: What the hell were you *doing* during the war?

Lionel's story of the fighting at Kumsong was convincing even to the first sergeant who was listening. It sounded plausible. But what the private didn't know was that he was in the presence of someone who had actually been there. The colonel was a battalion XO during the battle of Kumsong. And although he nodded politely as Rook told his story, when he departed the mess hall he ordered the first sergeant to find the adjutant at the HHQ company and check into it. "Sounds fishy to me."

Captain Harold Weeks didn't even have to make a call. A quick check of Rook's service date showed that the math didn't add up. He had never been to Korea.

The colonel was livid. "First Sergeant, Private Rook has ten minutes to take that CIB off his uniform. Then he walks a few tours."

When Lionel got the word, he told the first sergeant, who was not even in his company, that he would comply. But he didn't. He calculated the chances of ever seeing the colonel or that first sergeant again, and he kept the CIB on his uniform.

That turned out not to be a good plan.

Two weeks later, Private Rook was standing at a phone bank outside the PX, trying to place a call—his company commander later found out that the call was to a teenage girlfriend downtown who was trying to learn English—when his battalion commander strolled by. There were perhaps twenty-five soldiers and junior officers smoking and joking near picnic tables and such. All of them stood at attention and popped sharp salutes. But Private Rook looked up briefly and tried to duck. That also was not a good plan.

The colonel approached Private Rook. "Soldier, if you want to be in this battalion, you had better damn well salute when the commander walks by."

Into the phone receiver, Lionel said, loud enough for the colonel to hear, "I'd just as soon not be in this battalion." Then he turned, faced the colonel, and saluted.

The colonel did not return the salute, instead leaving Rook to hold his. He said twelve words that could have summed up everything anyone needed to know about Lionel Rook. "You are a sack of shit from the word 'go,' aren't you?"

There were witnesses. If faces could speak, then the colonel's face spoke of an impending explosion. Some thought it was an overreaction, but not knowing the mess hall encounter, they didn't fully understand the boss's anger.

The colonel didn't say another word. He knew his rank insignia spoke louder than words. He removed a large folding pocketknife from his uniform trousers, opened it with his thumbnail, and began working on Private Rook's uniform. One NCO stepped forward, thinking the colonel might be stabbing Rook. No. When the colonel stepped back, he had cut a large circle of material from Rook's uniform that included three items: a black-embroidered combat infantryman badge, a black tape with gold letters that read US ARMY, and a scrap of white jersey T-shirt stained with a fresh spot of blood.

Unfortunately, Rook's comments, overheard back in the barracks, did not include remorse or contrition. Rook's focus was solely on the humiliation he had taken at the hands of a "nigger."

"I am not going to forget that."

By 1955 the US Army was drawing down at Hohenfels to hand the training center to the newly formed militaries of NATO alliance partners. Private Lionel Rook—along with a letter of reprimand for beating a German civilian and the memory of his CIB behavior and falsification of honors—was shipped off to Fort Hood, Texas.

Lionel Rook's reckless and callous disregard for authority—in an organization built on the concept of respect for authority—defied reason. Dozens of notable examples could demonstrate the point that this soldier was a special case.

Sergeant Rook served a relatively uneventful tour at Fort Hood: a son out of wedlock, a mysterious crib death, a quick divorce, a tearful wife in the commander's office screaming, "Keep that psycho away from me!" Just everyday occurrences in the life of Lionel Rook. His company mates were incredulous and took to using the phrase "You got Rooked" to specifically note some antic Lionel had pulled.

In part so that his infractions would be swept under the rug —and so that Sergeant Rook would be placed out of sight and out of mind—he was reassigned to Fort Gulick along the Panama Canal, to serve in an unspecified role at "The Latin American Center—Ground Division." Since 1946, the army had been providing Western Hemisphere armies with counter-insurgency training there.

Lionel didn't like Panama. He didn't like the fact that Fort Gulick was in the middle of nowhere. He didn't speak Spanish. The girls were brown, so of no interest to him. And he quickly established a well-deserved reputation as a malingerer. Aches and pains, sick call, unfounded claims of malaria, late to work, and early to depart. The HHQ company commander was exasperated, and he decided to put Rook close, where he could keep an eye on him.

July 1959 marked the forty-fifth year of the opening of the Panama Canal. The project officer for the big event was Major Dave Sanchez. Major Sanchez was up at battalion. He needed help. "What better help than an NCO?" thought the HHQ company commander.

"He's Latin, sir," Rook commented.

"What in the hell does that have to do with the price of tea in China?" the captain screamed.

Rook didn't have a clue what China had to do with it, but he nodded anyway and then started planning a way to make the major look bad.

The Fort Gulick garrison commander and other distinguished guests would soon attend two days of celebration, on the invitation of the Panamanian government, in Panama City to the south. In recognition of the importance of the canal to world commerce and the direct role the US armed forces had in defending it, the chief of staff of the army responded to the invitation by sending his deputy chief of staff for operations, Lieutenant General Gary Kingery. Major Sanchez would work with the DA G3 staff to ensure everything was in protocol order to receive the general as the CSA's representative. This was a big deal for the colonel who was garrison commander and who would be escorting the general.

Sergeant Rook's job was to coordinate with the Panamanian staff to work the general's attendance at the main function, a commemorative ball to be held in the most luxurious hotel in Panama.

Rook got his hands on the project book from the fortieth anniversary, opened the three rings, and extracted the section on the dinner. Over the coming weeks he had the opportunity to compare the current program to prior years and noted that in the past all the attendees had worn traditional Panamanian dress, including a formal, and expensive, guayabera shirt. To Americans this shirt looked informal. In Latin America it could serve as wedding attire.

This year, however, Rook learned in meetings, the Panamanian government had responded to concerns among the invitees of the difficulty in finding the guayabera before the event.

So the dress, on this forty-fifth anniversary, would instead be dark suit and tie, and dark shoes—Latin standard.

So Rook pretended he didn't notice this change. He coordinated, via a poor phone connection with DA G3, and later with Major Sanchez, that the general would need only his short-sleeved uniform combinations, owing to the heat and humidity, no blouse, and just a wheel hat. And for the dinner he would need the guayabera. Major Sanchez would accompany the general to the town of Colon to make that purchase after he arrived.

"We could buy the general one ahead of time," Rook told the general's protocol officer, "but he'll want to make sure it fits, and he might want something fancier."

On the day of the event, General Kingery landed at the airfield in Colon in the army chief's plane, a C-121 Super Constellation. They were met by the American ambassador to Panama and the commandant of the Panamanian National Police.

Because Major Sanchez was of Mexican descent, appeared Latino, and carried the name Sanchez, everyone in Panama assumed he was fluent. He was not, and that became apparent when he opened his mouth. The sum total of his Spanish had come in his childhood, from trying to communicate with his grandparents.

After the greetings died down on the tarmac, the Panamanian project officer for the event asked if he could hitch a ride back with the US group in the afternoon.

"*Absolutamente que si,*" the major replied.

The shopping trip in Colon went off without a hitch. The major had pre-arranged a visit to a Panamanian tailor who had several guayabera shirts to choose from. The general liked the idea of owning one of these. He was culturally astute and imagined he could use it in the future. There was a high-quality haberdasher next door to the tailor that happened to have an oversized Panama hat that fit the general perfectly. It had been sitting on the shelf for a few years waiting for the right head. Extra-large. It came after some negotiation and a sale price.

The garrison commander's staff car was set aside for the general, an OD-green 1959 Ford Galaxie 500. When they picked up the Panamanian project officer, there was plenty of room for him in the front seat. The ride to Panama City would be two hours. The general had everything he needed. That is, the general *thought* he had everything he needed.

The main entrance to the Hotel El Panama was buzzing with valet parkers, bellboys, and all manner of assistance. The three got out of the staff car, removed the general's luggage from the trunk and exchanged pleasantries with the police captain.

"*Mi General, ha sido un placer.*"

"The pleasure is mine. Will we see you tonight?"

"Yes, my general." This time the captain spoke in English.

Major Sanchez and the police captain shook hands, and the captain said, "Tengo que *cambiar la ropa. Nos vemos pronto en traje y corbata, mi mayor.*"

Major Sanchez's face didn't show the blush he felt. "*Que?* Again?" He thought he had heard the captain say that he would see them tonight in coat and tie— the gala event was just two hours hence.

The major's first call was to Sergeant Rook at Fort Gulick. "The police captain just told the general he had to go home to change into a suit and tie for the function tonight."

Rook pretended to search through papers, loudly shuffling them so it could be heard over the phone. He spoke into the receiver: "Whoops, sorry sir, I guess I was looking at an old schedule. I'll bet he has a suit anyway He knew full well that the general did not.

"He didn't bring a fucking suit, you idiot! His aide said you told him he wouldn't need one!"

"I don't think I told him that, sir." Rook nearly laughed, but he held it back until he hung up. Major Sanchez was highly embarrassed, and Rook knew it. He smirked to himself. *Serves that wetback right for not paying attention.*

A major scramble began. A dozen frantic phone calls to find a dark suit, tie, and shoes for the general. A colonel in the military office at the American embassy came through. The American ambassador to Panama was about the general's size—big. He would lend a suit.

At the general's direction, the aide took a note remind his boss to talk to the garrison commander "… about this goat screw."

For nearly fifty years the area of the world that would become Clark Air Force Base on the island of Luzon in the Philippines was known as "Fort Stotsenberg." Over the years following the separation of the air force from the army, the fort was absorbed by the base and relegated to diminutive status as "Stotsenberg Station," a small, battalion-sized unit known as the Ninth US Army Security Agency Field Station, a classified listening operation and cryptologic center that gathered early intelligence on communist intentions in Southeast Asia.

In 1962, Staff Sergeant Lionel Rook had not a clue in the world why he was stationed in this hellhole, stuck in the asshole of the world surrounded by long-haired, sloppy, and otherwise worthless airmen. Nevertheless, the girls in Angeles City outside the gate were pretty nice—and Rook was getting over his aversion to skin color when it came to women. He still couldn't get it up for any kind of Latina chick, but the Filipino women were fine. Plus they were cheap. Shacking up with one of them was one of Rook's rights.

Staff Sergeant Rook was not a cryptologist, was not a linguist, could not operate technical communications gear, and could not perform 90 percent of the tasks required of the personnel assigned to the field station. Nevertheless, he had a lot of practice in setting up for war. And like any army unit, this one had a periodic requirement to conduct a field exercise, a field problem, "maneuvers." The real problem, in Rook's mind, was a bunch of security agency and signal pussies had to go set up tents, sleep in the outdoors, and operate a tactical operations center while the Boss Man walked around in his once-a-year TA-50 lying to everyone about what a great job they were doing.

There was a lot of talk about everyone deploying to Vietnam one day, so he took his job of mobilization NCO more or less seriously. And, to the degree that he could use his position to harass others, it was his dream job.

In the conduct of his duties, which Rook routinely shirked and made excuses for, he frequently ran afoul of the field station XO, one Major Daniel Hill. "Danny Boy," as Rook called the major, was a gigantic pain in Rook's ass. Major Hill viewed himself as the Boss Man's expert on going to war. *No shit, someone had to do it. Most of these guys couldn't find their asses with a mirror.*

Staff Sergeant Rook, as mobilization NCO, was necessary to ensure mission success. Rook didn't like jobs where he had actual responsibility, so he devised a plan that would get the major thinking about other things, while netting himself some cash.

Late in 1963 one of the air police, AP—or, as every soldier referred to them, "the Apes"—was serving gate guard duty. He was a young kid and got nervous when one of the Filipino foreign nationals who worked on Clark got in his face. The airman cooked off a shot with his M-14 rifle that sadly killed the Filipino's toddler son, and all hell broke loose. There were screaming civilians all over and demonstrations outside the fence. The poor airman was sent back to the States for his own safety. But in the end, the only thing that was important to Lionel Rook was the hush-hush news that the Filipino family was paid off with thousands of dollars. *So, they pay off the Flips.*

Lionel's hoochmate was a twenty-two-year-old pretty young woman named Ramie Guzman. Ramie was a foreign national employed by one of the officer households as a maid. She was authorized unimpeded access to the base on a special permit and ID card. Ramie's long-term plan was to marry an American and emigrate to the United States. She was working diligently to learn English so she could work her plan to perfection before dumping the sap stateside.

Lionel endorsed the part of the plan he knew, and he legitimately wanted to be Ramie's sponsor and perhaps husband, but he didn't want to be the father of Ramie's full-blooded Flip brat. But over the course of a year, living with Ramie and mistreating her daughter, he got her to agree to a course of action. He wanted everything to be finished with cash in hand before he was due to rotate back to the States in the summer of 1964. Ramie was a mental wreck at times over the ensuing weeks, but in the end she was also a willing participant.

Major Hill drove a VW Microbus. It was red with a white top, canvas sunroof, and eight tiny skylight windows, four on each side of the sunroof. The rear window of the vehicle was higher than most others out there to accommodate the engine, so it was difficult for the driver to see behind him when backing up.

Rook and Ramie were driving around in his junk car trying to keep an eye on the major. It was Friday afternoon, and a stop at the officers' club was the routine order of the day. They found a semi-secluded parking spot around the side, on gray dirt filled with shells. At around 1930, when dusk was falling, they saw Major Hill depart the club, maybe just a little tipsy.

Ramie was crying, but Lionel didn't hesitate. He took Ramie's sleeping two-year-old from the bench seat between them, looked around furtively to ensure no one was watching, and placed her on the ground behind the rear wheel of the Microbus.

It happened quickly. Major Hill started the VW, crunched it into reverse after double-clutching the transmission, and ran the little girl over. He recalled feeling a bump, but he was as yet unaware of what had really happened when Ramie came around to the windshield, pounding on it and screaming, "You killed her! You killed her! She was walking and you murdered her!"

Rook watched from his car. There was no acting needed. Ramie was the mother of a dead little girl. Rook, more detached, was characteristically sitting in the car pumping his fist in victory.

For Rook, the plan worked—in part. Major Hill was preoccupied with the matter for months, thus leaving Rook to ignore the mobility operation. And Ramie got a large payment. Unfortunately for Rook, by then she was bunking with an airman, and Rook never got his half. Except for the odd beating and having killed her daughter, Lionel could not for the life of him understand why their relationship was over.

The incident, combined with a few others, forced the 1965 ratification of the first-ever Status of Forces Agreement between the United States and the Philippines. Had Rook known that in advance, he would have figured out a way to take credit.

CHAPTER 13

15 July 1967

Landing Zone Regulator, near Thuong Duc, Quảng Nam Province, South Vietnam

Second Platoon was a reflection of the America it fought to protect. Oriental, black, white, and Latino. Lieutenant Bross guessed that at least one member carried Indian blood in his veins, but to his knowledge no one in the unit was Native American. He would come to learn that the crucible of combat had forged these men into a close-knit group that, in general, got along well with each other. He was the newcomer. Like a single living organism, the platoon came to Darren with an innate ability and willingness to compensate for each other's weaknesses, to back up when backup was needed, and to back down without question when the situation dictated. This synergy helped keep the men alive even when the odds were stacked against them. In seconds, someone you barely knew would be the person you trusted with your life. On your behalf, they would make a life and death decision that more often than not was the right one. Summed up as "trust," it was there.

Darren had spent a lot of time thinking about what his mark

would be. How would his leadership style fold in with this team? In his short time since landing at Tan Son Nhut Air Base, after hearing countless horror stories and living a couple of them, he wanted to lead a platoon that kept its humanity, that took the fight to the enemy, but remembered that the Vietnamese people were human beings and basically good. The vast majority were living hand to mouth, a subsistence existence. They had little understanding of, and less interest in, the politics of the country they happened to live in.

It was the first meeting with his new platoon. In the shade, but with no hope of avoiding the humidity, everyone found a place to sit around the north side of the mess hall. Initial introductions went off without a hitch, and included a great deal of laughing about hometowns, who had a girlfriend or wife back home, who got a "Dear John" letter, and the like, and all this banter let Lieutenant Bross know that he had a good group of tight-knit guys. In particular, Darren noted that Sergeant Masterson was a cut-up. He helped break the ice by telling everyone he had gotten a "John Deere" letter while in Basic Training.

"I'm from farm country in Ohio, Lieutenant. If you try to say 'Dear John,' it just comes out 'John Deere.'" About half the platoon had no idea what he was talking about. The other half laughed just from listening to Masterson talk in an affected hayseed accent.

Two of the men were brand new. The casual, friendly atmosphere was destroyed by one of them, the new platoon sergeant, thanks to a brief, bizarre, and inappropriate megalomaniacal rant that ended with him red-faced, screaming,

"We're going to rip their fucking heads off and shit down their necks!"

Lieutenant Bross gave him a glare and a confused look that said, *Sit down. Are you crazy?* Then he changed his tone a little. "Thank you, Sergeant Rook. We'll talk later."

"Just Rook," the man responded.

A pause. Darren turned to Rook. If he'd been wearing reading glasses, he would have been looking over them with his chin tucked. "Thank you, Sergeant Rook," he repeated.

Lieutenant Bross looked over the men in his platoon and waited until the hormones cooled down. He knew no better way of getting men to listen than by just sitting quietly and then talking softly, so that they had to strain to hear. This, he knew, had a way of getting them to pay attention.

"Men. I really do want to get to know each of you better. This has been good, but we will have more time. Of that, I am certain. Just one admin item, before we get up from this formation: give me some contact information." He unclipped a stenographer's pad from a clipboard. "My name is listed first. Fill it out just like that. Basically I want to know who I can write to about your exploits here in Nam. After your names add your parents, or your girlfriend, or your wife—you decide. The only requirement is it has to be a relative. Any one of you who doesn't have such a person?"

Private First Class Stanley Peckham raised his hand.

"Your name, soldier?" Lieutenant Bross asked.

"Stan Peckham, sir. Alamogordo, New Mexico, like we just talked about."

"Alama goo? Isn't that what you just told me?"

They all chuckled again.

"Yes, sir, Alama goo."

"No family I can reach out to?"

"No sir, that's not it. I got family. I wanted to mention Beans over there."

"Beans?"

"Yes, sir, Vicente Mejia. We call him Beans because when he says his name 'Vince' in Mexican, it comes out like 'Beans.'" Stan said it aloud for emphasis.

Beans had only just figured out he was the topic of conversation. Stan had pronounced his name with a perfect Mexican Spanish accent.

"Why doesn't Beans speak for himself?"

"Sir, Beans speaks some English, but not much. He actually is from Mexico. A big city called Guadalajara in the center of the country. It's really hard for him to contact his family. The APO don't send letters to Mexico."

"You're kidding, right? Beans is Mexican, a Mexican citizen, and in the US Army?"

"Yes, sir, I think the recruiters got some kind of program to make him legal after he gets back to The World."

Lieutenant Bross searched his memory for the three years of high school and two years of West Point Spanish he had suffered through. He directed his gaze to Private Mejia, "*¿Cómo estas usted, Vince?*" Mixing up the formal and the familiar in Spanish, he tried to pronounce the name the way Peckham had just said it. It came out

"Beans." He smiled.

"*Muy bien, Teniente.*" Mejia then unfolded from his seated position and stood at attention while addressing the lieutenant, the first soldier to do so since Darren had arrived. Bringing his M-16 to port arms, he looked straight ahead. "*Estoy tratando de aprender Inglés.*" Then he switched to heavily accented Spanglish. "My promise to you, *mi Teniente*, is I always understand *ordenes.*"

The lieutenant responded, again, in the Spanish he knew. "*Entiendo soldado. Estoy tratando de aprender Español. ¿Tienes alguna parte de tu familia en los Estados Unidos?*" Then, looking at the other guys and smiling, he added, "I think I asked him if he has any family in the US."

"*Sólo una tía y su esposo gringo, mi Teniente.*" (Only an aunt and her gringo husband.) Mejia had served some time as a conscript in the Mexican army when he turned eighteen. When addressing an officer in the Mexican army, the respectful form always included "my Lieutenant," or the correct rank: "Mi Capitán," "Mi Coronel," et cetera. Old habits die hard.

In later discussions Darren would come to discover that Mejia had deserted for reasons that were not well explained, and had crossed the border at Nogales, Arizona after a long bus/train ride from the south.

"*¿Pueden pasar cartas a tu Mama o Papa en México?*" Darren asked. Then, again translating for the others: "I'm asking him if his aunt and uncle in the States can get a letter to his family."

"*Si, mi Teniente.* Sometime her husband visit Guanajuato to his job."

"Guanajuato? I thought you said he was from Guadalajara."

"*Guanajuato es corecto, mi Teniente.*"

"Okay, *su direccíon.*"

Everyone was looking around at each other in disbelief that the new lieutenant was speaking Spanish. He noticed. "Hey, guys, I grew up in Texas and took a lot of Spanish in school. I never thought I'd need it." He looked back at Beans. "Take a seat, Private."

Then, addressing everyone again. "Now, back to the contact info. If you know it, add a phone number. You never know when I might want to make a call."

Bross couldn't have known it, but through that minor act of understanding and compassion, through his simple attempt to reach out to Mejia on a human level, he had laid the cornerstone of an unseen level of loyalty and commitment. Prior to this moment, the typical treatment Beans had received from everyone was to be ignored, to be treated as stupid, or to be cast down as a "spic" or "wetback." But while he was taking his seat, Beans thought to himself, *Este líder me ve como un verdadero soldado del pelotón. This leader sees me as a true soldier in the platoon.*

Lieutenant Bross got on to his real reason for the meeting and changed the subject. "We are in someone else's country. And we are fighting a war. No one wants to be here less than you do, less than I do, but our country says get on with it. Americans have a lot of years of standing proud when their country calls." He took half a minute to collect his thoughts and was just a tiny bit overcome by the thought of patriotic service. Choking up during public talks was something he needed to work on. "I want you to think for a minute about what that would mean to you if there was an occupying force fighting battles, waging war in your hometown."

He looked at the faces of his guys. For now, they looked pretty intent on what he was saying, some leaning forward and moving from the back to get a better vantage point. Bross recognized one soldier, the boy-man who had been throwing the Frisbee to the dog earlier in the morning. Darren looked him in the eyes to get his attention. "Name and where you're from."

"Corporal Sean MacNulty, sir. Las Vegas, Nevada."

One of the other men in an OD T-shirt piped up, "No shit! Las Vegas? Why didn't you ever say anything? Love those casinos."

"Shut up, asshole, I'm not old enough to gamble."

From the back, "He's Mormon, dipshit."

"What?"

Lieutenant Bross held up his hand. "You guys can discuss the finer points of gambling and religious convictions another time." He looked at Sean. "Las Vegas." He gave it a second and said, "Sorry, not a good example for the point I'm trying to make. Is that your mutt I saw today?"

"Yes, sir, when I'm at the LZ. He's a good boy. Nutsy. I'm trying to keep him off some gook's Sunday dinner table."

Bross looked at the man with the John Deere story. "Where are you from in Ohio, Sergeant?"

"Staff Sergeant Jim Masterson, sir. Guys call me *Bat* for obvious reasons. Born and raised in Chillicothe."

"Where's that?"

"East of Cincinnati, south of Columbus."

"Perfect." Lieutenant Bross turned to the rest of the men. "So imagine you're fat, dumb, and happy in Chillicothe, Ohio, and several thousand Chinese soldiers are walking around with guns shooting at you and your family and blowing stuff up."

Everyone laughed.

"I know it sounds funny and improbable. Impossible. But just imagine that for a second." Lieutenant Bross paused. "I'm not kidding. How would you like it if those Chinese soldiers were all over tarnation, killing your livestock, burning down your houses, shooting your sisters, dragging your dads off for interrogation? Think for a minute. How would you like that?"

He looked around.

"No? Not good, right? These people outside that concertina wire," he waved off over his shoulder, "have no choice. But I can guarantee you that if they *did* have a choice, they would want us gone. They would want us gone *right now*. They still can't believe we came back after the French left."

"We're getting rid of the fuckin' H ồ Chí Minh commie bastards," Rook said.

Bross held up his hand again. "We are not here to discuss the politics that got us twelve thousand miles away from home. That's not our job, but I will say that sometimes the solution is worse than the problem. That's all I'm saying." He looked around at each of them. "I know you guys are looking at me now like I'm from the planet Mars. What does this cherry boy know about Vietnam? Well, I can't argue. Not much. I am totally going to rely on you to help keep Sergeant Rook, me, you, and Kook over there alive."

Rook returned a puzzled look that said, *How does he know that's Kook?*

"But what I do know is that every man out there is a son, and most likely a brother and possibly a father. Every woman is a daughter, perhaps a sister and a wife and maybe a mother. Every kid in every ville has never seen anything but killing. And all I'm asking you to do, each and every one of you, is to remember that these people are human beings. I don't have any interest in who's religious, but every religion has a form of the Golden Rule. In this platoon I intend to practice it. I want you to do the same. When you kill a son, or mother, or sister, or child, that person will be missed." He looked around and saw interest in just about every face, except the face of Sergeant Rook, who was tossing his head back and rolling his eyes in disbelief.

"LT, I gotta differ," Rook interrupted with a southern accent so thick he was barely intelligible. "You do not want these guys hesitatin'. That's what's gonna get 'em killed."

Lieutenant Bross had a passing thought that he and Rook might not get along, but for now he ignored the comment. He didn't want to break his chain of thought, but he incorporated Rook's thinking.

"Golden Rule. If that man in your sights is going to do unto you with a bullet, then you do unto him first. No hesitation. Again, let's remove the people who need removing, but let's take some time to make sure it's the enemy. I am *not* telling you to give bad actors a break. Get it?"

He looked around. "Any questions?"

Masterson held up his hand as if in school.

"What is it, Bat?"

"Sir, I been doing this for over seven months. You are platoon leader number three for me. We all have our baggage, but I can say sir, you now hold the world record for *weirdest pep talk ever*."

Nervous chuckles all around.

"Screw you, Masterson," MacNulty stepped in. "Sir, I agree it's strange, but it's like you been here before. Like you know what some of us are thinking." MacNulty looked at his boots. "Sometimes I cry when I shoot a slope. I'm not ashamed to admit that. There's some mother, somewhere, bawling her eyes out. It keeps me up at night thinking about it. My mother would be crying up a storm. I bet they are too. I completely understand they're shooting at me and want to kill me, but I don't think that old man out there in that paddy gives a shit if Hồ Chí Minh is in charge."

"Thanks, Corporal MacNulty. I don't expect all of you to get it right away. My promise to you is to do everything in my power to get each and every one of you back on that silver freedom bird in a seat, not in a box, not in a bag, not on a gurney. You will never hear that speech or anything like it again, but when you wonder if I'm going to beat the crap out of you for killing some poor farmer's water buffalo, remember this day."

There were some nods of agreement. But Lieutenant Bross caught Sergeant Rook feigning a wide-eyed puzzled look while mouthing to one of the squad leaders, *What the fuck?*

The platoon broke ranks. It was near chow time. The

lieutenant noticed that the Frisbee dog was sitting next to a pile of disheveled sandbags. Had he been listening too? No, he already knew the game. He stood up and wagged his tail when Sean MacNulty reached out his hand in a tiny, below-the-waist "come here" wave. Like a dog at a show, he glued himself in a heel to MacNulty's left leg while he walked. The dog looked up with love, and Sean looked down with love. Darren was a dog person, so he got it. He smiled, thought back to his border collie, Race, back in Lufkin, and then looked again at MacNulty and Nutsy. There it was: the Golden Rule.

16 July 1967
Landing Zone Regulator, near Thuong Duc, Quảng Nam Province, South Vietnam

Sunday. Darren was not what many would consider a religious man, but at morning chow he had overheard a couple of his guys, more devout, talking about the battalion chaplain being on the LZ. If he took the time to attend the service, then he would be able to write his mom to let her know he had been a good Christian boy. This would provide her some comfort, on this, his last day in relative safety before taking men out in the field to die.

The GP-medium was otherwise a meeting location that kept soldiers dry in this moderate rainfall, but for today, it was a chapel, a place of worship. The chaplain was non-denominational by order, but Darren learned after the service that he was ordained

Presbyterian. Chaplain, Captain Roy Davis was from Boise, Idaho. His short sermon was on the righteousness of the war with "God on our side." He talked briefly with each soldier as they departed, blessed their service and such. Darren made sure he was last to depart and pulled the chaplain aside just inside the flaps of the tents while the steady rain fell.

"Do you really think God takes sides?"

"Of course he does, Lieutenant."

"Don't you think the enemy is praying to their God as fervently as we are praying to ours?"

"Perhaps you are right, but unless they are praying to the one Christian God, they are misdirected."

"What if I have some Jews or non-believers in my platoon? How about them?"

"As a chaplain, I serve them all."

"But my Jews aren't praying to a Christian God."

"They should be."

"I'm going to pretend you didn't say that, Chaplain."

"As you will," the chaplain responded.

Darren held a scrap of cardboard over his head as he ran back to his bunker. He couldn't shake the thought that nothing about this conflict was right. *How are we on the right side, when the entire thing is a goat screw?*

He thought back to West Point football games when a

halfback in the end zone would kneel and pray, thanking God for the touchdown. *Could God really be on the side of West Point instead of Navy, Colgate, or Rutgers? What did the other guys do wrong?*

He thought back to a tie before Ranger School, when he was in the "rent-a-crowd" as a major was promoted to lieutenant colonel at Fort Benning. The major addressed the gathering and thanked God for seeing fit to "raise his poor young soul." *There were a couple of majors in the audience who didn't made the cut. Did they tick God off?*

It all seemed ludicrous, but Darren would play along with his men. Some needed the hope their faith provided. If that was an advantage, then it was needed.

Monday, the seventeenth of July, 1967 would be Lieutenant Bross's first test of mettle in combat. He could not deny that he was nervous. Flat-out scared, truth be known. The rain was coming down in buckets, a less than perfect day to prepare for battle.

He wasn't the only one who was new. His platoon sergeant was new to the men, but he had at least survived a difficult tour as a squad leader, and then platoon sergeant down south somewhere. Darren wasn't worried about him. But he harbored a nagging feeling about Sergeant Rook. In Ranger School, one of the NCOs drilled into them the mandate to make certain the entire platoon, including the platoon sergeant, knew who was in charge from day one. But here was Rook, already questioning Darren's decisions in front of the men. He'd have to deal with it at some point.

Before the noon meal he gathered Sergeant Rook, First Squad Leader Staff Sergeant Whitsun "Witz" Carper, Second Squad Leader Staff Sergeant "Bat" Masterson, Third Squad Leader Staff Sergeant Scotty Johnson, and Weapons Squad Leader Sergeant Kimball Elphick for a short talk.

"I'm counting on you guys. Tomorrow is a big day for me, but it's not lost on me that you've all been there. It must scare the bejeezus out of you that the least-experienced guy is in charge, but that's the way the army is. I have a lot of training, but promise me you'll tell me when I'm screwing it up. I will listen. I promise each of you that I will listen."

The lieutenant saw a lot of head nodding. "Sir, they call me Elf. You're gonna do fine. Don't sweat it."

"Thanks, Elf. I appreciate it."

Darren looked around at his men. "The plan is this," he said. Now he looked directly at Sergeant Rook. "Get everyone together after noon chow. This is prep day. I want everyone one hundred percent ready to move out before they hit the sack tonight. We'll meet again at fifteen hundred hours right here. I want to walk through our orders, and everything we can think of about how we're going to spend the next four days together."

Scotty Johnson spoke up in a deep Mississippi drawl. "Sir, there's not much room here. I'd like to bring my team leads." The others joined in agreement with head nods and raised thumbs.

Carper piped up, "Saw you at church this morning, boss. We could meet there. It's a general purpose spot. I can move the tables to the center so we can lay maps out."

"Perfect," Darren said. "Make sure it's available. We'll take two hours. Then before we eat I want thirty minutes with the entire platoon." He motioned to Sergeant Rook, who responded with a smug look as if he'd just heard a bad joke.

"Sergeant Rook, do we have a problem?"

"Nope. Got it. And it's Rook. Just Rook."

Everybody smoked. Or at least that's how it seemed. Darren recalled that when he was at West Point all the cadets had been required to read and initial a warning report that was put out by the Surgeon General. He pondered its purpose while working with PFC Van Wright, who had a cigarette hanging magically from his lower lip while seeming to touch nothing else. They were cutting the baling wire on a box of C-rations—"Meal, Combat Individual, C"— to divide them up before the patrol. Heavy, more than two pounds each. A determined soldier facing a five-day patrol might attempt to carry thirty pounds of C-rations in his rucksack. He'd do that early on in his tour, but when he was more experienced, he'd make half as much last. If re-supply choppers could get in, they'd drop cases to you.

Turkey Boned, Ham and Eggs Chopped, Chicken and Noodles, Beef Spiced with Sauce, Beans and Wieners, White Bread, and Pound Cake in cans. On its face there was variety, but in practice everything was just about identical in taste and texture.

PFC Wright took the cigarette from his mouth and held it

between his first and second fingers while hoisting a can. "Sir, this one is Beefsteak with Potatoes and Gravy. The factory sliced raw potatoes as a joke and added them in the mix. We all call it "Beef and Shrapnel.""

Lieutenant Bross laughed. "Private Wright, where are you from?"

"They call me Van, sir. Been living Olympia, Washington since my dad retired at Fort Lewis in sixty-four. Before that I was an army brat. I lived all over, but I guess Olympia's home since I was twelve."

"I've never been there, but I understand it's a beautiful area of the country."

"It is, sir. All the rain of Nam, but not the steam bath."

"I hear that!"

At night, if you opened up a ration can with your P-38 opener, you could be eating Beef and Shrapnel, but someone could tell you it was Ham and Lima Beans. You'd believe them. Twelve units to a case, and every soldier had their favorites. Trading began from the get-go. If you could call it meat, some liked ham, others turkey, others beef, but the highlight of every box was the accessory pack with chewing gum, instant coffee, toilet paper, sugar, creamer, salt, and the favorite of all, a slim pack of ten cigarettes and matches provided by the tobacco industry for the benefit of soldiers at war.

On three meals per day with two thirds of the platoon lighting up, everyone who wanted to could begin a two-pack-a-day habit free of charge. Winston, Old Gold, Marlboro, Lucky Strike, Newport, Pall Mall, and the occasional surprise of Tareyton and

Benson & Hedges Menthol. Christmas every day in Vietnam as the necessities of life were stripped down to Maslow's hierarchy of needs, modified to add coffee, tobacco, and fruitcake that even the local rats wouldn't touch.

To the lieutenant, who'd tried a few times, but never could take to it, the ritual of cigarette-smoking in his platoon was a window into the soul of the soldier. The smokers all carried Zippo lighters, so the matches in the accessory pack were saved for emergencies. Only, more often than not, they were soaked with rain and sweat. Like legerdemain, a corporal could calmly light a cigarette during a break in a firefight and be transported in his mind for a moment to a far-off peaceful place. Rounds zinging overhead, mortars incoming, he could pull the smoke into his lungs while a cylinder of ash grew to impossible lengths. Another sergeant would fiddle with matches, working to get one of the twenty in the book lit and to the end of his cigarette. He'd fidget, looking in all directions simultaneously, eyes in the back of his head. A thousand nervous flicks of the butt would ensure that not the tiniest piece of ash remained.

That juxtaposition was a lesson for Darren in the human condition of war.

For a platoon that would take all possible precautions to hide from the enemy, to conceal the all-important "position," it was anathema to even consider reducing the human signature by prohibiting soldiers from lighting up, except perhaps at night when a soldier in the open would cover himself in a poncho before striking his Zippo. "Smoke 'em if you got 'em." In a platoon of thirty, after forty-five minutes humping concealed trails, whether in elephant grass, along stream beds, or in jungle triple canopy, any enemy within miles knew Americans were nearby when twenty of the thirty lit up and were able to smoke two, perhaps three cigarettes before packing up again and stepping off. In the worst case, in the calm breezeless early morning, a lazy sniper might simply fire into a column of sunlit smoke and find a target. In Nam, the Surgeon General's warning was right: smoking could indeed be hazardous to your health.

Darren thought back to the introductory talk he'd had with the platoon the day prior. He'd laughed it off at the time, but Masterson's comment about the strangeness of his message hit home. He wanted to start out as a good leader, and that might not have been the best start, even though he believed his words and he knew they resonated with at least some of the guys.

Far and away his favorite pre-battle talk was the Saint Crispin's Day speech that Shakespeare had put in the mouth of King Henry the Fifth before the eleventh century Battle of Agincourt.

> *... If we are mark'd to die, we are enow*
> *To do our country loss; and if to live,*
> *The fewer men, the greater share of honor...*

> *We few, we happy few...*

And gentlemen in England now a-bed
Shall think themselves accursed they were not here,
And hold their manhoods cheap

When he was a plebe, a first classman had forced Darren to memorize all fifty-three lines of the speech and stand in his room to recite them with as few breaths as possible. The firsty and his roommate counted the breaths, and then ordered it up again, with one fewer. Then again with an English accent, then a Southern drawl, then from Massachusetts like President Kennedy, then back to Darren's native Texan: think LBJ reciting *Henry V*. They laughed at him. It was pure torture at the time, but it was so burned into his neurons that he could recite the lines today as if he were in the play off-Broadway. The gifts leaders give that stick with you forever.

Speaking of weird—if he recited those lines to his troops...

He thought better of it.

"You guys have done this, and I've only practiced, so I'm not going stand here and give you some sort of rousing speech about the glory of battle. I can see it in your eyes, your time here has worn you down. You may question the reason you're here. You might be focused on the A&W back home and that girl on roller skates who will bring a root beer float to the door of your convertible just for the asking. We're all there. Don't feel like you're the only one questioning why your country took your names from a hat and decided you had to go to a far-off land to fight in a place you wouldn't have been able to point to on a map a few years ago. I'm the new guy, but I don't think I need to explain to you why I'm in charge. Like I said yesterday, it's just the way we do business.

"Tomorrow we step outside this LZ. Tomorrow Sergeant Rook and I join a team of seasoned professionals. Some of you may be wounded. Some may die. All are scared. I would be more scared if I didn't know the incredible reputation this platoon has built. I talked to Lieutenant Jacobs over noon chow. Yeah, I know. He was supposed to go to Battalion with the old man. But he got permission to stay at the LZ for a couple of days to finish up your evaluations and some other admin stuff. He mentioned every single one of you by name. I am embarrassed to say he knows you better than I do right now, but that will change. You are his family forever, and he yours. Trust me, I'm going to get to know each of you. I will keep you in my heart. As we discussed yesterday, I plan to reach out to each of your families. In my short talk yesterday I may have made you think twice about your decision to shoot, to take a life. But I promise you, my priority is to bring you all back. This time, we have four nights in the bush. When we meet the enemy, make them remember us. Be ferocious, but be wise.

"Are we all ready to go?"

The response was unrehearsed, a resounding: "Yes, sir!"

Darren thought back to his training and half-expected someone to belt out, "I CAN'T HEAR YOU!" but it ended there.

"Any questions?"

There was tension. The kind felt when no one has questions, but everyone wishes someone else would break the ice and ask the first one.

PFC Francisco Hernandez—"Paco"—had a voice like the cartoon character Speedy Gonzalez. He was born and raised on the north side of the Rio Grande River in Zapata, Texas, but in a household with English as the second language. He was quiet, humble, and unassuming, but when he spoke, it was memorable. "Sir, you sort of lost me when you were talking about root beer flotas. *¡Hijole Jefe!* You making me thirsty. That A&W in Brownsville. Those *chicas* got *nalgas* that don't quit. *¡No nos chinga Teniente!*"

"It's Paco, right?"

"Yes, sir!"

"You know I speak some Spanish, but I didn't get that."

"Don't worry sir. Just me being a wise-ass. I said those chicks' asses don't quit. And don't fuck with us, Lieutenant."

Every member of the platoon turned and looked at Paco. They couldn't remember the last time they had heard him say anything, and now here he was, the class clown. They all burst into knee-slapping laughter.

Lieutenant Bross joined in. Paco added in perfect English, "We got your back, Lieutenant." Then, "*Todos nosotros* gonna be just fine."

"That's right, boss."

"Fuckin' A, boss."

"Let's kill some dinks, LT."

Darren looked around. High fives. High morale. This was a

team.

This was his team.

2nd Platoon, Bravo Company

Platoon Leader: 1LT Darren Bross -- Lufkin TX

Platoon Sergeant: SFC Lionel Bodean Rook -- Arcadia FL

RTO: CPL Clayton Kook "Kuykendahl" -- Franklin Park NJ

Medic: CPL Sean MacNulty -- Las Vegas NV

1st Squad

Squad Leader: SSG Whitsun "Witz" Carper -- Marblehead MA

Rifleman Team Leader: SGT Dick "Robin" Grayson -- Gainesville FL

Rifleman: CPL George "Peanut" Washington Carver -- Valdosta GA

Rifleman: Vicente "Beans" Mejia -- Guanajuato MEX

Rifleman: PFC Kennan "Pixie" Pixton -- San Antonio TX

Rifleman Team Leader: SGT Carter "Maple" Maples -- Sacramento CA

Grenadier: PFC Stanley "Stan" Peckham -- Alamogordo NM

Rifleman: PFC Peter "The Knife" Mack -- St Petersburg FL

Rifleman: PFC Wellington "Loo" Chamberlain -- Arlington VA

2nd Squad

Squad Leader: SSG James "Bat" Masterson -- Chillicothe OH

Rifleman Team Leader: SGT Norman "Nick" Nicolletti -- Bellevue NE

Grenadier and Rifleman: PFC Cesar "Switch" Torrens -- San Juan, PR

Rifleman/BackUp Medic: CPL Michail "Mickey" Grosvenor -- Ft Collins CO

Rifleman Team Leader: SGT Craig Message -- Belleville IL

Rifleman: PFC Martin "Marty" Byers -- Montgomery AL

Rifleman: PFC Daniel "Jiggles" Schmidt -- Falls Church VA

Grenadier: PFC Francisco "Paco" Hernandez -- Zapata TX

3rd Squad

Squad Leader: SSG Scott "Scotty" Johnson -- Gulfport MS

Rifleman Team Leader: CPL Timothy "Lassie" Langman -- Beavercreek OH

Rifleman Team Leader: SGT Charles "Chuck" Warren -- Cocoa Beach FL

Rifleman: CPL Andrew "Russ" Russelvage -- Vienna VA

Rifleman: CPL Mark Owens -- St. George UT

Rifleman: PFC Mitchell "Smitty" Pholoong -- Peyton CO

Weapons Squad

Squad Leader: SGT Kimball "Elf" Elphick -- College Station TX

Bearer and Rifleman: CPL Gary Cole -- Chico CA

Bearer and Rifleman: PFC Ernest "Ernie" Salisbury -- Portland ME

Assistant Machine Gunner: PFC Van Wright -- Olympia WA

Machine Gunner: PFC John "Jack" McCloskey -- Nederland CO

Machine Gunner: CPL William "Willy" Hartsdale -- Gifford FL

CHAPTER *14*

17 July 1967

Lampshade Valley, near Thuong Duc, Quảng Nam Province,

South Vietnam

The incongruity of fighting a war in a beautiful place was lost on most of the platoon. They'd become jaded. Under constant fear for your life and counting every day in this eternity could blind you to the stunning landscapes, vibrant colors, bluest skies melting into greenest terrain. Whitest puffy clouds as far as the eye could see. Sunsets ablaze. Morning mist obscuring tiny villages until they were just silhouettes on a steaming horizon. In many ways it was impossible to believe lives were at stake.

But they were.

Sean MacNulty brought it home for the "dog guys" at least. Sitting cross-legged on the dirt, rucksack weapon and medical kit by his side, he held his dog Nutsy around the neck, cradling him in the space made between his crossed legs. He might just as well have been saying goodbye to a toddler son. Nutsy knew the drill. Embodying the word "hangdog," he walked around with his head low. Somehow he knew it was goodbye for now. Nutsy was

MacNulty's dog, no doubt about it. For however many days it took, he would pace the LZ, searching and panting through the fence, waiting for his master to return.

Thirty-three Americans, as far out of their element as was humanly possible, stepped one after another, single file, out of the LZ. On this first patrol with the new lieutenant, there would be no transport in a five-ton to start the patrol; they'd be on foot from the get-go.

The damp ground from the previous day of rain was giving up its moisture in rising vapor, steam from every living thing in sight. The sun continued its ascent so that everyone was marching into a 0800 shadow—not a good idea, since full sun was a better ally to spot the inevitable booby trap, tripwire, or punji stick. When a group of this size started out, they tried to ensure a separation of "four parallel parking spaces." With one hundred feet between them, the string of humanity was over a half mile long—so far apart that if one or two soldiers lost sight of the one in front, the cohesion of the platoon could be lost in an instant. Human nature and the need to be close invariably caused the line to compress like a Slinky. They had to work it constantly to ensure separation. To maintain contact, the squad leaders—Witz, Bat, and Scotty—were tied at their hips with a squad-level radio operator, a team leader working double duty. Maples, Message, Warren, and Cole carried AN/PRC-6s, fancy "Prick 6" walkie-talkies to maintain contact with the platoon RTO, Kook.

There are a few qualities a platoon needs in the RTO. Kook had them all. He was quick-thinking. He could call in fires before the platoon leader even asked. He was smart. Working the radio-telephone required a daily recoding of the crypto using a "whiz wheel" and a code sheet to ensure transmissions were not made in the clear. Map reading was vital. It was a skill lost without practice and repetition. The platoon lifeblood was knowing where they were at all times. An RTO's additional duty was to shoot geographic features with a compass, calculate the back azimuths from at least two, preferably three locations, and plot the intersections. Knowing where you were every second could be the difference between life and death. In range of a fire base, supporting fires could stop an enemy sniper attack or an ambush in its tracks. It could mean the difference between Dust Off arriving in fifteen minutes instead of thirty. One problem was that a good RTO was usually more accurate than the chopper pilots. But if the platoon could get them close, popping smoke and directing an approach over the radio was the key to ultimate success working with army aviation. Kook kept up with map-reading and maintained a constant mental reminder of grid coordinates.

The heat and humidity were unrelenting. Everyone felt damp all the time. If you didn't repeat the mindless motion of pulling your jockey shorts out of your butt crack you'd wonder if it would close around the cotton like some oak tree growing around a strand of barbed wire that was strung next to it when the tree was just a sapling. Jungle rot, boils, mosquitos, leeches, and everyone's favorite: impetigo that seemed to rear its head just when the doc was fresh out of antibiotics to treat it.

Against the advice of two squad leaders, Lieutenant Bross

made the decision from the first step out of the LZ to walk point. Well, not exactly *point*, but within fifty feet or so. He wanted to establish his bona fides. Evans had told him the platoon leader should be "up front." Leading from the rear never worked. One hundred feet of separation was the goal, but Kook stayed with the platoon leader to ensure instant radio contact to Company.

Sergeant Rook wasn't thrilled with the lieutenant's decision, especially since it was his first day. He spoke to Carper. "Put Beans up there in front of the boss."

"Why Beans?" Witz asked.

"Just fucking do what I say!" Rook whisper-screamed. "Put Mejia on fucking point. Do I make myself clear?"

"I got it top, but didn't you hear Beans yesterday? No speakee da English. How's he gonna tell us what's up?"

Rook stopped, turned, got in Carper's face, and in a stern whisper said, "Witz. Just do what I fucking say!"

Rook had a year of experience walking around in Vietnam, so Witz acquiesced, noting that Rook took up the rear, or near the rear, ensuring he wasn't too far from Third Squad Rifle Team Leader and the Prick 6.

To help prevent fratricide, the platoon had adopted a controversial technique of having the point man keep his M-16 on "semi-automatic," when the rest of the line was clicked to "safe." Lieutenant Bross was willing to try it, but at the first indication it was placing them in extra danger, he was planning to put everyone on "semi."

The platoon missions were threefold: find, close with, and

kill the enemy. In addition, they were ordered to search two villages that had not been investigated in quite some time, and then touch base with Delta Company's Third, who was taking turns with other Delta platoons guarding two bridges along Route 14. The four-night, five-day route would take Second Platoon thirty miles on foot in an expanded loop ending up back at the LZ.

Two semi-permanent bivouacs, defensive positions, were marked on maps, hills that were within LZ supporting fire's range, and had been kept clear of the enemy by a constant stream of US units. The squad leaders were trying to convince Lieutenant Bross and Sergeant Rook that those places were ripe for overrunning.

"Yes, sir, they have latrines, but no showers. I've been in one of them close to the river. You can't even dig a foxhole without the water table making it a bathtub before you get two feet down. A two-day night defensive position is a lot smarter than hanging out at some place Charlie knows about and is ready to pounce on. No latrines, but NDP is the way to go. If we move every couple of days we can stay ahead of 'em."

Route 14 headed west toward mountains close enough they could almost be touched. To PFC Jiggles Schmidt and PFC Andrew "Russ" Russelvage, the view reminded them of the Blue Ridge Mountains of Virginia as seen from the windshield on the way to the Skyline Drive. It turned out that Jiggles and Russ had grown up in Northern Virginia just a few miles from each other. Russ had been a defensive tackle at Oakton High School in Vienna, while Schmidt was a star running back for the Falls Church High Jaguars. It took them a while to figure it all out, but Russ had tackled Jiggles more than once during the Oakton High homecoming game almost two years prior. Now they were inseparable.

Their route took them along the Vu Gia River that paralleled Route 14 west of LZ Regulator, past roadside shacks and endless Vietnamese workers, old men and women working the fields and paddies all around them. Day one for Darren Bross was uneventful. A walk in the park, so to speak. They were able to make it to the established bivouac by 1500 hours. There was something about this place that tugged on the lieutenant: passable bunkers, well-constructed defilades, latrines. But he looked around, conferred with Rook, and said, "Move it out, guys. I agree with you guys. I don't like this place."

While pacing away, it was Masterson who pulled up near Lieutenant Bross and talked him through what they all wanted to find in a suitable NDP. "Sir, there's old rice paddies everywhere— great places to take cover. We're looking for rocks, stands of trees, even cemeteries are fantastic."

Under an hour later they found unused high ground with some old empty rice paddies on the gentle slopes. This place was suitable to create the night defensive position. There was ample time to dig in, set up perimeter defenses, lay some claymores, and prep for night, the scariest time in Vietnam. Soldiers rotated guard duty. Scared shitless, they were skittish, trying not to fall asleep. They had a set of clackers for the claymores, and if there were no trees nearby, hand frags at the ready. Sergeant Rook employed a pretty good method of ensuring alertness, but it only worked a few times.

"We were down south with the best triangular-shaped NDP

anyone had ever seen," he told the men. "Soldier on the northeast apex fell asleep. NVA regulars crab-crawled in, turned the claymores around, and then made a racket to wake the night guard up. He hit the clacker, and boom, cut himself in half. So stay the fuck awake." The story, while a bald-faced lie, was not that outlandish. Things like it happened in Nam.

As the sun set, Message was scanning the horizon with a strange-looking pair of small binoculars and taking notes in a tiny memo book. Darren made a mental note to thank him for his diligence. *Why don't I have a pair of binoculars?* he wondered.

It was his first night in charge in Indian Country, and he was in and out of fitful, fear-ridden sleep. His own turn at guard duty was a non-event. Sergeant Rook had told him not to worry. "The dinks aren't magicians. If they happen on it, this NDP scares the shit out of them. They know we've surrounded the place with claymores. Yeah, they own the night, but we own the firepower."

For night one, it turned out that Rook was right: the night was quiet. But Darren would have to get used to sleeping in uniform. In time, he would come to know the pleasure of uniform parts seeming to grow into your skin.

19 July 1967

Lampshade Valley, near south of Tây Hoà, Quảng Nam Province, South Vietnam

Tây Hoà was a hand-scrawled spot on the grid map, three

clicks north of Route 14. Captain Evans transcribed it from a battalion S2 briefing chart. It had not been investigated in eighty-four days—now eighty-six or eighty-seven—and a lot could happen in three months. It was time.

There was known Charlie activity in the area. Willingly or not, Tây Hoà could well be a stronghold. On paper, the plan was straightforward. One, find a village. Tây Hoà was as good as any, particularly since Battalion wanted it cleared. Two, scout its approaches and all potential exits. Three, find probable exit routes. Four, set up an ambush along one or two exits. Five, approach the village in a conventional manner from one or two cardinal directions. Six, wait in ambush for the roaches to flee. Seven, engage. Eight, take prisoners. Nine, count bodies. Ten, work a system to search the village for weapons caches. Eleven, depart.

What could be simpler? Sergeant Rook had spent his first tour becoming an expert in the tactics, techniques, and procedures of clearing and securing. Bross learned that Rook was an expert because that's what Rook told him: "I am an expert." And since that's what Lieutenant Bross was after, he let the platoon sergeant run the show. Which was a mistake. Instead of a lesson in real-world operations, he and the rest of the platoon were about to get a clear-eyed view of sadism at its finest—or its worst, depending on your perspective.

Rook wanted full sun. No early wake-ups or departing too

soon. "No need to interrupt anyone's breakfast: not ours, not theirs." The lieutenant didn't think that sleeping in felt like much of a military operation, but this time he'd take cues from Rook and step in only if necessary.

Rook had Second Squad peeling out ahead of the others. "Split in half and mark every fucking trail these gooks could run away on. Meet us here." He pointed at an intersection of two streams. "Just north of this. Find someplace with cover. We'll locate you."

From the NDP, the platoon crossed the Vu Gia on foot, fording the rushing stream that was swelled and muddy from monsoon rains and late thunderstorms the night before. There was no easy way to get across, and over twenty soldiers were soon soaking wet to their armpits. No one wanted to imagine what was in the water around them. By the time they crossed and found Second Squad, they were a third of the way to the Tây Hoà village center.

Second had conducted their reconnaissance during nautical twilight under cover of mist, near fog. They were confident they hadn't been seen by any villagers. Staff Sergeant Masterson pulled a grid map from a plastic protective envelope, opened it up, and spread it across the ground while Lieutenant Bross, Sergeant Rook, Kook, and MacNulty looked on. Rook sent MacNulty out to summon Witz, Carper, and Scotty Johnson. They would need to hear the plan.

The arterials feeding the village radiated as one would expect in Vietnam: along the dikes between rice paddies, or straight across meadows as created by beasts of burden, and then one to the north leading toward another village about halfway to the horizon. Cover was good along this path, so setting an ambush would be easy compared to a more open landscape. Since Second Squad had seen the terrain, they had the best understanding of the battlefield layout. Masterson would split his team into two, flank the village wide to the east, and set up on either side of the trail. First and Third Squads would place one team each in a pincer movement from the four o'clock and eight o'clock positions.

The remainder of First and Third co-joined with Lieutenant Bross. Sergeant Rook and Corporals Kuykendahl and MacNulty would walk in two files, line abreast, into the main north-south entrance to the village, the path to the village water source.

Lieutenant Bross stepped forward and said, "Guys, just a reminder. Battalion brass made it clear to Captain Evans and me that the MACV"—this referred to Military Assistance Command Vietnam, the military headquarters in Vietnam—"strategy is 'clear and secure.' Men running north as we enter are fair game, but this is also a village of humans. If we determine they're riddled with VC, we'll deal with that, but let's take some time to figure it out."

Everyone but Rook responded in the affirmative. They conducted a final radio check, synchronized their watches, and moved out. It was 0922. Second Squad already had a few extra miles on their feet, but they had the most work to do to get in position. The remainder of the platoon would lay low until 1015 when Sergeant Message would triple-key the mic on his AN/PRC-6. A triple-key said, "Ready."

They were in position. First Squad Rifle Team Leader

Sergeant Dick Grayson and his counterpart from Third Squad, Corporal Tim "Lassie" Langman, shook hands under the shade of a tree. One took his team west, the other east. Their progress was slowed by having to zigzag along rice paddy walls. Sergeant Rook took point with the twelve remaining platoon members and marched with his M-16 at port arms north toward the village. For safety, Lieutenant Bross and Kook took up a rearward position. The soldiers passed the time with mindless banter as only soldiers can do.

"Sarge, I was just thinking. This is the first year I haven't had a summer vacation."

"Whaddya you call this, asshole? You get a round-trip, all-expenses paid visit to a faraway land. And if you're lucky, you win the Kewpie prize. You get to stay a whole year!"

Maple raised his head with a huge grin. "I'm not shitting you, Sarge, last year I had a summer vacation before senior year. This year I'm killing dinks for a living."

"Stop thinking, Maple, it'll hurt you."

At the agreed-upon safe separation of fifty to seventy-five feet, Lieutenant Bross was two football fields back. An excited soldier can march at four miles per hour without much exertion. That made the trip to the first village shack a little less than fifteen minutes.

A lone old man accompanied by two elderly women approached the soldiers from under a bamboo archway marking the southern end of the village, the main entrance of sorts. They were accustomed to seeing soldiers in the distance, but they knew that in close proximity the encounter might not be good. The man turned and stepped a little to his side and motioned his hands in a welcome gesture, as if sweeping the soldiers toward the arch. The women stepped aside as well, making way. The old man said something in Vietnamese. From its tone his words sounded like a greeting: "Welcome to our village." But he appeared nervous, which may have contributed to Rook's knee-jerk reaction.

Sergeant Rook took one step toward the old man and in a single movement of blinding speed, lifted his M-16 from its ready position and butted the old man in the face.

He went down like a sack of rocks, out cold before he hit the ground. The two women screamed. Rook grabbed the barrel of his M-16, swung his weapon like a baseball bat, and hit one in the side of the head. The other moved fast, intending to run. But Rook was ready. He tripped her to the ground and stomped her head with his right combat boot as he continued into the village.

Sergeant Carter Maples was closest in proximity to Sergeant Rook when the carnage began. Maples was a First Squad team leader. From Sacramento, California, where he had attended SACTO State, he had earned his PFC rank before leaving Basic Training— this in recognition of his college time. He'd been in Nam a few months on this tour, his second. He'd lost two toes to a booby trap his first time around. He'd pleaded to stay in the army, and throughout the healing process he'd begged to attend Ranger School before going back to Nam. He got his wish. Maples was one of a handful of Rangers in the platoon. He estimated he'd walked around seventy-five patrols. Until now, every excursion since his return was with Lieutenant Jacobs, an average, but in his opinion, caring military leader.

Maples's innate reaction was to do something, whether it involved disrespecting the senior NCO, or not. "SERGEANT ROOK! WHAT THE *FUCK* ARE YOU DOING?"

Rook spun around and aimed his M-16 at Maples's face. In an eerie, quiet way that stopped time, he said, "Shut up Maples, or I will shoot you. I am not kidding."

Maples dropped his weapon to the mud and raised his hands like someone being robbed. "You can't do this, Sarge. You can't do this."

"Watch me." Rook pointed to Peckham, The Knife, Waterloo, Smitty, and Torrens, and screamed, "*Every hooch! Clear out every one! EVERY ONE!* Burn this bitch to the ground."

Apoplexy was uncharacteristic of Darren Bross, but this, his first patrol as the boss, put his mind in a far-off place. The little respect he had for Sergeant Rook was tempered by the fact that this guy had "been there and done that." He was alive after over a year in Vietnam, and according to Rook, had survived some of the most vicious combat of the war.

But now, on seeing a sociopath in action under his command, the lieutenant's initial reaction was to run forward, with Kook in tow, take charge, and calm things down. Yet already the entire platoon was in fluid motion, and a plan, Rook's audible plan, was taking hold. Bross hesitated just long enough to see a dozen soldiers taking cues from Rook by pulling palm fronds from hut roofs and lighting them with Zippos—ready-made torches to carry out the order to burn the village.

Even with the daily afternoon rains, the huts went up in roars of flames. For Bross it was like a scene from a movie, the action seared forever in his head. He stood back, underneath the bamboo arch, and observed the destruction. When Kook reached down to help one of the injured women to her feet, Lieutenant Bross did the same for the other. While they brushed their skirts of dirt and mud and rubbed their wounds, Kook knelt with the radio on his back and tended to the unconscious old man. He was coming to, but the open wound on his forehead was bleeding into a puddle. This would not heal fast.

In Ranger School, Lieutenant Bross had learned that "clear and search" was a tactic to wear the enemy down. The Viet Cong, and in some cases the North Vietnamese Army, were locally supported. The logistics tail from the north was too long and the movement methods too primitive to keep an army of tens of thousands on the move indefinitely. So MACV strategy had determined that local villages were *centers of gravity*. Without that direct village support, the enemy would shrivel up and die. It was a doctrine, a strategy, and a plan, developed by REMFs wearing starched fatigues with embroidered rank insignia and custom-sewn patches, sitting in air-conditioned buildings back in The World.

What did an army need for support? The answer to that simple question was complex. It depended on the army. A GI might carry eighty pounds on his person: food, water, weaponry, ammo, armor, clothing, ID, photos, letters. What they carried was an individual thing and told you not only what they did, but who they were. The enemy was a little more agile, say, ten pounds. Uniform, perhaps. Hồ Chí Minh sandals made from old tires and inner tubes. Straw hat. Weapon. Ammo. A small cache of food. Traveling light mandated constant resupply. From their perspective, cooperative villages were reliable resupply depots.

But while some villages had close ties to the Viet Cong, for others, the Viet Cong were sworn enemies. Unfortunately, given the ever-present cultural and language barriers, for the average GI it was impossible to discern the difference between the good, the bad, and the ugly. So clear and search started out as a tactical approach with the best intentions.

However, "search and destroy" became the reality, and a pillar of the theater strategy.

There were two primary aims of both "clear and search" and "search and destroy": find food storage caches too large to be explained by the size of the village that harbored them; and find ammunition. How? There was the distinction. One way was to "burn the bitch down," round up the population, kill anything that fled, and search everything left. That method was not Lieutenant Bross's first choice. He wanted a little more subtlety.

Lieutenant Bross surveyed the carnage. He found himself wondering if every village in Vietnam had a central plaza like this one. A hardpan about the size of a basketball court was constructed from rectangular crumbling cement bricks laid out in a herringbone pattern. "It must be multi-purpose," he said aloud, to no one in particular.

Corporal MacNulty was nearby. He took his eyes off Sergeant Rook at the end of the plaza—Rook had his hands on his knees and was taking gulping breaths; the effort of destruction had its limits on the human body—and looked around wondering who the boss was talking to. He decided it was him.

"Yes, sir," MacNulty said. "Looks like they could use it for meetings, and games and such too." The *too* because they were both standing on what was now a drying platform for threshing rice. Three handmade wooden rakes stood nearby; these were used to keep airflow in the rice on this dry morning as the sun headed toward zenith.

They both surveyed the inferno. "What have we done, Sean?" the lieutenant asked. "What have we done?"

It sounded to MacNulty like a rhetorical question, so he didn't answer. He and the lieutenant stood with their M-16s hanging on outstretched arms below their waists and watched the village burn. Considering the potential danger, it was a sight unto itself seeing the platoon leader transfixed by the scene before him.

After several minutes of staring though the village to the

horizon, to the mountains in the distance, Lieutenant Bross said, "This is taking a lot longer than I imagined."

"Yes, sir, those fronds and the thatch and the bamboo walls still have a lot of wet in them from all the rain."

From the north, marching this way and that while rubbing their eyes against thick white smoke, Second Squad arrived from their ambush location. Sergeant Message led the loose formation with his binoculars swinging back and forth and bouncing on his chest. He took a second to look behind him for Witz, but couldn't see him through the smoke.

"Sir, not sure if you got it on the radio, but we didn't have any activity at all. Not a soul tried to escape by our position."

"That so?" Lieutenant Bross asked.

"Yes, sir."

"Could you see anything?"

"Funny you should ask. Looks like the breeze is from due south. Once you guys torched the village we couldn't see our hands in front of our faces for the smoke."

"What if VC ran by you on the trail?"

"Sir, there's no way they could have seen the trail. I really don't think there was anyone in the area." Staff Sergeant Carper stepped up beside the lieutenant and joined a rough square with MacNulty and Message facing each other. "Sir, he's right, nothing. No one. Not a dink, not a dog, not a pig, not a twig."

MacNulty, the wiseass, cracked, "Who are you, Message, Dr. Seuss?"

Everyone laughed except the lieutenant. Carver and

Peckham joined the group.

"Witz, what did we do wrong?" Lieutenant Bross asked.

Carper looked around to be certain the lieutenant was asking *his* advice. "Well, sir, coming to Nam for starters."

Everyone laughed again, except the lieutenant. "No, really," Bross said. "This looks like a giant waste of time. Now these people hate us. How do we get them on our side when we're doing this kind of crap? If this is the way we're gonna fight this war, everyone in the entire country will despise us before it's half over."

Witz spoke again. "Sir, with respect to the platoon sergeant, this ambush shit never works, at least not the way we execute. We would have to be a lot smarter. Look at all this rice. It's everywhere. How many villagers do you see? Maybe forty, forty-five if you count the infants. We're standing on enough rice to feed a battalion for a month."

They *were* surrounded by piles of rice. The six men looked at the drying rice and the large burlap sacks on the edges of the cement.

Witz continued, "I'd say there's no doubt this village is supporting at least the VC, maybe the NVA. Maybe it's coercion, maybe it's voluntary, but there's plenty growing season left, so they haven't started hoarding for winter... whenever that is."

Lieutenant Bross looked bewildered. The other guys were shuffling around, kicking rice like beach sand. More of Second Squad joined the group: Mickey Grosvenor and PFC Marty Byers.

Witz went on. "LT, these guys aren't stupid, but we treat them like they are. We got up too late. We started too late. If this village was supporting VC, then they knew exactly where we were. I guarantee you they had lookouts reporting back. We strolled into the NDP at fifteen hundred yesterday with thirty-three dudes. And the fourth guy in our line looks like Sasquatch to these people." He pointed at Kook.

Everyone laughed one more time—except, again, the lieutenant.

"Sir, they have this platoon pegged. So this morning you sent my squad out to recon. I think we were probably undetected, but I could be wrong. So, around ten hundred hours, or later, twenty-four guys start approaching the village from the south, southeast, and southwest. These guys can do arithmetic. 'Gee,' they think, 'nine guys are missing.' It takes their scouts about fifteen minutes to locate the ambush. We sit around holding our dicks while the rest of the platoon destroys their way of life."

Witz stopped there. There was a pregnant pause while Lieutenant Bross contemplated what he'd heard. *So obvious now. So simple*, he thought.

Peckham shifted his grenade launcher from one hand to the other. "Welcome to fucking Nam."

Bross spoke up. "So, Witz, you think this village is supporting Charlie."

It wasn't phrased as a question, but Witz said, "Yes, sir."

"How do we search the place when it's on fire?"

Witz was a little uncomfortable. He looked behind his right shoulder to the ten o'clock position in the village. They all followed his eyes to the commotion of Sergeant Rook, who was in the full role of a certified maniac: hitting villagers, pushing them with the barrel of his rifle, threatening them with burning palm fronds, and, deep somewhere within his psyche, leading his version of "the attack."

"Sir," Witz said, "this wasn't my idea. This is not the way I'd do it."

20 and 21 July 1967
Lampshade Valley, south of Tây Hoà and northeast of Nhon Ky, Quảng Nam Province, South Vietnam

Back at the NDP, after thirty minutes on the radio with Captain Evans to give a SITREP on the failed operation, Darren got to the priority task of writing another letter to Christy. He mentioned that he'd thought about Lex being four months old on the seventeenth, and wished he could have been there. Knowing he'd even miss Lex's first birthday brought some emotion to his chest and a tear to his eye. He wouldn't be able to drop anything in the mail until he got back to the LZ, but remembering the song he had sung before departing for West Point a lifetime ago, he made a personal commitment to write her every day. He sealed each with a kiss, and just like every other day, even with danger in the air all around, the song ran through his mind to the point where he couldn't get rid of it while trying to sleep.

Just two days short of a month in country, he made another note on the blank page in his prayer book before *The Order for Daily*

Morning Prayer: Letter #28. Today he wasn't sure what else to say. He couldn't shed the image of three dozen Vietnamese people rounded up inside their burning village. The women and children had been bawling their eyes out. There wasn't a man who appeared to be younger than fifty. In sign language and through the hesitant interpretation from Sergeant Warren, who seemed to have a knack for languages, Lieutenant Bross was able to question the village elder about the quantity of rice and the lack of younger men. Their story seemed well rehearsed. It elicited from one of the women and one man, perhaps the "assistant elder," a string of English phrases, including: "We help army. We help our army."

"Which army are you helping?"

"South Army."

"The South Vietnamese Army gets rice through its own supply chain."

"No, army get rice here."

"Are you working with the Viet Cong? The Cong?"

"No. Never. No help Cong. Cong kill brother."

"Where are the younger men?"

"They in army."

"Which army?" Lieutenant Bross had a rhythm going. By now he was pretty certain that, if the village really was supporting the South Vietnamese Army, the elder's answer would come across with a tone of exasperation. A response like "Which army do you think, dumb shit?" at this point would be convincing.

Instead the answer came out matter-of-fact and rehearsed. "Men in our army. South Army."

Sergeant Rook spoke up. "LT, we should call in a chopper and send a couple of these dinks back east for questioning."

Lieutenant Bross contemplated the suggestion in a moment of deep thought. He stared at the flames, scrunched up his eyes a little, and said, "No, we're not gonna do that. We screwed this up. These people have paid enough for now. Gonna recommend to Battalion a future op to get back to ground truth on this one."

The second letter Darren wrote was to his parents. It was a little more fact-based, but he had been well warned not to share too many details of the patrols. He wanted to soothe them, his mom in particular, and tell them everything was okay. He was learning fast and would return home on time.

A soldier's DEROS—his date of estimated return from overseas—was twelve months from the day he stepped on the plane at Travis or the ship from Oakland. Darren knew it was no lesson in leadership to count the days until DEROS, but doing so helped him retain his sanity. One of the sergeants at the out-processing center at Fort Benning kept a bowl full of dog-tag chains cut to exactly 365 links. With a pair of nail clippers, Darren cut a day. The tiny steel ball shot off into the dirt at his feet. Today, Darren Bross was at 344 and a wake-up. He had forty-five weeks left.

Their second mission was not unlike the first: clear and search Nhon Ky, a village on the south side of Route 14. Battalion sent intelligence through Bravo Company suggesting the village had cleared muster many times in the past. On a scheduled rotation, that was the type of intelligence that Lieutenant Bross later would deem "dangerous." It made him and the platoon complacent. But he was careful not to share too much of the intel with the men. He leaked word to his squad leaders, who passed it to their team leads, who made sure everyone in the platoon knew that Nhon Ky was an innocuous place, but they still all had to go through the motions of ensuring it was not a VC stronghold.

Days later, while watching Delta's Third Platoon guarding a bridge on Route 14, Bross would thank his lucky stars that no one had died in the debacle. They had overreacted at Tây Hoà, and they underreacted at Nhon Ky. Though over half the platoon had been through Nhon Ky more than once, Bross learned fast that it was not the men who were responsible for their own lives. *Orders* killed. He wanted to be cautious. And after Tây Hoà, the lieutenant had admonished Rook that in the future, village clearing would be just that: search and *clear*. Search and destroy would be reserved for the aftermath of a firefight when it was clear the village was siding with the enemy.

The setup for the search and clearing of Nhon Ky was similar to what they had done for Tây Hoà; the only difference was timing. On Thursday night, they returned to the NDP in squads and portions of squads in an attempt to confuse anyone paying attention. Lieutenant Bross positioned scouts in copses along the way, and they kept an eye on the paddies for undue attention. Message, with his binoculars, was a perfect choice for the task. Third Squad waited until dusk, after local area thunderstorms died, to make the trip back to safety. This was intended to confuse the enemy, making it harder for them to tally the total numbers. Their reward for coming in late was being last to depart the following morning. All in all it was much more difficult for an attentive enemy to discern the size and intent of Second Platoon the following day, the twenty-first. That was the hope.

First Squad set up the ambush along what appeared to be the most obvious village exit, toward the southwest, with the first hint of hills looming in the background. The trail appeared to go nowhere. They discovered after further inspection that it was a shortcut back to Route 14, as the main road there curved south.

This time they saw no initial evidence of logistical support to anyone. The village appeared to be harvesting just enough rice, husbanding just the right number of water buffalo, and raising a reasonable number of goats and pigs to support just the subsistence of the village.

Lieutenant Bross was surprised that the ambush setup to the southeast worked like a charm. This time Bross took a position near point and stepped toward the village from the east with ten men, the others on flanks to the southeast and northwest. The sun rose at their backs, making it difficult for the villagers to see their approach. There was a bell ringing in the village; they would think back on that later and realize it had been an alarm—an alarm just a minute or so before a village elder "welcomed" the platoon. It would also turn out that Rook knew the signs, but didn't bother to share.

From the southwest, First Squad took up position under cover on each side of the exit road. They were on time and on location. Given they knew the village had a low chance of harboring Charlie, they relaxed, happy for the opportunity to rest.

When PFC Chamberlain heard the bell from the village, he assumed it was an alarm clock of sorts for the breaking day: "Wakey wakey, sun scorch your eyebrows." He heard the phrase in his mother's voice. She was English, a World War II bride. He'd never heard that quip anywhere else.

They had time to think about the incessant barking of dogs. "They're not eating 'em, Sarge," Rook said. "Those are fucking watchdogs. We need to go into the villages ahead of time and kill the pooches."

And on that cue, a half dozen young men, three dressed in black "pajamas," ran down the path. Each was carrying an AK-47, and they were moving fast. First Squad was lined up on each side of the "expected escape route," but nevertheless they were surprised at the sudden appearance of the enemy. The sun was rising into their eyes. The squad might have missed the gaggle altogether had the six not been jabbering to each other in high-pitched, excited Vietnamese.

About a klick from the village, close to the ambush, one of the six stopped while holding his left hand up in a "wait a minute" gesture. Maybe he'd heard a noise. Perhaps he was thinking something was amiss in the elephant grass in front of him. Light was on the side of the escaping enemy. A lingering mist began its rise over the terrain. Dull silhouettes of mountains appeared in the distance. But what Charlie noticed was elephant grass with unnatural splits in its otherwise smooth drape. The first man held his hand up a little higher to stop the advance and to quiet his comrades. Their chatter ceased, leaving a ringing silence broken only by the sounds of a flock of singing sparrows in a nearby tree, a calling buffalo behind in the village, and the otherwise quiet sounds of nature. The man on point leveled his AK-47 in his right arm and began firing on full automatic into the elephant grass before him.

"Fuck, *they see us!*" Witz screamed.

Fact is, no one saw anyone. The six-man team from the Viet Cong was acting on instinct. First Squad could only see the flaming ball of the sun in the distance. A sun so bright it would leave latent retinal images long after eyes were turned away. No one had to tell the squad to hit the dirt. Bullets from multiple directions whizzed overhead. The entire squad was petrified, unable to see, unable to return fire, unable to call for help. Pinned down.

But not quite the entire squad. PFC Cesar Torrens, a grenadier from San Juan, Puerto Rico, was partly obscured by the thin shade of a tall bush. A member of Third Squad, he wasn't even supposed to be on ambush, but Stan Peckham was fighting a nagging cough that didn't lend itself to the quiet required in ambush duty. Stan and Cesar were both Latinos, and with no intention of being racist, Staff Sergeant Carper had thought Torrens was a good swap for Peckham. Besides, he thought to himself, Torrens went by "Switch." "We're gonna 'switch' you for Paco," Scotty, Staff Sergeant Scott Johnson, told Switch as they were leaving the NDP before sunrise.

Torrens was the most recent arrival in both squads. An FNG, he had only been in country for a short time, so he was untested. Yet the decision to put him on ambush probably saved the lives of most of the members of the squad.

Everyone was frozen, trying to find a stump or rock or tree to hide behind. Most were kissing dirt with their hands on top of their steel pots, waiting for the cracking of automatic fire to stop. But Switch was unfazed. He casually looked up and saw the outline of Charlie, backlit against the rising sun, spraying the squad-filled vegetation. Later on, he wouldn't be able to explain why he did it, but he stood slowly in the long shade of his protective bush and raised his M-79 grenade launcher, the equivalent of a single-shot, large sawed-off shotgun—or at least that's what it looked like. He made a quick mental calculation, an unconscious measurement born of recent experience. The spinning M-406 grenade would arm after thirty meters. *A little longer than the length of a swimming pool. Too close,* he thought.

Torrens knelt down, broke the barrel of the M-79 from its stock, and reloaded from his bandolier with M-576 buckshot, sliding in a cartridge filled with twenty large encased metal pellets. This would be delivered with no short-distance arming issues. He stood calmly again, as if unaware of the death around him, aimed, sensed a couple of AK-47 rounds whizz through the bush to his left, and pulled the trigger. Even with the noise of the direct fire, the squad could hear the telltale "bloop," the discharge of a grenade round.

He scored a direct close-range hit. The firing stopped. The 40mm round, releasing twenty steel balls traveling at around six hundred miles per hour, was an awesome display of power against flesh. That is, awesome for those who were not looking down the barrel when the shot was fired. The effect on a human was devastating and brutal at that range. The body count would include a note showing *one torso missing.*

One down, and then, for a few seconds, absolute quiet. Absolute until Pixie—PFC Kennan Pixton from San Antonio, Texas —let a fart rip so loud, long, and complex it could have been mistaken by the enemy for another weapons discharge. And what's a good fart without some cracking up? So PFC Peter Mack, "The Knife," started laughing—the kind of knee-jerk laughter you can't stop at a funeral even when you know the gravity of the situation and its incongruity with mirth. It was ingrained in his psyche: teenage fart jokes. He tried to stop, covering his mouth, but couldn't. The fear of death was running alongside the comedy neurons in his brain, and was losing the race.

The squad would learn soon enough that Pixie had passed his gas with some liquid included. A slippery wet fart, and they'd all smell it as a reminder until the next river crossing.

Though history shows that fart jokes are universal comedy, Switch ignored everything but the task at hand. In seconds he had reloaded. No one in the platoon knew it then, but he had gotten the nickname "Switch" from his instructor at grenadier school. Torrens could switch and reload multiple types of rounds faster than anyone they'd ever seen, a born grenadier, if there was such a thing.

If the enemy was chuckling over the fart, Switch never knew it. There he was, standing, kneeling, firing, reloading. Explosives, flechettes, close-range, long-range, wide pattern and close pattern. He even grabbed one illumination round by mistake, but still managed to hit one of the fleeing VC in the left upper thigh. Switch kept it up until even ragged enemy firing stopped.

When it was all over the silence was palpable. The smell of cordite hung in the still morning air—a mist of gray lazily rising on the heat of the morning sun.

There were five dead enemy soldiers and a sixth running out of range before the rest of the squad got back to their knees and stood into the layers of rising smoke.

Over the radio-telephone the company commander relayed his immediate priorities. The men were all reeling from a near-death experience, and the question over the bitch box did not fit the situation. Soldiers looked at the R-T like a confused dog cocking his head. The question from Company was not, "Are you guys okay? Any dead, any WIA?" No, nothing like concern for the platoon. Rather, the captain wanted only to know: "What's the body count?"

What's the body count? Are you kidding me? It all pretty much gets down to this, Darren thought. *They almost died. What's the body count?* He kept the frustration to himself and responded, "Five, all probably VC."

What the captain said next could not have been any weirder. At first Darren thought the man was trying to make a sick joke, but after the third patch of silence over the radio he figured out that he was serious.

"That one who took the direct hit," the captain said. "If he's cut in half we can count him twice. Any way to make it six vice five?"

The lieutenant made sure the mic key wasn't squawking, held it at arm's length, and said to no one in particular, "Get—me—the fuck—out of here." Then he keyed the mic. "No, sir, it's just five. Five VC."

The Third Squad leader, Staff Sergeant Scotty Johnson, stepped forward and held his index finger up in a "wait a second" gesture.

"Bravo six, six-two, stand by one," the lieutenant said. He removed the mic from his mouth and asked, "What's up, Scotty?"

"Sir, I'm pretty sure one of 'em is NVA."

"What?"

"Yes, sir, I think the VC were mixed up with a North Vietnamese soldier."

Rook stepped in with a radio-telephone-like question, "Why say you?"

Scotty turned to the platoon sergeant and pointed. "We rolled that one over. He's got different web gear, a different pack, a mess kit, a canteen, and a pistol on his web belt. But most of all, he's wearing a belt buckle with a red star on it."

Rook perked up, shifting his focus to "me," thinking of how he would collect that buckle as a souvenir.

Again Lieutenant Bross spoke into the mic. "Bravo six, six-two, stand by one more. We think we have one NVA regular." He lowered the mic and looked over to Sergeant Rook, who was now leaning over the dead soldier. Rook turned around with a thumbs-up and said, "NVA, LT. Not a doubt."

"Six, six-two. Best guess is four VC and one NVA regular, over."

"Copy six-two, four and one. Nice job."

The treasure trove was an intelligence score. It made Lieutenant Bross think of not only the stark reality that a squad in his platoon had been saved from a potential disaster by a young soldier who was so well trained he did the right thing without even thinking, but of how a present can just be tossed in your lap without warning.

He had no sentiments for the five dead soldiers who lay before him, but at the same time he didn't feel good about it, even when surrounded by high-fives and fist-pumping. While the rest of the platoon was gathering around, taking turns capturing posed images on a couple of Instamatic cameras and wasted flash cubes in full sun, he thought back to all his study of war and came around to a common theme, a theme that for him defied origin. Perhaps it was his upbringing. Perhaps it was an evolutionary mutation bent toward compassion in some that was designed to balance the hardheartedness of others. But he couldn't shake the inner feeling that someone, somewhere would miss these men. A wife, a son, a daughter, a mother, a father, a brother, a sister.

Darren shook the maudlin thought when Sergeant Elphick held up one of the Cong rucksacks and said, "LT, you might want to take a look in this one." He handed it over with a smile. When Lieutenant Bross took the ruck and peeked in, Elf added a thumbs-up and said, "Fuckin' A, guys. Fuckin' A."

The backpack was crude, but factory-made and functional. Green canvas, worn shiny in places from use, it had a drawstring on top covered by a flap that could be secured with two leather straps and rusty buckles. The top was already hanging open when the lieutenant started pulling it apart to look inside.

First he noticed cash. A later count, which devolved into an argument over what they could do with the money, tallied thousands of piasters. There were also some black and white photos of friends and cohorts. PFC Ernie Salisbury took one and held it up to the face of the deceased to verify that it included the man who lay dead before them.

"That's intelligence," Sergeant Rook commented. "Kook, start recording a list of the good stuff like that so when we shoot a SITREP to S2, we're organized."

Under the banded stacks of cash were dozens of documents, three annotated terrain maps, and one larger, color photo of a woman, inscribed with what was probably a message of endearment. "Come home safe. I love you," Darren guessed, a thought he couldn't shake until hours later.

Company called in the news to the Battalion Tactical Operations Center, Battalion TOC. S2 had a field day. Word would spread through the platoon days later that intelligence analysts had found a ledger among the documents. This guy was carrying payroll, enough that it might be back pay. The ledger included names, ranks, pay periods, amounts due, and even some additional annotations that were probably leave calculations.

"LT," Rook said, "we can keep that cash and have a party, or pay it out for information in villages, or hand it out to kids, whatever."

Of course Bross was skeptical. On the advice of Rook, combined with the squad leaders in a group, he agreed they'd hang on to the piasters until someone asked. No one ever did.

There were countless rules in Nam about taking souvenirs, knives, uniform items, and especially firearms, but unwritten custom implied that no one at higher headquarters was looking for anything more than an accounting of how much cash was found. Where it ended up was not a question anyone contemplated. Every outfit in every military in every country on Earth maintained a unit party fund, but in the normal sense, the enemy rarely provided donations. This became a welcome windfall investment to add to the kitty.

On the trip back to LZ Regulator, everyone was calling Switch a hero. And like the best heroes, he didn't accept the adulation. *"Nada mas que mi cargo, Sargento. Mi cargo, nada mas."*

Sergeant Johnson smiled, laughed, patted Torrens on the back, and said, "You gotta start speaking English, Switch. English. No one has any idea what the fuck you and Beans are talking about."

In thick, Spanish-accented English, Switch said, "My job, Sergeant. *Nada mas que* my job."

22 July 1967

Landing Zone Regulator, near Thuong Duc, Quảng Nam Province, South Vietnam

Back at the LZ, Lieutenant Bross stood by the entrance gate with an outstretched hand for every member of the platoon as they lumbered through. He thought back to his conversation with Torrens before the firefight and slapped him on the back as he stepped through. "Great job, Torrens, I'm going to put you in for something."

As he was walking away, with Kook in tow, he heard one of the other guys comment, "Fuck that's gonna happen. We never get put in for shit."

That comment made the lieutenant pause for a moment.

"Kook, how are you as a writer?"

"Not sure where you're heading with this, LT."

"Nothing super important, PhD and all, I just need you to take notes on incidents. Who did what and when, stuff like that. We'll give them to Battalion so they marry our details up with the S2/S3 daily logs and write our guys up for decorations. Elbert told me the only award you can't fake is a Purple Heart, the rest require a good write-up. I want to make sure our guys get recognized."

"I hear you, sir. Your predecessor, Lieutenant Jacobs, was a great guy, but if anyone got put in for anything while he had lead, I am not aware of it."

"That's it. Just what I'm talking about. Do you think you have time?"

"You're kidding me, right, sir? I have time to do whatever you order me to do."

"I don't want to order you. Call yourself platoon adjutant if you want. Just keep track of the things going on that are awardable. I also need to make sure we follow up with the right paperwork for the CIBs."

"Sir, did you notice Sergeant Rook has a star on his, his CIB?"

"Yeah, just like that battalion commander we had when I got here, you get a star when you earn a CIB in two wars. Rook must have been eleven bravo in Korea."

"Thought so. I wasn't sure if you get a second CIB on your second tour in Nam."

"Two wars. Check out that command sergeant major at Chu Lai. He has two stars. Served in World War Two, Korea, and now Vietnam."

"Due respect, sir," said Kook, "but I don't see how a guy at that level could get a second star after a month of close contact with enemy here in Nam."

"I'll bet you money he got in country and attached to a platoon like ours long enough to teach soldiers and to earn the CIB at the same time."

"Must be something like that, sir."

"So, back to awards and decs."

"Got it, sir. Thanks for taking care of the guys, sir, it means a lot. You're the only platoon king anyone has ever seen that doesn't treat the FNGs like they're from another planet. Seems like Switch got here in country last week. He's still shaking like a leaf, but when the shit gets deep he's a swimmer. I think we might have enough to put him in for a Silver Star just for the crap he pulled yesterday."

"Switch?"

"You were talking to him earlier: PFC Torrens… killed five VC… Everyone calls him Switch."

"Ah, Torrens. Does he speak any English? He was nodding, but I don't think he picked up a single word I said. Maybe I should stick to Spanish with him."

"No, sir, he speaks English. He's Puerto Rico, I think. Gutsy dude, I'll say that. I'm not sure of the statistics, but I think I read somewhere that guys from Latin American descent have won a disproportionate number of Medals of Honor."

"Only a corporal with a doctorate in history would know useless information like that. But it wouldn't surprise me. In Mexico they say *huevos* for balls. In Puerto Rico, I think it's *cojones*."

"Speaking of useless information, boss."

They both laughed and continued the walk back to Company headquarters.

24 July 1967

Landing Zone Regulator, near Thuong Duc, Quảng Nam Province, South Vietnam

"See any dinks, Message?" Bat Masterson asked.

"Nah, just playing around," Craig Message replied.

"Just playing around? Those are the weirdest-looking binoculars I've ever seen. Can I take a look?"

Sergeant Message shrugged and handed the pair of tiny silver and black binoculars to Masterson.

"They look like opera glasses or something," Masterson said as he took a look through them into the distance outside the LZ.

"Nope, they're real binoculars. I should have spray-painted them green or black before I brought 'em out here."

"Quit cleaning 'em. They'll be covered in mud soon enough. No sweat." Masterson kept looking around, scanning the horizon. "Man, these are tiny, but really amazing! Nice plan. Gonna help us find dinks."

"That's not exactly why I got them."

"Fuckin' A, what else?"

"Everyone's gonna figure it out soon enough, so I might as well let it out."

"Let what out?"

"I got these things for bird watching."

"Get outta fuckin' town!" Masterson blurted out.

"I'm not kidding."

"Bird watching? Give me a break, Message. You think you have time for fucking hobbies? Are you sending bird love notes back to Grandma?"

Message blushed a little. He knew he was going to take major grief from the guys, but it was worth it.

"No shit, I'm not kidding. I've been studying birds most of my life, as far back as I can remember. And you aren't half wrong;

my grandmother is the one who got me into it."

Masterson took the binoculars away from his eyes and took a look, reading out loud: "Asahi Pentax, prism binoculars, coated lenses, six by twenty-five, wide field."

"I got 'em in Bangkok on R&R."

"What the fuck for?"

"Birding, asshole!" Message was getting a little frustrated.

"I just feel like you're bullshitting me. What's the real story?"

"You're right, it's an unusual hobby. But I got hooked when I was just a kid. My grandparents live in Mascoutah, just down the road."

"Where're you from again?"

"Belleville, Illinois. My dad and mom retired there. My dad was air force."

"Air force, no shit?"

"Full bird."

"Fuck you!"

"I shit you not. Bird colonel."

"No wonder you're hooked on fuckin' birds—you're a pussy!" Masterson laughed out loud.

Message looked at him with an instinct to laugh it off, but instead he blurted out what was destined to become the platoon motto. "Bat, why don't you put a double lip lock on the snotty end of my fuck stick?"

Craig was stunned, but not because he was upset. Not because it hit home, but because up until that time, it ranked as the funniest thing he'd ever heard. "A double lip lock on the snotty end of my fuck stick?" He laughed again. Out loud. It struck him as so hilarious that he was unable to repeat the phrase to anyone without bursting out laughing. Tension of war. But soon enough, the entire platoon caught on. You could get a smile just by saying "snotty end." If you pointed at your crotch, index fingers, both hands, and said "fuck stick," you'd get a big laugh. "Double lip lock" resulted in everyone present completing the whole line, including "Bat." "Bat, why don't you put a double lip lock on the snotty end of my fuck stick?"

Masterson stopped laughing after a bit, and Message continued, "Okay, I'll take it—pussy it is—but I'm telling you, it's a lot of fun. My dad and I would go birding all over the place. Nature preserves, Mississippi River. There's some Indian mounds in East Saint Louis. One of the only places in the US to see Eurasian tree sparrow."

"There's about a million Asian sparrows right here at the LZ."

"You're close—more like a couple hundred. Looks a little bit like our house sparrow, but actually they're called plain-backed sparrows. We don't have those in The World."

Masterson handed Message the binoculars. "You *are* serious." Half statement, half question.

"In my first seven months I saw a zillion birds all over the place. I took a lot of notes and drew some sketches, but so many of them were new, I didn't have any idea what I was seeing."

"What do you mean 'new'?" Bat asked.

"New to me." Message put the binoculars to his eyes, trying

to locate something he'd seen before Masterson showed up. "Look over there on the ground next to the red pole by that pile of rat's nest of concertina wire." He handed the binoculars back to Bat who held them up to his eyes. "Find something you recognize, like that red pole. Now follow that down to the ground." Masterson took the binoculars away from his face and adjusted them a little. Message continued, "See that bird rooting around?"

"You mean that crow with brown wings."

"Exactly! Brown wings, red eyes. That's a greater coucal. Like the sparrows around here, you've never seen that bird in the States either."

"Those things are everywhere." Masterson lowered the binoculars. "They have that weird call like they're dying."

"The locals think it's their ancestors talking to them."

"No shit?"

"That's what one of the village elders told me. He was showing me the only photo he has, heard the call, and pointed to some old man in the photo. I think he was telling me it was him. He even mimicked the call and pointed again."

"Are you counting them too?"

"And markin' 'em on a map. And sketching each one in my memo book."

"What the fuck for?"

"In Bangkok, I was staying at the Windsor. I ran into an American ornithologist. Guy named Ben King. He went crazy over the fact there was a GI in Nam who was a birder. He's writing some kind of book on the birds around here. He knew a shop in town and the owner." Pointing to the binoculars in Masterson's hands, Message said, "He got me a great deal on those, and I think he might have even paid some out of his own pocket. He asked me to keep some records and send them to him. He's been all over Thailand and plans to get all over Asia, but it's a little hard to do this crap in Nam right now."

"Yeah, people trying to kill you and all."

"Exactly."

Masterson handed the binoculars back. "Well, if we need them to see dinks, you better hand 'em over." He laughed to himself. "And not while you're drawing sketches of them."

"I'll stick to birds, promise."

Lieutenant Bross sidled up to Sergeant Rook while handing his tray and silverware to the soldier on KP duty behind the window in the mess hall. "Sergeant Rook. Where have you been? I've been looking for you."

Rook looked over his right shoulder, tossed a balled-up napkin into a galvanized can, and gave a lackluster response. "Around."

"What does that mean, 'around'? There's no place to go."

"Just around, LT. Catching up on sleep. Getting my shit cleaned up."

"Step outside with me. We need to talk."

They walked around the building together back to relative

privacy, to the same shady place where they'd had the platoon meeting the week before. Lieutenant Bross motioned to a couple of sawn logs standing on end, makeshift seating. "Let's talk."

They sat facing each other.

"It's been just over a week," Bross said. "One op. No KIAs. No WIAs. How do you think it's going?"

"Okay."

"What does that mean? Okay? I need more from you than 'okay.'"

"I mean it's going pretty good." Sergeant Rook said this with a sneer in addition to his unusual slow southern drawl that sounded like an affectation, like he was putting it on—a character from some movie filmed in eastern Kentucky.

Darren felt himself getting mad. "Do you ever address officers respectfully? Perhaps you're familiar with the respectful form of address to superiors? A 'sir' here and there?"

"Sometimes."

"Sometimes? What does that mean?"

"It means I say 'sir' sometimes."

"How the hell did anyone put you in charge of anything, Rook? Sergeant Rook."

"I respected my platoon leader down south. I called him 'sir' a lot. He's the one who pulled me up from squad leader to platoon."

"So, by implication you don't respect me?"

"He was a badass." Rook kicked at a rock embedded in the ground. "You gotta earn respect, LT."

Darren was not a cursing man, but he made an exception,

while trying to keep himself from screaming. "I have to *earn* your respect? So when the fuck are *you* going to start earning *my* respect?"

With his head down, Rook rolled his eyes up. "LT, I got no answer for that one."

The lieutenant lowered his voice, but his angry tone was unmistakable. "Well I'll answer it for you. At your current rate, never. We've been back at the LZ for two days. By all appearances you've been avoiding me. A platoon sergeant has a leadership role in the unit. I do not need you to be *around, catching up on sleep,* and *cleaning your shit.* I need you to be a key player in leading this platoon in combat. Am I making myself clear?"

Sergeant Rook maintained his slouched posture and stared at a spot of ground between his jungle boots, still working the dirt with one toe.

Bross lowered his tone with restraint and repeated, "I said, am I making myself clear?"

Talking to the dirt: "LT, you're going to get us all killed."

"What the fuck do you mean by that?"

"I mean, you can't be pussyfooting around with Charlie. Those motherfuckers are trying to kill us. This ain't the time to be nice to them. They gotta be scared of you. VC has to know that if we're out there, they better run and steer clear of us."

Clearly Darren wasn't getting through to Sergeant Rook with his humane approach. "How many KIAs did we score on the last patrol?"

"Five or six, thanks to Switch."

"Do you think those guys were VC?"

"They were VC, except for that one NVA."

"Did we pussyfoot around with them?"

"Guess not, they're dead."

"Exactly. They are dead. How many people did we terrorize last week?"

"I don't get it, LT. What do you mean by 'terrorize'?"

"I mean how many people did we fill with terror? How many people now hate us forever? You seem to think brutality is some sort of leadership trait."

"You mean dinks?"

"I mean the Vietnamese!"

"I thought you were talking about people."

Hitting an NCO violated the Uniform Code of Military Justice. Lieutenant Bross came very close to doing it anyway. "Look at me, Sergeant Rook."

Rook lifted his gaze from the ground and drew his vision to Lieutenant Bross's right ear, still avoiding direct eye contact.

"Are the civilians out here people to you?"

"Not really, LT. More like dinks, slopes, zipperheads. I seen 'em kill a lot of my friends, soldiers, Meericans. I hate the motherfuckers. How we're gonna stay safe is to kill everything that moves. Battalion wants body count. We're supposed to bag dinks. We don't want 'em baggin' us. If we don't engage with those fuckin' slopes, we're gonna lose the body count tally to the other platoons."

Darren looked to his left and his right and into the branches of the tree above them and wondered for just a minute if he could ever be reduced to this level of harboring abject hate for human beings he had never met. Pure, raw, stereotypical hatred. Would he stay in Vietnam long enough to get so jaded that he felt everyone should be treated like the enemy? He couldn't imagine any scenario or any future that would cause such a transformation in his psyche. So he must be sitting with some sort of crazy man.

"Well, Sergeant Rook, I would call you a racist."

"And proud of it, LT. White people are better'n dinks. No doubt about it."

Lieutenant Bross just shook his head and pondered the hand he was dealt. "Listen to me, Sergeant Rook, and listen to me well. Here's the way it's going to be. You might view me as cherry, or greenhorn, or FNG, or any other negative term you like, but in this man's army I am the platoon leader. I make the rules, and you follow them." He rose from his seated position and stood. "Stand up."

Rook stood. Lieutenant Bross looked around to see if they were in sight of anyone. An inviolable lesson of military leadership for him was to praise in public and correct in private. What he didn't know was that a gaggle of soldiers had heard the commotion and had hidden from view while remaining in earshot. This was too good to miss.

"Stand at attention."

Rook did.

"Four days ago we were in Tây Hoà."

Rook interrupted, maybe in an innate attempt to break the lieutenant's rhythm. It didn't work. "Five days."

"What?"

"It was five days ago."

"Four day, five days, I do not give a damn. Five days ago we were at Tây Hoà with a mission to clear and search the village. Clear and search is not, I repeat *not*, search and destroy. Do you know the difference?"

"I guess."

"Jesus Christ. What is the matter with you?"

"LT. We are at fucking war. One day you're going to wake up and notice that it's not all roses."

Darren paused, paced around a little, admonished himself for blowing up, and pondered how he could get rid of this idiot. *Should I tell Evans? Should I pop him with an Article 15 for insubordination? He's walking a fine line. On the other hand, maybe I am a terrible leader. Maybe Rook is right. Maybe I am to blame. Maybe this is the kind of leadership challenge that's been waiting out here for me since I marched plebes as a cow during Beast Barracks. I can fix this guy. He just needs some army leadership. I can fix this guy.*

Darren Bross was so wrong. A line of others had already been passing along the Lionel Bodean Rook problem for over thirty years. Perhaps someday it would catch up to him. Perhaps not. But for now he remained an exercise in extreme frustration.

"What happened in Tây Hoà is never going to happen again. Do I make myself clear?"

"Yes, sir, I got it."

And thanks to Rook's first effort at replying to Lieutenant Bross with a respectful form of address, with the simple use of the word "sir," Darren felt like he had won this round. He hadn't; it was just an example of Rook's psychological manipulation.

"Soldier, you are dismissed."

And with that, a dozen hidden eavesdroppers skedaddled. Lieutenant Bross stood alone, a little bewildered.

26 July 1967
Lampshade Valley, near Thuong Duc, Quảng Nam Province, South Vietnam

It was just about dusk. The platoon seemed to be dug in at today's NDP as well as could be expected. The rain that had been falling lightly all day took a break, but they guessed it would start up again in the wee hours of the morning. Darren had just finished his first letter to the parents of one of his soldiers, PFC Cesar Torrens. He hoped they would be able to read English. He decided not to relate the details of Switch's heroism and the fact that he'd saved some lives the prior week outside Nhon Ky. Rather, he kept it short, saying that he was proud to serve with their son and he would do all in his power to send him back home safely—a promise that, in eleven months, would be kept. Switch would survive.

He wrote another letter to Christy and a short letter to his parents. He needed this ritual to maintain his sanity and to remind him why he was doing what he was doing. While he wrote, he imagined they might be able to hear him, might sense his thoughts of them from this faraway land.

For the past few nights the moon had been near full. If the rain broke and the clouds cleared, it might have a chance to peek through tonight. A mixed blessing: the moon served Second Platoon in the bush, but it also served the VC and the NVA, who were more comfortable operating at night anyway. Darren looked up as he had at West Point, imagining that Christy would see the same moon and that it would somehow establish a connection between them. He knew that by any definition his thoughts weren't rational, but if Christy was waking up as Darren was watching night fall and the moon rise…

Corporal Carver broke Darren's reverie. It was a good thing. There was not much good to come from dreaming. "Sir, do you have a minute?"

"Corporal Carver, please join me." Lieutenant Bross reached out a hand to shake. "Please, sit down. What's on your mind?"

"Thank you, sir. Somethin' weighing heavy…"

"Hang on a second." Lieutenant Bross pulled an Episcopal prayer book from his flak jacket. "Can you tell me your home address again? I think I got it mixed up with Byers."

"We all look alike, sir." Peanut laughed out loud.

"Now I want to go on record. You have never heard me say anything like that."

"No, sir, in fact the colored boys want to thank you for treating us just like anyone else."

"Why wouldn't I?"

"Sir, it won't surprise you to know that not everyone thinks like you."

"No, I do know. But I want you to know I wasn't raised like that. My dad is Alex and my mom is Margaret. They would be proud to know you. Both of them have been involved in the civil rights movement in my hometown for the past couple of years."

"No shit, sir? White folk?"

"No joke. Since President Johnson signed civil rights into law and people started protesting and all."

"You know Marty Byers is from Montgomery?"

Darren looked in his prayer book on the inside back flap. "That's what I screwed up. I have you from Montgomery and Byers from Valdosta."

"Bass ackwards, sir."

Darren crossed out the errors with his ballpoint and made a correction. "I'm not going to lose this book." He held up his Episcopal prayer book and shook it a couple of times for emphasis. "My plan is to write your family from time to time."

"Or when we eat it, sir."

"That too."

"Anyway, sir, Byers knows Mrs. Rosa Parks."

"No way."

"Yes, sir, they went to the same church. And Marty used to see her in some store down in Montgomery."

"I'll have to say something."

"He would probably wish you didn't, sir."

"Understand."

"Anyway, the reason I wanted to talk to you is 'cause of Sergeant Rook. I ain't here to get no one in trouble, but that man hates coloreds."

Lieutenant Bross feigned surprise like this was new

information. "How so?"

"Sir, you probably don't notice it, but he treats us different —me, Byers, Willy Hartsdale, and even Scotty."

"Staff Sergeant Johnson, that Scotty?"

"Yes, sir. Scotty's got stories about some colored school in Gulfport, Mississippi. Those crackers are still fighting the Civil War."

Lieutenant Bross smiled, but he didn't doubt it. "Define 'different.'"

"Now, sir, you're going to think we're making this stuff up, or imagining it, but please keep an eye out. We get all the shit jobs. And I do mean shit. One example for you: back on the LZ the three of us get the honor of emptying out the shitter drums—those ones filled with diesel and poop."

"But that's some kind of rotation, right?"

"No, sir, every time. Even when they don't need emptying, like some other platoon already took care of it. He uses the 'nigger' word all the time. Maybe you hear us saying it, but that word offends us. A lot. Tells us if we ran into him back in Florida, we might be strung up from a big tree."

"Seriously?"

"Sir, those were his words, not mine. Friend of mine over in the weapons platoon from Macon told me Sergeant Rook pals around with one of their lifer NCOs. Says he's seen KKK stuff in the platoon sergeant's hooch. Crap, sir, he carries a Confederate flag in his ruck."

"I wasn't aware the flag was a problem."

"Might as well be a swastika, LT. When the Germans lost their war, the swastika was outlawed. Freedom of speech and all, wish our government had outlawed the flag from our losing side in the Civil War."

Darren had lived in The World like everyone else. He knew racial strife was rampant. And now he had no doubt in his mind that Sergeant Rook was a card-carrying member of the Ku Klux Klan. It fit straight in line with everything else he knew about the character of his platoon sergeant.

"Is Carper working out?"

"Sir, Sergeant Witz is a great man. And I am not kidding. And Willy Hartsdale loves his squad leader, Sergeant Elf. Switch, I mean Torrens, is from somewhere in Puerto Rico. He's a white guy married to a black woman. He showed me the pictures. Could have knocked me over. Says it's no big deal in Puerto Rico."

Darren smiled and wondered if a day would come when it was no big deal in the US.

"Peanut, you are named after a great man."

Carver didn't realize the lieutenant knew his nickname. "Thanks, sir, been dragging George Washington Carver around my whole life."

"Hey, five hundred uses for peanuts. Could be worse. I heard about a guy in Tennessee who named his kid Adolf Hitler. Can you imagine that?

Carver shook his head in disbelief. "Racist, peckerwood cracker, sir." He mused for a second or two, then added, laughing, "That wasn't Sergeant Rook, was it?"

The lieutenant smiled and let out a chuckle as well. "No, he's Florida, but if he has kids, the names might be interesting. Corporal, I will keep an eye on Rook. This I promise you: when we get back to LZ, you will not be emptying the johns."

"Thanks, sir. And while you're at it, you might take note of the number of times we get named to walk point. Squad leaders is s'posed to assign that, but Sergeant Rook seems to step in and volunteer one of us blacks, the Spanish too."

The lieutenant made a face that looked like he'd just bitten into a lemon slice.

Carver saw the tacit acknowledgement and said, "Sometimes when we bring it up to the brass it gets worse."

"It won't get worse this time. Trust me on this." They shook hands again, and Peanut started to stand, but Darren held on to his hand.

"Hang on a second, Corporal. Tell me about your brothers, sisters, girlfriends. Stay a while."

Lieutenant Bross wanted to get to know his guys. He was genuine, and they knew it. He and Corporal Carver talked for half an hour. Darkness fell, the moon continued crossing over the night sky, and all was good in the world. The Nam world. For now.

Kook approached. "I was trying to track you down, boss."

"What's up, Kook?"

"Couldn't help overhearing some of your conversation with

Peanut."

"He's something, that's for sure."

"And how, sir. You know there's a lot of rumors out there about him." That he was now talking about Sergeant Rook was implied.

"What have you heard?"

"He's a killer."

"Well we're all killers. Carver thinks he's in the KKK."

"There's no doubt about that. He's probably a grand dragon poohbah back in Florida. What I mean is the guy is a sadist."

"How so?"

"No proof, boss, but one of the rumors going around comes from his last tour. They say Rook took a baby, put him face down in a puddle, and stepped on the back of his head while calmly talking to some villagers. They went fucking crazy, but he just stood there like a statue and kept asking them to speak English while they were all wailing at the top of their lungs. Rook just smiled and laughed."

"What happened to the kid?"

"That's the end of the story, especially for the baby. Dead."

"Fuck."

"Fuck is right, sir."

"Is Rook really singling the colored guys out for mouse duty?"

"I never really thought about it, but I guess my opinion would be different if I were black. Point is a two-edged sword. You need a good guy up front to protect the platoon. Most NCOs would say *you're all city boys*, they want the country boys up front, the ones who have spent time in the woods, hunting and stuff like that."

"Are the colored guys country boys?"

"I don't really know, boss. I can ask."

"Don't bother. I'm going to get involved and change the selection criteria."

28 July 1967

Lampshade Valley, near Thuong Duc, Quảng Nam Province, South Vietnam

They could hear the bullets that missed. That was a good thing. But too often, they were too close. Human ears, bilateral and therefore in stereo, are an amazing thing. Likely evolved to help a human duck in the face of a hurled stone, human hearing was nevertheless also capable of judging with accuracy the distance from a steel-jacketed, AK-47, 7.62mm bullet traveling twice the speed of sound. Some of the residual generated noise was from the explosion in the cartridge, but to the target, it was a bullet breaking the sound barrier. At two shots per second, Doppler shift registered instantly, enabling the human head to turn toward the source even in a hail of cracking bullets. No one had to be commanded. The pucker factor was high when the sound of shots finding their marks was imminent. Someone managed to toss a grenade into the mix, but it fell short. Way short.

Over it all, they heard Sergeant Rook, in a rare moment of

combat leadership, booming. "Lay down a field!" Everyone knew which direction. Everyone. Then fear became revenge, then fear again. GIs, always anxious to lighten their load, emptied their clips and filled the jungle with hundreds of rounds. Whether they hit anything was secondary. *Let Charlie learn a little about sound waves and Doppler shift.* Then silence, dead silence. Then a shot-up banana tree falling. Then a moan. Then screams as the unfortunate on both sides realized they'd been hit.

"Kook, do you have our position locked in?"

Kook stayed low and crab-walked to the lieutenant. "Yes, sir, got it."

"How about theirs? Got theirs?

"Yes, sir, about three hundred meters due northwest. Plotted, sir."

"Double-check and call it in. I'm not sure if we're in range of an FB. On July fourth I saw some mortar unit to our west. If they're fixed, they might have eighty-ones."

"Could be, sir."

"I want them to walk fires toward us from a hundred meters behind Charlie until we call cease."

Kook already had Company on the radio and was relaying the message as the boss spoke, but meanwhile, from Weapons Squad, Gary Cole was calling in on the Prick 6 trying to talk over top of his transmission.

"Bravo six-two, six-two-four, I'm hit, I'm hit. Over."

"Standby one, six-two-four, I'm on with bravo six."

Sergeant Elphick grabbed the mic. "Copy six-two. Six-two-four is standing by, but we need the medic ASAP."

Kook heard it and changed his priority. "Bravo six-two, stand by. We need supporting fires at…" He passed coordinates. "Breaking over to six-two-four. One WIA. More to follow."

"Copy six-two. Bravo six is on. How far are you from six-two?"

"Passing to six-two now, over."

"What's going on, Bross?"

"We were taking a break when all hell broke loose." There were a few potshots in the background, all on semi. Lieutenant Bross couldn't tell if it was return fire or if they were taking fire. "No details yet, but we have at least one WIA. Sounds like Cole. We're going to need—"

His transmission was cut off by earth-shaking explosions to the northwest. These weren't mortars. *Must be howitzers,* he thought.

"Stand by, six," Bross screamed into the mic. "I can't hear a thing!"

"Say again, over."

"Send Dust Off! Stand by. Awaiting fires to cease."

"Six standing by."

Overhead they all heard the telltale noise of a light aircraft, O-1 Bird Dog. An Air Force Forward Air Controller, FAC.

"This is Sandy eight-niner on guard. Who's down there? Need help?"

Guard was the universal frequency. All radios were keyed in to guard in case of emergency. An emergency like this. Kook took the mic from the lieutenant and flipped a switch on the R-T to activate the external speaker, making it a "bitch box." He had dealt with these guys a thousand times. "Eight-niner, this is bravo six-two on guard, request you move to the freq of the day."

"Roger that." He called back. "Bravo six… six-uh, this is Sandy eight-niner. How copy, over."

"Six-two has you Lima Charlie, Sandy."

"You guys need help? I got a fast mover with half a load on the way back home. He has to drop 'em somewhere."

Kook held the mic and looked at the lieutenant who shrugged and said, "Can't hurt. Can't hurt us." Then he marveled at this giant and how he worked the radio and the life-and-death coordination under the most extreme pressure.

"Eight-niner, six-two. We'll kindly accept the help. See two lines of fire, southeast and northwest. See a clearing between. We are southeast, I repeat, southeast of the clearing in the bush. Charlie is northwest, I repeat, northwest, over."

"Roger, copy six-two. Tally-ho. I will mark 'em in a jiffy. If I screw it up and you get some rocket fire on your position, let me know soonest."

"Roger that, eight-niner, wilco."

They all thought it was amazing that some air force lieutenant or captain up there in a tiny Cessna was in a steep bank and launching smoke rockets. They could see it across the clearing. Rifle shots sounded again. Charlie was trying to shoot him down. The O-1 was well within range of an AK-47, but seemed not to care.

A few minutes passed. Distant potshots and the sounds of

wounded humans continued. With zero warning and nothing like *I hear an airplane headed this way,* an F-4 Phantom made a low pass over the action over the enemy and then, in a split second, over their position. It was loud as hell, but a sound they all relished. More than half the group thought he might have dropped his bombs in that pass. A slight miscalculation and they'd be on the receiving end.

"Sandy eight-niner, bravo six-two. Request a northeast to southwest pass from your mover."

"Copy that, six-two. Gonna check. See if he has enough gas."

Those with a view could see the Phantom climb in a maneuver that appeared to be straight up. "Speed of heat," Sergeant Grayson commented to Lieutenant Bross. The pilot pulled and turned so they could see the bottom of the jet, a centerline tank and two large bombs. The talk later was that they were "thousand-pounders," more for taking out factories than enemy combatants. The plane seemed to float at the top of its arc. Now moving toward the northeast, the exact opposite of what they asked for, but still safe, the pilot pointed his nose at the platoon. No one saw the bombs pickle off two, maybe three seconds later, but they felt the roar of the jet noise again. He must have pulled five Gs yanking back on the stick, out just above the treetops. And just as he passed over, dangerously close, the bombs landed on target, on the smoke. The shockwave on Second Platoon knocked some of the soldiers over. There was no more shooting from the other side of the clearing.

Ten seconds of silence was interrupted by spontaneous

cheering from thirty-three soldiers of Second Platoon, Bravo Company. Even Cole was screaming, but now happy cheers.

Without direction, or orders, Masterson took Second Squad across the clearing to ensure the area was safe. They found eleven North Vietnamese regulars and what appeared to be two VC. Of the thirteen, twelve were KIA on the spot, surrounded by US soldiers yelling at them all. Beyond hearing, beyond caring, the bodies were in full receipt of an angry enemy.

"Motherfucking dinks!"

"Death from above. Shit falling from the fucking sky, you fucking assholes!"

"How'd ya like them fucking apples? Five hundred-pound apples? Fucking dinks!"

Catharsis, the lieutenant thought. *Stress relief.* Shooting additional rounds into the dead bodies was verboten, as was kicking them or pissing on them. But yelling? *Sticks and stones, and all that*, he mused. *Who's that going to hurt?*

If an enemy combatant had escaped, it was not apparent. One NVA was vertical, but he was weaponless and walking in a daze, and had blood streaming in rivulets from his ears. The white sclera of his eyes had turned blood red from overpressure. Masterson declared the area clear. Sergeant Message called it in on the Prick 6.

Turns out Corporal Cole, from Chico, California, took a through-and-through in his left shoulder. MacNulty was able to patch him up pretty well before Dust Off landed. Cole was lucid, and proud. The only thing worse than getting hit in Nam and living to talk about it was getting hit in Nam and dying. Two weeks after he landed at the field hospital on Chu Lai, he would be back at the LZ. The brigade commander would fly in to pin a Purple Heart on his fatigues, a new pair starched for the occasion.

Captain Evans called in an armored Huey to take the dazed NVA prisoner back to Battalion. Intel types there would "marry him up" with South Vietnamese interrogators. They could be brutal, but they were much easier on the regular army than they were on the VC, whom they considered traitors.

Early August 1967
Lampshade Valley, near Thuong Duc, Quảng Nam Province, South Vietnam

By the second-to-last day of the platoon's third operation as a solidified unit, Lieutenant Bross was getting the hang of it. Though he'd been in charge only two weeks, he felt as though the constant level of excitement and anxiety, combined with a heightened state of awareness, had contributed to rapid learning. He began to wonder whether he'd be able to stick with it for the coming months and found himself daydreaming already about a cushy job back at Company, Battalion, or Brigade. The squad leaders had grown comfortable with the new boss and had returned to a relaxed sense of autonomy. The group had been together long enough that they were able to sense each other's needs before being asked. And they all felt better because the lieutenant was no longer on pins and needles. He was beginning to act like the boss even when the orders were mundane but necessary. He'd walk the line, reminding everyone to maintain separation, and at every stop he'd ask if everyone had taken their weekly horse-sized orange malaria pill, a troop favorite—or not. If there was one silver lining to that pill, it's that it gave you the shits. That didn't sound good at first blush— until you'd experienced the thrill of C-rations binding you up.

The third operation was supposed to have been a carbon copy of one and two. But Darren learned that the only constant is change. A clear and search of another small village later in the week had turned nothing up. But Darren had one strange encounter with a boy about ten years old. The kid called him by name in English. The words were thickly accented, but "Bross" was unmistakable. At first he thought it might be a mistake, but then the boy asked about "Rook."

Bross thought this was important enough information to pass along to the intelligence pros at Brigade S2. They proved to be less interested in the fact a young boy had their names, and much more interested in newly discovered proof that one village was talking to another.

"That can't be a big surprise," Bross said. "But I've never seen that kid in my life. How did he know my name?"

The reply hit him flatfooted. "The Vietnamese written language has letters too, Bross. They can read. You might notice there are English words all over the place. Take a look at your soda next time you have a Coke, or the writing on your C-rations, or... your name tape."

Bross couldn't believe an explanation so simple—his own name tape—had not even occurred to him. He signed off on the radio and scratched it with his fingernail. Then he keyed the mic again and said, "One last question. How do they happen to ask for Rook and me?"

"You're wearing your rank." A pregnant pause. "Are you okay, six-two?"

Bross felt like the butt of the joke about the idiot who was taking nails out of a bucket and throwing half of them away because the heads were on the wrong ends.

Three weeks passed in north central South Vietnam without a KIA. Bross was becoming more adept at leading a platoon, though he was still cognizant of the fact that death lay around every corner, every bush, every tuft of elephant grass. And he got to know the other platoon leaders well enough. One question they always pumped him on was his *luck* with not getting his soldiers killed. He did count it as luck, but he also knew the detailed planning he'd picked up early was helping to keep them all alive. He recalled the luck he'd had on August second, when Corporal Russ Russelvage stepped on a "Bouncing Betty" and not only lived to tell about it, but would be back from the hospital in Chu Lai soon to do exactly that.

The Bouncing Betty is found in countless forms. The one Russelvage stepped on was a crude contraption, probably handmade and placed by VC. Eighteen soldiers walked past it—they counted later—before Russ placed his foot in just the right spot. Or just the wrong spot. He felt a "click," and as he lifted his foot a Chi-Com grenade popped into view in front of his face. He was holding his M-16 in his left hand, and as casually as anyone might swat an annoying insect, he backhanded the explosive with his right hand a fraction of a second before it exploded. His quick, mindless reaction saved his life, and maybe that of a platoon mate or two. By the time the grenade exploded it was sailing like a handball out of his right peripheral vision. A piece of shrapnel took the tip of his right little finger off. Another ended up in his armpit. A third tore through his right sleeve, leaving a scar on his right forearm.

"Could have been a lot worse," Darren commented out loud later.

"No shit, sir," Kook said with a smirk.

Village searches became uneventful. Every local seemed to know the platoon before they arrived. Kook was first to figure it out, and he was at fault. His size was the talk of the region, and might have explained why Charlie had evacuated every ville before the platoon arrived. Twice in the same village, but a week apart, Kook was paraded around by the elders and kids alike. Everyone wanted to stand next to him, the tallest human they had ever seen. Platoon mates took photos with their Instamatics.

On Friday the fourth of August, one day back at the LZ,

Doc MacNulty had to be restrained to prevent him from killing Sergeant Rook. The platoon was falling in on the platoon sergeant for a unit muster and SITREP. While milling around, Doc was tossing the Frisbee to Nutsy, who wanted to please and was still reveling in the return of his master. Everyone was just about formed up. Sergeant Rook was standing out front of a loosely arranged unit. Nutsy knew Frisbee time was over as soon as his master sauntered over to join the others. The mutt always had to take a piss after exercise, so with the Frisbee still in his mouth, he trotted over toward the platoon and lifted his leg on Rook's right jungle boot. The result was tragic, but it didn't stop the group of deranged soldiers from joking later: "Nutsy knew exactly who deserved to be pissed on—his final act of vengeance."

Rook carried a Walther PPK sidearm. He had fallen in love with the pistol and its mystique when he'd seen Sean Connery as James Bond in *Dr. No* at the Clark Field Base Theater in late 1964. He wasted no time locating and purchasing his own, fashioning himself a British MI-6 agent. Unfortunately for Nutsy, Rook had it on his right hip when the piss started flowing, making a hollow sound on the toe of Rook's boot. In a practiced motion, Rook pulled his weapon from its leather holster and right there emptied his clip into the poor little guy's head and body. A mass of fur and blood and dirt was all that remained. There was even a clip the diameter of a bullet taken out of the outer sole of Rook's boot; he had come that close to shooting himself in the foot.

Doc was apoplectic. He grabbed his M-16, which was now loaded, whereas the PPK was empty. He knelt down crying next to his dog, a bleeding mess of death. Then he stood, holding the flaccid remains of Nutsy under his left arm, and began screaming at Sergeant Rook, "You motherfucker! You murdered my dog! You fucking asshole! I'm going to shoot you where you stand, you steaming hunk of shit!" Sean took two steps back, held his M-16 in the crook of his right arm, and leveled it at Rook. Rook raised his pistol, but with its slide locked back, everyone, including Doc, knew it was empty. They all later thought it was amazing that Doc didn't pull his trigger.

When Bat Masterson pulled the barrel of the rifle from Doc's grasp, he noticed the selector switch was on "full auto." If he *had* pulled the trigger, the scene would not have been pretty—but a lot of the guys sided with Doc and wished he'd taken the asshole out right then and there.

Doc never forgave Rook. Never spoke to him again unless forced to. He joined others in an informal daily prayer that someone would kill the bastard. And that day, he began a plan to take Rook off the planet. Had he not been gravely wounded a month later, he might well have carried the plot out.

Craig Message continued his birding, and he developed the annoying habit of telling everyone who would listen his daily count of species. "Just bagged number five oh two, a Burmese bushlark. He flew into the trash pit, looks a lot like an Indochinese bushlark. Probably rare for this area."

The reaction was pretty common. "Message, do I look like someone who gives a shit? If I had a dime I'd give it to you so you could call someone who cares."

"If I had a pay phone, I would. Dipshit."

During Thanksgiving week 1977, Craig Message would be named Deputy Chief of the Migratory Birds Division in one of the regions of the US Fish and Wildlife Service. He would thumb through his little green Vietnam memo book from time to time just to recall what it was like to catalog birds in the midst of hellfire.

Pixie was an odd case. When the last mail run arrived, he looked like a kid on Christmas morning. His brother sent him a Yahtzee set, a blue and yellow cardboard box with five dice, a cup to shake, some tiny pencils, and four pads of score sheets—a distraction to carry around in the ruck during combat. Pixie ditched the box and the cup and spent every spare minute playing Yahtzee with the guys. *Call it poker with dice,* he said.

He had a good group of followers going right up until the end. They continued without him long after.

One final night in the bush before the platoon got their new marching orders, Bross was practicing the age-old, time-tested methodology of "leading by walking around." He was filling in the gaps of his quest to establish a personal connection with everyone.

At the moment, they were all the unhappy recipients of a driving rainstorm that seemed to come in waves. Everyone was drenched. A lightning strike, too close for comfort, cooked off a claymore that was set for defense. The explosion scared them all, but with its proximity in space and time to the lightning, they all knew the score.

Bross came across Staff Sergeant Whitsun, who was sitting next to Beans Mejia, both on watch. He noticed Beans had a hand frag at the ready.

"Got the pin in?"

In accented but passable English, Beans replied, "Jes sir, not *estupid*."

Then, thinking back to Ranger School where a classmate had almost suffered a fatal accident, Bross added, "You're not going to throw that in the jungle at night, are you?"

"*Solamente* if need to."

"What if there's a tree right there?"

"What if? No *entiendo*, LT."

"If you throw that grenade in the dark and hit a tree, it could bounce back into your lap. Ever played golf?"

"Golf, LT?" Beans missed the analogy.

"Put it away," Bross said. He turned to Sergeant Carper. "Get one of the Latinos to explain to Beans why you can't throw hand frags at night into trees."

"Wilco, sir."

"How'd you end up with the nickname 'Witz'?"

"Sir, you probably know my real name is Whitsun."

"Yeah, pretty unusual."

"You got that right, sir. When you have kids, be careful what you name them. It sticks. My parents are kind of religious. I was raised Episcopal."

"So was I, Witz."

"Turns out I was born on a Sunday—the seventh Sunday after Easter. There probably aren't ten people on Earth who know that day has a name. It's called Whitsunday."

"Where the heck did they get that?"

"I don't know if you've ever seen that little Episcopal black book *Common Prayer*, but it's somewhere in that—according to my parents." Witz paused and reflected for a moment. "Something about the day the Holy Ghost appeared before the disciples and told them to get their act together."

Bross smiled, unconsciously picked up his right hand, and touched the left breast pocket of his flak jacket. "And the nickname followed?"

"Yes, sir, since about the second grade. On the first day of school, seemed like every year, the teacher would do roll call and would screw my name up every time."

Lieutenant Bross rolled over on his knees in preparation for moving down the line. He patted Sergeant Carper on his back, and said, "I was an altar boy for years. If you ever want to get together for some Sunday readings, come find me."

"Thanks, sir. I'm really not too religious, though I have been thinking about it more since getting over here to hell. I was in the choir, but I never really paid any attention to anything except where Father Louis hid the communion wine."

After Bross moved on, he found a blank spot on the trail to pitch his poncho and get out of the rain. He pulled *The Book of Common Prayer* from his flak jacket pocket and unclipped his flashlight. Even in the red filtered light he could read. He was curious. There it was, right there in Psalms and Lessons for the Christian Year: *Whitsunday*.

"You learn something new every day," he mumbled to himself.

CHAPTER 15

22 June 1957—Ten Years Prior

Xa Ruh Village, Hien District, Quảng Nam Province, South Vietnam

Kiep had his eye on Thia from the first time they met at an inter-*toring* gathering of just children. For complicated reasons that selected males over females among the DeGa, girls were scarce commodities, and age-appropriate options were few. Kiep knew making his intentions known and staking a tacit claim early could help ensure long-term success. He had seen the men in his village fight over women. So over the years Kiep took every opportunity to steal a glance, or to pass by her village and longhouse on return from a hunt. The bond grew.

Thia, for her part, was smitten with Kiep, too, though he could not have guessed it. On the celebration of her eighth birthday, after lamenting Kiep's failure to appear, Thia did a bad thing by crossing the valley alone and climbing the ridge line to deliver a hemp armband she'd woven. It fit well, and between the two adolescents it sealed a future for them both.

DeGa marriage rituals are encased in a long-forgotten

history of tradition. They were practiced by Kiep's and Thia's *torings* without a hint of skepticism. And among the requirements for marriage was that a man must reach the age of fifteen years.

There was no precise recorded date of Kiep's birth. When he was born, his father had been gone for months, traveling with, as Kiep later learned, French soldiers. However, the family remembered that it had occurred close to the solstice, and thereafter it was marked and, from time to time, celebrated. So with permission from his grandfather, on the first day of Kiep's fifteenth solstice, he crossed his valley and climbed his ridge to arrive in Thia's village, Xa Ruh.

She saw him coming—had been hoping for this day. For a week she'd spent every waking hour sitting in the window gazing toward the openings in the jungle canopy along the path that came down from the ridge above. "Mother, Kiep is coming! Quickly, we don't want him to think we're expecting him. Hand me your embroidery. I must look uninterested."

Kiep climbed the steep side-by-side notched logs of the two-family home and declared his presence on a small, covered platform at the front door—the only door. "Family Pholoong, I am Kiep from Ri'Ga Village, a member of the Co-Tu Toring Briu Thi in the next valley."

There was no response, nothing.

"Family Pholoong, it is Kiep Dool. With your permission I seek an audience with Thia."

Thia's father was a giant among the DeGa. He was over twice Kiep's age and stood a full head taller. He rarely smiled and never offered a kind word. Kiep was in fear every time he found himself in the man's presence. Today was worse. Her father came to the main doorway of his home sucking on a long pipe with a small bowl while blowing smoke from the side of his mouth. He could not be considered an older man—he was roughly the same age as Kiep's own father, perhaps thirty harvests behind him—but he had adopted a characteristic that Kiep saw in the village elders. He had filed his four top front teeth almost to the gum line and had painted his bottom front teeth with a black lacquer. When he pulled the pipe from his lips with a final deep draw, he presented Kiep the visage of an angry man, affecting a smile but with his top lip covering the space where teeth were missing and showing only the black of his lower teeth.

Kiep was terrified, but he spoke nevertheless, knees shaking. "Sir, it is my hope that you know me well. I am Kiep, son of Hlong. I am Co-Tu, *toring* Briu Thi, from Ri'Ga Village, over the ridge and across the valley."

Thia's father carried on with his role in this theater. He gave the evil eye and paused for an uncomfortable length of time while Kiep stood looking to the left and right, fearful of making eye contact.

Finally, Mr. Pholoong spoke. "Kiep, welcome to our village. It is good to see you again. Please give my regards to your mother and your family. We have had the opportunity to hunt, plant, and harvest together many times. What brings you to our home?" He returned the pipe to his pursed lips and began his habitual sucking.

Over the sounds of insects and birds, Kiep was so close to

Mr. Pholoong, he could hear the tobacco burning in the bowl, a nearly imperceptible crackling. Kiep's knees knocked while his upper lip quivered. "Sir, I request an audience with your daughter Thia."

Thia's mother came to the landing and joined her husband. They interlocked arms—her right in his left. She wore the simplest of clothing: a floral cotton blouse over a long black skirt. Silky black hair extended halfway down her back and was pulled into glistening ponytail. "And why is it you need to speak with our daughter?" she asked.

Kiep squirmed. His grandfather had assured him that the entire *toring* would know why he was there. *Why are they making this difficult?* He held up a bundle wrapped in brilliant hemp cloth, yellow and red. "I bring a gift for Thia. I made it myself."

Thia's mother reached out with her left hand. "Why thank you. I will tell Thia of your generosity."

Kiep retreated a single step, pulling the package to his chest. One foot almost slipped off the landing. "Please, ma'am." Kiep lowered his voice to a whisper, guessing that Thia was just inside. "Please, Mr. and Mrs. Pholoong, you know I must give this to Thia myself. She must receive it from me alone."

Her father had done well at pretending he didn't know why Kiep had come to see Thia. In a bellowing voice that confirmed his stature, loud enough for the longhouse next door and the entire village of Xa Ruh to hear, he asked, "And why must you present this gift in person?"

Kiep looked into Mr. Pholoong's eyes. He imagined he was levitating down the short steps without moving a muscle, because

Thia's father seemed to grow taller and taller while Kiep shrank beneath him. Mr. Pholoong once again locked what appeared to be angry eyes with Kiep for a silent but brief moment. And just before he thought Kiep would faint right there, he stopped his game.

With a smile, Mr. Pholoong announced to all within earshot, "Young Kiep, welcome to our home and Xa Ruh Village." Stepping aside and reaching out for Kiep's shoulder, he added, "Our entire *toring* asks that you make yourself at home."

The blood returned to Kiep's face and appendages as he took a step inside.

Mrs. Pholoong called out: "Thia, you have a visitor."

Thia recognized the bright yellow embroidery and the embedded glass beads on the indigo scarf, the signature pattern from Kiep's *toring*. In anticipation of this day, his grandmother, mother, and sisters had been stitching it off and on for months. It was stunning. She unwrapped the bundle, held up something that glittered, and beamed.

"Kiep, where did you find this? It's beautiful. This is an amazing thing! Is this for me? Did you make this with your hands? How is it possible?" Thia admired a delicate necklace of gold interwoven skillfully with round black beads. It was accompanied by a matching bracelet.

Kiep was choking up, so much so that he had a problem getting his words out without humiliating himself. "Thia, I knew when I was eight years old we would marry. I wanted my gift to commemorate your beauty and your grace. You are the most spectacular girl in the highlands. I wanted my present to be the most spectacular in your village. I want you to be the envy of every wife, mother, and girl in the *toring*."

Thia touched her forehead to Kiep's. She could not be permitted any other demonstration of affection here in the presence of her family.

"I love this," she said, loud enough for the family to hear. Then, in a whisper for Kiep's ears alone, she added, "I love you. I have always loved you. The women in our *toring* won't envy me for this gift. Not at all, Kiep. They already envy me because they have known for many years that you are unavailable to any other."

Kiep's chest filled again with emotion. His eyes filled with tears. He wanted to reach out and hold Thia. And hug. And then cry, perhaps. He thought of something to say to break his tension and avoid breaking down. "I must tell you, Thia, that this is not gold. I wish that it were. My promise to you and to your family is that one day you will wear a necklace of gold, but today I ask that you settle for this."

Mr. Pholoong made believe he did not notice; he pretended to be busy repairing sandals on the central table in the living area while picking at his teeth with the needle. But Thia's mother was attentive. She stood from a squat, reached for the bracelet, and asked, "Settle? How could you have made this? Will I have a jeweler for a son?"

"No, but perhaps a warrior." Kiep explained, "I have been

collecting the remnants of bullets I found in the jungle. For as long as I can remember, walking with my father, I have gathered every one I've seen. For many years my father let me believe they were gold, but I know now they are another form of yellow metal, not quite so rare."

"But how can you make bullets into something so delicate, so fine, so beautiful?" Thia could not imagine she would be the owner of this.

"My mistake—they are not bullets, Thia, but the metal left behind when bullets leave the gun. When I was young, I found a way with the blacksmith's hammer and some smooth stone to work each one into a tiny medallion." Kiep beamed with pride. "Each year I was able to complete a handful, knowing this day would come. I am happy you like it."

Thia could not contain herself. Tears of joy flowed. She broke tradition and extended her arm, took a step toward Kiep, and offered a sobbing embrace. Kiep returned a pat on the back before Thia retreated with a few steps, a bow, and a sheepish smile.

Mr. and Mrs. Pholoong exchanged a look and a smile. Finding a home for a daughter was important. They knew they could not have done better.

CHAPTER *16*

13 August 1967

Landing Zone Regulator, near Thuong Duc, Quảng Nam Province, South Vietnam

Five nights outside the LZ was a record for Bross since he'd taken the platoon. Some of the guys said they'd been out two weeks in the past. When they got back to Regulator, the G4 logistics guys met them at the gate with an assortment of new jungle fatigues. All their old fatigues got tossed in fifty-five-gallon drums with burning diesel fuel "like the shit it is," said one of the guys in reception.

"Who's sewing our stuff back on?" Staff Sergeant Carper asked.

The company first sergeant was there to greet Bross. "Sir, Captain Evans wants to see you and Sergeant Rook in his quarters before you guys get chow."

"What about?"

"Can't say for sure, sir, but there's been a lot of radio chatter and the battalion commander is here. I think you guys might be getting some kind of special mission."

"Special mission?

"I don't know much about it, sir, but there's some Airborne Ranger Green Beret Special Ops stud flying in tomorrow."

Lieutenant Colonel James Long had survived his second tour in Vietnam and was lucky enough to step back on the silver freedom bird on July twentieth. Lieutenant Bross had not yet met his replacement, Lieutenant Colonel Lorne O'Neill, but today was the day. There was something up, but Darren had not a clue what it might be.

Darren reported to Company Headquarters as ordered, but alone—he couldn't find Sergeant Rook anywhere. Captain Evans met him at the flapping screen door. Colonel O'Neill heard the greeting at the entrance, stood up, and offered his hand. "Chip O'Neill. It's great to meet you, Lieutenant. I've heard nothing but good things. MACV noticed. It's easy to get noticed for being a screwup in Nam, but it's not easy to get recognized for good. Yet here you are, fewer than two months in country, and MACV, Division, and Brigade have singled you out for something special."

Lieutenant Bross stole a look at Captain Evans. He asked with his eyes and face: *Do you have any idea what the heck the boss is talking about?*

Captain Evans answered aloud, "The colonel will get there. Be patient."

The colonel continued, "Short story, Bross, they want you to head into the mountains to find out what's there."

"Sir, I think there's a bunch of troops already in the mountains."

"Not here. We got nothing over here." Colonel O'Neill pointed to the map on the planning table with a swagger stick. Lieutenant Bross had heard of swagger sticks. There were famous photos of General Patton wielding a swagger stick, but to Darren it looked like something Alec Guinness might have carried in *Bridge on the River Kwai*. It made the colonel look like someone with an elitist affectation, which didn't align well with his current position in the mud, heat, and squalor of Vietnam. *What kind of jerk carries a swagger stick?* he thought to himself.

The lieutenant almost gasped when the colonel pulled a blade out of the contraption and stuck it in the map. "We are in Quảng Nam Province. You probably knew that." The colonel moved the thin blade. It was twelve inches in length, pointed and square in profile, with a subtle flair from tip to hilt. "We are here between Thuong Duc and An Diem. On a bearing of two fifty degrees true, sixty-two klicks, forty miles, is Laos. Don't go there."

He paused for fifteen or twenty seconds pondering the map, then pointed south. "Don't go down here either. General Peers is down there in Kon Tum Province with two corps kicking ass in Operation Greeley."

Darren wasn't known for adding levity to the conversation, particularly not with a new, serious commander, but he couldn't help himself. With his best comedic timing while pointing to the map he said, "Promise, sir, I won't go there, or there."

The comment did not get a laugh, but it did get a quick reply from Captain Evans. "You're gonna get close."

"Right." The lieutenant joined in the joke.

"We're not kidding around, Bross. That's the mission. MACV has a bunch of special operations guys tripping all over themselves to conduct covert long-range patrols. Call 'em LRRPs, *lurps*. Long Range Reconnaissance Patrols." The colonel moved his pointer blade, tearing a hole in the best planning map on the LZ. "See Ta Ko right here and Rah right there? The jungle is thick as thieves. We can't see it from our recon birds, but we know NVA and VC are there. The Hồ Chí Minh Trail goes from the north to the south. You hop in, look around, avoid the enemy, report back what you see, come home. Pretty simple."

"Long walk, sir. Forty miles one way."

"Won't be that bad. An air cav unit will drop you and a couple of squads as far in as they can reasonably get you."

"Sir, got it. And while I'm talking here, I am saluting smartly, but I have to tell you: Ranger school taught me a lot about what I need to know to find and eliminate the enemy, and that's worked pretty well. And I've learned more since I've been here; in fact, I've jotted down a few lessons and already sent them back to Benning."

Darren had expected to be interrupted, so he didn't have his entire train of thought worked out. But he found that Colonel O'Neill was listening quietly

"What I'm trying to say, Colonel, is me and my guys don't know anything about avoiding the enemy at long range and collecting intelligence."

"Oh, you will," the colonel said. "There's a senior SOG

NCO, a snake eater. He's gonna fly in tomorrow to spend some time teaching what you need to know. Pick the two rifle squads you feel most comfortable with. Your weapons squad won't work. We'll add a South Vietnamese Tiger Scout as a guide. Questions?"

Lieutenant Bross was just about to speak up when the colonel spun on his heel, making it clear he wasn't interested in questions. While walking away, he said, "Nice to meet you, Bross. Brigade picked you out of the lineup because you seem to have a knack for keeping your soldiers alive. That's a key skill for a LRRP. You're gonna kick ass. I'll leave you here with Captain Evans."

Colonel O'Neill sheathed his swagger stick in its pigskin scabbard, grabbed his cover from a nearby chair, and in a single fluid motion began heading out the door. Then he stopped and came back to the table. "One more thing. You might run into some Yards out there. We don't see any Yard villes on recon, but there's a lot of clouds blocking the pictures and the jungle is a thick as a double ditch, so we might have missed 'em." The colonel paused a second —but just a second. It was hard to get a word in. Looking at Lieutenant Bross, he said, "You know about Yards?"

"Montagnards, sir. I've heard about them, but don't know much."

"Well learn, and learn fast. That SOG sergeant major is an expert. He's been working with 'em down around Dak Pek for months. VC are trying to get in their shit. Pick his brain."

"Copy that, sir."

The colonel looked around. "Did I miss anything?"

Captain Evans piped up, sensing the colonel's impatience.

"Got it, sir. We are all over this."

The next thing they heard was the screen door slapping shut behind the colonel. He must have had some important stuff to do elsewhere.

Darren lifted his hands, palms up, spread them apart, and said to the captain: "Thick as a double ditch?"

"Guy is second-generation Irish. Must be Irish slang. He's always dropping crap like that. Half the time when he leaves we look at each other and ask for confirmation amongst ourselves of what he was talking about."

Darren pondered his new life for a quiet ten seconds or so while it all sank in. Then he looked at Captain Evans and with a puzzled look, said:

"What—the—fuck?"

14 August 1967

Landing Zone Regulator, near Thuong Duc, Quảng Nam Province, South Vietnam

"Let me introduce Đinh Quảng Tý," said Master Sergeant Stargardt. "He goes by Ty. Ty was a VC officer until he found out they tortured and murdered his parents and burned his village. The marines have an entire program of using these turncoats. MACV is just getting around to figuring out how we can use guys like this to our benefit."

Sergeant Rook spoke up. "So this guy is a traitor to his own cause, after being a traitor to his own cause? What benefit is this motherfucker to us?"

The master sergeant smirked a little. "You don't have a choice. Ty is a Kit Carson, Tiger Scout, a Chiêu Hồi. He's vetted. The general says we use him. That's all the fuck I need to know."

Stargardt was an imposing figure, almost as big as Kook. At six foot six and around three hundred pounds, he looked like a Norse god. So when he fixed his steel blue eyes on someone, they usually turned away. Not Rook—he was wired different.

"How about you?" he asked Rook.

"Me?" Rook looked around at the others. "Tell the general he's not out here in the fucking bush with us. We don't need a dink tagging along."

Stargardt's jaw dropped. "Did you really just say that? Respect much?" He pulled his gaze from Rook and gave Captain Evans a *what-the-hell* look.

Lieutenant Bross held up a hand as if he were stopping traffic. "Got it. Sergeant Stargardt, what's next?"

But Sergeant Rook wouldn't stop. He either didn't get the hint or he was just too dense to understand that his opportunity for input had passed. "Does he speak English, or just fucking slope-ese?"

Stargardt started to answer, "That's going to be a prob—"

Lieutenant Bross raised his voice and ended the discussion. "What's next? Right now." He glared at Rook, and then turned back to Stargardt. "Master Sergeant, what's next?"

Rook turned to Sergeant Masterson, and, under his breath,

thinking no one else could hear, he muttered: "Wonder if he'll go back to Mr. Charles when we burn some villages?"

Masterson pretended like he wasn't listening and continued focusing on Master Sergeant Stargardt.

"I've been in the central mountains south of here," Stargardt was saying. "Hard to describe. It's kind of a no-man's land. There are people here and there, but they look more like Filipinos than Vietnamese. If you think the valley here is uncivilized, get ready for the Stone Age out west. The French called these mountainfolk Montagnard. We call 'em *Yard* for short. They don't seem to mind. There are a hundred different tribes, all with different dialects of some language that is not Vietnamese. So if you run into them, even Ty won't be able to communicate, at least not perfectly."

"Maybe Sergeant Rook has a point then," Lieutenant Bross said. "What good is Ty?"

"Sir, this guy is going to get you where you need to be. He knows the jungle, and he can smell out booby traps. He knows which trails were made by wildlife, which by wild men, and which by Charlie."

Lieutenant Bross pressed his lower lip to his upper in a facial gesture of understanding and shook his head in agreement. Sergeant Rook rolled his eyes.

Sergeant Stargardt continued. "Think the hills of West Virginia down some scary remote trail in the most backward place you can imagine. You're gonna feel like you'll come across a moonshine operation at any turn. This area"—Stargardt pointed to the map—"is completely unknown. We have some of the French intelligence reports, but they're too old. If they were ever here, it's a fading memory. You guys will be first."

Lieutenant Bross spoke up. "We learned a little about LRRPs in Ranger School. Other than me, my entire platoon only has five soldiers with Ranger tabs. Four are already in Squads One and Two. I pulled Corporal Owens from Third Squad and swapped him with a greenhorn."

"Good plan," Stargardt said. "I've been evaluating your other troops, sir. I have one more recommendation. PFC Mejia, I think the guys call him Beans. Sorry to say, but I recommend you pull him from this op."

"I was thinking the same thing myself," Darren said, "but he's a proud soldier."

"Got all that, sir, but he can barely speak English. You don't need any more challenges out there than you already have."

"Okay. I agree. Consider it done. But, I thought LRRPs were supposed to be really small, inserted covertly, and extracted the same way. Two squads, plus RTO, plus Ty is going to be over twenty men. Pretty hard to be stealthy with that many guys humping it through the jungle."

"Lieutenant, I agree with you. This is different. Consider yourselves a test program. MACV wants to see if part of a qualified platoon can be morphed into a LRRP."

"Okay." Bross thought for a moment. "Colonel O'Neill said we'd be forty miles from the LZ. We've never been farther than ten miles or so. Kook, my RTO, did some testing. Best he can get out of the Prick 25 is about twenty miles. And that's stretching it. How're we going to stay in contact?"

"You're thinking ahead, LT. Range is only part of the issue. Battery life. You're gonna need five extra batteries, at least. Good question though. Kook and your squad leaders will work with my commo guys after chow tomorrow morning. We've done this successfully before with forward-deployed repeater stations. A special ops commo team will install them before you go out. Comms with the LZ and Company will be seamless to you—well, let me qualify that a little. *Should* be seamless to you. Battalion is too far, but Captain Evans will relay. Dust Off is an issue, but manageable. Response times will be quite a bit longer if you get in the shit. Nothing we can do about that unless we forward-deploy Dust Offs. That's not gonna happen. We asked."

For the next three days, Sergeant Stargardt had everyone's attention teaching the basics of long-range recon, intelligence collection, reporting, and moving with stealth. Third Squad and Weapons Squad were hanging close by. They had heard a rumor, that during the Second Platoon's LRRP mission—however long that lasted—those staying behind would be broken up to fill temporary holes in the other three platoons. The thinking was, if they stayed close to their unit, everyone else would forget about them. That strategy worked until the day the Second LRRP departed the LZ. Then Captain Evans got his hooks into them.

Stargardt was a guy who lived up to his name—sounded like

some kind of astronaut. He was a no bullshit, all business, we-are-here-to-keep-you-alive stud—a seasoned instructor from MACV's Recondo School, the Special Forces "LRRP finishing school" in Nha Trang, Most of the platoon ended up developing a man-crush on Stargardt since he personified everything in a badass that they themselves were not, but wished they were. Even Sergeant Rook was impressed. And normally nothing impressed Sergeant Rook short of a passing glance in a mirror.

With deft skill, passable Vietnamese language skills, and the ultimate authority earned only by having "been there," Stargardt taught unit deception, stealth, and moving in the jungle as a part of the jungle that belonged. He taught personal camouflage—to a level that made the field manual's instructions look like bad Halloween makeup—chopper insertion, investigation of spider holes, quick claymore setup and takedown, alternate routing, ambush defeat, intelligence collection management, and highly accurate map symbol annotation of items of interest. For the Rangers in the platoon, much of this was review, although with added techniques applicable to the terrain and location. For the infantry grunts, it was mostly new.

The fear of death can focus the mind. There was not a single member of the platoon who was not paying utmost attention and working the practical exercises until they felt like experts in the new methodologies. Truth be told, they were all scared of what was to come, but they were also proud to have been selected for this special recognition. It was something different. Something to break the monotony. Even Third Squad and Weapons Squad got into it and shared in a pride and camaraderie that had already been solidified by war, but which was now intensified by their being deemed unique.

18 August 1967
Movement to the western edge of Lampshade Valley, West of Kadap, Quảng Nam Province, South Vietnam

Lieutenant Colonel O'Neill had made the trip from Battalion the prior evening. At breakfast he sat with Captain Evans and Lieutenant Bross.

"Basically MACV-SOG wants to know what the hell is out there," he explained. "That's why I volunteered you guys. If this works out, Brigade wants to use your model to build some more LRRPs. The whole task force is getting wire-brushed. By the time you get back from the field, four disparate brigades are going to be reorganized into a new division called *Americal*. It's gonna take over Chu Lai, but that's no concern of yours." Colonel O'Neill looked at Darren. "Try to stay out of the action. Keep in contact with your CO and let us know just about everything you see. If you capture Charlie, we'll send some choppers in for a quick extraction. You won't have to deal with him long."

Everyone was packed up, and there was a lot of nervous anticipation about what was coming. Six armored Hueys had landed in the past hour—an indication to the rest of the company that zero hour was near. The battalion commander wanted to address the group; Sergeant Rook formed them up and brought them to attention. Captain Evans and Lieutenant Bross were ready for the admonition they were going to get from the colonel for showing every sniper in range who was the boss, but he didn't do that.

"At ease, guys. At ease. In fact, everyone take a knee, sit on your steel pot, relax." The commander was new to just about all of them, but they took orders well. The new LRRP collapsed from vertical like a deflating beach toy and got comfortable while Colonel O'Neill and the officers stayed standing. Lieutenant Bross expected that Sergeant Rook might stand alongside the company first sergeant, but no such luck. He was more comfortable acting like a PFC than taking his dutiful leadership position.

Lieutenant Colonel O'Neill began. "Men, I have looked at the files on every one of you. So if paper can speak, then I know you a little. You guys were chosen for something special because you have demonstrated that you *are* special. I have too many platoons loaded with fuck-ups that I could never trust with something like what I'm sending you out to do." The colonel surveyed the group. Some of what he was saying was true. The rest was just to pump everyone up. "Yesterday in our sister brigade we lost a solid NCO to the stupidest thing I have heard yet. A sergeant first class slid off a paddy dike into the mud. He worked at it, but couldn't extricate himself from the sucking slop. A squad leader. And I am not bullshitting you, a squad leader offered him the business end of his M-16. You know, grab on to this, I'll pull you out." The colonel pantomimed the scene, holding his feet akimbo pretending to be pulling someone out of the muck. "So the stupid sergeant first class, encouraged by the stupider squad leader, grabbed the rifle. They told the company commander there was a lot of slipping and sliding until the weapon discharged on full auto."

There was some laughter, and then there were other soldiers looking at their boots, thinking about their own dumb luck and the angels that must be looking after them in their equivalent stupidity.

"You're right. It's funny as shit, but unfortunately that dumbshit went home in a bag. How do we tell his family their son survived almost two tours in Nam—that's right, two tours— only to be shot by one of his own?" It was a rhetorical question, but it gave pause.

There was an uncomfortable silence, the kind that some people feel like they need to fill by speaking up. Sergeant Maples was one of those people. "Sir, mind if I tell a quick story like that from my first tour?"

"Go ahead, soldier."

Maples nodded. "We were down south a ways. The battalion XO wanted to come and shake everyone's hands after we had taken a hill and zapped a lot of Charlie. He flew down from the fire base and landed on the side of a hill—"

The colonel smiled and interrupted. "I've heard this one. You were there?"

"Yes, sir, too close."

"Go ahead, soldier."

"Anyway, the chopper didn't have a really good flat place to land." Maples looked around at all the guys. "Listen up, this is the good part. Always exit the chopper on the downhill side. Anyways, the major hopped out of the idling chopper, all badass and everything. We were all formed up on the hilltop above. He stood there next to the chopper adjusting his TA-50, pulling at his starched jungle fatigues and all. The door gunner tried to stop him but it was too late. He got out on the uphill side, on our side, and when he took a couple of double-time steps toward us, one of the blades took the top of his head off while we were all standing there in formation at parade rest."

Everyone sat and stared at Maples. Again, uncomfortable silence. "Took his steel pot and most of his head clean off. I am not shitting you." He looked around again at grimacing faces while the members of the patrol considered the scene.

The colonel spoke up. "Guys. Another dumb motherfucker. One of those lessons learned in blood. Needless to say, we didn't select that major or the other fucking rice paddy unit for LRRP duty."

The colonel removed his steel pot and sat down on it in the dirt, avoiding a puddle. "I'm guessing you guys haven't been keeping up with the news or even on what was going on when you were still in The World, but here that doesn't matter. Why we're here just doesn't matter. Sorry. Your job is to fight for that guy sitting to your left and sitting to your right. If this mission goes right, and I think it will, it will be a break in the action. There shouldn't be much fighting." He motioned over his shoulder. "Master Sergeant Stargardt tells me you guys are ready. If he says you're ready, then you are ready, even if looking in the mirror you don't think you are. We just want you to keep an eye out and tell us what you see. It's that simple."

Another pause to collect his thoughts. "We don't have any choice whether we do this. We do this because we are Americans and our country tells us to, no questions asked. I can't tell you guys too much about it, because I don't know too much, but there are a lot of American resources up there," he pointed to the sky, "trying to look through that jungle in the mountains. We think it might be loaded with Charlie, but they can't always see through the clouds. When the clouds are gone, they can't see through the trees. When the trees are gone, they can't see through the bushes. When the bushes are gone, they've run out of excuses, but they keep making excuses anyway. That's where you guys will make the difference. You're going to get a good understanding of what *triple canopy* means. Now, I'm preaching to the choir, but you're out there to mark trails, locate villages, collect intelligence, find old French roads —anything that might help a conventional force know what they're dealing with as we take this fight to the enemy toward Laos."

Colonel O'Neill didn't take questions. When he stood, the entire patrol came to attention. Leadership saluted. The colonel stepped off. "Take care of yourselves out there, don't shoot each other, and, oh yeah, disembark helicopters on the downhill side." His chest heaved with the start of a laugh, but he caught himself and just smiled while scanning the patrol. "Carry on. We'll be in touch."

Long-Range Reconnaissance Patrol LRRP

Platoon Leader: 1LT Darren Bross -- Lufkin TX

Platoon Sergeant: SFC Lionel Bodean Rook -- Arcadia FL

RTO: CPL Clayton Kook "Kuykendahl" -- Franklin Park NJ

Medic: CPL Sean MacNulty -- Las Vegas NV

Tiger Scout: Đinh Quang Tý -- Chiêu Hồi

SSG James "Bat" Masterson -- Chillicothe OH

SSG Whitsun "Witz" Carper -- Marblehead MA

SGT Carter "Maple" Maples -- Sacramento CA

SGT Craig Message -- Belleville IL

SGT Norman "Nick" Nicolletti -- Bellevue NE

SGT Dick "Robin" Grayson -- Gainesville FL

CPL Michail "Mickey" Grosvenor -- Ft Collins CO

CPL George "Peanut" Washington Carver -- Valdosta GA

CPL Mark Owens -- St. George, UT

PFC Cesar "Switch" Torrens -- San Juan, PR

PFC Francisco "Paco" Hernandez -- Zapata TX

PFC Stanley "Stan" Peckham -- Alamogordo NM

PFC Kennan "Pixie" Pixton -- San Antonio TX

PFC Martin "Marty" Byers -- Montgomery AL

PFC Peter "The Knife" Mack -- St Petersburg FL

PFC Wellington "Loo" Chamberlain -- Arlington VA

By the time everyone got their stuff together it was almost

noon. There were three armored Hueys on the corners of the helipad. All were running idle, rotors turning. No one could hear a thing, and visibility was poor from all the dust. The patrol took a cue from Lieutenant Bross, who stepped up on the chopper closest to the group. He sat in the sling seat next to the door, facing forward. He held up six fingers and motioned for everyone to climb aboard. Kook and Doc joined the lieutenant. Rook went to chopper two. The squad leaders split up, as did grenadiers and the other riflemen. The communication was silent. Everyone seemed to know what to do. Before they took off with seven in chopper three, each bird contained a fully functioning lean fighting unit complete with goods, weapons, ammo, and communications.

In the lead chopper a chief warrant turned around, lifted his helmet visor, and with a thumbs-up asked Lieutenant Bross if they were ready to go. Bross returned the gesture and gave a nervous smile. When the pilot turned around, he and the co-pilot saw one of the combat journalists who had been on the LZ for the past couple of weeks approach the front left quadrant at a dead run. Hippie haircut, two cameras swinging from his neck, and a large, paper-laden clipboard held in one hand. He was motioning a desire to board, but the warrant waved him off before goosing the throttle and yanking the collective.

"Who was that?" Bross yelled up front. The co-pilot responded by motioning to the headphones hanging on a hook over the lieutenant's right shoulder. Bross fitted them over his ears below his steel pot and moved a microphone on a gimbal to a position just below his lower lip. On intercom, he pushed the black mic button and asked, "How copy?"

"Five by, LT."

"What was that about?"

"MACV wants us to start hauling reporters around. Might have taken him, but we're already heavy."

"Got it." Bross gave a thumbs-up. He recalled the battalion CO talking about the press, but he hadn't given it much thought at the time.

Bross and Evans had pre-briefed the pilots beforehand, but this was a horse of a different color for these guys. They were used to flying in on smoke and a ground-pounder directing them in by radio, but now they had to rely on map-reading. Unfortunately, the clear morning had given way to a formation of thick puffy clouds and a broken cloud deck below them. Staying above the clouds made map-reading all but impossible, and staying below the three-thousand-foot "deck" made small arms fire a potential problem.

The dirty deed of finding the drop point was relegated to the crustiest old fart the air cav unit could drum up. Chief Tracy Kisa might have had more combat flying time than any other army pilot in Nam, but even he hadn't flown the western mountains of Quảng Nam Province. It was impossible to know whether they would be landing in a hot zone or not. There was no area recon that could provide details. No intel.

To make matters worse, three guys in the patrol had never flown in a chopper before and were scared shitless—a complication Lieutenant Bross hadn't even considered. Just after liftoff, Paco Hernandez panicked, and had to be moved to a seat farther away from the open door. During the swap, he somehow managed to fall out of the chopper. Had the door gunner—who was strapped in—not grabbed Paco's TA-50 webbing in a knee-jerk reaction, the kid would have flown out the door like Superman. Only, the result would have been less "leaping over tall buildings in a single bound," and more "grease spot" on the ground with one pissed-off aircraft commander. Bross thought back to Ranger School, when he had come close to falling to his death from the side of a Coast Guard cutter.

As they approached the area near what everyone thought must have been the LZ, it appeared to the men that they were going to land when all three choppers pulled up. They pulled up hard in the beginning of a "helicopter dance": pretending to land here, then changing their minds to a klick over there, then changing again to a different clearing on the other side of a river, then over a ridge line, then to this open spot, then to that. No one had briefed the patrol on these maneuver tactics, which they found out much later were designed to confuse any enemy on the ground regarding where a force would eventually alight. *Note to self,* Lieutenant Bross thought. *Include chopper insertion instructions in LRRP training.*

The person these maneuvers didn't confuse was the luckiest and unluckiest VC sniper in Vietnam. He was walking alone back to his home village when three helicopters began doing a strange set of movements in the distant sky. By the time they calmed down, the three landed one after the other in an open pasture adjacent to his position. From a kneeling position, he took aim with his single-shot rifle, and from two hundred meters he scored a KIA with one shot.

One of the soldiers jumping off the helicopter landed in a pile. It was the sniper's lucky day.

The unlucky part began when the door gunner saw the muzzle flash from the sniper rifle and filled the area with 7.62mm automatic machine gun fire at the rate of over five hundred rounds per minute. The door gunner screamed while fanning the area, "You lose, motherfucker!" An accurate assessment.

The sniper was tallied for a body count. Only one of over a hundred rounds in the gunner's burst found purchase—but that was enough. Brigade would argue later over who got credit for the kill. Those details didn't matter to the gunner, but he unbuckled and spent twenty-five seconds begging Chief Kisa for permission to hop out to retrieve the sniper rifle as a souvenir. No dice.

The other unlucky soldier that day was the Kit Carson scout Đinh Quang Tý. Tý was gone just like that, bullet in the forehead. As the two gunners dragged Tý's body back on board they marveled at the accuracy of the shot. "Lucky son-of-a-bitch," one commented. "Skill," the other replied.

For all intents and purposes, the patrol was alone and on their own in an area of South Vietnam that seemed to be unknown to the US or its allies.

So, on landing, with everyone nervous and their scout dead, they all assumed they were landing in hot zone—one with enemy nearby on the ground in contact. They didn't know it was a lone gunman who had taken one shot. The reaction was reasonable: twelve of the twenty remaining guys switched to full auto. Each soldier unloaded a clip into the surrounding bush. Innate training took over so that there was little crossfire and no one dead from this display.

This deafening burst had to end before Rook screaming "Cease fire!" was heard. In the process, he took a grazing bullet across the outer edge of his left shoulder. It scored a line across his unit patch and drew a tiny spot of blood. Weeks later, he would work that graze hard to keep it from healing. In his mind he'd ensure he could add a Purple Heart to his ribbon rack. More than the medal, it earned him the derisive nickname "Scratch." But everyone knew not to say it to his face or risk an eruption of fist-pounding anger.

Kook and Lieutenant Bross talked about it. They both realized that until that afternoon they'd never had any concept of what real jungle was.

"Holy shit, LT, I thought I was an expert on jungles. Hey, I've seen a lot of Tarzan movies. This doesn't look like any of 'em."

Bross laughed. "Yeah, no platforms to swing from. I don't see or hear Jane anywhere."

"I never figured out why they called the chimp 'Cheetah.'"

"Maybe he could run fast."

In the Tarzan films the jungle was black and white, or maybe that was the TV. The human mind had that to relate to, although this was 100 percent in color, but with hues that were difficult to discern. No one in the patrol was prepared for triple canopy forest so thick it felt like twilight all the time, almost dark at high noon.

"Reminds me of a solar eclipse I saw one summer a few years ago in Maine," Kook said. "The whole place turned sort of like dusk. It was really eerie."

Thankfully, sawgrass—which, according to one of the guys, *would grow on the surface of Mars*—was less successful without direct sunlight. But they were still surrounded by wet and slimy, huge hardwood trees that made Maples, who had grown up in Sacramento, think of Muir Woods out near the California coast. And there were "wait-a-minute" vines, so named because their thorns would grab fatigues so convincingly, everyone who got snagged would say "wait a minute" during their extrication. But most fun were the leeches. Everyone had experienced the pleasure of leeches in the foothills and flatlands, but in the jungle they were another thing altogether. Every break required a leech search. Every soldier had his own "best-ever" method of getting them off. The techniques ran the gamut, from burning them with cigarettes to squirting them with bug juice. The latter method seemed to work well, but they were running out of the juice fast. And they would need to save some for the coming Biblical insect swarms of mid-summer.

The jungle was like being trapped on an endless obstacle course, with dirt, sweat, stink, and a constant supply of natural "things" that had to be approached and scaled. Lieutenant Bross thought of the trials and tribulations of Ranger School, the terrain in the southern Appalachians of northern Georgia, and how primeval that had seemed at the time. *A walk in a pasture compared to this place.*

"Why are we here, boss?" someone asked. "There's no way any human could live here."

"And yet, here we are," Lieutenant Bross replied.

The jungle seemed to absorb sound. Someone just feet away to the left or right of the trail would disappear both from sight and from the range of hearing. Darren was reminded of Gandalf's warning in *The Hobbit*: *If you stray off the trail in Mirkwood Forest, you will never find your way back.*

Despite the dead silence, the squad leaders were concerned about announcing their presence to Charlie. Night was the worst. Lieutenant Bross took the lead trying to get the guys to keep quiet and stealthy while eating, smoking, making coffee, opening tins, coughing, clearing throats, and generally acting like the group of young men they were. While he was at it, he stayed true to form in demanding proof that everyone was taking their malaria medication.

But sleep was a capable enemy as well. In his short time in Indian Country, Bross had come to learn the power of exhaustion over the human body. Unlike in Ranger School, no one here had to tie their weapon to their TA-50, but sleep was nevertheless a constant nag. Even at 1500, in bright sun, a soldier could go into deep sleep in under a minute. The lieutenant would check guard posts and find soldiers dozing while standing. When the body said *sleep*, the body slept, plain and simple.

Kook and Doc told Bross that checking up was a job for the platoon sergeant. In one of his rare moments of profanity and public display of frustration, the lieutenant responded, "Fat fucking chance." Until then he had kept his disdain for Rook in check, but those in the platoon closest to him had felt the constant tension. Something was going to break. Eventually. They knew it.

CHAPTER 17

12 September 1957—Ten Years Prior

Xa Ruh Village, Hien District, Quảng Nam Province

Kiep had planned Thia's abduction weeks before he thought about how to present her the necklace and bracelet. After the gift, the next step in DeGa tradition required that Kiep steal his bride-to-be away from the safety of her village. It would be an actual kidnapping, though an expected one. Kiep secreted himself in the jungle in a spot where he could overlook the village and ponder a plan of attack.

Kiep's and Thia's distant ancestors, after being driven from Vietnam's coastal regions to the Highlands, had slashed and burned flat locations in their valleys to build their villages. Thia's village was a near carbon copy of his own, as if many years ago tribal elders had commissioned a traveling architect who ensured a measure of uniformity among neighboring tribes. This was atypical, since most DeGa villages, while similar in the construction of buildings, were beholden to the terrain for a suitable layout.

And that layout was quite deliberate—the result of a Co-Tu tradition that had evolved over two thousand years. In most DeGa communities, the structures, and the orientation of their entrances, were designed to prevent easy access by evil spirits. Most were designed as an ellipse with a central plaza—an open area where all outdoor ceremonies and sacrificial rituals were held. The longhouse marked one side of the plaza, while across the square was the Guol.

The longhouse was the most apparent vestige of a South Pacific heritage tracing its origins back over two millennia, from Polynesian islands, to Southeast Asian beaches, and finally to the mountains of what became Vietnam. The longhouse in Thia's village was over forty meters in length and fifteen meters deep. The original design was half that length, but with the addition of each new family a section had been added to each end, symmetrically, to accommodate new residents. Built on an interlaced structure of massive bamboo stilts, the floor of the longhouse sat two meters above ground, leaving enough space below to elevate it above the worst possible floods, to protect it from all but the most inquisitive wild animals, and to provide cover for caged rabbits, chickens, and dogs.

Under the longhouse were play areas for children—with protection from the elements and the sun—and large grain storage bins for rice. A corner area was reserved for storing firewood; the cover and protection of the longhouse was essential to keep the wood dry. A small, enclosed shed was secured as an armory. The longhouse interior was marked with a central corridor on each side of a central meeting room that contained a large clay hearth—for cooking and warmth during winter and the monsoon season. With no exit port and no chimney, the hearth exhausted smoke into the rafters, an open attic of sorts that extended across the entire length of the structure. But this was an intentional feature, as a twice-daily dose of billowing smoke rose and filled the beams to ward off critters, bugs, and mosquitos. For the most part the design served the residents well, but if cooking and fire-building were not tended with care, the entire longhouse could become a smoke-filled chamber, where, unfortunately, a resident would die of toxic inhalation from time to time.

Along each side of the corridor, rooms were separated from the hallway by embroidered curtains of cloth, hemp, beads, or the rare drape of hanging seashells, a show of opulence. These rooms included sleeping quarters, meeting rooms, shrines, and kitchens. Throughout the structure, homemade oil lamps hung on interior walls, sharing space with hammocks, spears, machetes, knives, and articles of clothing. Floors of bamboo and wooden planks and parquet held rolled mats and wooden or rattan and bamboo chests of all sizes.

One small window in each room was covered by makeshift curtains in bright colors and double layers. One curtain was always thin gauze that let light in, but a heavy blue hemp covering could be dropped when a darker interior was desired. From the exterior, a rattan awning was held open by a carved stick, so that it could be closed for inclement weather. Both interior and exterior walls were woven of bamboo strips in intricate, repeating designs, adding cross-patterned grasses where additional detail was desired. Ceilings rose to two meters above the floor and were intricately woven from palm and bamboo. Interior beams of monkey wood were carved with ornate bas-relief images of local flora and fauna.

The longhouse was always oriented north and south. The ends of the building, as with all Co-Tu structures, were rounded with heavy thatched roofs and hipped from end to end. Roofs pitched down to a level that matched the height of the exterior walls. This design not only presented proportions pleasing to the eye and provided ideal angles to repel incessant rainfall, but the rounded ends and smooth thatched roofs prevented easy access by evil spirits coming from either of the two cardinal directions.

Across the square from the long house was the Guol—the common house, the bachelors' residence. Less than half the length of the longhouse, but deeper, it had a steep pitched roof seven to eight meters tall. The primary purpose of the Guol was to house unmarried village men, a significant proportion of the village population. Nevertheless, the structure was also elaborately constructed for the conduct of rituals; it contained male guest quarters, meeting rooms for instruction from village elders, and space for communing with spirits who also found sanctuary within.

At the base of the central plaza was a conclave of three houses of worship. Built for show as a space for the spirits, these buildings lacked space enough for human occupants. They were tiny, useless structures with no apparent function, but were reserved for the spirits that protected the village. They were maintained as the cleanest facilities in the village.

In Xa Ruh there were sixteen separate houses arranged in concentric ellipses facing the square. On each side, four houses in front and four behind, but staggered so the main entrances to each had an unobstructed view of the plaza. From a distance it appeared the houses matched like twins: cookie cutter, all designed by the same architect. Closer inspection showed that each owner had added personal touches, like carving supports and beams in unique patterns, or weaving exterior walls into spectacular designs, some depicting hunting or farming scenes. For entry, some homes had ladders, some had notched logs side by side, and some even had stairs—copied from more upscale homes on the coast near Da Nang. Scattered at the base of the ladders to each structure was a variety of homemade leather sandals, an indication that removal prior to entry was the custom.

Finally, to the southeast of the plaza, outside the ring of homes and beyond the spirit houses, was a workhouse. It had the base dimensions of the Guol and was set aside for working rice and other grains during the monsoon, dressing game, drying meat, keeping firewood dry, storing boong'boong fruit, and building furniture. One end was a portico reserved for the village blacksmith, who crafted tools and weapons from iron—and, more recently, from brass, salvaged from military artillery shell casings and delivered by entrepreneurs who hauled them on their backs from the coastal plains.

The workhouse was owned by no one and everyone. Any village adult was permitted to make use of this outbuilding for any reason whatsoever.

Kiep stayed hidden in the jungle on the outskirts of Thia's plaza and contemplated the execution of his plan. *I will wait for nightfall. I will approach the Pholoong house after everyone is asleep. I will quietly make way to the room where Thia is sleeping with her family. I will step in quietly, cover her mouth, wake her up, and command she go with me. This will startle her, but won't be a surprise. She has been anticipating this day since I presented her the gift of the necklace.*

It was a plan, but not a good one. Kiep had approached two of his older married cousins to seek assistance, but they reminded Kiep that he was responsible for a flawless kidnapping to begin his life together with Thia. They would assist later, they promised. Kiep was not convinced.

Slapping at insects, and wishing he had brought his father's canteen, Kiep kept an eye on the village goings-on as he waited for nightfall. But then an opportunity presented itself. With a large aluminum jug on her head and a *gui* basket on her back, Thia emerged from the longhouse and headed down the steps, disappearing behind the communal house adjacent to the plaza.

Kiep knew she was headed downhill to the stream to collect water. He took a parallel wildlife trail down to the stream, a steep shortcut that got him there ahead of Thia. He wanted to be there when she arrived so he could surprise her.

He brushed the mud from his legs and rear end, sat on a log next to the running water, and listened to the movement in the brush as Thia made her way down the path. When she stepped down a rock staircase and around large boulder, she didn't see Kiep at first, sitting in the shade. She dipped the jug into the rushing water and began preparations for the walk back to her village.

Kiep wanted to surprise her, but he didn't want to scare her. "Hello, Thia," he said under his breath.

She was alarmed, not terrified, and happy with relief. "Kiep! What are you doing here?"

"Thia, today is the day. If you agree, I'll take you back to my village." Thia was taken aback, but the realization hit her. She beamed. She smiled. She had been waiting for months.

"Today is the day? Today is the Zij?"

In Kiep's eyes, Thia's smile lit the jungle. "I wonder if a hundred years ago the Zij was a true abduction?" Kiep asked.

"I suppose it was," Thia replied. "I have heard that other larger villages to the south are not taking the time to do this kind of thing anymore. The old ways are beginning to die out."

Kiep raised his eyebrows. "My grandfather and cousins would never stand for that." He paused and reflected a moment. "When I was discussing my plans for the Zij with my cousins, our grandfather told us about his experience and why he thinks the tradition took hold. Have you seen those human skulls hanging on the wall in our hut?"

Thia grimaced. "That's awful, Kiep! Human heads? Our longhouse has skulls from buffalo, boar, and monkeys—there is even a tiger skull in the center—but we don't have human skulls!"

"Grandfather said when he was young, men outnumbered women three to one. If you wanted a wife, you had to go to another village and steal her. Even then, like now, marrying someone from your *toring* was forbidden. But when a woman came of age, men would fight over her… sometimes to the death. He told me when he married my grandmother he knew there was a boy from another village who was going to be a problem, so he and his brothers went on what was called a 'blood killing' party. They hunted the boy down and killed him."

"Do you think his skull is in your hut?" Thia asked.

"I asked Grandfather the same thing." Kiep raised his eyebrows a little, wrinkled up his brow, and nodded his head.

Thia made a face that indicated her disgust. "I wonder why that tradition ended."

"You and I think alike," Kiep replied. "Grandfather said in those days there were five men for every woman because girl babies would disappear in the jungle when they were born. A daughter could not care for the family—only take food out of every mouth. She brought little honor to the family or the village."

Thia thought for a moment. "I think that happened to a baby girl in our village when I was small. The mother died in childbirth. They buried the crying baby with the mother. I am so glad it's different now. I am so glad you didn't have to fight for me."

Kiep smiled. "Me too. Grandfather told us that so many DeGa died when our villages were fighting with the white man, against—against whatever it was they were fighting against—that village elders decreed that we would stop the practice."

Kiep shook his head in bewilderment over the story he'd told Thia. Perhaps he should not have shared the horror. "Take my hand," he said. "Let's walk back to my village."

Thia wanted to go. But she was concerned that the longhouse needed the water she was sent to gather. "Kiep, is there any way we can take this water back to the longhouse now, before we depart?"

Kiep replied, "It wouldn't look much like a Zij if we did that. Eventually somebody will come to look for you. They'll find this jug and your *gui* and begin searching. The smarter ones will guess why you're gone. By that time you'll be back at my village. If there's a problem, my cousins and grandfather are standing by to make the trip over the ridge line to tell them where you are."

Kiep was not nervous in the least as he walked hand in hand with Thia along the stream and then followed a game trail across a grassy clearing that climbed toward the trees and the ridge. This was the route any number of animals took for a reliable source of water from the stream below. It was still early morning, yet the sun was visible, with a wide expanse of rays in the jungle canopy like spokes on a wheel. Dew on the leaves formed curlicues of steam that rose and coalesced into a white, light-filled radiant mist.

The jungle and its gargantuan succulent trees and mist, and the second and third layers above, made Kiep think of the uncertainty of the life before him. But as he walked, those unknowns dissolved into the raw love he felt for Thia. He could not be happier. He had contemplated this day since the age of eight. He loved Thia. That superseded any concern for the future. His *toring* had already begun adding a section to the longhouse, a room where Kiep and Thia would begin their lives together.

Talking together nervously, they worked their way around two village houses on the south side of the plaza. As Kiep's village was a mirror image of Thia's, he had to remind himself he had not walked in a circle back to where he came. There were old and young alike peering around the corners of buildings and from open windows. Marriage remained a special ceremony for everyone involved.

When the couple arrived at the plaza, two young girls ran arm in arm—free hands over their mouths to cover their high-pitched giggles—to the open entrance of the longhouse. Kiep knew their job was to announce to the elders that the Zij was successful, that Thia and Kiep had returned.

Kiep pined for his father, who would have helped to lead the coming procession. Instead his mother appeared at the main entrance of the longhouse while his great-grandfather stood in the doorway of the bachelors' common hall. Two uncles helped Great-Grandpapa down the bamboo ladder.

One of Kiep's aunts carried a large, shallow open basket containing a dead chicken and a dead rabbit. The animals represented villagers who had passed: ancestors. Keeping with tradition, Great-Grandpapa did not take any time for pleasantries or greetings, rather he approached the couple and took the dead rabbit from the basket. He held it high above his head in front of Kiep and Thia and spoke in a high-brow ancient language/song that few understood. Then he stood silent for a moment, before asking Thia's ancestors to release her from her *toring* in order that she might join a new village. With the rabbit still held high, and with the help of Kiep's uncles, he circled the couple, who bowed their heads.

He came back to the basket, swapped the rabbit for the

chicken, and held it high. To the widening crowd, he spoke again. The words sounded identical, but this time Great-Grandpapa was instead asking his ancestors permission for Thia, now released from her village, to be admitted into his *toring*.

Thia's eyes followed the chicken corpse as it circled around her head and Kiep's in a figure eight. Great-Grandpapa returned the chicken to the basket, clapped his hands twice, and opened his arms for the first village embrace of the new couple. "Let the wedding begin!" he tried to bellow. But his voice was frail. One of Kiep's uncles nudged the other, and in unison the two men belted out, "Let the wedding begin!"

As planned, two of Kiep's cousins made the trip to Xa Ruh to let Thia's parents and village elders know that she was in good hands. In accordance with tradition, she would remain in Kiep's village for the first wedding feast, which was the responsibility of Kiep's family. This was also the notice for Thia's village that the couple would return the following day for the continuation of the marriage ceremony—a feast and ritual in Thia's village, with her elders, and a payment to be passed from Thia's father to Kiep's grandfather.

Mr. and Mrs. Pholoong were all smiles when they got the news. Like Thia, they had been waiting for months, expecting the Zij any day. They had immediate work to do. Thia's father was wealthy by Co-Tu standards, and Thia was his only daughter; he and Thia's mother wanted the marriage ceremony to be a spectacle. He would sacrifice a water buffalo to honor Thia and Kiep and to honor his village. The village would eat well the following evening.

CHAPTER *18*

22 August 1967

South of Letia Dadiou, Quảng Nam Province, South Vietnam

Four nights in the foothills walking toward the mountains was sort of like hiking with the Boy Scouts, in the sense that no one was apparently trying to kill them. Colonel O'Neill was right: there was no enemy out here. Somehow the enemy had missed this patch of South Vietnam. But Bross and his men still had to face a formidable foe: the jungle.

Mickey Grosvenor hailed from Fort Collins, Colorado. A Ranger School honor graduate, he might have been the smartest soldier in the entire group. He put "the mountains" of the Central Highlands in perspective: "Mountains? These are fucking bumps. Reminds me of visiting relatives in North Carolina. Now the bugs, I'll give 'em that. This place has some fucking bugs. But mountains? If you want to see mountains come to Colorado. We got some fuckin' mountains. Who named these hills *mountains* anyway?" He was hiking along talking aloud to himself, too loud, but he got the point across, at least to those in earshot.

Nick Nicolletti was the only one who responded. "Tell you

what, Mickey, when we get back home I'm gonna drive over from corn country and visit. Show me some mountains."

"Deal," Grosvenor replied. "Smitty and I will hook you up. He's from a little town in the grasslands called Peyton. I'd say it was 'in the sticks,' but there's no sticks, only grass, thunderstorms, and hail." He loved talking about Colorado, so he went on, "And Jack McCloskey in Weapons Squad is from Nederland, uphill from Boulder. Lots of hippies up there."

In truth, Lieutenant Bross also wanted to visit Colorado. It seemed like half the guys in his hometown had gone out there to ski at one time or another. He'd keep that in mind.

LRRP training taught them to stay off the trails whenever possible. "Where would you put a booby trap?" Sergeant Stargardt had asked. And then, answering his own question, "Exactly right, where people walk." A pause, a look around at interested faces. "And where do people walk? Exactly right, on trails. Ergo"—hardly anyone knew what that meant—"don't walk on trails."

Like many things in life, this was a lot easier said than done. It was a toss-up whether to risk being blown to bits by a booby trap or to let oneself be ripped to shreds by a jungle that seemed designed by the Creator to do the job. On the first day, they strictly followed the "rules," and they moved at about a quarter of a mile per hour. By day two, after a powwow between the lieutenant, Sergeant Rook, and the squad leaders, they decided to make use of whatever trails they could find. And they did exist, although in many places they were grown over.

A dozen and a half men, each positioned about twenty-five

feet from the ones ahead and behind, they were stretched out just over a tenth of a mile—a little over five hundred feet. At times, with a break in the cover, and perhaps a sunlit meadow, the lieutenant could look back and see the entire tired line.

Bross reported back to Company twice per day, sometimes three times, and more if there was something to SITREP. The standard practice was to navigate in the jungle using a primitive, featureless map and a compass. The navigation taught in Ranger School was advanced by comparison, since the maps there were accurate, and provided the ability to triangulate based off of observed features: a hilltop here, an antenna over there. But here, with unreliable maps and so few breaks in the canopy, reckoning where they were was a bigger challenge. Marching west using the compass and sighting large trees as markers became the best practice. The truth was, they barely knew where they were, and they fretted over whether they would be able to adequately triangulate and plot coordinates for radio passage to a resupply chopper "RS bird," or, God forbid, Dust Off.

They were in no hurry. Other than a fervent desire to get the hell out of this mess, this mission was in many ways a relief from the monotony of Lampshade Valley patrols and the alternative mission of guarding bridges on main thoroughfares. The slow pace led to a decision to begin setting up an NDP around 1500 each day, and no later than 1600 hours. Sergeant Rook would gather the squad leaders and outline the NDP layout. They would all make provisions to protect the platoon leader, and to ensure, to the extent possible, a line of sight for Kook's radio-telephone. Finding flat ground was a challenge, particularly when leadership wanted the night defensive position set up in a specific manner. But everyone tried their best. Sometimes that meant sleeping against a tree to keep from rolling downhill. Sometimes it was a case of meticulously setting up only to discover you were on an ant pile. Ants don't wake up until they are knelt on or stepped on, but when they do wake up, they're determined to protect their territory—and a good guess was that where there was one ant, there were a million more underfoot, so stomping them out was a bad plan. Moving was the better option. The only option.

It was during this lazy preparation on Tuesday the twenty-second of August 1967 that Private First Class Marty Byers lay screaming while he bled out and died in the arms of Corporal Peanut Carver.

Marty Byers grew up in Montgomery, Alabama, the great-grandson of a sharecropper who had worked the Butter Creek Plantation in Watsonia, Alabama. Marty's ancestors didn't know where the name Byers had come from, but one of his grandnieces would learn from an ancestry web site in 2009 that one Horace Byers, a childless white man, a lawyer, and devout abolitionist, was killed while trying to save two former slaves from being lynched near Butter Creek in 1871. Subsequent marriage and birth records showed that those slaves honored Mr. Byers by keeping his name alive for posterity.

Unfortunately, Marty would not be able to carry on the tradition. He attended George Washington Carver High, a segregated school for colored students. This was a humorous coincidence not lost on Peanut, his best friend in the platoon. Marty was an average student, but an exceptional athlete. He was a star running back for the Carver Wolverines. He'd had his eye on a scholarship to Alabama State when he was drafted into the army.

Marty also knew Rosa Parks—if not quite as well as he bragged to his friends and fellow soldiers, and whether she knew Marty is lost to eternity. What is certain is that when Marty was ten years old he earned fifteen cents an hour doing odd jobs and clean-up at the department store where Mrs. Parks worked in the alterations shop. Though she was thirty years older than Marty, she may have recalled him from teaching Sunday school at the African Methodist Episcopal Church in town. Marty was immensely proud of even having rubbed shoulders with Rosa Parks, but the only guys in the platoon who knew it were the Negroes. It was a snippet they kept from Sergeant Rook, who would have found a way to use the association as a negative.

Marty was an excellent and reliable soldier. He talked to some of the guys about going to jump school before starting his second tour. He saw the army as a way out of the poverty he grew up in, and had early eyes on becoming a "lifer." But he didn't share this plan with his black platoon mates. They'd have ribbed him for consorting with *The Man.*

When it wasn't raining, Marty liked to place his poncho on the damp ground as a protective cover. At around 1545, he stepped about twenty feet off the trail with his eye on a dip between some trees, a suitable place to prepare his spot for the coming night. He snapped the poncho out, catching warm air above it, and worked a move to land it on the ground between the trees and under the corner of a thicket of bushes. The poncho got caught up in the branches of a bush. He knelt down on it to lean forward and spread the material flat. His left knee landed squarely on top of a land mine.

The explosion wasn't massive, but it startled every member of the LRRP. The position of his body shielded the other twenty guys from potential destruction. Marty looked at his crotch—what was left of it—and screamed.

Doc was at his side in less than fifteen seconds. He had his medical kit opened in a single, unrolling motion. Peanut Carver pushed through the gathering soldiers, sat on the ground behind Marty, spread his legs in a "V" and made a sort of recliner for Marty to lean back on while Doc went to work. Peanut tried to calm Marty down, but the pain was too great—he was inconsolable. Screaming, wailing. Doc had scissors out in a flash and cut down the legs of Marty's jungle fatigues. Lieutenant Bross was standing over the group while Kook called in Dust Off through Company.

"Tell Captain Evans I'll give him a SITREP ASAP." Bross looked around for Rook, but—no surprise—Rook was MIA. He grabbed Witz by the sleeve and said, "Get three guys out there with smoke, *now*! Find a clearing. Make sure you send them with a Prick 6!"

"Got it, boss! Why three guys?"

"Kook has a position estimate, but we don't really have any idea where the fuck we are. You're gonna need extra smoke. Put your best guy on the radio—the guy who can vector Dust Off in fast."

"LT, it's pretty early for smoke. We're pretty far out here. I don't think Dust Off could arrive in under thirty minutes."

The lieutenant scolded himself for his stupidity. "Right. Find a clearing and perk your ears up for rotor noise."

"Roger that, boss."

Doc got the pant legs off and paused. Then he looked up at Peanut and burst into tears. Not the typical reaction from a trained medic.

Peanut looked down at the carnage before him. Marty had little left between his belly button and his right knee. His genitals were gone. They could see both ends of his right femur, blown right in half. A large blood vessel—Doc knew it was his femoral artery— was shooting blood toward Marty's left knee to the tune of Marty's fading heartbeat.

Peanut put his hand over Marty's mouth to quiet him down for a second. He leaned in to Doc. "Morphine, Doc, now." He hugged Marty from behind, pulling his head back a little so Marty wouldn't be able to see what was left. "You gonna be okay, Marty. Doc says you gonna be okay. Lean back on me, brother. Dust Off's on the way. You goin' home, brother. You goin' home."

Marty stopped his wailing and fell into serenity. He looked back into Peanut's eyes. "I'm tired, Peanut. I love you, man. Tell my moms I was a good soldier. Tell my moms I love her."

With that he took his last breath, just a gurgle, his eyes still staring back at Peanut.

Peanut's eyes were full of tears.

Within five minutes Sergeant Rook was back, casually strolling over to the scene while tucking his T-shirt into his pants. "Sorry boss, I was off taking a crap." Carver was still holding Byers, rocking him.

Lieutenant Bross was on the radio, back-briefing Company, calling off the Dust Off, and asking for transport and a body bag. "We need some stuff. I'll have the guys vector an RS bird in. We can wait. Almost three hours 'til sundown." He listened for a minute to squawking from Company. Kook was pretty sure it was Captain Evans, but they might have been patching the colonel in as well. "Yes, sir, that's right… We're not sure, sir."

Rook understood the conversation back at Company and chimed in. "It was an M-14."

Bross spoke into the mic. "Stand by one, sir." He held his hand over the mic. "An M-14?"

"Yep. Not the rifle, an anti-personnel mine. An M-14. I heard too many of 'em. Knew it as soon as I heard it pop. It's made for blowing feet off. How Byers got it in the balls is anyone's guess."

The lieutenant stood silent for a second until the radio lit back up. "Six-two bravo, six-two. Are you there?"

"Yes, sir, the platoon sergeant says it was an M-14 mine. Somehow Byers got it in his lap."

"He probably sat on it. What the hell is a mine like that doing out there?"

"Must be Charlie in the area, boss. But it's strange. This thing wasn't near a trail, at least not a trail we can see. How lucky would you have to be to snag someone off trail?"

"Set your NDP up in a different location."

No shit, Darren thought. "Copy that, six-two. Send that ReSupp, over."

"Got it, S4 is already talking to the unit. They should be at your position within an hour. Correction, near your position. I say again, be ready for vectoring. Find a spot comfortably distant from your actual position. Recognize movement of the body will be required. When they depart, hightail it until sundown to try and maintain some stealth. We're gonna be making a lot of noise."

"Wilco, six-two. Got it. I'm gonna pass it to Witz. He'll tell you what we need. Bug juice for sure. It's the only thing that'll take the leeches off. We're almost out."

So much for the lazy afternoon until sunset.

The radio crackled to life once again. Kook was packing up for movement so he wasn't quite ready, but nevertheless he answered quickly. "Six-two, six-two bravo, copy. What's up?"

"Six-two bravo. The ReSupp is on the way to your general area. Estimate twenty minutes. Assume a smoke marker in the vicinity will be ready."

"Copy that, six-two. We have comms with the vector team. Will advise."

"Got it, Bravo, tell them there's a reporter on board from some magazine. He's taking pictures and asking questions. We have not told him, repeat *not* told him the special nature of your mission. Approved story is standard ops, enemy fire. How copy?"

"Copy all, six-two. Putting six-two bravo on the horn. He wants to know more about this guy."

"Six-two bravo, six-two. What guy? Over."

"The reporter, six-two."

CHAPTER 19

12 September 1957

Sông Cả River, Hien District, Quảng Nam Province

The first order of business was to bathe the bride and groom, a ceremony in itself, since bathing, apart from special occasions, was normally an annual occurrence. This day dictated a second dip in the Sông Cả.

Ri'Ga village had used a Sông Cả River bathing location for decades. An accident of geology enabled both women and men to wash simultaneously without being in view of each other. At a turn in the river, a well-established sandbar, peppered with smooth round river stone, jutted out into a valley oxbow, a sharp bend in the stream. The village shaman was able to stand on the end of the bar and, facing left then right, bless both groups from that single location. Like everything else in nature that surrounded the village, the river was sacred. Bathing required an apology to the river spirit and a plea for permission to foul the water.

Kiep and Thia waited patiently for the shaman's words and singing to conclude. Then they stepped into the warm flowing water and dipped themselves. Kiep let a loincloth fall to the ground, his only clothing. Thia, on the other side of the sandbar, hidden by brush and distance, removed a simple hemp dress. They permitted relatives to scrub their bodies clean. Kiep with cousins, Thia with village women.

After stepping out of the water, they were led to a clean rock where each would stand naked to drip dry. The women combed out Thia's long black hair and braided it with the inclusion of colorful blue glass beads. They wrapped the result into a beautiful chignon in the style of all the other village women, but with more ornate woven-in decorations, as was custom.

By tradition, Kiep's family was responsible for preparing the wedding garments that would be donned for both the festivities today and those tomorrow with Thia's family. This could not be Thia's responsibility, as her family had to profess to have had no advance notice of the wedding—even though the presentation of Kiep's gift to Thia months before had provided all the blessing Kiep needed to commence the Zij—and the Zij, in turn, commenced the wedding.

Thia's bath was complete. The village shaman said a few tonal words to once again thank the river spirits for permitting the washing. Kiep's mother approached Thia with what appeared to be a bolt of deep blue folded cloth. She walked with the material in extended hands with one palm up, the other down. Thia knew this was her wedding dress. She wondered if it would fit properly, but then realized that was a silly thought since all the village women her age, including a younger cousin, were of nearly identical stature. Later, she was ashamed of herself when she wondered if Kiep's mother understood how to properly set the indigo dye to prevent the near-permanent blue stains many villagers across the Central Highlands carried on their bodies.

"Thia, we are so proud to welcome you to our family. We do appreciate you not fighting against the Zij. Had you done so, the work of my sisters and I would have been wasted."

Thia smiled. "Mrs. Dool. I have had my eye on your Kiep since we were children. I would never let him get away."

Kiep's mother held the dress up before her and turned a pirouette so everyone could see. The sun was high overhead. Reflected light danced off the water to display the dress in all its glory. A fine and intricate weave of jute and hemp, it was stunning —befitting of a beautiful young woman like Thia. Ankle-length, with long sleeves, it was decorated with horizontal embroidery in red, white, gold, and green. One pattern went from shoulder to shoulder and was carried over to the tops of the sleeves. A second, wider strip of embroidery would encircle Thia's breasts and back. As wide as three of Thia's hands was a waist sash that matched the pattern of the other embroidery.

"Mrs. Dool, this is beautiful beyond description." Motioning to the gathered aunts who faced Thia in a loose-knit semicircle before the rushing river, she said, "You have made me proud to join the Dool family. I will wear this dress today and tomorrow, but then I will treasure it the rest of my life."

"Thank you, Thia. We all worked hard on this. Please, from this moment until eternity I ask that you call me Mother."

As if on cue, Kiep's aunts held their hands up in rapid

clapping and giggled like schoolgirls. An omen for the success of the marriage was acceptance of the first family gift to the bride: this wedding dress. Kiep's mother hooked her arm in Thia's and walked her around the spit of land. In this way Thia could see Kiep and Kiep could see Thia.

The feast in Ri'Ga Village was a fitting start to the further joining of the two villages. There was food aplenty. Most of the sixty-seven residents—now sixty-eight with the addition of Thia—looked forward to any reason for celebration. It meant a hearty meal in times that were otherwise scarce.

Once the boar had roasted through, the village butcher made the large cuts to take the meat from the carcass. One of Kiep's aunts led the preparation of the meal, moving meat into bamboo vessels and supervising the preparation of delectable "sticky rice," also served in long cups made from bamboo. There were bananas, beans, sweet potatoes, and a casserole-type dish made from boong'boong fruit. From neighboring villages, invitees came prepared with dishes of maize, cassava, yams, onions, and the rarest of coastal delicacies, pineapple.

Kiep's Uncle Y'Nen was the village purveyor of spirits. He continued the long-standing tradition of keeping elders and select women supplied with "ta vak," coconut and manioc wine distilled from the shoots of the ubiquitous tropical yucca-like cassava plant.

Auntie H'Juel Ya—Y'Nen's wife and Kiep's aunt—was the village tobacconist. She delivered well-rolled cigarettes to all interested village adults. It was easy to identify the smokers —they lived with a pipe like an appendage. Some carried a personal tubed pipe-like contraption, ready-made to accept a cigarette placed vertically in a narrow cylinder made just for it.

The entire day was a festival, a party, not with a care in the world except for fawning over the soon-to-be newlyweds, who would be sealed as a couple in Xa Ruh the following day. To music produced by a sort of pan flute made from bamboo, men danced a showy tung'tung, and everyone joined in the fun of folkloric dance. Village women co-opted Thia into joining them in several versions of a ya-yá. She was a quick study, learning the familiar, but new, steps—just a little different from those danced in her own village.

Hours passed. As the sun set over the mountain range to the west, it was clear the revelry was dying down. The village shaman called a halt to music, dancing, singing, smoking, eating, and finally drinking. With no apparent direction, the villagers formed on the south side of the plaza near the spirit houses. The shaman led them in a short ceremony to give thanks to their spirit protector, Giang.

Then every member of the village, even the children, was handed a smooth yellow stone. Yellow was an unusual color and therefore special. The stones had been collected from the river over years. The shaman marked this day and directed all villagers to place their stone at the altar for Giang in their individual homes or rooms in the longhouse.

The village bowed in unison. There was a final chorus of beating drums. The ceremony and the festival were over. Village women moved Thia to a special room in the Guol that had been set aside for her in preparation for her trip to Xa Ruh with Kiep the following morning.

CHAPTER 20

24 August 1967

Southwest of Letia Dadiou

Quảng Nam Province, South Vietnam

The RS chopper run was a success. The platoon held a silent vigil for a few moments while the "vector team" rigged up Byers's poncho—what was left of it—into a sling to assist in transporting his body to a clearing they thought might be large enough for a chopper to land.

The bird came complete with a resupply sergeant, a variation on a supply sergeant, who was experienced and savvy. He knew better than even the platoon did what they'd need: water, ammo, a couple of entrenching tools, a few claymores, some medical kit replacement items, trip flares, smoke flares, hand frags, bug juice, oil for small arms and some new thick synthetic stuff for the machine gunners.

The M-60, "The Pig," combined with linked 7.62mm ammo, was way too heavy to lug around on this patrol, but the supply sergeant didn't know that. It was designed to be a crew-served weapon—that is, two guys—but in normal ops a dedicated gunner would leave food behind for the perceived safety of The Pig. They preferred the thick oil, something that wouldn't vaporize under heavy fire.

But the item that made them all realize the value of a man who was thinking ahead was a bag full of mail. "I left the care packages back at the LZ," the sergeant said, "but I thought guys might want to read their mail."

The sergeant had also brought an extra body bag along, which the team thought might be a bad omen. But when they were looking for some way to carry all the supplies back to the NDP, they realized the genius of the vinyl bag. It wasn't made for carrying supplies, but they loaded it up, and it was pretty easy for the three men to take turns like carrying it like a zipped-up hammock.

"I heard the guys joking. I should have got it sooner," Kook said while pushing a vine away from his face.

"Gotten what?"

"Your nickname."

"Robin?"

"Right—Robin. I was never much on comic books."

"Yeah," Grayson said. "It follows me around everywhere, even when I try to shake it. Me and Batman and all."

"Funny really," Kook said.

"Then you're not going to believe this."

"Try me."

"One of my teachers in Gainesville was named Bruce Wayne."

Kook gave him a puzzled look that said *I don't get it*. "I told you I don't keep up with comics."

"Bruce Wayne, moron. Batman's real name is Bruce Wayne."

"Now that's funny. What are the odds?"

"Exactly, only no one called my teacher Batman. He weighed about one thirty soaking wet. Just out of college, he looked like a freshman."

Kook laughed. It was a brief interlude for reflection on the things they never had any time to think about. "Hey Robin, I forgot to mention something vitally important."

Grayson was just putting a towel over his eyes to catch some Z's, but he looked up.

"Sorry," Kook said, "but this can't wait. I got a letter from my Auntie Emma. She's upset. Her new wall-to-wall shag carpet doesn't pick up the colors in the drapes the way she'd hoped."

Robin pulled the towel from his head, sat up, and reached for the letter. "Tell me you're kidding. A relative wrote that in a letter to you in Nam?"

"I shit you not."

They both burst out laughing. "We'd better check the carpet in the bunkers back at the LZ. I thought it matched the fucking plywood pretty good, but now I'm not so sure." Laughter.

"I knew you'd love it. You're the only sick fuck out here who gets the irony."

"Cut the shit with the big words, Kook."

In a word, this place was "spooky." Over the weeks prior to this mission, the guys had become accustomed to hearing the distant sound of chopper blades, jet noise ("the sound of freedom"), the odd mortar attack on the horizon, the occasional sound of distant gunfire reminding them they were at war. And for some bizarre reason, Bross mused, the sounds of combat were a comforting reminder that they were near friends. Enemies for sure, but friends were close by too. But it wasn't like that here. There were no sounds of combat, of friends or enemy, nor of human activity of any kind.

Bross began wishing again that his Kit Carson scout was not taking a "dirt nap," in the words of Craig Message. Just that one guy, that professional guide, would make him feel like he wasn't leading the patrol into a morass. He wasn't a particularly religious man, but in his improvised shelter the night before, he'd held the prayer book to his forehead and prayed that no more of his men would die like Marty Byers.

Doc was the one to see it first: there was something out of place. Considering he was the medic, it didn't make too much sense, but eyes were eyes. He called from behind, a shout in the form of a whisper. "Hey, LT, there's something here."

The guys in the lead all looked to their right, up on the side of the steep slope. Above them, live trees appeared to have been laced together to produce a gate of sorts. Bross thought of his

Auntie Katherine, who had a plant in her house with several trunks that looked like they had been woven together when the small tree was being trained in some greenhouse. This spot was nearly invisible even from here, only twenty-five feet away. There was no possibility that any forward air controller or chopper observation could see it. Behind the woven macramé of trees there was a small entrance, about five feet in diameter, cut into the side of the hill. A tunnel.

Lieutenant Bross set the example without even considering he was doing so. He stepped toward the entrance first. Rook quick-stepped from the back of the patrol and grabbed Bross's shoulder. "Not so fast, boss. This stinks like a booby trap waiting to spring."

Witz and Nicolletti were renowned for finding booby traps. It took them about five minutes to clear the area, then Lieutenant Bross ordered everyone back and stepped in first. He unclipped his flashlight from the right side of his TA-50 webbing, unscrewed the front, and removed the red filter for use at night. It fit as intended in a screw cap on the base of the olive drab Bakelite. Rook, Witz, Nick, and Mickey Grosvenor followed. They fired their lights up as well.

The initial entry required some duck-walking, but after a few feet it opened up into a larger tunnel, almost tall enough to stand. The lieutenant heard Mickey mutter from the back: "We could stand if we were five feet nothin' like Charlie."

"Everyone shine your flashlights over here," Bross said.

"You know, boss," offered up Mickey, "in the army these aren't flashlights."

"Oh yeah?" the lieutenant half asked, half spoke. "What are

they then?" They were lighting up cobwebs and moving them aside with raised arms.

"The army has a special supply name for everything," Mickey said, "Check out your jungle fatigue top. It says *Coat, Man's Tropical.*" He waved his beam around and said, "And these babies are *Battlefield Darkness Penetrators.*"

"Bullshit," Rook cut in.

"Just kidding. A joke from Basic Training. Thought everyone heard it."

They all smiled, but this dark tunnel was too creepy to be overcome by any comic relief.

Stooped over, they continued forward about twenty-five feet. From their vantage point it appeared the tunnel ended, but when they got to the back wall, they saw that it turned sharply to the left, more than ninety degrees. Witz moved his darkness penetrator around and surveyed. "If the entrance takes an artillery blast, or a five-hundred-pounder from above, the explosion can't turn this corner."

"But they'd be trapped," Nick said.

"Nah, they built exits, I guarantee it," Rook said. "Saw one like this down south, but the turn was vertical after we went down some, since there weren't any good hills."

They took the left turn. After another thirty feet or so was a turn to the right, at the same angle as the one they'd just taken. The result was that they were headed in the same direction, into the hillside, that they had started, but by now everyone was getting disoriented. Fifty feet more and the tunnel opened up into a larger cavity, a room.

"How would anyone use this?" the lieutenant asked "There's no lights, no wiring, no furniture, no nothing. This place doesn't look like it's been used in a decade."
Rook held his flashlight under his chin, giving him the appearance of the goblin he was. "Betcha they have this marked on a map. They're probably all over the place. Hideouts. Saving the locations for the future." There was no evidence of an exit route. Just dark, dank spider webs and bugs. "Wish we could destroy it," Rook said.

Witz said, "Hell, sir, we could mark the coordinates, but no one's going to be able to locate this from the air unless we put a smoke grenade on it and call it in. And then we'd give away our position."

"He's right, boss, Mikey said, "I suggest we mark it and give S2 the grid coords next time we call in."

"Good plan. At least we have something to tell them for the SITREP."

That afternoon they were able to find a superb spot to set up the NDP. Just a short walk up a steep grade in a drainage that couldn't get past a stone outcropping. Years of flooding had created a stairway of sorts from river rock. They took turns climbing and doubled back to a large flat area, free of trees, a welcome change. The downside was that the ground was nearly solid rock, but the guys welcomed the new surroundings and hoped for fewer bugs, crawly things, leeches and such.

Everyone was getting settled in with the NDP set when they heard a claymore mine explode in a twin draw on the other side of the larger rocks. With an effective kill range of over one hundred meters—the length of a football field end zone to end zone—the claymore sends out seven hundred pellet-sized ball bearings in a sixty-degree arc out to two hundred and fifty meters in about half a second. Think simultaneous shots from seven hundred 0.22 rifles all firing in the same direction. If a man is close, he's pulverized. If he's far, there's still a high probability of kill. If someone rigs the claymore with a tripwire as a booby trap so the intended target is around fifty feet away... Short of misfire, there's no hope of survival. None.

PFC Kennan Pixton had just played his last round of Yahtzee as the sun set over the rising mountains dipping into a western valley. Three others had joined in: Carter Maples, The Knife, and Loo Chamberlain. Pixie had kicked their butts, filling the thirteen boxes on his score sheet with two Yahtzees, for fifty- and one-hundred-point bonuses. No one else had a chance. He sported a shit-eating grin and a thumbs-up while grabbing some toilet paper from his ruck. Yahtzee was important to Pixie. It helped him get his mind off things. He had headed down into the draw to find a quiet place to "drain the lizard and pinch a loaf," as he had said to Loo when he swaggered off a winner.

When he tripped something that set off the claymore, the rest of the platoon was protected by the terrain. The mine had probably been placed by someone who viewed the draw as a likely ingress route. Pixie never felt a thing. And there was little of him left; the claymore had done its work. No screaming. No other noise except the uncomfortable silence that rings after an explosion in the middle of nowhere. When every bird and every bug goes quiet. Everyone dove for cover, grabbing weapons, feeling for hand frags, waiting for the next foot to fall. But most of them thought back to Byers—and who would be next.

Rook broke the silence with a maniacal yell: "CHARLIE MOTHERFUCKERS! MOTHERFUCKER!" His maniacal response and its potential to impact others was not high on his priority list, but he had started a chain reaction that spun most of the platoon into a frenzy. Rook had had almost no reaction to Byers's untimely death, but now he stood on the edge of the rocky ledge looking down into the draw. With an M-16 in his left hand, it was he who first saw what was left of Pixton. He pointed his rifle, without aiming it, to the south off the cliff face and—with the maniacal behavior of a crazy man with a deadly weapon—emptied his clip into nothingness. It was a natural act of anger to be sure, but not what one would expect of platoon leadership. His reaction served no purpose other than to make himself feel better.

Kook tried to calm him down, but it was no use. "What is it? Who is it? Calm down, Sergeant."

"I don't know," Rook said, "but I can tell from here he's one of us. He was a white guy once upon a time." The comment didn't register as odd with anyone except for Peanut, the only Negro still alive in the LRRP. Peanut had certainly noticed that Rook had had no reaction when Byers died.

It seemed the immediate danger was over, that this was another spurious blast. Sixteen soldiers stood, walked over to the edge next to Rook, and joined him in screaming profanity at nature, at the tragic death of one of their own, and at an enemy they could not see.

Their rocky cliff top turned out to be a visible and adequate landing area for a Huey helicopter. Company seemed less concerned this time with pinpointing their position for an unseen enemy and more interested in what was killing their LRRP one soldier at a time. No one felt safe. Everyone was pissed off. Even after the chopper took to the sky with a bloody body bag on board, about half the patrol was walking around in frustration offering up a string of "Fuck fuck" to any tree, bush, or rock that might listen. Corporal Owens broke his big toe when he kicked a large boulder, and then he felt like such an idiot for picking up on everyone's anger.

They opened Pixie's final care package, left by the RS bird, mailed from San Antonio, to see if it contained the new Yahtzee score pads he'd promised. It did, but the real excitement was in sharing the box of "D" batteries his parents had sent. In its wisdom, the army handed out bullets, hand frags, and mortars like candy at a Mardi Gras parade, but flashlight batteries were scarce and had to be requisitioned individually in a one for one, bad for good swap.

The platoon continued the Yahtzee legacy and honored PFC Pixton by renaming the game forever as "Pixie." Kook would tell his kids years later, "It says Yahtzee on the box, but in this family we call it *Pixie.*" He often wondered if some others had followed suit. Then he wondered if any of the guys were even still playing Yahtzee at all. Then he wondered who might still be alive.

26 August 1967
West-Southwest of Letia Dadiou
Quảng Nam Province, South Vietnam

They were beginning to learn their lesson. Despite Company and Battalion insisting they keep off trails to the maximum extent, what was left of the patrol came to understand the danger was not *on* the trails, but *off* them. They revised their tactics, and that had proved effective for the past couple of days.

The near-exact map plot provided by the chopper that picked Pixie up did two things: it established their position to a high degree of accuracy, and it gave Kook confidence that he was getting pretty good at reading maps. The rock outcropping was well captured by the contours on the topographic map, but Kook knew that was because of a combination of low resolution of the charts and the fact that much of the surveying done over the years prior had been based on estimates and poor techniques. Kook wondered if adding a feature here and there might help a struggling S2 analyst for a future mission, so he started the process of adding some contours and shading in ink. If the map survived, perhaps someone could use the information to send another group of poor suckers out to this Godforsaken armpit of Earth.

With the correct location from two days prior and some expert dead reckoning, Kook annotated that they were just west-southwest of a little village named Letia Dadiou. According to Nick, who looked over Kook's shoulder and helped him record the grid coordinates—and who seemed to have a sixth sense about these things—they were closer to *B-F-E*.

"LT. Sorry sir, I gotta differ with your navigator Kook here. He says we're near 'Letty Doo Doo.'" Laughter from those close enough to hear; poop references never failed to elicit a chuckle. "I don't think he has a clue, sir. I can feel it in my bones. We are right on top of B-F-E, sir."

"B-F-E?"

"Yes, sir, not more than a klick either side. Bum Fuck Egypt. The middle of nowhere, sir."

The lieutenant and a half a dozen soldiers nearby needed a good laugh. Everyone knew in military parlance that BFE was "nowheresville," "dullsville," "the boondocks," "the north forty," and even "east butt fuck." But few knew 'B-F-E' was *Bum Fuck Egypt*.

"Nick," Bross said, "I think you're exactly right. I can feel it too. You're on to something. Kook, radio please, kind sir. Light up the bitch box. Time for a SITREP."

On "bitch box" everyone could hear from the speaker at Kook's back. They didn't see the lieutenant acting like a clown too often, so the impact was all the greater. A moment of levity to break the continual tension over who would be the next to die. Everyone gathered around as the line of tired soldiers began compressing from the rear.

"Six-two, this is six-two bravo, how copy, over?"

There was some static. They had a connection thanks to some poor, hot, wet, bug-bitten special ops commo guys posted on a hilltop at a different "ass end of space" to their east.

"Lima Charlie, six-two bravo. What's up? Over."

"SITREP, six-two, position report, over."

"Six-two is ready to copy, Bravo, press ahead, over."

"Roger." Then the LT did something unexpected: he went into a perfect impression of Jerry Lewis in *The Nutty Professor*. "Six-two bravo is positioned dead center on Bum Fuck Egypt. How copy, six-two?"

They all heard laughter on the receiving end before the mic there was un-keyed.

Sometimes the human psyche is tuned to humor at the right place and the right time. They all got the giggles. More than giggles —there were guys on the ground laughing. Perhaps it was the incongruity of the platoon leader doing an impression, perhaps it was the laughter on the other end, but in a rare moment of levity and tension release it struck everyone as hilarious. And they acted their parts.

On the right side of the trail, near a rotting stump in the bramble, Sergeant Message saw what appeared to be a piece of trash. The area was pristine since it had not yet been overrun by GIs tossing C-ration cans, cigarette packs, candy wrappers, and every other type of trash that could be left in the jungle. When Craig was little he visited relatives in Staunton, Virginia. He was playing with neighborhood kids in a ditch that had no business being where it was—as there was no water to drain. A US Civil War belt buckle fell out of the dirt along with a handful of huge bullets corroded to white, looking like fishing weights.

His Uncle Pete had told them all the area had been the site of a lot of action during the Civil War ninety years before. "It's a trench," he explained. The soldiers from the north had had a lot of gear, so were wasteful. "If you find a CSA belt buckle from the South, that's something I want to see. The southern soldiers had nothing, so they wasted nothing. It's impossible to find their stuff. Union crap is easy pickings."

So the light bulb came on. *The VC and the NVA have nothing, so we don't find any evidence of them out here in the jungle,* Message thought. *When we, we the mighty Americans, leave an overnight NDP, it looks like a bunch of teenagers trashed the woods after a party.*

Weary of booby traps, he poked with the barrel of his M-16 at what appeared to be a little white book. It was about the size of a large note card folded in half, and still damp from rainfall, a tiny book softbound with a paper cover the color of a grocery bag. Inside it had stylized human stick figures and some kind of oriental characters. He ran it forward to his squad leader. "Bat, I think I found some intelligence."

"Sure as shit it's not in your head," Masterson replied.

Message held out the pamphlet. "This was back on the trail."

Sergeant Masterson took the little book and leafed through it. Some of the pages were stuck together from the moisture, but the paper was strong enough that it didn't tear when he pulled them apart. He laughed out loud. "What the fuck? This is some kind of guide to teach Charlie how to use a toilet, but it's for Chinks, not Dinks."

"What the fuck's the difference?"

"It's Chinese characters. Dinks use pretty normal writing, what with curlicues and such."

After passing it around, and before letting Lieutenant Bross in on the joke, it was Kook who hit pay dirt. "This is Korean. Look at the way the characters are written in block form, no swirls or curves. That's Korean."

Sergeant Maples spoke up. "Sergeant Rook, you were in Korea. Is that Korean?"

Sergeant Rook, who had been bullshitting people for thirteen years about serving in Korea and who wore a star on his CIB that he never earned, was put on the spot with a question he knew he couldn't answer with any authority since he had never set foot on the Korean peninsula. But no matter—he could weasel out of this one with the best of them. He took the little book and scanned it. "Damn, I almost didn't recognize it. Kook, you're right. It's Korean. This thing shows 'em how to use a shitter."

Maple made a face that looked like he'd just stepped in dog crap. "Who the fuck needs instructions on using the john?"

Kook answered. "They poop in holes in the floor in Korea.

This tells 'em, 'If you come across a toilet, don't stand on the seat. Put your ass on the seat and your feet on the floor.' See the X through the guy standing on the seat."

Walking back from point and joining in on the conversation, Lieutenant Bross said, "Whatcha got?"

Sergeant Rook handed him the pamphlet. "Shows dinks how to take a shit using a toilet."

Lieutenant Bross laughed with the rest of them. "Who believes in UFOs? It's like some alien spaceship dropped this to confuse us all."

Maple said, "Do you see any cameras? Maybe we're on *Candid Camera* or in an episode of *The Twilight Zone*."

Everyone laughed.

Lieutenant Bross couldn't make heads or tails of it. As he put it in the cargo pocket of his fatigue trousers, he wondered to himself, *This is pretty new paper. Are the VC working with Koreans? Are we working with Koreans?* Few below the level of MACV knew the answer to either of those questions.

27 August 1967
Between Rah and Letia Dadiou, Quảng Nam Province, South Vietnam

Kook spent a lot of time thinking about the necessity of war. He seldom vocalized his internal questions and thoughts, but he did jot some of them down every day in blue university exam books his parents had found in his stuff and sent to him.

　　—*If communism is so bad, then why are the NVA and VC fighting so hard? How could it be worse than what we're dealing these people now?*

　　—*How many villages will burn under the guise of making friends and searching for VC?*

　　—*Aren't we creating VC with every village destroyed?*

　　—*Needs of the Vietnamese people: water, rice, roof, sleep, poop, piss. Luxuries: cloth, scrap corrugated steel, footwear. Needs of the GI: I don't have enough paper in this little book.*

He stowed his pen in his pocket. He'd never leave it on the ground, though he did imagine that every ballpoint he had ever lost would be returned to him in heaven one day.

They all stood from the thirty-minute break, stretched, and tried to pull their sweat-soaked T-shirts away from their skin. Paco Hernandez stepped off the trail while tugging at his web gear and belt. He had a bad case of the runs and had already left a few squirts off trail here and there during breaks. Not wanting to step in something he'd already left behind, he worked his way through the brush and trees to a new spot. He understood the danger, and he tried to be careful, but he picked a spot where it was easy to enter the underbrush—and therefore had been recognized as a potential entrance by whoever placed a mine to protect it. Hernandez tripped the claymore and instantly lost both his legs to mid-thigh. He was unconscious before Doc could get to him. Dead before anyone else showed up.

Fifteen were alive. All were furious with the world.

CHAPTER 21

27 August 1967
Quảng Nam Province, South Vietnam
The Culprit

By mid-July 1953 and the end of the Korean War, the Republic of Korea, ROK military had established itself as a stalwart defender of democracy and capitalism against a determined communist enemy. In the earliest days following the end of the conflict and the final defeat and retreat of the French in Vietnam, leaders there were reaching out to South Korea to assist in their fight against a well-supported communist aggressor from the north.

In summer 1965 the request was formalized. South Vietnam's Prime Minister Nguyễn Cao Kỳ reached out to South Korea for assistance. And before the end of the Vietnam conflict in the mid-1970s, more than three hundred thousand ROK Army, Air Force, and Marines were supporting the allied effort in South Vietnam.

In a tri-lateral agreement between South Korea, South Vietnam, and the United States, the US agreed to equip ROK forces and to pay for all their associated expenses. What was known to few was that the US paid, in part, by the soldier, airman, or marine—and at a pay scale that equaled that of the equivalent ranked US soldier. It was a windfall for South Korea, as they paid their soldiers and marines a pittance and pocketed the difference as a buttress to support a post-war, still-struggling economy. In public discourse, the Korean National Council voiced the reluctance of the Korean people to provide Vietnam support—but it was also, in part, won over by the economic argument.

By August, just two months to the day after Ky's request, South Korea had boosted the size of the Second Marine Regiment to brigade proportions and moved them on US troop ships to South Vietnam. The majority of the soldiers in Vietnam had no knowledge of Korean involvement; however, they did reuse those same ships for large US troop redeployments, and US GIs found evidence the Koreans left behind: tiny pamphlets prepared by some strategic communications team to teach the Korean regulars to use western toilets, icons of western civilization many had never encountered.

The Korean effort was intended to be coherent and part of an overall plan. But to ensure complete, if unintended, adherence to Clausewitz's "fog of war," the units were initially trained at Pohang, then moved to Cam Ranh Bay, then Tuy Hòa, then Chu Lai, and then to the four winds.

One military genius, whose name is lost to history, determined it would be best to combine ROK Army and ROK Marine units into a single brigade-sized organization. For reasons of military cultural difference, that plan turned out to be a dismal failure. An absolute disaster. The larger force was ROK Marines, and so the army was voted out. In mid-1966 a company-sized unit of the ROK Army was split out of the brigade and covertly moved to conduct a mission in an area of the Central Highlands where activity was not well understood. That was an understatement. Their mission was to seize, hold, defend, cordon, and search a swath of territory in the South Vietnamese Central Highlands in the western quadrant of Quảng Nam Province, near and east of the border between South Vietnam and Laos.

In rugged terrain, enveloped in impenetrable triple-canopy jungle, the new company, led by a Korean War veteran, took the reins and far exceeded any possible expectations. They dug in for the duration. Flown to Da Nang on cargo aircraft, and moved west in five-ton and deuce-and-a-half trucks as far as primitive roads would take them, the company commander was determined to place his force on the "X" that had been haphazardly drawn on a map by his battalion commander while a US Army colonel looked on.

One hundred percent equipped by the US military, though with some Korean-war-era weapons that were being replaced at a snail's pace, the South Korean Army company was a four-platoon fighting force built on the US Army model. A heavy weapons platoon lost three soldiers to death by heat exhaustion in the effort to move about twice as many 82mm mortars as were needed to supply a firebase supporting a battalion.

Instead of demolishing a portion of the jungle to set up a small firebase for coincident operations, the company commander, though experienced, took his orders at face value. He was on the "X." He owned the terrain. He and his four platoons dug in and awaited orders.

Though tactics and techniques were shared between the ROK Army and the US Army, with just over a year in country, the Korean soldiers had never imagined a mountainous jungle like the one they found themselves in. South Korea has a reliable monsoon season, but the peninsula is encased in wooded northern forests, not tropical rainforests. At least that's how it seemed to them.

Months passed: July, August, and September. Weekly airdrops kept the unit resupplied, but the soldiers were miserable. No enemy, no mission, just working to stay alive against the elements. And the elements were a capable enemy. Radio contact was intermittent or non-existent. The best the company commander could hope for was passing an occasional message to an aircrew back to his battalion commander. But the two individuals in the company who had some facility with the English language spoke with such a thick accent, they were not well understood by anyone in the air—that is, the US Air Force. The US Air Force had no idea the ROK Army was even on the ground in the first place, so they assumed when they took a radio transmission that it was a counterintelligence scheme from Hanoi. Even when a hapless pilot would listen, Battalion rarely had any idea what it was the company was attempting to transmit. It was like the exercise in communications class where a message starts on one side of the room and is 99 percent changed by the time it passes from thirty mouths to thirty ears.

Morale went from bad to worse to none. October ninth was Hangul Day, a national Korean celebration to commemorate the invention of the Korean written language. Many of the soldiers wondered if they would be stuck in the bug and leech-infested jungle until Christmas. Though Christmas was not a national holiday, sixty percent of the soldiers were Christian.

When a company digs in for the long haul, an accepted practice is to surround encampments with perimeter protection. Where the US Army had chain link and concertina, the ROK Army had a US supply of anti-personnel mines, chiefly M-14s and M-18 claymores. They would serve the purpose of defense well, the inventory was limitless, and ROK Army soldiers were well trained in mine deployment.

Mostly. A key procedure in deploying mines, and mandatory for a US unit, was to annotate, in detail, the location of all mine deployments on a common-use map. But these platoon leaders were an apparent comedy troupe of bungling idiots. So when, in November 1966, the company was given orders to move out, to hump east where trucks would meet them, and the company commander ordered the deactivation and recovery, or safe explosive release, of all defensive mines, the platoon leaders saluted and trotted off to comply. But all four were well aware, from weeks of conversation on the matter, that no one had anything other than a vague idea of where any of their deployed mines were located. Everyone in the company knew well which lines of trees, rocks, streams, and other features not to cross—but nothing more specific. They'd been lucky that, with the few exceptions of a soldier here and there being blown to smithereens, their bodies buried *in situ*, they hadn't suffered more casualties.

The mines had been placed haphazardly. There were no maps to mark. They were camouflaged well when first placed, and by now, after months of water-fed jungle undergrowth, even with the monsoon on the wane, they'd never be found. Except by accident. Except by tragedy. The M-14 toe poppers were set-and-leave, intended to maim, not necessarily to kill. Textbook claymore deployment normally required the use of a "clacker" operated by a human about to be overrun. The soldier produced a manual electric charge to the firing pin—no batteries were required. They'd run out of juice quickly in the jungle anyway. The Koreans, however, devised ingenious methods to set the mines with trip systems for ambush-like power. That is, if you tripped the wire, you generally got the bad side of the mine. *Front Toward Enemy.*

The Third Platoon leader was selected by the others to break the bad news to the company commander. He was nervous. His fear played out when he was summarily beaten with the butt of a rifle for insolence. Pressure increased on the others. In the process of working in parts of the jungle where no one had walked in months, eight more soldiers lost their lives attempting to clear mines without the benefit of any suitable tools to do so

On November 12, 1966 the Korean company began the difficult march to an eastern valley where they would meet again with some semblance of civilization. Behind them in the Central Highlands of Vietnam a short distance east of the Laotian border, they left an estimated two hundred and twenty activated claymore and toe popper mines. Participants in a secret mission, their presence in the area was lost to memory.

CHAPTER 22

28 August 1967

East-Southeast of Rah, Quảng Nam Province, South Vietnam

The last thing that went through Masterson's mind was a chunk of steel. It was about the size of a bottle cap folded in half. It tore through the strap on the inside of his helmet just before it entered his skull, going from one side straight through to the other.

Rook took Masterson's helmet off. A couple of the guys saw him inspect the shrapnel and then look around like he was planning to swipe it. Perhaps it was a puzzled look as he wondered, "Why not a ball? Why a piece of folded metal?"

As usual, Rook stormed off while screaming obscenities that might have been heard all the way across the valley if not for the interference of the jungle. Once again he unloaded a full clip into nothingness, the nothingness that had just taken the life of one of his best. "Show your faces you motherfucking cowards!" Then the sound of automatic fire to accentuate his point. Once again, the actions of this "leader" spun the survivors into a frenzy. The platoon was upset and frustrated. Everyone was pissed off, crying, screaming, and shooting into the sky. There was a momentary loss of control.

Lieutenant Bross had a passing thought about the poor example Rook was setting, but he got his mind back on his dead man. "Kook, get Dust Off moving."

"Already done, sir."

Bat was KIA. KIA just like that. They'd heard a click, then Bat took a half a running step and crumpled to the ground like a marionette whose strings had been cut. When Bross held Bat's head, he imagined he could hear the man's heart screaming, fountains of blood spreading like the bubble voice of a cartoon character in the Sunday comics. But this wasn't funny. It wasn't a bit funny.

Now we are fifteen. Or is it fourteen? Bross thought. *What have I gotten myself into? There are men dying while walking where I ordered them to walk.*

The dead in Second Platoon would be remembered by their families only through pictures—except for James "Bat" Masterson. He had recorded tapes over a tiny reel-to-reel deck his father had sent him in a care package. The whole thing was a giant pain in the ass—tapes and batteries and trying to keep it all working in this Godforsaken climate—but he was committed.

He had told everyone, "Twenty years after I die, my daughter will be able to hear how much I loved her." Now this was real. Now she would be able to hear—if her own sobbing wasn't enough to drown out the voice of a father she never knew.

Sergeant Nicolletti stepped over to where Lieutenant Bross sat cross-legged on the ground, his lap full of blood, stroking Masterson's head. And shedding a few tears.

"Sir, no doubt a bounder, but not what we've seen so far. This one was larger, too good and too effective to have come from China. I think it was probably US-made. If we'd been tighter, there'd be three dead instead of one. Masterson took the main part of the blast. It looks bad now, but if you hadn't been haranguing us to keep our separation we'd have two or three dead." He took a pondering look around. "At least."

Lieutenant Bross held up the shrapnel they'd found in Bat's helmet. "Doesn't take much. Doesn't take much." He regained his composure and stood, brushing off his pants and looking at the spreading bloodstain in his lap. "Looks like I pissed my pants." Looking over to Nicolletti, he said, "Your squad now, Nick."

"Got it, sir. Message'll be my number one."

"Right," Bross responded. He looked at Kook and added, "Tell Dust Off, no rush. In fact they can send a slick. No docs needed here. We're going to cool it here for a while and think this out."

"Yes, sir."

Lieutenant Bross looked up the trail and saw what was left of a textbook infantry patrol spread out at the ready in defensive positions, sitting on fallen logs, leaning against trees, hiding in the shade of Jurassic-era plants. To the rear was a worthless platoon sergeant sitting on his haunches, smoking a bent sweat-soaked cigarette, content to let everyone else do the work. "Sean, wrap him up best you can," Bross said. "If you need more supplies, ask Dust Off if they can spare some. No need to get that chopper bloodier than it already is."

He looked ahead to the first two riflemen he saw, Jiggles and The Knife. They turned their heads without adjusting their defensive positions. "You guys come with me," the lieutenant said.

When they were out of earshot of the mayhem, the three hopped to and followed Lieutenant Bross to the shade of a tree where Sergeant Rook was taking a siesta.

Lieutenant Bross looked over his shoulder and said, "Keep a watch out while Sergeant Rook and I talk."

"Yes, sir," the two men replied in unison.

"No listening in."

"Not a chance, sir," The Knife said, hoping the lieutenant would shoot Sergeant Rook on the spot. He wondered to himself, *Isn't there something in the UCMJ that says you can shoot shitheads in combat? US shitheads?* He could only hope.

It was no surprise to Darren that Sergeant Rook didn't stand when he approached. He could have been the four-star MACV CG and Rook would just as soon have given him the finger. Bross thought to himself, *If this sack of crap is an army lifer, God save the army.* Every leadership lesson he'd ever had said there was no need to scream, nor to even raise your voice with the troops. Your rank insignia did the screaming for you. *Though one could argue whether a first lieutenant outranks anyone.* The power was in your words. Subordinates would listen when superiors spoke.

But Lieutenant Bross was not in a leadership mood. What came next was a rare display of uncontrolled emotion. The Knife and Jiggles later used the words "maniac" and "popped a cork." "The LT screamed like a dad whose teenage son had just hit Mom. I think he was taking Bat's death out on Rook." "Motherfucker deserved it. That's what I say. Fucking had it coming."

Lieutenant Bross approached Rook and, in a controlled yell, said, "STAND THE FUCK UP!"

Rook flicked his cigarette butt into the woods and slowly rose, slapping dust off his butt.

"WHAT THE FUCK WAS THAT?"

"Guess I lost it," Rook said while kicking the ground and looking at his boots.

"GUESS YOU FUCKING LOST IT?" Lieutenant Bross heard PFC Mack snickering, so he toned it down. "You guess you lost it? You're supposed to be one of the leaders of this platoon. What kind of leadership was that?"

"Not the good kind."

"No shit, not the good kind. We've lost five guys. It does us no good to have you running off all half-cocked like some psycho." It was a moment filled with emotion for Darren. He was simultaneously choking up with sadness while screaming at Rook in anger, snot from his nose commingling with tears.

"Four."

"What?

"Four guys. We lost four guys."

"Five, and I am counting," Bross snorted and sniffed, shaking in anger. "Everyone is in a nightmare. They are on me, motherfucker. Ty, Byers, Pixie, Paco, and now Masterson."

"I don't count Ty, he was a VC traitor."

"Give me a break. Ty was attached to this platoon with

orders from MACV. He was ours. He's lost. Dead. He's on us. Fuck, if he had been here Masterson might be alive." Lieutenant Bross paused for a pregnant moment and wiped his face with the backs of both hands. "It doesn't matter. We need to focus on the soldiers who are still here. I promised these guys I would do everything I could to keep them among the living. I cannot keep that promise without your help." He tried to keep his emotion in check, but his voice was filled with desperation for assistance. "I need your help, Rook." He wiped his angry face again. "I need your fucking help. Do you get it?"

Rook looked up, nonplussed. He showed no remorse, no contrition, nothing that might be a normal response to an angry and distraught superior in his face. "We need some Charlie to kill," he said.

"What the fuck does that mean?"

"This is shit, Lieutenant. They're killing us and we have no one to take it out on. They're fucking cowards."

What Darren heard in that exchange was the word "Lieutenant." This may have been the first time Sergeant Rook had ever addressed him by his rank. That was progress. He straightened up a little and regained his composure as if speaking to a peer. "Nick thinks it was a US bounder. Where does the VC get those?"

"Steals 'em. Down south we were guarding a bridge for two months. The locals would steal anything not nailed down. Search and destroy."

"I told you, we are not on a search and destroy mission."

"Got it, but sir, Charles can't use anti-personnel mines they don't have, so torch the fucking villages and find that shit."

Bross ignored the comment, thinking back to how long it had been since he'd seen a village. "Can I count on you, Sergeant Rook? I know you've lived through more crap than I've ever seen, but I need you to use that experience to keep these guys alive."

"I will work on it, but it frustrates the livin' shit out of me when I can't find the assholes that're killing 'em."

29 August 1967

Southeast of Rah, Hein District, Quảng Nam Province, South Vietnam

PFC Chamberlain broke the lieutenant's morbid daydream. "Hey LT, do we ever get to do anything but fucking walk?"

Sergeant Maples responded, "Shut up, Loo. The lieutenant ain't got no time for your stupid-ass questions."

"Sarge, on that TV show *Combat*, those guys get to ride in Jeeps sometimes. How come we never get to ride? How come we always gotta fuckin' hike? If we'd been ridin' instead of walkin', maybe Bat would be alive and we'd be changing a flat tire."

"Flat tire? Fuck you," Maples replied. "We're on trails, Loo. See roads much? Anyway, mines can blow the whole front end of a Jeep off. Woulda killed everyone when it landed on top of them upside down."

Waterloo gave it some thought. "Okay, we'd be Jeepless, but maybe we'd be alive. Maybe Bat would be alive. I wouldn't be carrying his shit around in my pockets. Look at my fuckin' fatigue pants. I don't see any of his brains on you. I don't really have room for all his shit in my ruck. Do we really need to carry his fucking tape recorder around?"

At that, Lieutenant Bross stopped the march to let Maples and Loo catch up. He'd had enough. He stepped over, looked at Private First Class Chamberlain square in the eye, and said, "Waterloo, I don't want to hear any more crap like that. You're carrying Bat's gear for two reasons. His family is going to want it and I trust you to take care of it. Do I need to pass this job off to someone else?"

Loo hadn't realized the lieutenant could hear him from way up front. "No sir, I got it."

Maples added in, "Loo, if you don't shut the fuck up, it's gonna be *your* brains. Now shut the fuck up."

Spread out, ten to twenty meters apart—a lesson reinforced after losing Masterson—what was left of the patrol continued climbing. This break in the pace gave the first squad grenadier, Stan Peckham from Alamogordo, New Mexico, time, like Paco before him, to step off the trail and into the bush to use "the facilities." The nightmare happened again. He was tiptoeing, being careful, and looking at the placement of every footstep. The sequence of explosions was deafening, but recognizable to both squads. A string, a daisy chain of claymores. A rip of lightning and a crack of thunder feet away, then again, then again. Ringing in the ears as Peckham flew out of the brush, jungle fatigue pants and skivvies around his ankles, into the middle of the trail with the top of his head sheared off. Blood. Chunks. *Fuck!*

A short, timid investigation, full of concern for the potential of other mines in the area, revealed that he'd sidled up to a large tree, taken off his steel pot, and had probably set his M-16 and M-203 on a tripwire. It just didn't look like a place where anyone would set a string of mines.

This time Sergeant Rook kept his cool. Or rather, this time Sergeant Rook outwardly kept his cool, while fighting internal demons telling him to react like a madman.

The Dust Off door gunner, the same guy who was on crew Sunday and the week before that, commented just before loading everything back up, "You guys are in the shit. Never seen anything like it. Death, but no enemy. We're hopping in with door gunners but they don't see nothin'. And trust me, those guys are looking, and looking hard."

Once again, Lieutenant Bross called a halt to the patrol. "Sergeant Rook, gather the squad leaders, team leads, and anyone else you think might have an opinion on this."

They sat in a shady circle. "Captain Evans is asking me what the hell is going on. Why would anyone put a daisy chain of claymores off trail in the middle of nowhere?" He looked around.

Message spoke up. "Boss, looks like classic tactics to me. Protect your position."

"Your night position," Waterloo added.

"That's what we're all thinking, but what position? There's no one here, no one there."

Message continued, "Maybe it was a position before we got here."

"I hear you, Message, but I gotta trust that MACV SOG guy. The reason we're up here is because this territory is unknown. No one has been here since the French left. They sure as heck didn't have claymores."

Sergeant Rook said, "Lieutenant, I know you don't want to hear it, but it's VC. There's no other explanation. Fuckin' Chuckin'."

"I have no better ideas, Sergeant Rook. You're probably right, but in my short time in Nam I have come to respect these guys. They don't seem to be stupid. Tell me, why does VC daisy-chain claymores where they'll have no effect?"

"Sir, with respect," Message commented, "looks like they had an effect to me. Stan is flying home in a bag."

30 August 1967
South of Rah, Quảng Nam Province, South Vietnam

"Maples, Owens, Mack, Mickey and Rook—front and center." The group hopped to, guessing something was up. They'd all figured out the lieutenant had called together the remaining Rangers.

Lieutenant Bross sat down on the edge of a fallen log and crossed his feet in front of him. "Everyone take a seat."

Rook took a seat to his left. The others found spots within talking range. Kook joined them, knowing the boss wouldn't want to be far from the radio.

"I want ideas," Bross said. "What the hell is going on? How in the world are we in a patch of land with no human habitation but swimming in sophisticated mines all booby-trapped to kill?"

Rook spoke first. "Boss, I've said this before and I'll say it again. It's fuckin' VC." When he was excited, his southern accent was so thick it was difficult to understand.

"Thanks, First Sergeant, but I really want to hear what these guys have to say. I have some first-hand understanding of what they might have picked up at Ranger School regarding booby traps and remote activation of mines."

Maples was drawing circles in the dirt with a stick, but Darren could see on his face he wanted to talk. "Maples, what do you think?"

"Looks to me like this place was once a US encampment," Maples said. "Lots of soldiers. Spread out. Spread out too far. Some of this stuff is set up the way we prepare an NDP, but I've never seen these methods. Could be special ops guys, probably someone else, but it's really weird, LT."

"Thanks, Maple." The lieutenant looked over to Owens, who was seated next to Maples. "Owens, thoughts?"

"I agree with Maples, sir. This is the strangest thing I have ever seen. I hear what the platoon sergeant is saying, and he has a lot more experience in Nam than most of us put together,"—Rook sat up straighter and stretched out his chest—"but this doesn't feel like

VC. We seen VC in Lampshade Valley, but never saw anything like this."

Mickey chimed in. "Sir, I keep thinking back to that little shitter how-to book we found. Could there have been some other force here?"

"I was wondering the same thing, Mickey. Battalion 'went back to MACV,' or so they say. Word from the guys who are supposed to know is we're the first in recent history."

The Knife spoke up. "Sir. I've done a lot of hunting in the southeast US. This place kind of reminds me of the Georgia mountains where we all had a fun time during that block in Ranger School." The Rangers laughed. "This place is overgrown. No one has been here recently. It's not easy to rig a claymore as a booby trap."

Maple interrupted. "They told us it was against the law, or something like that."

"Geneva Convention," Mack said.

"Yeah, that."

The Knife continued, "LT, I doubt they taught you how to do it. None of you guys was in my Ranger class, but we had the old crusty lifer first sergeant who told us that one day we would want to place some defensive mines out there along trails to give advance warning of enemy approaching. Said it was really dangerous, because friendlies use the same trails as the dinks. But he did show us how. It wasn't in the official training syllabus… at least I don't think it was."

Lieutenant Bross was interested. "You're not wearing your

Ranger tab. You must be really close to sewing on corporal."

"Actually, one September, tomorrow, boss."

"Okay, Corporal Mack, do you remember enough to run everyone through it? We need to know enough to disarm if we find them before they find us."

The new corporal said, "Sir, from what I can tell, there is no one better at rooting out booby traps than Witz and Nick. I asked their secret. Say they look around and ask themselves 'Where would I put it?' We should bring them in on this before I start. To me it looks like every KIA is right where I would place the defense. It's also the place where we go to take a crap. Two plus two." The Knife was already removing an M-7 claymore bandolier from around his neck and shoulder. "I never intended to bring these along, but the ReSupp chopper didn't know."

Witz and Nicolletti hopped to and joined the group. Maples said, "The Knife is going to show us how to make a claymore into a booby trap."

"He called 'em mechanical ambushes, MAs for short. Illegal, I think," Nick replied.

"But, golden rule applies," The Knife said. "We need to know how they're fucking unto us so that we can fuck unto them first."

Heads nodded all around.

Corporal Peter Mack stood and held the bandolier open, exposing the contents. "As you know, we have to charge the blasting cap with the clacker. No batteries out here. Since there's no one around to push the clacker in a set trap, you have to have another way." He pulled the claymore from its pouch. "Obviously I don't have any on me, but you need a mechanical, non-electric blasting cap that you can rig up to a tripwire. They make 'em; I've seen 'em. Not made for this purpose, but they work just fine." The Knife had their undivided attention.

Rook spoke softly, under his breath really. "Makes sense. Fuck, those batteries we used were fuckin' worthless. Didn't last two weeks."

Owens said, "Ah, now it's coming back to me. MA, mechanical ambush. That's it! There were a bunch of guys doing this in secret. Now I know what they were talking about."

Mack nodded. "Two guys. The guy placing the mine holds the clacker, just like normal. Place the mine." He bent down and picked up a smooth round stone. "I'm going to pretend with this rock." He sounded like a seasoned military instructor, careful to cover every detail. "You take the mine out of the bandolier like this, turn the legs toward the back, then down. Spread the legs just like normal."

Rook spoke up, "We know how to set a claymore, Knife. Get to the good part."

"Got it, Sarge, I don't like fucking with these things. It helps me to go over every step so I don't end up like Pixie and Stan."

"Go on, Knife," Lieutenant Bross said.

"Yes, sir, I can cut some corners with the rock here. Front Toward Enemy. Aim the mine... all that shit." He looked at the rock, then the claymore in the bandolier. He tossed the rock and removed the claymore. "Now for the good part. Take your blasting cap—pretending here since I don't have one. Squeeze it to the firing device. Get some tape and attach the device to a tripwire of your choosing."

"Guys down south had family send monofilament in care packages," Rook said.

There were confused looks. Rook mistook the reaction for them not knowing what monofilament was; the truth was, they were just surprised that Sergeant Rook seemed to know all about MAs.

"You know, that clear plastic fishing line," Rook said. "Clothespins, too."

"So you've seen this in the field, Rook?" the lieutenant asked.

"Not with a claymore, LT, but I'm not gonna try to tell you there's not some guys out there who are pretty good at setting MAs. But again, I don't really know one way or the other." There it was: Rook weaseling out of any and all responsibility for knowing anything whatsoever.

The Knife resumed the lesson. "Now you have to secure the firing device to something that won't move. That means beating a stake into the ground or having a small tree exactly the right place. Now put another blasting cap on this end of the cord. Put that cap in the detonator well right here." He pointed. "Then you have to tape it in so it'll stay. Take the tripwire and attach it to the firing device—the ring is good here. Now, stretch the tripwire, connect it to two other stakes, and you're ready to go."

"Not sure I get it completely, Knife," Owens said.

"Me neither," Maple added.

"Fuck. We don't need this one." The Knife held up the claymore. "Let's do it for real."

"Everyone gather 'round," Sergeant Rook called out. "Let's move over there where there's more room."

"Owens, I'm gonna need some help," The Knife said.

He walked through the steps. "Mine here." He extended the legs and placed the mine, being careful to face it in the right direction and taking pains to actually aim it. "Anchor stake here behind the mine. Attach the firing wire to it here, but leave some slack. Now, unroll the wire like this." He pulled it from the bandolier. "Now pull it over here to the right of the claymore. Anchor it here. Now it's getting fun. Normally you would need a clothespin, like Sergeant Rook mentioned, to keep the contacts from touching each other, but I didn't plan on drying clothes so I'm fresh out." He took his knife and whittled off the end of a stick, cutting a smooth split in one end. "This is crude, and won't last long."

"Bamboo works the best," Rook added. Everyone turned to him in further wonderment, beginning to think they were listening to the wrong expert, Ranger tab or not.

"I'll bet it does," The Knife said. "Now, who has a C-ration plastic spoon?" Someone pulled one from the tiny slot above their breast pocket. "This keeps the contacts from touching. Put that here. Then caps here. Then pull the wire like so. Then tighten it up here. Then cover it up a little without tripping the wire."

By the time he was finished it was a work of art. Everyone was impressed. "So what we're all looking for is something that looks like this—but it will be covered over even better and impossible to see. They might not have spoons or clothespins. If the tripwire is thin enough, monofilament like Sergeant Rook said, you'll never feel it. Boom! This one is set up a little tighter than I would do it for real, and this loop over here is not going to be on anything you see."

"What's that for?" the lieutenant asked.

"So we can pretend someone walked into it and pulled the tripwire. Ready to blow, sir?"

Bross nodded. "Everyone back up, let's don't tempt fate."

When everyone was out of lethal range, Mack called out, "Ready on the right, ready on the left, ready on the firing line." Like a dutiful range controller he looked left, looked right, looked behind him, and got a thumbs-up from Lieutenant Bross. "Fire in the hole!" He pulled the loop.

Nothing happened.

"What the fuck?" Rook said.

Lieutenant Bross also had a puzzled look.

"Told you sir, we need those special mechanical blasting caps. I just simulated them with electrical tape."

They all laughed, a little relieved they wouldn't have to risk an explosion in front of their faces.

"You had us going," Bross said. "Thanks for the lesson, Mack. Hook up a clacker and get rid of that thing."

"Yes, sir."

Four minutes later they did get a first-hand reminder of the destructive power of a claymore mine. And they all agreed that the sound of a claymore was unique. Some of their guys had been killed by claymores—they'd heard that sound—and some not. It was curious.

31 August 1967
South of Rah, Quảng Nam Province, South Vietnam

They were skittish, jumpy, and terrified of their own shadows. The group lesson on the use of claymore mines as booby traps hadn't made anyone feel better; rather it had reinforced in their minds the awesome power of this staple weapon and kept them confused regarding its ubiquitous presence here in this remote area of Vietnam. But they did get better at finding the claymore traps.

After becoming convinced of their personal prowess, the lieutenant put Witz and Nicolletti on a semblance of dangerous point and slack, though others were in a shared lead with rifles at the ready. Witz and Nicolletti acted as a team, using their "Where would I put it?" methodology. Bross further ordered that no one would go off trail to defecate. When they needed a nature break, they would poop on the trail behind the last man.

They found one, then two. Disarming was straightforward— a simple cutting of the arming lanyard. Then they'd attach a clacker and safely dispose of the claymore. Later, they thought the better of making so much noise and just removed all possible firing mechanisms.

They got better and better at this, and saved some lives in the process, but in that process everyone failed to reconsider the potential presence of any other type of mine, particularly the M-14 toe popper that might have been renamed with a more ominous moniker after one blew half of Witz's foot off. It had been over ten days since Marty Byers bled out from an exploding M-14 mine in the crotch. The one that got Witz worked the way it was designed.

"Fuckin' slopes got their hands on a fucking M-14 again, LT!" Rook screamed. "I can hear *those* motherfuckers. Now *we* carry claymores for everything, but M-14s are a lot better and lighter for setting up night defense. Only problem is they're plastic, so they're hard as a motherfucker to locate after you place 'em. But, I repeat. How'd those zipperheads get their hands on 'em?"

Nicolletti stepped over. "Thought you said they stole 'em." He turned to Bross. "He's dead on, LT. Little three-pound plastic can with a sort of round convex spring inside. Ever seen one of those mint cans you have to press the center to get the top off? Like that. Spring pushes a spark into some C4 and blows straight up. That's what blew half of Witz's foot off."

The war was over for Witz. Doc saved most of his foot by moving the tourniquet below the ankle. It was a more difficult placement, but Dust Off would take some time, so he had some flex. The stump was gushing at a rate that would have led to bleed-out. But Doc was good. He affixed a web belt just above the ankle to stop the flow. Every bone in Witz's left foot had been shattered. Morphine relieved most of his pain. Witz was conscious and watched Doc as he stopped the flow of blood and was able to clean and dress the wound.

"Witz, how're you doing, my man?"

"Good thing it's my left foot. I do most of my ass-kicking with my right."

Rook and Lieutenant Bross were standing by. Along with Doc, they all laughed.

"Looks like you're gonna live, Witz," the lieutenant said.

"Yes, sir. I'm going to miss you guys. I'm already teary-eyed. No long goodbyes, please. We'll always have these times." As he said this, he pantomimed flicking a tear from the corner of his right eye.

Kook joined in. "Fuck that, we're planning a farewell party for you. It involves a free ride in a helicopter and an all-expenses paid vacation trip to The World."

"Probably take you to Japan first, Witz," Doc added.

"Then that's where I'll start ass-kicking again." Witz looked down at the mess and was unable to hold back his emotions. This was real. He was wounded, but he knew it could have been worse. His mind raced to the weeks to come: a return home, rehabilitation, and a life with the possibility of a missing foot. "Can you save most of it, Doc?"

"It's just about impossible to stop the blood flow if I use a tourniquet below your ankle, but let me see what I can do. It'll be at least an hour until you're in front of a real doc. That could be too long to save any live tissue."

"Then put it on my foot"—Witz reached down and pointed to his heel—"and let me bleed a little. I'd rather bleed a little than lose the foot."

Doc finished the dressing on the wound, left the tourniquet in place above the ankle, and crafted a smaller tourniquet from clacker wire that wrapped from the arch to the heel and over the instep. He used a metal spoon to cinch the three-way contraption. To test it he released the top tourniquet and watched the dressing saturate with blood. A single additional turn of the spoon made Witz cry out in pain.

"Can't do it, Witz."

"Yes you can. Leave it just like that. I can take the pain. Next time I see you we'll play a little kickball."

While they were all waiting for Dust Off, Sergeant Rook joined the group. His M-16 was bent at a thirty-degree angle between the stock and barrel. Witz was eye level with the rifle and noticed the damage first. "Sarge, what the hell happened to your weapon?"

They all looked down. Lieutenant Bross turned on his heel and shook his head at another notch in Rook's lack-of-leadership column.

"Nothin', I dropped it," Rook said. He addressed Witz: "Where's yours? We're gonna trade. You're not gonna need yours for a while."

They had all heard commotion in the near distance—someone beating the crap out of something. There was a tree back there somewhere that had been on the receiving end of the wrath of Lionel Rook.

Rook stepped over to Lieutenant Bross and said, "I saw your

look. Not much I can say. At least I tried to keep it pretty much to myself this time. Can't take much more of this, boss. Not sure if you've noticed, but I'm not the only one pissed off. Look around at the guys."

Bross did look back, but he noticed nothing untoward. He reached out to take the weapon, which Rook was reluctant to give up. "What are you, twelve?" the lieutenant asked. "How're we going to explain this?"

"Boss, no one's gonna give a shit. I'll toss it on the litter with Witz. We'll clear it up with the armorers when we get back."

"Might cause a Report of Survey. We can lose and screw up just about anything, but an M-16 is a different story."

"Got it, LT. Next time I'll use the business end with lead flying out."

"Next time, grow the fuck up."

"Trying to, LT. Just tired of our guys getting whacked."

Lieutenant Bross looked at this guy, ten years his senior, and wondered why he was in war and in a position near the armpit of Earth having to give advice. "We're all tired, Sergeant Rook. We're all tired of losing guys. They need you. They need us. We have to keep it together to get out of here with the pieces we have left."

Rook sat alone in the dirt and raged. The army was supposed to have been there for him to deal with his demons. He spoke aloud to himself as if there was someone else in his poncho-covered foxhole who needed his lesson in leadership. "Now I'm stuck with a fucking lieutenant, a pussy platoon leader, a goddamn pacifist, a wimp. War is about killing people. What does this fairy idiot not fucking understand?" Whispering to himself, he added, "Did I say that too loud?"

In Darlac, operating out of Ban Me as a squad leader, he had found his sadistic soulmate in one Sergeant First Class Stockman. *Blue Stockman. No shit, his name is Blue,* Rook recalled writing in a letter to his uncle back in Arcadia. His uncle was the only one who called him Red and got away with it. *It's like this guy and I were made to meet each other. Me red hair and him fucking Blue! And we're both fucking White! Red, White and fucking Blue!*

"Sarge, you okay in there?" Corporal Owens called out.

"I'm good, just writing a letter and making sure it sounds right," Rook lied. Muffled, but still aloud, just not loud enough to be heard over light rainfall on the ponchos all around, Rook went on talking to himself as if carrying on a conversation with an alter ego. "Fuck, I need to quiet down, it's The Knife. Or was that Owens? One of those Ranger fucks. Who the fuck do they think they are, anyway?"

A passing wave of sadness passed through him. Rook was not a maudlin person. Not sentimental. In fact, since he didn't care much for *any* humans, he was confused over why he was so angry about losing guys in this patrol. That faraway cloudy look in their eyes jazzed him a little. *One second they're looking at me. The next second they're looking at heaven. Or hell. I'm gonna be looking at hell.* He smiled.

But he thought again about Blue, Blue Stockman, until tears

welled up. He felt somehow responsible for Blue's death. In fact, Rook himself had shot Blue in the side of the head, but Rook felt neither remorse nor culpability. "It wasn't my fault. The moron went all idiot on me. Motherfucker deserved it. He killed himself. Yeah, really it was suicide," Rook said aloud. Too loud. "That .762 round could have come from anywhere. No way to track it to me. Not out in this shithole with bullets flying everywhere."

Owens shifted in his tiny, muddy spot, now straining to hear. They were all worried about the platoon sergeant. "Sergeant. Let me know if you need any help over there!"

"MIND YOUR OWN FUCKING BUSINESS, KNIFE!"

"Owens. It's Owens, Sarge. But got it."

Now keeping his psychotic thoughts to himself, but still speaking inside his mind, Rook mused, *My life was really made for this. There's guys like me all over the planet. If not, then why is there war where you can shoot dinks between the eyes, fuck dinkettes, strangle old dinks, slide a knife between the tits of dinks right under their solar plexus, and no Judge fucking Miller, no Bob Hagen, no Mister fucking Sherman, no Bidwell, not even poor old Major Hill to tell someone over and over that I'm a bad man.*

As his rant built to a crescendo, he once again spoke aloud. "Someone is going to pay for this. Someone is going to pay for this. Someone is going to pay for this. SOMEONE IS GOING TO PAY FOR THIS!"

Owens heard that and made a mental note to talk to Nicolletti.

Rook opened his green memo pad and clicked his flashlight on with the red filter in place. The pencil was hard to make out in the dim light, but he said the names of the dead aloud. "Fucking Dink Tiger Scout. Marty Byers—nigger, but still one of the guys. Pixie—good man, could have fought at the Alamo. Paco and Peckham—spics, but better'n niggers. And Bat Masterson. I really liked that guy. Tears? Is them tears? No, I got something in my eye… Someone is going to fucking pay."

Again, aloud, but not too loud: "Fucking Miller thought I was killing dogs. That dipshit." Rook thought back to the glassy eyes of that colored kid he'd held under water at the spillway while his uncle shot him in the heart. "Those dumb shits, they send me to reform school for killing dogs. If Willie had just worked it like I told him to, he'd probably still be alive. If he hadn't beat my brother up, he'd be alive."

That thought gave Rook what he called "the feeling" in his crotch. He worked himself a little—it didn't take much—before turning on his side and calling it a night.

1 September 1967
Southwest of Rah, Quảng Nam Province, South Vietnam

Early morning, still near trickling water, the mountain climes were teeming with birds. Peeking through the multiple layers of canopy, crepuscular rays of morning sun were able to find a way through from the east, lighting the trunks and branches of the largest trees any of them had ever seen. Craig Message was having a field day—a literal *field day*. He found some time with his open memo book to draw fine facsimiles of some new bird species that had remained quiet in poorer weather up until now.

"Yes, sir, God knows when they eat during crappy weather. Seems like when the sun pops out they come alive. Plus I can see them better, colors and all."

"Today starts September. Will they start migrating?" Bross asked.

"I expect they're already in it, LT. That's probably why I'm seeing more species than ever before. Three new warblers this morning alone."

"Keep at it. Interesting pastime and one way to keep your mind off the mayhem around here."

Rolling up the NDP was a well-oiled process by now. Everyone had a common goal and a list of personal tasks. Each soldier followed a mental checklist with the most important jobs being relegated to those who were proven entities. One such task was disarming the claymore mines placed on the NDP perimeter the night before. No one had seen Charlie, or any enemy in this part of Indian Country since dropping off the chopper, but the lieutenant wouldn't let them take any chances letting their guards down.

The sole remaining claymore expert was Nick Nicolletti, a new buck sergeant. The lieutenant asked Nick if he needed help. "You guys were great as a team, Nick, but I'm not sure a helper is going to help much. Witz's toe popper was unfortunate, but you guys found, what, a half dozen yesterday?"

"Five, LT."

"Five. You saved five guys, maybe more, from getting killed.

That's gotta make you feel pretty good. I know I appreciate it."

"Thanks, boss. I got it. Don't want to let these guys down."

Kook and Doc had left some miscellaneous clothes to dry hanging on stubby tree branches outside the defenses. "Nick, are we good to go?"

Nick had disarmed the claymore, but had not pulled it from the ground yet. "Yeah, you're good."

Kook and Doc stepped out of the perimeter and walked toward the hanging laundry. Nick reached for the disarmed claymore, and at the second he touched one of its legs, the weapon exploded—*front toward enemy*. Only this time, there was no enemy, only friendly. The one thing worse for a platoon leader than explaining enemy action for the death of a son, husband, and father, was explaining friendly fire.

At the far edge of the range of the claymore, Kook took a single pellet through the back of his right ear. It made a perfect hole in the cartilage in the center. When he had it repaired and sewed up by a nurse at the LZ later, the medical record would say "shrapnel through pinna conch." A half inch to the left and it would have entered his brain. He was bleeding like a teenage girl with new ear piercings, but otherwise was unharmed.

It was Doc who took the full force of the blast. He was twenty-five feet to Kook's right when the mine released its fury. Had he not been wearing his rucksack, he'd have been dead instantly. As it was, Doc took one to two hundred balls the backs of his knees, to his buttocks, across his back, and up to the back of his head. He fell face forward, unconscious.

Sergeant Rook was like a kid with a learning disability who can't remember instructions from one minute to the next. His immediate reaction had nothing to do with ensuring the safety of his patrol. Assuming another enemy mine explosion, he attempted to throw his steel pot down the hill as far as his arm and twisting torso would let it fly. Instead, the helmet hit a tree branch about six feet away with a loud "clunk," ricocheted back, and struck Rook square in the forehead, increasing his rage to a fever pitch.

Lieutenant Bross was preoccupied with response to the carnage, but later he would pull Sergeant Rook aside in private to tell him he would be relieved of his duties as platoon sergeant when they all returned to LZ Regulator. He had had enough.

For an uncomfortable minute, no one knew what to do. They had seen repeated life-threatening injuries too many times, but every one of those times, it was Doc MacNulty who would appear in the field of view with the speed of a lightning strike. Who was now going to respond to Doc?

He wasn't screaming. He was probably dead. Face down, dead. Kook was in mild shock, assuming he'd been hit worse than he was, but also because he was closest to Doc, who was now a bleeding mass on the ground to his right. He began screaming, "Medic! Medic! Medic!" as if they were in a World War Two movie where medics seemed to be available at your beck and call.

Mickey Grosvenor surveyed the scene. It took him fifteen

seconds to realize that it was MacNulty face down in a bed of tall ferns. He'd forgotten he was the backup medic. When he remembered, he yelled aloud, "Fuck! That's me. I'm the medic. I'm the fucking medic!"

He ran back to find his rucksack. For weeks he'd been carrying the backup medical kit in a roll of canvas. He was out of practice, but he ran to MacNulty with no hesitation.

There was panic in every corner of the NDP. Nicolletti stood up and screamed, "Everyone stand still for a second! Stand the fuck still!" He looked over at Sergeant Rook who appeared to be performing some sort of tribal dance while screaming. "Sarge! Sergeant Rook, *stop!* There is unexploded ordnance here. I do not have this place disarmed yet! LT. Help. Everyone needs to hold their positions for a second while I think this through."

Lieutenant Bross took charge. "Patrol. Stand down! Hold your positions!"

The pandemonium settled. Nick took stock of the situation. "Mickey, get to Doc. That corner is safe." Turning to the lieutenant while already choking up to hold back flooding emotions, he said, "This one's on me, LT. I think I killed Doc with our own claymore."

"We'll sort it out later. What else needs disarming?"

"Just that corner, boss." He wiped snot from his nose and pointed to his left. "I just want to make sure I'm a hundred percent secure before anyone exits the perimeter in that direction."

"Does everyone copy?" Bross called out. There were thumbs up and acknowledgement all around from everyone except Rook.

The area was secured while Mickey was kneeling next to Doc. The doc was still out cold, but Mickey was able to get a pulse. "He's alive! We need Dust Off."

Everyone was so used to Kook calling in Dust Off before being asked that the simple task was forgotten in the bedlam. Kook was leaning over MacNulty as well, trying to help Grosvenor.

"Should we turn him over?"

"No, not yet. Just make sure his head is turned so he can breathe."

The lieutenant stepped in. "Kook, I know you're trying to assist"—he had just noticed Kook's bleeding ear—"but it turns out you're the only one who can operate the radio."

Kook snapped out of it, realizing where he could be the most help. The radio had been left in bitch box mode, a mistake, so everyone heard him in a frantic, uncharacteristic state as he put a call in to Company for immediate Dust Off support.

On the other end, Captain Evans was careful to put the mic down so that no one in the mountains could hear him as he said, "We gotta get 'em out of there. Soon."

2 September 1967
West Southwest of Rah, Quảng Nam Province, South Vietnam

Bross decided that today was a day of rest. The climate was changing. Even in the dead of summer, the air a few hundred feet above Lampshade Valley put the platoon in a different thermocline.

They were starting to dry out. He spent some time on the radio-telephone with Battalion, pleading for extraction. They had found almost nothing of note but had plenty of needless KIAs and WIAs to show for their efforts.

Mickey heard water running up a draw to the north-northwest. He took off, searching for tripwires with The Knife. Over one well-defined but low ridge line, they found the source of the racket: a waterfall coming from dense foliage above, emptying into a clear, shallow pool below.

It took less than an hour for most everyone to relocate from the NDP to the little oasis. With a rotation of posted guards they took turns bathing and rinsing out their ragged, filthy, and often-bloody uniforms. In the more arid air at altitude, the material, hung on branches and makeshift clotheslines, dried well. All in all, it was a day to relax and rest, to steal the deep-sleep catnaps they could only get when feeling clean.

Lieutenant Bross gathered everyone around a clear spot that overlooked the pool. "They're not going to get us out of here yet. We only have a few more klicks to get to Laos. Plan is to give us a couple more days moving west, then they're going to let us stand down at Chu Lai for a week. We'll meet the other guys there on Monday the fourth."

Maples spoke up. "Labor Day, how appropriate is that, LT? We can stand on our heads in a bucket of shit until Labor Day."

"Exactly," Bross replied while loading up with a couple of sticks of Teaberry gum.

"LT, I did that Chu Lai thing on my last tour. It beats the

shit out of being out here, but it's about the weirdest time off you'll ever have. There's an area set aside for guys like us that they don't want mixing with humans. I felt like we were all in a zoo with visitors looking at us through the fence."

"Fence?"

"I shit you not, they separate you from the rest of the REMFs and gawk at you like you're animals. Don't get me wrong. Like I said, it beats the shit out of this slog. We're gonna get to spend some time at the beach. There's clean water, real shitters, showers, soap, and relative safety. Some rich asshole in the States donates cigars. Everyone gets sick smoking them, drinking beer, playing poker, hearts, and spades. Stuff like that."

"Sounds like heaven to me," Nick said.

"Fuckin' A, compared to this hell."

Sergeant Rook said, "I got a week there last year. Best deal was a USO show, but you have to catch it just right. But like Maples said, they cordon you off from the REMFs like astronauts coming back from space. I think it was spring of '66. I got to touch Ann Margaret's leg. I didn't wash my hand for a week."

"You never wash your hands anyway, Sergeant, what's so special about that?"

Everyone chuckled.

"Sarge, what we don't want to know is what you got on that hand later while you were thinking about touching her leg."

Everyone laughed again.

Rook looked up and said, "It was this hand. Look close." And he gave them all the finger. It was a rare moment when the platoon sergeant reminded them of a human being, and there were smiles all around.

Sergeant Rook went on habitually flicking the ashes of his cigarette while he said, "It's just like Maples says, volleyball, a barber shop, a stand of PACEX catalogs, Class Six store, a fresh ration card, just about everything in life that's important."

"Life's little favors," the lieutenant added. "It's amazing how little we need to live and how good something like a tiny slice of The World sounds."

"Hear hear," Kook replied, pantomiming lifting a glass for a toast. "Here's to Witz. Praying he's okay. Here's to Doc, hope that motherfucker makes it. Here's to Bat, and Marty, and Paco."

"Don't forget Pixie, Kook."

"Right. Here's to Pixie. Let's make a pact to play a few rounds of Yahtzee at Chu Lai."

"Hear hear," everyone answered in unison.

When the commotion died down and everyone was thinking about the splendor to come at Chu Lai, Peanut whispered to Kook, "Where did 'hear hear' come from anyway?"

Kook thought for a brief moment. "Fuck if I know. Sounds stupid when you think about it."

In a more perfect world, the two-hundred-meter hike back to the NDP from the pool and the waterfall would have been uneventful. They felt safe, so they had no real need to form up and put someone on point or slack. Each of the thirteen soldiers remaining was dry and dressed and felt much better for the wear. The waterfall and idyllic nature of the place instilled a sense of comfort in them all.

Peanut Carver led the gaggle through the thick underbrush and canopy. The sound of the waterfall attenuated behind them until it was inaudible. They were approaching a rock outcropping that overlooked the NDP—in fact, The Knife and Loo had set up one of the corners of the defensive position on this high ground.

But at just that moment, the spot was occupied.

Peanut spotted the beast first. He held up his hand and felt the accordion of the other dozen men closing in behind him. He could not have known it at the time, but he did the right thing: he stopped. He was quiet. Everyone was skittish, but they kept the noise down. From near the rear, Lieutenant Bross worked his way to the front.

Sitting on the rocky patch in full view was a tiger. An actual tiger. "Like the ones in the zoo," Maples later commented. It was resting on its haunches in a regal pose, its tail slowly wagging like a pendulum from side to side. Unfazed, it stared at the group below. In the aftermath, everyone would overestimate its size, but it *was* huge. Some nine feet from nose to hind end, this cat weighed around four hundred pounds. A light golden yellow with jet black stripes, and a line drawn down the center of his nose outlining its perfect symmetry. It was beautiful.

Craig Message had, by now, well established himself as the platoon and LRRP naturalist. He whispered in the lieutenant's ear:

"Tiger, sir."

Lieutenant Bross turned his head and shot Message a sideways glance with a sarcastic reply. "Tiger? No shit, tiger? You're a genius, Message."

"Got it, sir. Just that there are about ten different subspecies of tigers. Not sure what this one is, but he's fucking huge."

Another reply dripping with sarcasm: "Thanks for that second piece of important information."

So still and quiet was the jungle, they could hear the sound of the waterfall and stream again. All manner of insects were creating a bath of subdued sound enveloping them on all sides. Birds chirped, whistled, and called. Tree frogs on the banks of the stream croaked a high-pitched scrape. The tiger sat looking at the group of men below and yawned, providing the men a full view of the killing machine present in those teeth.

"Stay together," Bross said. "Maybe he won't attack if we stay together."

Mickey Grosvenor spoke up in a whisper. "Sir, I'm gonna guess that all large cats are similar. In Colorado, if you come across a mountain lion, the word is to back away real slow without turning your back. And don't look him in the eyes."

The advice was solid, and perhaps they all would have acted on the recommendation, but before they could, the tiger lifted his head, took a long, slow lick of his nose and lips with a bright pink tongue, and then stood up on all fours. After surveying the group for the longest thirty seconds any of them could remember—since many thought he was preparing to leap toward them—the tiger turned to his left and made a lazy leap off the rock, disappearing into the jungle.

He went uphill. The same direction they all guessed they'd be headed in the morning.

One more thing to worry about.

CHAPTER 23

27 March 2000

Franklin Park, Middlesex County, New Jersey

On Mondays, his workday ended early. *Oh, to move the eight o'clock class to noon*, he thought. *I need to buttonhole the registrar. Who comes up with early Monday classes anyway?* It was a rhetorical question, even in his own mind, and one he had been asking himself since he was eighteen years old. But in truth, he preferred the early return home. He could deal with the wakeup.

It was getting lighter out now that spring was in the air, but the weekend snow and the lingering patches on the north side of the house reminded him that winter was trying to retain its grip. He walked out to the mailbox. Donna didn't often check the mail, which was normally delivered midday. He sifted through the junk—the Publishers' Clearinghouse giveaway and the electric bill—and then studied a hand-typed letter. It looked as though it had come from an old manual machine.

"Can't be," he said aloud. The return address read *The MacNultys, Pahrump, Nevada.* "Can't be," he repeated to himself. As he stepped back into his home, he was going to open the letter on the spot, but he was met by his very insistent border collie, Fire.

The unwritten custom was to name this breed with a single syllable, a throwback to the days when border collies were bred only for herding sheep. The kids had chosen "Fire" for this little girl. She was an unusual red and white *merle* mixture of colors, and when she ran, she looked a little like flame. Perhaps "Flame" would have been a better name. Jogging in the park, screaming, "Fire! Fire! Fire, get over here!" always got a reaction from others. Donna remarked, "Could have been worse. Kids could have picked *Rape*," a thought that still drew a smile if not a laugh.

His usual three-o'clock arrival was a treat for Fire. Relying on her inner clock, she would begin her wait by the door around then, adjusting every few months to the new semester schedule. But he swore she knew it was Monday. She knew he'd be early. And her greeting at the door was her demonstration of this. And it meant one other thing. Fire loved him, but what she really wanted—absent of a herd of sheep—was a trip to the park to engage in the pastime that was her true reason for living: Frisbee.

He set the mail down in the laundry room, gave Fire a big hug and lots of strokes, and then extended almost equal treatment to Donna. Once upon a time this ritual had included the kids, but with one now at Stanford and the other at Cornell, he wouldn't see them again until the coming weekend when spring break began.

He was distracted at the park today. His tosses were a little off. He had never told a soul his little Frisbee secret. That every time he played with a dog, he thought back to Doc MacNulty. And today, he was thinking about the letter. *I should have brought it with me. The*

MacNultys. Nevada. Hmmm… Fire could sense the change, but she still took what she could from the opportunity to play with Dad.

The unexpected mail had opened up a flood of recollections, things he hadn't thought about in decades. He had secured many of those memories in a footlocker, brought home from Nam—and he had not opened that chest to ponder the subject matter for years. In the upstairs hallway behind bi-fold doors, under old linens, mismatched pillowcases, and threadbare towels, it rested. Wooden, four feet by two by two. He remembered the Air Force Red Horse guys had offered it up; it had been left over after they'd packed up some general returning to The World. Painted standard-issue, OD green, one side and the top were stenciled with his name, service number, and hometown.

Now he dragged the box into the hallway and found himself wondering two things that had nothing to do with his reasons for wanting to dig back into this memory vault he'd locked away: *Did they have a machine that made these stencils at the transportation management office?* He didn't have any recollection of working something up with cardboard and a can of white spray paint. And *Would this kind of signage, on the side of the box, stand the test of privacy in The World today?* Certainly not, since his service number was his social security number, then and now. He smiled and said aloud, "Some things never change."

The lid was secured with a hasp and a nickel-plated, spring-loaded clip. He opened it.

A jungle fatigue shirt lay on top, folded, with his name tape displayed and his rank insignia on the sleeves. *Was it frayed that badly when I was wearing it?* he asked himself. *Probably.* Under the blouse… *Why did we call this a blouse?* No recollection, but blouse it was. Under the blouse, the fatigue shirt, was a folded field jacket. Nearly brand new. He didn't even remember owning it. The name tape was his— white with black letters—but he hadn't worn it since he'd been a one-stripe private. *No need for cold-weather gear in the jungle.* He had never changed the rank on this one. Web belts, a khaki uniform, a tarnished brass belt buckle, a helmet cover folded neatly, a garrison cap fitted with a US insignia centered on a brass disc, two OD green T-shirts, a tie, a plastic name tag.

He picked up his ribbon rack. Somehow his brain picked the term out of the blue. Had someone asked him minutes ago the name for the ribbons that would be pinned to his "greens" he would not have been able to say. But reaching in the box, holding them in his hands, he knew this was a ribbon rack. Three rows, nine ribbons, each signifying something he'd won, or rather earned, or rather was handed. Other than the Bronze Star, the Purple Heart, and the *Alive-in-'65* ribbon, he could not recall why the others were on the rack. *Wait, this one is for service in Nam,* he remembered.

He set the ribbons on top of the field jacket and vaguely recalled that the associated medals were on the second level of the box, in folding display boxes of their own. There was an insert that could be lifted, giving the trunk two layers. The center of that top section was bisected by a piece of plywood that was fitted with finger-holds, making it easy to lift from the rest of the locker. The footlocker looked like something built by an expert cabinetmaker, someone with pride in the Red Horse unit. *A South Vietnamese carpenter,* he thought. *Who else would spend so much time making a shipping container look like a piece of furniture?*

He lifted the top layer, exposing a new set of memories. A smile came to his face as he reached in to investigate.

Of course a young man would think to save the important things in his life. And what could be more important than eight issues of *Playboy Magazine?* He thumbed through, wondering why he'd retained this random smattering from 1965 through 1967. He opened the one on top, thumbed to the centerfold, and held it vertically. The page dropped down and a young woman revealed herself after having been hidden away all these years. He recalled her immediately and vividly, like a girlfriend from a past life. Guilt forced him to look over his shoulder to be certain that Donna had not climbed the stairs and was spying on him. No. He let out an audible chuckle while refolding the image and putting the issue back on top.

Wedged in behind the magazines was a sheaf of letters wrapped in what had once been rubber bands, but was now just scraps of dried-out strings of rubber. He retrieved one letter, recognized his mother's handwriting on the written address, opened the envelope, and read for a moment. He wanted to re-read them all, but not right now.

Under the magazines he hit pay dirt, a treasure trove, a new set of recollections he had wiped long ago from his mind. But they made sense all the same. He remembered the letter to his parents that started his journals: "I need to write, to keep some of these memories. Can you send me some paper, maybe small spiral-bound, to help me organize my thoughts?"

He remembered laughing the day he opened the care package at the LZ. *Care package*—another term he'd long since forgotten. Inside it he'd found a stack of baby blue exam books. They must have been left over in his belongings at home from his days as a teaching assistant. Eight inches square, they opened like children's cursive practice books with lined paper inside. The front read: *BLUE BOOK, Examination.* Below was a rectangular box:

Name_____
Subject _____
Instructor _____
Date_____
Examiner's Grade _____

Then below the box in tiny letters:

American Seating Company

Again he laughed out loud. On every book in this stack he had recorded his name, the subject, and the date. He'd even given himself a grade on several of them: A-plus, C, B-minus, et cetera. On two he'd listed himself as *Instructor*. He thumbed through them, interested in his thoughts from that time in his life. The subjects captivated him: "Village Life," "Booby Traps," "The Central Mountains," "The Plains—Lampshade Valley," "Rain—Monsoons." Each book chronicled his thoughts as they had come to him thirty-odd years ago. He'd kept them organized by these tiny volumes. He'd made an entry in "Booby Traps" whenever they had talked

about them, discovered them, or encountered them. There were
other subjects, but the one he sat with for the next hour was labeled:

> Name: C.A.K. — CPL
> Subject: Thoughts on Revenge
> Instructor: 1LT D. Bross / 1SG Rook
> Date: Sept 02 '67
> Examiner's Grade: F-

He turned the page and opened the cover. Blue-lined paper
with faded pencil scribbling, almost too difficult to read. This one,
he recalled, was drafted in one sitting, after a single event. He
recalled the moment when he got to the end of his monologue. Doc
MacNulty wounded, loaded onto a Huey slick, blood dripping onto
the skids. How could he have lived through that? But live he
evidently did. Today's letter next to his recliner downstairs was
proof.

> *... hope you can make it, Sergeant Kuykendool.*
>
> *Your friend for life,*
> *Doc*

The misspelling of his name was something he'd come to
expect. But he failed to note, or perhaps failed to remember, two
oddities: that Doc had never once called Kook "Sergeant
Kuykendahl," and that Kook had never achieved the rank of
sergeant.

He reached up to his right ear and caressed the scar left
there so many years ago. Compared with the damage to MacNulty's

backside it was unfair, he thought to himself, that they were both awarded the same Purple Heart. He flipped through his thoughts from another life—the ones on "Revenge"—and recalled the feelings he'd had when he jotted down his notes.

Revenge — Good, Bad, Cause? Paper??

- Two weeks in the shit. The mountains. Different from the plains
- Kit Carson, dead.
- Pixie, dead.
- Byers, dead. Someone tell Rosa Parks
- Stan Peckham, KIA
- Jimmy, Bat Masterson, Dead. Tears. Anger
- Yesterday, Witz WIA… sent home
- Today… Doc. Fucking Doc. Nearly dead. WIA. Hope he makes it. Hope. Anger.
- What is going on? Except for that sniper when we landed hot, not a single combatant.
- No one to shoot. No one to kill.
- Who do we shoot back at?
- Anger is boiling.
- Rook is crazy. I am not far behind.
- War sucks shit, but we need someone to shoot back at.

- Where are these claymores coming from? Who is killing us? We need extraction. LT says no, part of War. Great leader.

- Rook is fucking nuts. Pity the dink who gets in his way.

- Revenge is a harsh master. Thinking evolutionary, what is the advantage to a species to exact revenge?

- Feeling good does not help pass on genes.

- Is the mate attracted to the perpetrator? Does the revenger get the chicks? We are all so angry. There is no outlet.

- Human nature yes, but human nature says evolution to me. What do humans get out of revenge? Some want out.

- Some are scared. SGT Rook is stoking the fire. People react.

- Rook is stirring this pot of anger "Cauldron of Revenge." Interesting term. Remember that one.

- Academic Paper? Peer review? Other examples from Nam?

- Need to think this out. For further study. Literature search: Anthropological studies on "value of revenge." Perhaps no value. Does deep revenge inhibit the tribe? Do those who enact revenge rush their own demise? What is mechanism that builds the psyche of revenge?

- No one cared when Tiger Scout KIA. Hot LZ expected. No personal feelings for Ty. Ty's gone, no one gives a shit.

- Aug 22. Byers KIA. Interesting dynamic. Colored apparently more upset than whites or Spanish. No sign of anger in Rook then... but later he's on fire. Racist or just too early? Not his tribe?

- Aug 24. Pixie KIA. Patrol steaming. Rook screaming head off. Firing into space. Spinning patrol up.

- Aug 27. Paco KIA... Another claymore. Guys yelling at the horizon

- Aug 28. Bat KIA

- Platoon ready to explode — Rook fucking nuts. Screaming. Shooting weapon into the sky. LT B pissed. Yells at Rook. Tension mounting.

- Aug 29. Stan Peckham killed

- Patrol pissed — Rook cool. Racist? Less reaction when it's Spanish

- Patrol shooting phantoms in the jungle

- Aug 31. Witz WIA

- Platoon beside self. Everyone scared. Everyone

   livid. 1SG wraps M-16 around tree

- Witz laughs it off... tries to calm everyone

- Sept 1. Doc Dust Off... friendly fire. Could be

   dead. Not sure

- Tears. Anger. Hate. Loved that guy. Will we

   make it?

- Mickey is new medic

- 1SG on edge of complete insanity. Throws

   helmet. Kabuki dance

- We were 21, now 13

- We need to get the fuck out of here

Sitting cross-legged on the floor, he closed the exam book and returned it to the pile. His chest filled with emotion. He remembered writing the words. He remembered his feelings at the time. He had just read a study on the positive effect of emotion on memory retention. But now he was more interested in what was missing. Of course he knew what was missing: the rest of this story. And he thought to My Lai and Lieutenant William Calley and Captain Ernest Medina and the weeks, the months he spent poring over their infractions. "There but for the grace of God go I—go us," he often thought in the years afterward. And he wondered what other events like this were missing from the annals of warfare. And the professor in him wondered if anyone had published on the science and anthropology of revenge and the potential evolutionary or anthropological consequence. And he thought to an article he'd read on primates conducting organized raids, destroying neighboring habitats and killing inhabitants. He imagined a possible causal relationship between destruction and revenge at that primal level.

He picked up a stack of mimeographed documents, faded blue print against a background of yellowing paper. There was no smell, other than mustiness, but the sight of the pages brought back the smell of the mimeograph machine buried deep in his neurons. He'd somehow gotten copies of the S2/S3 logs for the days to either side of their visit to the village. In his own handwriting, he saw the two words written in pencil on the top of the package: "Chicken Shit." He smiled and remembered the reason for his admonition while he thumbed through the papers. On days when soldiers were killed by mines, a platoon leader wound up dead, a village was in ruins, and there was a general sense of something gone horribly wrong, the verbiage from S2 and S3 was a silly record of mundane details about bunker and perimeter checks, food deliveries, arrivals and departures of the brass, and takeoff and landing times of choppers. There was little detail on KIAs, combat casualties, or operational and tactical facts. The first line under every dated page was enemy dead and wounded, emphasizing the need to count. He recalled being incredulous that the history of this war would look to historians like records from clerks who had been recording the wrong data.

He began returning the artifacts to the footlocker but paused. Instead, he stepped to his office and did a quick internet search on "the science of revenge." Would there be enough for a graduate student to have taken this topic on? A master's thesis, perhaps? Doctoral dissertation? Maybe even focused on war? He himself would be able to provide a willing candidate some first-hand, though undocumented, material. *Would that testimony send me to jail? Statute of limitations? Probably not—on murder at least.*

And his mind began toying with the idea of locating the lieutenant's family. If not inviting them to the reunion, then at least letting them know their son had saved his life.

Kook was not an emotional guy, but he welled up. Tears landed on the keyboard. He pushed it back to prevent it from getting wet. And he sobbed like he had not sobbed since he was a kid. He lost it. His chin quivered, his jaw shook. Tears, red eyes, running nose, and raw emotion he had not spent on this part of his life in... in forever.

A call from downstairs brought him back to reality. "Dinner's ready!"

CHAPTER 24

3 September 1967

East of Ta Ko, Quảng Nam Province, South Vietnam

In just a day Kook and Bross had come to know Mickey better than it seemed possible. As Mickey was the medic, the LT wanted him close—not for his own safety, but so that he was able to triage during a firefight and direct treatment where and when it was needed most. *Firefight. What a fucking joke*, Mickey thought when Kook and the lieutenant told him the plan. *Claymores in all quadrants is more like it.*

"How's that ear doing?" Mickey said. "We should put some goop on it so it doesn't get infected."

"I'll know if it's infected. Not getting hot or too sore yet." Kook spooned a mouthful from a can of C-rations. He wasn't even taking the time to heat them anymore. Too much trouble.

"What delicacy are you savoring tonight?" Mickey must have been class clown in his high school.

"This one comes to us directly from the Sorbonne, beef spiced with sauce," Kook read in a stodgy New England accent. "Executed perfectly by the chef. Note the way the light picks up the bright colors of the ingredients. It's a feast for the eyes as well as the stomach. Try it *tout suite*; I am certain that you will agree on all counts."

Mickey and the lieutenant laughed, even though Mickey didn't have any idea what the hell the *Sorbonne* was or what *toot sweet* meant. But he did know that Kook was the smartest guy any of them had ever met. Whatever those things meant, the quip made sense to someone, just not anyone in Nam. "Toot sweet?" Mickey asked. "Nice-smellin' fart?"

Then they all laughed, Mickey a little guardedly since he wasn't kidding.

To the lieutenant, to Rook, to Kook, to the entire patrol, the entire excursion looked like a losing proposition. Two weeks in the shit, slogging through some of the toughest terrain imaginable. It seemed to all of them like two months. They were tired, confused, unsure of their position, and plagued by the nightmares of dead and wounded friends.

The lieutenant assured the men they were near the end of this journey. "Guys, we don't have much more time, you have my absolute word on that. The colonel said we'd head west, but we can't cross the border into Laos. Best we can figure, we're close. If there's one silver lining, it's that the mines seem to have stopped."

Rook picked at the scab again. "LT, somewhere there's the motherfuckers what planted those booby traps. They didn't just fall out of the sky."

Bross replied, "Same orders as always: if we encounter enemy we close and defeat. But I do not see any enemy. Current plan is to get us out of these hills and back to the war we left behind, where at least we know where the bullets are coming from."

The thirteen sat in a loose circle, some on logs, some on the ground, and others on their steel pots. Lieutenant Bross motioned Corporal Kuykendahl over and pantomimed holding a microphone. Kook handed him the mike. "Bravo six, bravo six-two, how copy? Over."

The one aspect of the mission that had gone well—or at least better than Kook or Bross expected—was the long-range transmission to Battalion through Company. The spook commo troops had worked magic in making the radio calls seamless, as if they were not forty miles away. Perhaps that was owing to technology, or perhaps to the advantage of high-frequency radio in mountains overlooking distant plains.

"Bravo six-two, bravo six. You are Lima Charlie. What say you?"

The lieutenant switched the R-T to bitch box so everyone could listen in. Darren wanted the guys to hear so they would know he was working it for them. A tenet of command was to never blame leadership, but it was time they all knew he had their backs. This mountain jungle was wearing thin on them. They were scared, and just wanted a change of scenery.

But it was not Captain Evans on the other end of the mic. "Is the boss available?" Bross said. "Over."

"Standby one, six-two."

"Six-two is standing by."

Someone at HQ had kept the mic key depressed. They could hear yelling in the background. "Get the fucking captain! Anyone know where the CO is?" Then, harder to pick out, but intelligible, "He's coming."

"Standby one, six-two. We think we have a bead on the six."

"Six-two is standing by. Over."

It took an interminable ninety seconds, but Captain Evans keyed the mic. "What's up, six-two?"

"Nothing up, boss. We just want the hell out of here."

"Copy that, six-two. We're working it." Then, referencing the Laotian border, "We got you plotted about eight klicks east of your limit. Stand pat. Tomorrow find a spot near a suitable clearing. Call it in. We will have assets on call. How copy?"

Lieutenant Bross looked around at his remaining men. With his left hand he gave a thumbs-up in a circle making eye contact with each of them. Most returned the gesture. "Six, six-two, copy all six. Wilco. Request your suggested timing."

"Good question, six-two. Assets ready at eleven hundred hours. Be in place an hour in advance. I will await your call around ten hundred."

"Thanks, six. See you at ten hundred hours. Six-two is out."

With that, they all heard the mic double click for acknowledgement, preceding high fives all around. They were ready.

4 September 1967

Just south of Ta Ko, outside Ri'Ga Village, Quảng Nam Province, South Vietnam

"LT, can you see it between that giant tree on the left and that snarl of brush?"

Lieutenant Bross leaned left and worked to sight down Nicoletti's arm.

"It blends in pretty well, but that horizontal line looks to me like the top of a thatched roof."

"Got it, is that the only one?"

"Not sure, sir. We need to go back to get a better look."

"Kook, call Captain Evans with our grid coords and ask if they know of anything out here. Peanut, Switch, and The Knife, haul ass back to Sergeant Rook and bring him back here. Tell him the situation. I want the four of you to scope out that hooch. First sign of civilization. Let's find out what we've got."

"Yes, sir," Corporal Carver replied. "We're on it. Bring the platoon sergeant back here first, right?"

"Right."

It took Rook less time to figure out what they were looking for. Truth was, he didn't see anything, but he pretended he did. "Fuckin' Charlie. I'd bet on it."

"Slow down, Sergeant Rook, we're not there yet."

"Lieutenant. Let's review. Someone has been blowing the fuck out of our guys. Here's this village. Conclusion: this village is blowing up our guys."

"Kind of a stretch, don't you think?"

"Not a stretch at all. Someone has been laying ordnance all over the fucking place. This village is the only living thing we've seen in two days. Come on!" Rook was pleading, frustrated that Lieutenant Bross couldn't see the facts right in front of his face. "It's time to waste these zips. They have to pay for killing our guys."

Lieutenant Bross could see the logic, but he wasn't prepared to jump to conclusions.

Kook spoke up. "Sir, bravo six says this area is a completely unknown part of Indian Country. He thinks the H`ôChí Minh Trail is nearby, but wants us to gather intel about what we're picking up before taking action."

Lieutenant Bross took the mic and keyed it. "Bravo six, bravo six-two."

"Bravo six-two, bravo six, got you loud and clear."

"Got your message, will report back as soon as we have something, over."

"Copy all, bravo six out."

"Six-two is out."

Sergeant Message was out of breath, but he caught the last part of the discussion. "Sir, sounds like I might have got ahead of you. Nick sent me down the creek to get a better view."

"And?"

"Big-ass village, sir. Men, women, kids. About half of them

are dressed like some kind of natives in loincloths, women in bright blue shawls and shit like that. They look sort of like the Sioux."

"The Sue?"

"Yeah, sir, you know, Indians. I mean American Indians. Sioux. Like Sitting Bull. No feathers, but hair all wrapped up on top with sticks and shit sticking out. Lots of cats smoking pipes and shit."

"Cats smoking pipes? What the fuck are you talking about?"

"Sorry, sir, when I see beatnik sort of guys smoking pipes, they look like hepcats. Shit like that. You know, cats. Cool cats."

"So not VC, not Vietnamese? Think they're Montagnard?"

"Could be, boss, but a lot of them are in black PJs like the ones in Lampshade Vall—"

Rook interrupted in babble so rapid, he could barely be understood. "Fucking VC. Black PJs. See? See! What'd I fucking say? *Fucking VC!* I am telling you. Men in black PJs? Men. We fucking know that men are on one side or the other. Fucking black PJs? Men? Are you fucking kidding me?"

"Sergeant Rook, cool it for a minute. There's no rush here. Sounds like they have no idea we're out here." Lieutenant Bross looked at the faces of the men who were now getting antsy and cocked for some retribution. "I got a cram course from that SOG sergeant major, but who knows anything about Yards?"

Rook replied, "I've been in Nam almost two years. I ain't never seen a fuckin' Yard."

"Okay. So you're no expert." Bross asked again. "Anyone?"

By now Sergeant Grayson had moved forward. "Sir, not

much, but my brother was down near Pleiku last year. He talked about Montagnards in his letters home. They were friendly, fought on our side. They fought with the French. I've never heard anything except that they're friendly."

Bross keyed the mic again.

"Bravo six, bravo six-two."

"Bravo six."

"Captain, can you do a little digging to see if MACV has any joy on Montagnards up here? Over."

"Bravo six-two, bravo six. Did you hear what I said? I repeat, get some eyes on target so we don't look like dumb shits. Six is out. Do you copy? Out!"

Bross looked at the mic, then at his guys. "Bravo six-two is out."

Rook couldn't contain himself. "Boss, fuck Evans. I was killing gooks before he was born. Fuck *eyes on target*. We need fucking *lead* on target."

Sergeant Message spoke quietly. "It's a big village, sir, not like the small groups of huts in Lampshade."

Rook spun on him. "Then we get everyone loaded up, walk in, and torch the motherfuckers. They're going to get away." Rook looked around and saw wide eyes staring back at him. Then he lost it. Again. "Our fucking guys are *dead!* There is never any payback! *Senor Carlos is in that fucking village over there!*"

Bross was up to here with frustration. Uniform Code of Military Justice be damned, his reaction was knee-jerk and uncharacteristic. The rules during combat were different anyway.

With his right hand open, in a roundhouse, Lieutenant Bross slapped Rook full force on the left side of his head. The blow sent Rook reeling back unbalanced. He nearly fell.

In a stern voice that sounded like a whisper, but was loud enough for everyone to hear, Bross said: "Rook, I am telling you to *calm the fuck down right now*. Do you understand me?"

The guys in view were stunned. They looked at their boots, working the ground and trying to hide where there was no cover. The boss was livid. They had hardly ever heard him use profanity, much less slap the bejeezus out of the platoon sergeant.

But Bross was hopping mad. Pointing at each man, he said loudly, "You, you, you, and you: come with me. Kook, come with me. Turn the bitch box completely off."

The six of them circled around and headed toward the village.

CHAPTER 25

4 September 1967—Morning

Ri'Ga Village, Quảng Nam Province, South Vietnam

Lieutenant Bross didn't feel a thing. No sensation of pain, no sense of falling, no bodily indication whatsoever that there was a problem. But there *was* a problem. A big problem. Bross opened his eyes to a face full of dirt. He was able to move his head to the side in order to breathe, but otherwise he was immobile. For all intents and purposes his head might as well have been planted in the ground and connected to the root system of the small bush to his left. He couldn't move. Not a fingertip.

Peeking through the fronds, Tsov didn't understand what he had seen. The first green man had shot the second green man in the back with a small gun—and then had run away. On the chest of the man with the gun was the symbol of an animal: two black eyes and two black ears. It was a symbol Tsov would forever associate with death.

Tsov was too young to understand the concept of evil. This scene, the men, the gun, the shooting would be mixed up in his mind for decades along with the horror of corpses littered across Ri'Ga. *Live, son. Make a life.* His father's words were a jumble that Tsov would replay in his mind over and over in the coming years. In 1991, at the age of thirty-one, he would accept Jesus Christ as his Savior. This nightmare was a step on the road that he came to understand had led him to Christianity and provided him a tool to learn the language of his new home.

On the day of his baptism, he would hear Father Dunn recount some words about the devil. And Tsov would think back to this moment, on this horrible day, at this place on Earth, and know that he had looked into the eyes of the devil himself. And he would know, even as holy water was sprinkled on his head, that this man, this devil, was the evil spirit responsible for the death of his village. *Live, son. Make a life.*

But now, Tsov could only look on in confusion at the green man who lay face down in the dirt, unmoving. Tsov walked out to the man, not understanding the danger. He didn't know how he did it or even why, but with all his might, he rolled the green man from his stomach to his back. The man's eyes stared right through Tsov, to a distant spot in the sky. *He does not see me.* Or perhaps he did.

Blood. Fear. Gunfire and screaming in the village. Over it all, Tsov heard his aunt cry out in a wail that stopped him in his tracks.

In an inexplicable instant Darren was on his back looking at sky. His inner ear spoke to his brain to tell him he had been turned over, but he couldn't verify that that was what had happened. There had been the fleeting image of a brown boy over him, but he was gone now.

Darren was looking at clouds. He was able to move his eyes left and right. He heard soldiers from the platoon screaming obscenities. They must be yelling at villagers. No—they were yelling at each other.

He tried to speak, but nothing came out. The realization came to him. He was a head attached to a human body that had no connection to its brain. He was paralyzed; something had done major damage. But he was alive.

The screaming turned to gunfire. Looking left and right to the width of his peripheral vision, Darren imagined his platoon was involved in the firefight. *Perhaps Rook was right: VC. This village is VC!*

Two villagers ran toward him and jumped over his face. His mind told him to tackle them both, but his body would not respond.

The shooting was interminable. He took solace in the fact that if he took a stray bullet, at least he wouldn't feel it. But he was alive. There was that.

Time passed. The shooting waned—a shot here, a shot there in the distance. He was able to hear the whimpering, the groaning, and the tear-filled wailing of the wounded. The sounds were all in a language he could not understand. Unrecognizable. Not Vietnamese. All villagers. One particularly anguished scream, from a throat filled with tears and snot, ended with a gunshot. *Did someone shoot her?*

Time passed.

From the distance, over the trees and likely from the direction of the river valley they had crossed, came the sound of chopper rotors. But the sound was a phantom bouncing in his head.

Mickey Grosvenor appeared before him. Face to face. *Medic, thank God. Where's MacNulty? Dead, I remember.* The corporal's ear was so close to the lieutenant's mouth, Darren could have kissed him. He wanted to kiss him.

Thank you for finding me, his mind said without a sound. But he could not purse his lips for a kiss. He could not make a sound.

"Sarge! Sergeant Rook! Over here! The LT is alive! Sergeant! Get over here. He's breathing. His eyes are moving!"

Mickey had the rolled med kit open in a single motion from his hip. Quick triage. He lifted, removed the flak jacket, then wrapped the lieutenant's neck with a roll of gauze. "LT, you should be fine. Through and through your neck. The exit wound is only a little larger than the back. Probably nicked your spine. You'll be okay. Amazing, you're hardly bleeding."

Darren had been daydreaming, hallucinating, about his Christy, his career, his family, Lufkin, Texas, R&R in Hawaii over Thanksgiving, his mother, his father—a life to come. All the while he had a realistic assessment of his chances to ever see any of those things. In West Point parlance he was a "mort": already dead. A tear ran in a rivulet down his left cheek. Then another. Just his left eye crying. Then another.

Sergeant Rook swung his weapon over his left shoulder and hightailed it to the edge of the village square, to the perimeter of the central plaza and the hut where the lieutenant had fallen. He screamed at Grosvenor, pretending to be concerned with the welfare of the lieutenant. "Take up a post and guard me. Keep an eye out for Charlie! I got it. Move out! Find Kook. Tell him to call in a Dust Off. *Now!*"

Mickey stood, backed off, got his rifle to the ready, and ran toward the plaza, passing Sergeant Rook shoulder to shoulder. "Got it, Sarge."

As soon as Mickey was gone, Rook knelt, put his mouth to the lieutenant's ear, and whispered, "You son of a bitch. How the fuck did you live through that?" He looked at the tears on Bross's cheek. "Fuckin' crybaby. Dust Off is on the way. But you know what? You're never going to see it. Slap me in front of the guys? During combat? Fuck you, asshole!"

The patrol was searching and shooting and burning as ordered, well wound up after being told the first shot had taken their platoon leader. "They're just letting off a little steam," Rook said to the lieutenant. He smiled and in a focused whisper added, "Finally someone to shoot. Could be VC. Probably not, but could be."

Rook looked to his left and right; Mickey was facing away, toward the village square to his back. Out of sight of the platoon, Rook placed a bare hand over Lieutenant Bross's mouth. With his thumb and index finger he squeezed the lieutenant's nostrils shut.

In his mind, Darren struggled. But he could not move, could not react, could only bat his eyes in alarm. He made no sound.

It didn't take long. Darren's lungs weren't working well anyway.

Lieutenant Darren Alexander Bross was just one of a dozen dead humans on the ground at Ri'Ga Village, Quảng Nam Province, South Vietnam that day. His eyes stared skyward. The tears dried where they had cut through the dust on his face.

Every soldier was possessed by a demon: a demon of hate, a demon of revenge. A flaw in the human psyche. Something rising from the reptilian brain. They could tell themselves later that they were threatened, they were in danger, they were being attacked, but none of that was true. Some villagers were running, and most were pleading. All were summarily shot.

An old man walked to the center of the square, pressing the palms of his hands to his face to wipe his tears. He must have been the oldest man in the village. The demons passed him by over and over, ignoring him due to his age. To the onlooker, he appeared to be trying to speak to the demons. They would pass him, and he would reach out for a sleeve, his face a reflection of his horror as the demons' rifles cut his village to shreds.

Uncle Vak had inflicted enough violence on the soldiers who occupied his land—the VC, the NVA—that for a brief moment he thought that payback had finally come. It had been many years since he had seen white men. He could not understand what his village had done to deserve this carnage. *Given the opportunity*, he thought, *I would have welcomed them.*

In shock, he stumbled over his own feet, one sandal on, the other missing. He was dripping blood, not from himself, but from the half dozen family members he had held in his arms, trying to call a spirit back into their lifeless bodies. He felt humiliated to be shedding tears in front of his family, his villagers, his *toring*, and he tried to wipe them away with the open palms of his hands. But he looked instead like he had spread his face with red war paint, a mixture of blood and dust. It was paste, the blood of his family, the dust of the Earth spirit.

Amid the roar of gunfire and the screaming and the dying, he reached out to the soldiers who ran by, firing this way and that. They ignored him. At last Vak got one to stop in front of him. The soldier had the look of a wild animal in his eyes. With his left hand, Vak took the soldier's right sleeve. With his right hand, he held the soldier's left. Then Vak knelt in front of this giant of a man and thought, *He will understand me, this one.*

Kneeling, pleading with everything in his heart, he released the soldier's sleeves and bowed to the ground. He wailed. Wailing was not allowed, he knew that, but he hoped the spirits would forgive his transgression. In his own way he prayed to the spirits who were supposed to protect his village.

He communicated in the universal language of sobbing, crying so deep he could barely speak as his chin quivered. Through his wails he asked, "What have we done? What have we done? We are humble villagers. We are family. Our *toring* is of the Co-Tu. Please, sir. I ask you please, sir! I beg you."

And Vak, Tsov's Uncle Vak, again bowed to the ground from his knees and released a gut-wrenching wail of loss.

Corporal Kuykendahl felt an old man, the oldest man, hold his arm. Short, brown, gray hair, bare chest. Just a loincloth and large ivory plugs in his earlobes. The old man was covered in blood. He was beseeching in a language Kook could not hope to understand, but it was pleading—there was no doubt of that. He was begging, crying, sobbing. A human being seeking compassion.

This simple act of supplication brought Kook to a semblance of sanity. He surveyed the plaza. Though he'd only been standing by with the radio and had not participated in the slaughter, he gazed in no particular direction and said aloud, "What have we done?"

Then he screamed—to himself, to anyone that would hear, but the old man did not hear—"*What the hell have we done?*"

With the radio on his back, he let his rifle fall to the dirt, the barrel still cool since he had not fired a shot, and he bent to reach down for the old man. It was a simple act of empathy.

Sergeant Rook came from nowhere, pulled his pistol from

his holster, and while the old man was still kneeling on the ground and kissing the earth, Rook shot him in the back of the head, barely missing Kook's foot.

The moment was over in an instant. It was this snapshot of life and death that Clayton Kuykendahl would play back in his head a hundred thousand times in the coming years. Kook looked down at the limp body, decades of life gone in a flash. Then he looked up at Rook with tears in his eyes.

As if drinking a cool lemonade on a Sunday afternoon, Rook said, "Don't think too much, Kook, we have mopping up to do. Let's get this party finished."

Kook replied, "Fuck you. Fuck you." Then he threw his hands up, and from a face bright red with raw emotion, he repeated, "*Fuck you, Rook!* Fuck you. I am done with this shit." He looked down again and burst into tears. "That old man was trying to tell me something and you fucking shot him. What the hell are we doing? What the hell did these people do to us?"

Kook's words were unheard like a tree falling in an empty forest. Rook certainly didn't hear. With a smirk, he was gone, off perfecting his role as executioner somewhere else in the tiny hamlet.

Tsov knew instinctively to lay low and keep quiet. The green man wearing the animal symbol was back. And now Uncle Vak was gone at this beast's hand. Tsov crept around the smaller houses to the end of the longhouse where he'd last seen his father run while holding his sister. He climbed the rattan into the last window on the back side of the house.

Inside, he found his father, Kiep. Kiep began a low crawl toward him as if to say, *Let's play. Climb up on my back.* At first he looked normal, if a little slow. But Tsov didn't have the full picture. The left side of his father's head looked fine, composed. But when Tsov went to him, he knew it was bad. The right side of Kiep's face was nearly gone: a mess of shattered bone, spurting blood, and a deflated eye hanging from the remains of what had once been an orbital socket. Gray and white flecks formed a pattern on the straw-matted floor where his exploding face had sprayed.

From the bridge of Kiep's nose, blood dripped like tears to the mat. The tears, the blood, a simple finality.

Kiep reached out an arm. Trying to get it around Tsov's shoulder—a father's reaction to protect his son.

Heavy footsteps. Another green man in the doorway, pushing the beaded drape aside and ducking his head, too tall to enter without bending. He had skin the color of water buffalo. Tsov looked to his father, then to the man. Then to his father. Then to the man. A bouncing of frantic eyes. Then complete resignation.

The green-clad man with the dark skin aimed his rifle… then lowered it.

Tsov could not understand the words, but the man screamed something over his shoulder. "All clear here!" Then he turned and moved down the hallway.

Tsov reached for his father's hand and held it tight. Then he squeezed hard through the grizzle that had been a face, working to replace in his father's head what was coming out. Through the shards of bone, and through the blood around his father's neck, he tried, but failed. Kiep was going limp, lifeless.

"Don't give up, Papa!" Tsov's voice was too loud against the quiet outside. Without really understanding why, he lowered to a whisper. "Don't die, Papa. We need you. I need you."

Kiep was still able to form some words. He fell to his left, the good side, and pushed himself up on one arm. Still trying to protect his son. Still trying to be a father, when he knew all was lost. Stretching his neck toward Tsov, he said his last words with difficulty:

"Live, my son," he gurgled. "Make a life."

Kook half sat with his back against the hut's bamboo supports. He spoke into the radio loud enough to be heard, but quiet enough to keep the fighting away from his position, "Bravo six, bravo six-two."

No answer. "Shit, we're in a valley." Kook stood, placing himself in what he thought was imminent danger, but hoping his stature would get a signal to the long whip antenna over his shoulder.

"Bravo six, bravo six-two."

"Six-two, this is six. What's up?"

"Bravo six, this is bravo six-two. We're fucked. Bravo six-two is down. Giant firefight. We need Dust Off now. He's going fast."

"What happened?" Company asked.

"Six, we need *Dust Off now*! Over." He passed grid coordinates. "Plotting YC431380 in a valley. Things are dying down. We'll pop smoke in the plaza in the middle of this village."

"Got it, we're working Dust Off. Could be a while, but we're on it."

"Six-two, six. SITREP. What the fuck is going on out there?"

Kook tried to stay composed, but he was scared to death, tears streaming down his cheeks. "Sir, I think the LT is dead. Got shot, then the shit hit the fan, over."

"Six-two, six. How many Dust Offs will you need?"

Kook stepped around the hut, took a few steps, and walked toward the square. "One for now. Lots of dead locals. I can't see it all. Few shots here and there. Looks like cleanup."

"No other KIA or WIA?"

"Not that I can see right now, boss. Not ours anyway. Few kids running around is all."

"Find six-two-five ASAP and get him to your RT."

"Wilco, six."

4 September 1967—Noon
Ri'Ga Village, Quảng Nam Province, South Vietnam

Two young boys stared at the sky, transfixed by the display above them. They had both seen such contraptions in the distance through holes in the canopy, but here, with death surrounding them, and the near complete and total loss of their families and half the human beings they knew, they could not take their eyes off this machine heavier than stone yet floating in the air above them. There was time for emotion later. Death was then; this was now.

A man, a white man with long yellow hair, was leaning out of a door in the machine, trying to get their attention by waving his hand. In the other he held a small shiny black box that was affixed to his neck with thick black cord. Tsov didn't think it was a weapon. A green man with the head of a large insect had a grip on the yellow-haired man. Tsov thought that was a good idea. They were floating in this machine above the tops of the trees. Last year, a cousin from Xa Ruh had fallen while gathering boong'boong fruit. He died a painful death while the blood flowed from his legs out of wounds caused by bones protruding through the skin. All villagers had been paraded by as a warning to take care in the jungle. They watched him die knowing nothing could be done.

Like that cousin, the man at their feet was dead. One boy took his helmet, and Tsov took his outer garment. *For what possible reason,* Tsov asked himself, *would a man need something this thick and this heavy in the jungle?* And after examining the helmet he asked, *How could a man wear something that heavy on his head?*

With the force of a wind from the downdraft of a storm, the machine floated to the ground in the Ri'Ga village square. Tsov and Siu kept their eyes locked on it, marveling as green men jumped screaming from the contraption and others approached it like spirits without any fear. Perhaps they felt safe since they were all carrying weapons that Tsov now knew could kill. Three green men stood at equidistant points from the machine, facing away from it. They must be looking for evil spirits that might emerge from the jungle to fight this monster. Tsov posited that they might be here to rid the village of the men who had just assassinated everyone.

The man with the yellow hair ran in a crouch from one house to another. He ran to the longhouse, then to the Guol, then a hut, then back again. He crossed the square again and again. He stopped and stopped again while holding the small, shiny black box to his face. He moved a tube attached to it. And he made quiet noises with the box that could be heard over the cacophony of afternoon insects, since the flying machine in the square had now ceased its roar. Tsov deduced that this man was creating photos, like the image of his grandfather standing with other white men posted on the wall of the longhouse. The picture with inexplicable symbols below: *Tu es un vrai ami, comme un membre de la famille. Nous ne t'oublierons jamais.*

The yellow-haired man took a small green book from his back pocket and approached Tsov and his cousin. From a top pocket he removed a black plastic stick with a silver button on top. He held the stick to the paper and knelt in front of the boys. He began speaking to the only two village humans he could see had survived the massacre. The man made harsh sounds from his mouth, some similar to those Tsov had heard tan soldiers bark to his father in the past year, but these sounds had no tone, no fluidity, no semblance of language. Could this yellow-haired man be trying to communicate with them? Or was he capturing their image on paper?

The boys stared, wide-eyed and ignorant. One was comically

wearing a large helmet with a black lieutenant's bar sewn on the cover, and the other was holding up the full weight of a US Army flak jacket. It fit him like a clown suit.

"What happened here? I ask you, what happened here? Do you know what happened here? Do you speak English?" Michael Joseph Westfall was a freelance photojournalist, on no particular assignment, but he carried press credentials and had convinced the brass from public affairs at MACV to allow him access to the front lines when there was room on helicopters. This day turned out to be the day that would keep him in work for the rest of his life.

Then, in a language that had commonality with something they had both heard Vietnamese soldiers speak, but also could not understand: "*Những gì xảy ra ở đây? Tôi hỏi bạn, những gì xảy ra ở đây? Bạn có biết những gì xảy ra ở đây? Bạn có nói tiếng Anh không?*"

Westfall had more success than others of his ilk due in part to the time he'd spent learning to speak Vietnamese. He had been in country since 1964, but he knew the Montagnard. He knew better than to think these boys would be able to decipher him. But in his frustration he attempted anyway, just to know he had tried.

He failed with the boys, so he took to questioning soldiers. And he did pretty well until Sergeant Rook knocked him out with the butt of his M-16, a roundhouse arc that somehow didn't kill him.

Westfall didn't come to until he woke with a massive headache at 120 knots, at the nap of the earth, headed east over triple-canopy jungle. Shaking his head and rubbing his temples, he loosened his seat belt—which someone had secured much too tight

—and checked his camera for tampering. A brand new roll of Kodachrome was gone from his Nikon. With his free left hand he felt for his top left pocket. It occurred to him that he looked a little like Deputy Sheriff Barney Fife from Mayberry, who always kept a single bullet in the awkward-to-reach shirt pocket.

It was there: a roll of thirty-six shots. Just the beginning of unraveling what he knew was a cover-up from the second he was knocked unconscious. It was a windfall story that could make a career.

And did.

6 September 1967
Lufkin, Angelina County, Texas

It was just coincidence that Darren's parents, Alex and Margaret, were visiting Christy, who was back living with her parents in Lufkin. It was a Wednesday evening, and they had been invited for dinner and to watch an episode of *Bob Hope Presents Chrysler Theater*. Mrs. Allison Mudd had mentioned to Margaret a year back how much she liked an episode with Cliff Robertson that had aired some time ago. "The Game" told the story of a broke businessman who found himself deeper in debt as a result of his addiction to gambling. So when *TV Guide* said that a repeat of "The Game" would be airing, Allison called Margaret and invited them over.

Five minutes into the show—just about the time the sun had set and it was getting dark—the doorbell rang.

Owing to the time, Gary Mudd got up from his chair a little annoyed. "Who in the Sam Hill is that at this time of night. Blast it!" The Brosses sat next to Christy on a flower-print modern couch sealed with clear vinyl slipcovers. Christy's brother Ted, who would leave for his first day of college the following morning, leaned against a doorjamb with his legs crossed. Mrs. Mudd got up with Gary but peeled off to the kitchen and called out, "Can I get anyone a refill?"

Mr. Mudd peeked out the front window while reaching for the light switch for the portico. "There's a green army car out front and a couple of soldiers in uniforms." He looked back into the living room to stunned silence and wide eyes from everyone.

"Should I open it?" Mr. Mudd asked.

From the doorway to the kitchen, Mrs. Mudd said, "Of course you should open it."

"I don't want to."

"You have to."

Alex Bross pushed off the arm of the couch and peeled his legs from the vinyl, making a ripping sound from where his bare legs below his shorts had stuck. "I can get it, Gary. I think it's probably for Christy." He took a deep breath, trying to compose himself. He was certain this visit would not end well. His chest filled to the point where, he knew from past experience, he was going to have a problem getting a word out without breaking down. Still, he took another deep breath and turned the doorknob.

An army major and captain in dress greens stood under bad light from above—one of those yellow insect-repellent bulbs. Both had somber faces, their expressions presaging the bad news to come.

Alex was unable to speak. By this time Margaret Bross was at his side. "Why are you here? What do you want? Go away!"

"I'm sorry, ma'am, we're looking for Mrs. Darren Bross. This is the address we have for her."

Alex stood like a wide-eyed statue while his wife continued. "You can talk to me. I'm Mrs. Alex Bross. You can talk to us."

"I'm very sorry, ma'am, but I am under orders to deliver a message directly to Mrs. Darren Bross." He looked at the paper he was holding in his hand. A tear fell from his eyes to it. "Christy Bross," the major sobbed.

"Is it Darren? Did something happen to Darren?"

The captain and the major exchanged glances before turning silently back to Margaret. Alex put his arm around her body and held her tight.

The living room wasn't big. The front door was visible to everyone. The unsaid message was clear. Christy stood and approached the door in halting steps, barely able to stay vertical. She found passage between her mother and father.

The captain stepped forward. "Ma'am. Are you Mrs. Darren Bross?"

A nod and a mumble were all she could manage. Her chin quivered out of control.

The captain reached out and held Christy's arms, left and right, in an odd manner. It was not the way you greeted someone, but rather the way you might hold someone who had already begun to faint. He had done this before.

"Ma'am, I am Captain-Chaplain Mark Allison. This is Major Tom Burgess. We have the sad duty to inform you, on behalf of the United States Army and a grateful nation, that your husband, First Lieutenant Darren Bross, has been killed in action in Vietnam."

Christy's knees buckled. The blood drained from her face. Margaret fell to the carpet. Alex had thought he was holding her tight, but she slipped from his grasp before he could react. Only the chaplain's strong grip kept Christy from falling as well.

Major Burgess got on one knee, helped Margaret up, and escorted her into the living room, where Gary and Allison Mudd sat in stunned silence. Ted unfolded his legs and rose in tears. He moved to the front door and put his arm around his sister. He and Chaplain Allison held her up as they walked her to the living room and sat her down on the couch. Christy was a strong person, but she could not contain her emotions. She released cries from the depth of her soul.

Chaplain Allison pulled Ted aside. "I know this is hard, but you seem like a tough young man. Can I ask you to be strong for your sister? She is your sister?"

Ted wiped his face with the palm of his hand. "Yes. I'll try."

Alex was trying to console his wife. His own tears flowed.

"Mr. Bross, are you okay?" Ted asked.

No response.

"Mr. Bross?"

"I'm good, Ted. Can you get me a cold washcloth for the missus?"

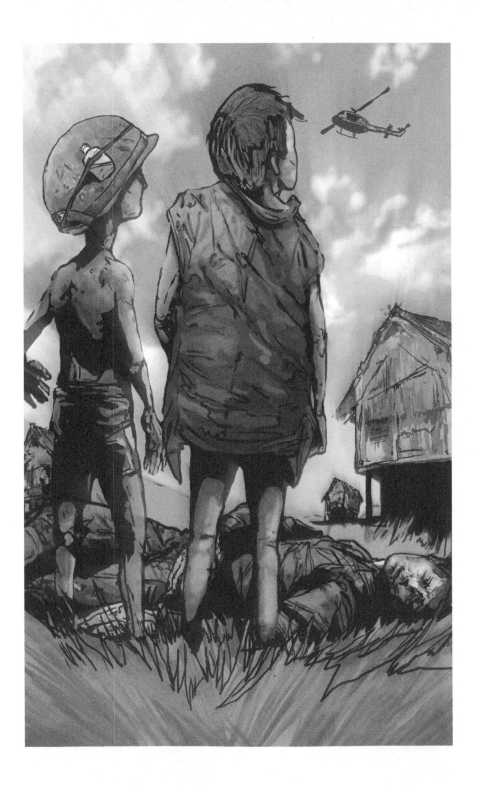

THE WORLD

I believe that all the fear you had, can gently fly away
We experience, we pull together lost in one embrace
We will love forever, this eternity

Jon Anderson

CHAPTER 26

6 April 1999

Lufkin, Angelina County, Texas

Mrs. Margaret Bross picked up the phone and dialed her husband at work. "Honey, I need you to come home now." She was upset, sobbing between her words.

"Margaret, what's wrong? What happened? Are you okay? Is everything okay?" His questions came out as fast as he could talk.

"It's a letter. We got a letter. It's about Darren. It's about how Darren died."

Alex Bross pulled into the driveway too fast, hitting the left front quarter panel on the dip. He exited the car and strode purposefully through the front door.

Margaret handed her husband two full-sized sheets of good quality paper. He unfolded them, revealing a letterhead embossed in gold and scarlet. And with a deep breath, he began reading.

DEPARTMENT OF HISTORY

April 2, 1999

Dear Mr. and Mrs. Bross,

It has taken me some time to locate you and even if I had done so sooner, I am not sure I would have shared the information in this letter with you then. However, my time in Vietnam manifests itself in an endless flood of memories that continue to haunt me. One incident is in my thoughts more than any other. It involves your son. I served with your son 1LT Darren Bross in Vietnam in 1967.

I am so sorry for your loss. I expect his memory remains with you on a daily basis. The Lieutenant and I only had a couple of months together, but first and foremost I want to tell you that your son was an exceptional leader of men. I had served for five months with his predecessor in the 2d Rifle Platoon. We all had some trepidation when your son took the reins, but learned quickly how lucky we were to have him as our young leader. Others were not so fortunate. There are a couple of dozen men alive today, spread across America, who think of Lt. Bross at this very moment and thank him for his leadership in keeping them alive during what was probably the most difficult time for all of us.

So many years ago I hope the Army contacted you in a positive sense to inform you that your son died an honorable death in the service of his country. I would add to that his service to the people of Vietnam. My words here will disturb you, but in order to work toward sleeping soundly at some point in the future I need to get this message off my chest. I apologize if you feel I have unnecessarily passed a burden to you. I am sorry. It cannot be helped. You need to know.

Your son died leading the 2d Rifle Platoon on a Long Range Patrol into the Central Highlands of South Vietnam. Our mission was to root out, identify, and report on the location and strength of enemy forces, both the North Vietnamese Army and South Vietnamese rebels (the Viet Cong). We were smaller than standard platoon strength and lacked the firepower to be an effective force against a determined enemy. For that reason we tried to remain hidden, but the worst of the war seemed to find us. The mountains of Vietnam are beautiful, but their beauty was interrupted by the untimely and unfortunate deaths of a number of men in our outfit. Looking back, it is difficult to explain, but we had repeated nasty and deadly incidents with land mines. The official Army story is that they were placed by the Viet Cong. Even at the time, I was not so sure. I have looked into it since and am even more convinced the Viet Cong were not responsible. My complete explanation is too long for this note to you, but I have done significant research into this matter and have come to the conclusion that somehow South Korean Marines were involved, trying to protect their positions. However implausible that may sound, you may not know

that South Koreans were US allies in Vietnam,
but they were.

With each man down, we analyzed the cause.
The issue is complex and my recollection is
fuzzy, but like the Army, our Platoon Sergeant
was convinced the Viet Cong were responsible.
Your son was the voice of reason. His leadership
skills kept us from going off halfcocked and
killing everything that moved.

In our patrol, losing a soldier per day, we
came upon an idyllic native village of about 50
individuals. Many were dressed in black pajamas,
the signature clothing of the Viet Cong. The
Platoon Sergeant wanted to destroy the village
and all its inhabitants. Lt. Bross started out
on a more conservative approach. In the end a
tragedy occurred. Your son was the first
casualty. That set off a chain of events that
live in my mind every waking moment and are the
source of a continual recurring nightmare.

The village is gone. But sadly, we never
found any indication they were the enemy. I
write you this because I think your son was
killed by the Platoon Sergeant Lionel Rook. I
have no proof of this, but I do have very strong
suspicions. I would not share them with you
unless I thought they had basis in fact.
Certainly you had the opportunity to review a
copy of the US Army Inspector General report on
the incident. It was investigated as an
"atrocity," but the conclusions of the
investigation did not support the allegations. I
was never able to see the entire report, only a
summary.

I expect this news will come as a shock.
The impetus for my contact now was a recent
magazine article I read on incidents of
"fragging" in Vietnam, when the troops murdered

their leaders. I believe your son was a victim of the practice.

Otherwise, I hope this letter finds you well. I am at your service should you want to discuss this matter further. I can be contacted here at the university.

On a side note, Lt. Bross and I shared an interest in history. For our few months together we were keeping a small notebook on historical observations. I have that little green book and reviewed it today with smiles. If you would like it as a remembrance, I will be happy to send it to you.

Sincerely,

Clayton Anthony
Kuykendahl, PhD
Professor

Alex handed the letter back to his wife with tears in his eyes. "It's a hard thing to read, honey, but we had to know."

From the top shelf of the closet in Darren's old room, now the guest room, Alex brought down a brown shoebox labeled with the words: "FLORSHEIM SHOES, Glendale Wisconsin, Founded 1892." He thumbed through the envelopes, every one of them identical: cross-hatching on the edges in red, white and blue; an embossed set of wings with "Air Mail" printed across them; a handwritten return address, cancelled in a circle by the A & AF POSTAL SERVICE APO 96374; and to the right of the cancellation, written in Darren's hand: *FREE*.

The return address was also handwritten.

1LT D. Bross

Co. B 2/18 12th Inf Bde /TF Oregon

APO SF 96217

Margaret had numbered each one, from #1 to #71, next to "FREE" in the upper right-hand corner. Darren had written nearly every day. Sometimes they arrived in Lufkin out of order depending on the military post office, but as far as the Brosses knew, they had everything he'd penned to them. Christy, they knew, had received exactly one hundred letters from Darren, and she said she'd read them a hundred times, but the Brosses were less comfortable with the pain of reminder the letters caused, and had tucked their copies away.

But now, Alex Bross wanted to do some review. It had been years since he'd opened this box, but he had some vague recollections he wanted to check. Darren's last letter was written on the day he died. Unlike the others, it had arrived with three others that had never made it to the military Air Post Office. Letters numbered 68 through 71 had come in a cardboard box with his other belongings, tucked in a pocket in his rucksack.

Yet before he turned to those last letters, he couldn't help but thumb through some of the earlier ones. These snippets of thoughts and memories were all that was left of his son.

#4: *This place has more humidity than Galveston…*

#13: *….not sure what you're seeing on the news, but it's not that bad over here. One of my guys has a PhD in history…*

#19: *….looks like I might get my own platoon before the end of the week.*

#21: *….the Colonel flew in, got the platoon as promised, met my First Sergeant. It's his second tour, so I'll be safe with him.*

#22: *It seems like a great group of guys ….most very tired ….some brand new, like me.*

#32: *My platoon sergeant argues with me a lot, but he mostly has good points…*

#34: *Sgt. Rook is from some hick town in Florida near that big*

lake. Some of the guys say he was a member of the
KKK. I think they're wrong. More like the Hitler Youth.
Ha, Ha.

#36: *My first guy was wounded today. Dan Schmidt from Falls*
Church, VA. Guys called him Jiggles. He got medevac'd.
He's going to live, I think. I'm going to write his parents
as soon as I close up this letter to you.

#59: *....gonna talk to my company CO when I get back to*
garrison. This is not working out with Rook.

#66: *I can't let the guys see my emotions. Private Hernandez got*
his legs blown off by a mine today ....bled to death before
Dust Off arrived. We couldn't get the tourniquet high
enough. Sgt. Rook went crazy. It's the only time we know
Rook likes anyone.

#69: *....mines are everywhere. The guys won't let me walk point.*

#71: *... near the Laos border ....can't cross ....Company CDR*
says they're going to pull the rest of us out with choppers.

Alex Bross folded letter #71 and stuffed it back in the
envelope. Then he replaced the box on the closet shelf, stepped into
the kitchen, and opened the drawer under the telephone. Even in
Lufkin, the phone book was an inch and a half thick, and about half

of it was the yellow pages.

There were three listings for private investigators.

Alex picked up the phone and first called his grandson Lex. "He's a spook and will know what to do," he mumbled under his breath.

18 June 1999
Las Vegas, Clark County, Nevada

Lex opened the thick manila envelope. He had been foiled in numerous attempts to get his hands on the army's official report on the "Incident at Ri'Ga Village." Finally a Freedom of Information Act request—and a letter from his congressman—broke through the red tape. He extracted a fresh Xerox copy of an old report:

INSPECTOR GENERAL
MILITARY ASSISTANCE COMMAND
VIETNAM

Report of
Investigation

11 November 1968

The 4 September 1967
Incident at Ri'Ga Village
Quang Nam Province,
South Vietnam

CLASSIFIED BY MACVG 19Nov68
DECLASSIFY ON 19Nov93

In addition to report numbers, release statements, and
redacted SECRET classification markings top and bottom, back and
front, the cover was adorned with the MACV patch and the crest of
the US Army Inspector General Corps. Its symbol was a crossed
gold sword and fasces, with the words "DROIT ET AVANT"—

which literally means "right and forward" in Latin, but is interpreted by the army as "do right and move ahead."

Lex read through the report's executive summary. It drew the conclusion that the destruction of the Ri'Ga village and the death of its inhabitants was justified.

There's a big surprise, Lex thought.

There was "evidence" the villagers were members of the Viet Cong, or at least Viet Cong sympathizers.

As Lex flipped through the rest of the report, he became increasingly convinced that it was all a cover-up. At least 50 percent of the verbiage had been redacted—that is, blacked out in permanent marker before the report was copied. If everything was "justified," why all the redaction?

In addition, he discovered that every surviving member of his father's platoon had been interviewed by the CID or the IG, even the ones who weren't at Ri'Ga. A part of him burst with pride when he read what they had to say about First Lieutenant Darren Bross:

"The greatest officer I have ever known."

"There was not a better platoon leader in Vietnam. He saved my life. Twice."

"… a huge loss. I cried for a couple of days."

The gushing went on.

Lex searched for anything he could find about the circumstances of his father's demise. There wasn't much. It seemed that not a single platoon member admitted to seeing him shot, although every single one agreed that the shooting of Lieutenant

Bross had caused the platoon to treat the villagers as "enemy combatants."

Forensic evidence was missing for the bullet that caused the fatal wound; it had been a "through and through" to his father's neck, entering from the dorsal and exiting the ventral severing the spinal cord. An appendix captured the full autopsy, and it was loaded with more medical jargon than Lex could stand. The short summary from Lex: *He was shot through the neck while not looking. That severed his spinal cord. He suffocated and died on the spot.*

With a little analysis—and Lex was an exceptional analyst— he picked up that only three weapons had been found in the village: a Nagant M1895 pistol, a VZ 58 Czechoslovakian semi-automatic rifle, and a French MAT-49 submachine gun. All three were found amid a collection of spears, knives, crossbows, and other primitive weaponry under a "longhouse." The report said that all three weapons were "badly corroded and/or rusted and had not been fired in at least five years."

Lex did a quick internet search. The Nagant pistol was not known to have been used by the Viet Cong. It had been issued early in the war only to North Vietnamese Army officers.

When asked about the lack of offensive weaponry from the villagers, many of the soldiers responded with nearly identical wording: "We were not able to get all the VC. Several ran off carrying armloads of weapons." To Lex, those statements stuck out as bald-faced lies. Two soldiers replied, "I don't know, sir," and two others directed the interviewer to talk to the platoon sergeant about "that one."

Cover-up? he thought. *No shit, Sherlock.* Lex was no stranger to cover-ups. A former air force officer, he now worked as a GS-13 in a US government agency, the name of which he would not divulge to family members. In fact, his family didn't even know where he worked.

Lex also knew something about the Privacy Act of 1974, so he was surprised to find that each interview began with name, service number, place of birth, and hometown, and that none of this information had been redacted. Although someone had gone crazy redacting text with a magic marker, they had apparently overlooked the fact that service numbers, even early in the Vietnam War, were also social security account numbers, and should not have been included in a report provided under a FOIA request.

Lex called one of his colleagues who worked in an adjacent division. "I need a recommendation on how to find people with just a name and a social security number."

"We have all that shit."

"It's not official. I don't want a record of the search, and I can't use government systems."

"There are a couple of new sites on the internet, but I'm not sure if they're worth a shit. Try *whowhatwhere.com*, they charge a little, but I found my high school girlfriend."

"Was that a good or bad thing?"

"Got me laid at the twenty-fifth reunion."

"I say again, good or bad?"

"Good for me, bad for her is how I'd characterize it," he said, laughing out loud. "Who are you looking for?"

"No one special. The guys who murdered my dad."

"Funny."

"Yeah. Might be funny if it wasn't true. Thanks my man, see you tomorrow."

Lex looked up the website and signed up for their online service. There was an online payment option, but he didn't trust it and paid with his credit card over the phone instead. Then he entered the social security number of one of the platoon members.

On his Netscape browser, a little clock with hands marked the passing time. Then the screen filled with a hit: Norman Maxwell Nicolletti, age 53, 8841 East Durherm Lane, Bellevue, NE.

To ensure it wasn't a fluke, Lex tried a second number.

Mark Swingle Owens, age 52, 12409 E 622 N, St George, UT.

"Wow," he said aloud.

Then he got to work.

22 November 1999

Arcadia, DeSoto County, Florida

In the parking lot of a grocery store, the man pulled into a space under a flickering light to survey his find. He took a black and gray heavy-gauge nylon case from the trunk. A tiny cloth label showed the image of a bighorn sheep. Two handles like those on a cheap briefcase made it easy to carry; hanging from the brass D-ring on one was a set of chrome keys.

He unzipped the case and removed a rifle from the fake sheepskin interior that had kept it protected. Light from the streetlamp revealed a beautifully crafted wooden stock. Attached to grommets on the front and rear of the wood, below the trigger guard, was a heavy leather sling worn from years of use—a sling that would help make the rifle deadly accurate when wrapped properly around a hand and arm. A solid stock composite bumper was fastened to the stock with two recessed screws. On the left side of the rifle, some engraved words peeked out from under a light coating of rust: "22 SHORT OR LONG RIFLE." And below that: "LONG RIFLE ONLY AS AUTOMATIC." The rifle had a gold bead bladed front sight and a dovetailed slot for the rear. Next to a smooth receiver top was a knurled thumbscrew for a scope, which was absent. On top of the barrel, just south of where the forward stock ended, were the words "SAVAGE, Savage Arms Corporation, Utica New York, Model 6A."

Savage. It made him think of *moi.*

Below the brand were eight gills on the left and one on the right—a large, round, concave, serrated and grooved charging handle.

He held the rifle to the light and admired it. It was a masterwork of craftsmanship and looked hardly worn for its age. But he couldn't help wondering how, with such a small caliber, it would do the job.

His search of the house had been nerve-wracking. He had been sure the owner was gone, but to avoid alerting nosy neighbors, he had kept the lights off, and kept tripping over the piles of junk strewn about the home. He had been intent on finding a weapon, something that could be identified, and had found this candidate in a back room closet behind piles of old clothes, boxes, and hangers.

Looking into the trunk of the car, he saw that an ancient, glossy, folded sales brochure had slipped out of the case. Below a black and white photo of the rifle before him he read with interest:

"Incredible," he mumbled. "Thirty dollars." He examined the business end of the rifle, unscrewed the magazine, and removed a long brass tube. From its end, two cartridges dropped into the trunk of the car. He couldn't quite see them with the light from the streetlamp, so he clicked on the tiny flashlight on his keyring.

Well-oxidized brass. He learned later they were rat shot—.22 caliber rat shot. He held the two cartridges in his hand, looked up to the trunk light with an empty gaze, and contemplated how he would proceed.

18 December 1999
Green Gate Village, St. George, Washington County, Utah

Lex strolled around Green Gate Village. It was unique. He read a sign that said that Brigham Young had given the residents a wagonload of green paint he couldn't use to touch up the local Mormon temple. The color theme stuck for over 100 years; the village was named. Lex could not imagine why Officer Owens had chosen this spot to meet other than that it was public and easy to find. An unmarked cruiser pulled into the parking lot. Lex had never met Mark Owens, but he felt as though he had when a garrulous gray-haired man stepped from his vehicle in uniform.

"You, sir, are a ghost," Owens said as he reached out his hand behind a huge smile. "I have never seen anything like it. No doubt about it, you are the son of Darren Bross."

"Yes, sir, family members who knew him say I resemble my dad."

"Resemble? They're messing around with cloning on some of the ranches in the area. I'd say someone already nailed it with you."

They took seats in the quaint restaurant attached to a historic inn on the property. There was no iced tea on the menu, so Lex ordered fresh-squeezed lemonade to start. "Lunch is on me, Officer Owens."

"Thank you, young sir. The club sandwich and fries are to die for. They dip the shoestrings in sugar syrup before putting them in the fryer. Not a bit good for your heart, but oh so good for the soul."

Lex took Mark's advice and ordered that exact meal. "Thanks for meeting with me, Officer Owens—"

"Please, call me Mark. I insist."

"Mark, then." Lex took a bundle of paper of paper from his leather valise, laid it on the table, and turned it toward Mark. "This one is a redacted IG report from 1967," he said. "The Incident at Ri'Ga Village."

"Amazing. I gathered that they had talked to the entire platoon, but this is the first time I've ever seen a report," Mark said.

"Yeah, it spent a lot of years classified as 'secret' by the military. Standing alone, it might not pique your interest. It admits an unfortunate military action against a small village in the Central Highlands, but it essentially comes to the conclusion that the result was justified."

Mark flipped through the report. "It wasn't," he said, then let those two words hang in the air between them.

"Sir, this is your copy, so you'll be able to read it carefully later," Lex said.

"Ten years ago I would have told you the conclusion wouldn't surprise me, but I would be lying to myself and to you if I agreed with this nonsense. We didn't have any proof, but everyone thinks Rook fragged the LT." Mark's eyes filled with tears as he stared at the documents, "Your father, I should say."

They talked over refills of lemonade about Vietnam, about the experience of combat, and about the special man Lex never had the opportunity to know.

As they were finishing up, Mark almost offhandedly mentioned an encounter that would prove to be a boon to Lex's investigation. "I don't know if this is of any interest to you," Mark said, "but not long back there was this oriental man—I guess I should say *Asian* to be politically correct—came to the station looking for me. He told the dispatcher he knew me from the war."

"Could that be?" Lex asked.

"No way. Donita said the guy wasn't old enough have known me in Nam. There's no better judge of age than Donita, and she said he was something like forty. She thought it was creepy and kicked the guy out on his ear."

"So he never came back?" Lex asked.

"Not that I know of, but…" Mark reached for his back pocket. "He left his phone number on a yellow sticky note." Mark presented a folded square of yellow paper and peeled the sticky apart. "Here you go. Take it. All yours. I'm not calling him. Have at it."

Lex slipped the paper into his pocket.

Mark looked at his watch and said, "Well, I'm one of the old heads in the department, but I still have to make it look like I'm working once in a while."

"Before you go," Lex said, "could I ask a favor? This takes someone wearing a badge."

"If it will help you come to terms with this, then I'll do what I can to help."

"I want to get a look at Lionel Rook's criminal record. I'm looking for anything he might have done as an adult."

"Good thing you're drawing the line there. Juvenile records are impossible."

"You'd think so, wouldn't you?" Lex said. "But strictly speaking, that's not exactly true."

"How so?"

"I can trust you, I guess. I ran into this a few times working security clearance investigations with the air force. It turns out that 'sealed' records are not so sealed when it concerns national security."

"So you found some of Rook's juvie stuff?"

"I can neither confirm nor deny that I have any information

on Lionel Rook's juvenile record, but let's just say that in today's world he would never have been allowed to enlist in the military."

"It wasn't that long ago."

"Right, but it was back in the day when a judge could order you in. That was Rook's path. There were no enlistment records to falsify since he didn't apply for enlistment." Lex began packing up his briefcase and getting ready to depart. "There's some good stuff in there. Kid was evil personified."

Mark stood. "What are you going to use all this for?"

"Well, there is no statute of limitations on murder. I'd love to build a case."

"Good luck on that one. Listen, I'll see what I can get you from the various crimes databases, but it's risky. They can tie my search back to me. I'll have to think about it."

"I understand." Lex stood. "Sir, thank you so much for meeting me and helping me to get to know my father." They shook hands. "Merry Christmas to you and your family. This looks like a nice little town to celebrate in."

"It is, but we have a cabin rented up at Brianhead. Everyone wants a better chance at seeing a white Christmas this year."

Lex knew Brianhead from a visit there with friends a few years back. "It's a beautiful place. You guys are going to have a blast."

Mark Owens phoned Lex two days later. "I called in a favor.

We're good. Do you have a fax machine? Not much here, really. Our guy got out of the army after twenty-two years' service in the mid-seventies. He's been pretty clean since then. But you might be interested in one arrest record from the late fifties."

"He was already in the army by then, right?"

"Right, but he must have been home on leave or something like that. Arcadia, Florida. He was arrested as a suspect in a murder, but then released. It's all in the report."

A few minutes later, Lex was pulling a copy of an investigator's arrest report from the fax machine. He scanned the salient points.

- 13 December 1960

- Spillway—DeSoto County flood control district, four miles west of Arcadia, Fla.

- William James "Willie" Johnson, age 14, found dead.

- Cause of death: Drowning.

- Post mortem shot in chest with a small caliber bullet. Rat shot.

- Suspects: Sylvan Bodean Rook, 38. Lionel Bodean Rook, 23; US Army on Christmas leave. Seen in area together. Recognized by two local fishermen.

It was the only place in the report that mentioned Lionel Rook. Lex had no idea who Sylvan Rook was. Too old to be a brother, and he was pretty sure Rook's father was dead or in prison at the time, so this must be an uncle.

The report was only two pages, and the second page was

nothing but a few irrelevant words above a large rubber stamp that read: "RELEASED ON OWN RECOGNIZANCE."

For Lex, this raised more questions than it answered. *The South. 1950s. Army soldier. Two white guys. Dead black kid. Perhaps no real reason to make a case of it.*

7 February 2000
Las Vegas, Clark County, Nevada

Since the call from out of the blue after the New Year, he had worried about meeting the lieutenant's son for weeks. But when at last they met, he found he'd worried over nothing. He recounted what he remembered from so many years ago—without going into too much detail, of course, and downplaying any elements of anger or revenge—and Lex Bross handed over the copies of what he had: a typewritten summary of Lionel Rook's criminal history and a copy of an army report on the village massacre.

He immediately keyed in on the report about the murdered Florida boy, and from that, he developed an idea. He asked Lex if had any idea where any of the other members of the platoon ended up. Could they be contacted?

Lex told him about the website he had found for locating people, and promised he would email what he had discovered.

The man then asked Lex if he had any interest in meeting the soldiers. He told Lex about a reunion that was going to take place back east. He thought it might be interesting to attend to find out who showed up.

Finally, the two men cordially shook hands and agreed to stay in contact.

Two weeks later, the man got the email from Lex with contact information for the other members of the platoon. Still in Las Vegas, he found a typewriter at a pawn shop off the Strip. It was just thirty dollars, and it would suit his needs—or at least he thought so. He didn't understand at the time that typewriters have individual characteristics like fingerprints.

The machine was old—manufactured around 1970—but serviceable. A tag reading "ROYAL" was affixed to the upper left, and was balanced by "*Century*2000" in the upper right. At the time it was built, the company deemed it so advanced that it would still be state-of-the-art in the year 2000. If only they'd known that by the turn of the millennium you'd have to locate a pawn shop or a collector to find a typewriter. And a new ribbon? Forget it.

He was not a typist, so it took some time to roll out thirty-three letters from the platen.

Dear Stanley,

Thirty two years pass like the wind. I hope this letter finds you good. It has been to long since we

seen each other. I am try to get the guys from the second together for a small reunion. I really really hope you can come so we can all play catchup. In a couple months on the weekend of Memorial Day a thousands of veterans like you and me are going to meet in Washington, D.C. You can look it up. Its Operation Rolling Thunder like when we bombed the shit out of north. I will see you and the others of our platoon mates next to the statue of the three soldiers by the Wall at noon on Sunday. Make that May 28. I hope you can make it Private Peckham.

Your friend for life,
Doc

Four down, twenty-seven to go.

Dear Dick,

Thirty two years pass like the wind. I hope this letter finds you good. It has been...

The man folded the letters into thirds and stuffed them into legal-sized envelopes—a task more difficult because he was wearing rubber dishwashing gloves. The return address on each envelope began with "The MacNultys." He figured the address he'd chosen should work fine. He'd found some MacNultys in the phone book up in Pahrump.

He had chosen self-stick folding-top envelopes so that he would not leave any evidence of saliva, but before sealing them, he sprinkled inside ten of them some of the detritus he had taken from the bathroom drawer and hair brush in Arcadia: some greasy dandruff, individual strands of hair, and dry skin.

Finally, he gathered up his short stack of crumpled mistakes from the round metal trash can and headed out.

After stopping for gas at the AM/PM Mini Market at the corner of West Charleston Boulevard and South Buffalo Drive—where he deposited the plastic bag full of his mistakes in a trash receptacle between the pumps—he took the scenic route past Red Rock Canyon, stopped for a soda in Blue Diamond, and made his way to the drive-in post office box up Nevada Route 160 near the center of town in Pahrump.

28 May 2000
The Mall, Washington, DC

For most of his formative years, Wellington Enoch Chamberlain was known by his given name—"Wellington"—until high school, at least, when most of his schoolmates called him Welly. Thankfully for him, in the United States few had heard of Wellington boots; he had read about a man named Wellington in

England, who picked up the nickname "Boots."

"Enoch" didn't lend itself to easy usage either. So Wellington grew up hating his parents for burdening him with these two anchors. At various times in his life he experimented with "Chip," and "Mac," and, once, "Cham." But his chosen monikers never stuck. What did stick was the psychological damage he carried from being teased for his name.

Had his name been, "Hunter Stone," perhaps the kids would have left him alone.

After a family visit to the Civil War Battlefield at Gettysburg, and learning of Joshua Chamberlain, he asked his father if he could change his name to Joshua and go by "Josh," but he got only a lecture on the value of ancestry and the importance of carrying family names across generations.

When Wellington's first son was born in March 1973, he named the boy "Hunter Stone Chamberlain." Screw ancestry and carrying on generational names.

Wellington was drafted into the army upon graduation from Washington-Lee High School in Arlington, Virginia. He had grown up close to Jiggles Schmidt and Russ Russelvage, but he didn't know them until the war. Russ and Jiggles played on their schools' football teams, whereas Wellington was Assistant Team Manager of his own school's team. His job was to ensure the ready availability of cups and water for every practice and game. Waterboy: a job commensurate with the name Wellington.

On day one of Basic Training at Fort Polk, Wellington was standing in a loose formation pretending to be in the military.

Everyone was in civvies; Wellington was in dungarees and penny loafers, real Bass ones with leather soles and heels, and a wheat-back penny in each. He had saved money mowing lawns to afford them. A drill sergeant was walking the formation taking turns screaming at each individual.

He stopped in front of Wellington and, at a volume sufficient to carry across a stadium, he yelled, "What's your name, soldier?"

"Wellington Chamberlain."

"Wellington Chamberlain what?"

"Just Wellington Chamberlain."

"That's Wellington Chamberlain—Drill Sergeant."

"Got it, sir."

"Not *sir*, dipshit, Drill Sergeant."

"Yes, Drill Sergeant."

One would have thought that particular lesson might have sunk in before this moment, since two dozen young men had already gotten the word ahead of him. The army is expert at ingraining new habits.

The drill sergeant looked at his clipboard. "And your middle name is Enoch?"

"Yes, Drill Sergeant."

"You're fucking kidding me. How are we going to work with that?"

"I don't understand, Drill Sergeant."

"You're a soldier. We can't be calling you Wellington until you're a brigadier general, and since that's never going to happen, from now on, you're Loo, and not Lou like Lou Costello, but Loo like Waterloo."

Of the fifty-one men in formation, in three rows of seventeen, perhaps two got the reference. But from then on, for the rest of his life, Wellington Enoch Chamberlain's problem was solved. He was "Loo" forevermore, and he dealt with the 99 percent of the population who misspelled it "Lou." By 1600 that afternoon he'd come to understand that the Duke of Wellington had defeated Napoleon at Waterloo a hundred and fifty years earlier. He'd gotten that information from some huge guy in the barracks with a name like *Kookydoll*. The guy seemed to know a lot about history.

Loo toyed with the idea of asking the drill sergeant if he could switch to "Duke," but there was already a famous actor named Duke. He looked into an imaginary mirror in his mind and came to understand that he was probably better suited as Loo.

All that was over thirty years ago now—thirty years since Loo had left Nam. But throughout those years, he stayed in contact with Russ and Jiggles. Jiggles, like Loo, returned physically unscathed from the war, but Russ was fond of showing off his missing finger and recounting the way he'd slapped a grenade like a handball. Jiggles lost his nickname after the war—to his family and friends he was simply "Dan." But to everyone he had served with, he was forever "Jiggles."

Of the three friends, only Loo still lived in his childhood home. He'd moved back after college when his parents died together during a freak volcano eruption in South America. He was also the only one of the three who received the mailed invitation from Doc.

But he phoned his Northern Virginia friends about it, and they arranged to travel together. Russ was planning to attend Rolling Thunder anyway—it was an annual event for him, at least when he could make it. He could don his leather chaps and vest, Ride to the Wall on his Harley, and stage at Pentagon North Parking with thousands of others. Unfortunately, Jiggles had to back out at the last minute, due to a family commitment.

Russ and Loo got hugs and kisses from Miss America who, for some reason, was at Pentagon North Parking dressed in full denim adorned with veteran, POW/MIA, and US flag patches and buttons. She was there in support of *the cause*, whatever that was. Russ thought she was a dead ringer for Phyllis George, who was closer to his age and had been Miss America at about the time he left the army. While the old farts were goggling Heather French —"the stupidest name for a winner in the history of the Miss America pageant," Loo commented—Russ was thinking of Phyllis George and wishing she were there instead of someone younger than his daughter.

It takes a while for ten thousand motorcycles, and scooters, and special-made motorized tricycles to make the trip, four abreast, past Arlington Cemetery, across Memorial Bridge, and to find parking along the DC Mall from the Capitol to the reflecting pool. The most popular spots were near the Lincoln Memorial and the Vietnam War Memorial, and at those locations you could find bikes and people crammed into every available patch of grass. DC parking enforcement was taking a rare day off from their sworn duty to harass tourists.

Russ and Loo arrived before the noon appointment. They roamed through the sea of humanity, visited a "Find Your Buddies Now" van, and made charcoal rubbings of the names of long-lost friends on the Wall, including Lieutenant Bross, Stan Peckham, Paco, Pixie, and Marty Byers. They both choked up when they recounted the death of Bat Masterson, and they had both forgotten, until that moment staring at the Wall, that his given name was James.

Then, pointing to a name, Russ said, "Jimmy boy, there's a mistake."

"I'm not Jimmy. I'm Loo."

"Whoops, sorry—daydreaming. I was talking to Bat. Take a look at this." He pointed again to the Wall, where "Sean Patrick MacNulty" was etched in stone. Fuck, you just got a letter from him, right? Doc, right?"

"That's right, Doc," Lou said. "Doc MacNulty. I think Sean was his real name, and he's right there near all our other guys. Must be him. Or at least they think it's him. I wonder how many other mistakes are on this wall."

"At least I don't see *our* names. There's that."

"Funny, I've been to this wall twenty times and have never noticed his name before. Probably my brain blocking it out."

"Nah, he's way down there. They're in order of death, right? They must think he died later from that claymore blast."

"Fuckin' idiots. He's coming today from somewhere around Vegas. We'll have to show him. He's going to laugh his ass off."

"Remember that Frisbee dog, Nutty or whatever? I thought

he was going to kill Rook."

"The dog?"

"No, dipshit, the dog was dead. Doc. I thought Doc was going to kill him."

"Wish he had, that sadistic fuck."

As they studied the Wall, they tried to avoid the rantings of a nearby crazy man, who was yelling unintelligible non sequiturs to the Wall about smells and death. But they both had a spark of recognition at the same time. They turned together and examined the scruffy, unkempt elderly man. It was the eyes that gave it away. Loo took a step and held out his hand in greeting.

"Sergeant Rook. Good to see you again."

"Who the fuck are you?" the man said in a deep, unmistakable Everglades redneck drawl.

"Loo, Sarge." He motioned to Russ. "And this is Corporal Russelvage. Russ."

"You I remember," Rook said to Loo. "You were at Ri'Ga."

"I was."

"Russ. Sorry man, I don't rightly recollect you right at this moment. You must have been fucking off with the REMFs."

"That I was, Sergeant. That I was, but not sorry I missed the snafu there."

Rook looked up with tired, bloodshot, watery eyes. He stepped toward Russ, too close, right in his personal space, as if entering a staring contest. Then he stepped back and shook his head. "Can't remember. Smells is what brings it back for me. Sometimes when I stomp on a juicy fat roach I remember Nam. It's not the killing or the other shit I remember. It's the smell."

Loo nodded. "I hear that."

"Yeah, but do you smell it? Five senses, motherfucker."
Rook was dead serious. He stared the two men down with crazy eyes
that made the hair stand up on the back of their necks. It struck
both Russ and Loo at the same time that they had found themselves
in the presence of this psycho—again.

Russ looked at his watch and gave the roundup signal to
Loo. "Guess it's that time," he said.

"Time for what?" Rook asked.

"Time for the meeting."

"What meeting?"

"Doc's platoon reunion."

"What platoon reunion?"

"Didn't you get the invitation?"

"What invitation?"

"Doc sent a letter. Meet at the soldier's monument at noon."

"Nope. I didn't get shit."

"Then how did you know to be here?" Loo asked.

"Fuck, I've been here every year since eighty-nine. You
could set your watch by it."

"You mean on the Ride to the Wall?"

"Fuck no, I mean right here. Every Sunday before Memorial
Day at noon I'm right here. Always a lot of other vets right here,
ridin' motorcycles and such."

"Did you ride from Florida?"

"Ride? You mean drive? Fuckin' A straight. I drove from

Florida. Drive every year."

"So you didn't get a letter?" Loo asked again.

"Letter? Do you have shit in your ears? No, I didn't get no fuckin' letter."

"Well, come along with us anyway. We're supposed to meet in about five minutes. Some of the old gang."

The Three Soldiers Memorial on the DC Mall is a stone's throw from the Wall. The walk would have been short if not for the sea of humanity between the two locations. The three of them muscled through the crowd of vets and came face to face with the monument.

Rook spoke first. "It says Three Soldiers, but any fucking idiot knows this guy"—he pointed at the one in the center—"is a Jarhead."

"I don't think the average Joe really notices the difference."

"Who the fuck is *average Joe?*" Rook barked.

"You know, the average guy."

"You said 'average Joe.' Never heard of him."

Russ looked at Loo, rolled his eyes, and gave the crazy sign with his index finger around his temple. Loo raised his eyebrows in acknowledgement, adding a grimace of his own.

Recognizing old friends after so many years was not an easy task, especially with everyone dressed in all manner of costume from biker gang to preppy. Haircuts ranged from waist-length ponytails emerging from do-rag bandanas to high-and-tight. There were hats of all kinds, sunglasses, and a wide range of ancient-to-current uniform options: dress greens, flight suits, and jungle fatigues. But in the end they did recognize some of the old crew.

Ernie Salisbury showed from Portland, Maine. Peanut Carver was there. He had lost his nickname back in Valdosta, Georgia, but none of the guys listened when he asked them to call him George. "So where's Doc?" he asked.

"That's what we're trying to figure out," Russ replied.

They all recognized Craig Message. He came with binoculars around his neck as if he'd never left the jungle or stopped looking at birds. He was still at the Fish and Wildlife Service, and his parents in Belleville, Illinois had called him to say he'd gotten a letter. Message then finagled a government business trip from his region headquarters to visit the Bird Grants and Conservation Divisions in Falls Church, Virginia.

He tipped his binoculars with his right hand. "Hey, it's May. We're right in the middle of migration. You never know what could show up. Besides, gotta make it look like I'm working. Taxpayers and all."

With one of those tiny smiles that shows no teeth, Loo offered his hand in greeting. "Message, you are a fucking dork!" They laughed and gave each other a big left arm hug while shaking hands with their right.

By 1230 hours, only nine of those thought to be alive showed: Kook, Robin, Peanut, Loo, Message, Jiggles, Russ, Ernie, and of course Rook, who appeared to be beginning to recall who these people were and the past he had shared with them.

They spent army-quality time, smokin' and jokin', catching up to the present, bragging about kids and a couple of grandkids.

No one was surprised that Kook was a full college professor. Dick "Robin" Grayson still lived in Gainesville, Florida and was foreman of the industrial plant for the university there. George Washington Carver managed a truck stop on Interstate 75 just outside Valdosta.

Ernie Salisbury had landed as a brewmaster in Portland, Maine, where he crafted beer for three microbrew pubs in the area and another out in Bar Harbor for the tourist crowd there. He told a story about starting the place as a regular bar. He'd put a sign in the ladies room that read, "Ernie has a big dick," and then over the bar he put another sign that read, "I'm Ernie." The bar became a brewpub about the time craft beer took off, but the sign persisted. T-shirts were offered for sale emblazoned with "I'm Ernie," over a graphic image of a beer growler with a simple logo: "BERT'S ALE."

The get-together was fun, if a little awkward, but they found the camaraderie they'd built and solidified in combat was a human condition that could never be broken. Some had been members of the LRRP, some had not, but everyone had something to contribute as they recounted story after story of this village, and that attack, and this patrol, and that "fucking captain," and the long sad memories of the friends they had lost in the jungle, and the stink, and the humidity, and the mosquitos, and the malaria pills, and the jungle rot, and the tiger.

The tiger. Peanut and Message had seen it first-hand. Two others had built a personal memory from others' stories, but Peanut corrected them: "It was just me, Craig, Maples, and the LT."

It was the first time anyone had brought up the LT. Russ

asked, "What the fuck happened out there anyway?"

Of the nine at the Soldiers Memorial, only Russ and Ernie hadn't made the trip to Ri'Ga. The others—those from the LRRP—shuffled around and gazed at their shoes.

"What the fuck happened?" Russ repeated. "CID grilled me like I was some kind of murderer."

The silence was deafening. Kook wiped a tear from his eye, but no one wanted to talk anymore. Russ's question was the drunk uncle who ended the party.

Still, they hung around until 1330 just in case, but no one else showed. The atmosphere among the nine had become somber, but still cordial. They headed over to a line of porta-potties set up between the Wall and the reflecting pool. On the way, they passed through an unexpected group of Montagnards, some of whom were dressed as US soldiers in a hodgepodge of uniform items. They were lounging under a banner stretched between trees, reading "Montagnard, Kernersville, North Carolina," but someone had spray painted a neat line through the word "Montagnard" and had sprayed instead, in the form of gang graffiti, *Dega*. Out of context no one had any idea what the message was. None of the nine platoon mates were surprised to see the group in Washington, DC—although they might have been had they known more about the harrowing journey the dozen men had gone through to get to this spot, on this day.

They continued their way through the crowds, until Message suddenly held up his right hand in a stopping motion. More than one of the nine thought back to their time on patrol. Even after more than thirty years, the group instinctively stopped. For a brief second, until Message pulled them all together with a hand signal and closed fist, Dan Schmidt wondered if his separation from the others was sufficient, then he smiled at his stupidity.

"Don't look, don't stare," Message said, which of course caused six of the nine to begin looking and staring. "Over my left shoulder, leaning against the trunk of that tree—see that guy?"

"The one in the ball cap?" Kook asked.

"No, next to him."

"Holy shit!" Carver said. "It's the LT."

"You have to be shitting me! Can't be the lieutenant, but that guy looks just like him," Ernie agreed.

"Can't be is right," Rook said under his breath, almost inaudible—but not quite. "I wasted that mutha."

Kook's ears perked up at that comment. "Say that again, Sergeant Rook?"

"Nothin'."

Kook turned to face Rook and grabbed him by both shoulders. "Did you just say you *shot* him?"

"I didn't say nothin'," Rook said, while forty feet away, the lieutenant's doppelganger, his son Lex, tossed a little wave at the group and started strolling over.

Dick Grayson knew. He had kept quiet until now, but he knew. "Rook, you're a murdering asshole. I've spent my life wishing I had told someone. I came this close," he pinched a space between his thumb and index finger, "to telling the IG when we all got interviewed."

Now Kook turned on Robin. "Tell us now, or I *will* beat you."

Kook wasn't kidding. His face was red, his fists drawn and squeezed tight.

Robin's eyes welled up. "He plugged the LT right in the back of the head. Murdered him. Cold blood." Dick was sobbing before he got the whole admission out.

What followed was one of those uncomfortable moments of silence that goes on just a little too long. Everyone was looking back and forth between Robin and Rook. Some became aware that the lieutenant's twin was now standing among them. Hadn't aged a day.

"It was the neck. Back of the neck," Rook said quietly. He couldn't deal with the inaccuracy of the description. "He was going to get us all killed."

As the saying goes, time flies. But Kook remembered it in slow motion. He was now a full college professor, with tenure at Rutgers University, yet he could not recall a time in his life, even in combat, when he'd reacted so quickly without thinking. All six foot six of him, with hands like dinner plates, he decked Lionel Rook with a single right hook to the left temple.

Rook went down like a sack. Out cold. Like the movies.

Kook rubbed his hand, wondered if he'd broken something.

Lex reached out a hand to no one in particular. "Hi, guys. Not sure what's going on, but I'm guessing some of you guys think you know me."

"No shit, dude. Who are you?" Message asked.

Everyone turned to face the new guy, even as Rook was out cold on the ground at their feet. Some onlookers looked on in mild concern, but things had calmed down, so no one interfered.

"I'm Lex Bross," the lieutenant's twin said. "My dad was Darren Bross. I think he was your platoon commander."

"Platoon leader, to be exact," Carver said. "You look just like him."

"I never knew him, but I get that a lot," Lex said.

Dick was still wiping the tears and anger from his face. He pointed at Rook. "You never knew him because that motherfucker right there shot him fucking dead. Fucking psycho."

"Not gonna lie," Lex said. "You're not the first one who's told me that." He looked over at Kook.

"You guys know each other?" Dick asked.

Kook lit up. "Full disclosure, guys. I *have* met Lex, but only recently. I made contact with the LT's parents. They reached out to Lex. We made the connection."

"Well fuck me naked," Dick said. "Thanks for telling us."

"I was going to get around to it. All in good time," Kook said.

Rook awoke to find Russ cradling his head and pouring bottled water on his face. He had been out nearly twenty minutes. Unlike his earlier mumbles, now his voice was clear and direct, and he said something that could never be taken back: "If you tell

anyone. If you tell a soul. Even a peep, you're next. I will find each
and every one of you motherfuckers and I will kill you dead."

Eight men heard it.

Five lived to repeat it when asked.

Three would be dead before the end of the weekend.

Then Rook stood and brushed his trousers and the back of
his shirt, the part he could reach. Nothing came off. Dirt was at
home on him. He backed away from Kook, not interested in any
repeat, and bumped into Lex. "Whoops," he said. "Sorry. Fuck.
Don't have my balance right yet."

Then he saw Lex. He stepped closer, too close. His habit
was to enter the personal space of those he encountered. Lex held
his ground. Rook said, "Fuck are you?"

Without blinking, Lex crooked his neck forward until he was
inches from Rook's face. He said, "I'm Lieutenant Bross. Who else?"

Rook never knew the truth, but he ran.

The others laughed like they had not laughed in some time.

May 28, 2000

Somewhere near Washington, DC

The last thing Dick remembered was sitting on a brass-clad
barstool in Georgetown. *Three or four of those homebrew beers… that*
lawyer… that chick grinding the chair… my bike out front, safe and sound.
His mind jumped in flashes from thought to thought. *What the fuck?*
How'd I get here? Fuck is in my mouth?

With more time to think he could have made some guesses about how he got here. As it was he was utterly terror-stricken.

It's a locker room. Ben-Gay. Old cigar smoke. Fuck, I can't move my head. Training table. I'm strapped to the trainer's table. Can't see. Bright light. Hangover. I'm gonna puke.

He rolled his head back, the only direction available. He stretched. His neck tendons were bulging, but his forehead was secured to the table legs with some kind of tape. *Probably duct tape. Can't move.* He could tell there was someone behind him, but it was impossible to get a good look. All he could see was a tripod, and—

Fuck! Fuck! It's a fucking rifle! Get me the fuck out of here!

Time passed, and Dick's captor didn't move, just observed. Dick's mind wandered. *Bright light. No blindfold. He wants me to see something, but I can't move a fucking inch. I'm gonna die. Why me? What did I do?*

Dick panicked. His eyes bugged and twitched left and right, the only parts of his body not secured. He screamed, or tried to. But all the man in the shadows could hear was a retch and the sound of dry heaves.

Dick cried. He sobbed. *Too much beer. I'm gonna piss my pants.* He did. Urine pooled at his buttocks and dribbled down to the concrete floor.

More time passed. Dick heard nothing. Nothing. Eventually, against all odds, he fell asleep. When he awoke, he felt instant terror again. *He's back. Feet shuffling. What the fuck does he want?*

Dick could see one hand in a black leather glove holding a magazine in front of Dick's face. *All this. Why all this to see a*

magazine? Some kind of photo. Wait. Wait! Fuck, it's that picture! Oh fuck.
It's that picture! He wants me to know. He wants me to feel his terror. Oh fuck!

The man pulled the trigger.

CHAPTER 27

29 May 2000

Near the intersection of I Street NW and Sixth Street NW

Chinatown, Washington, DC

Memorial Day was a federal holiday, so there was not much reason for Miss Huan's House of Oriental Massage to open. Her shop was just a few blocks from the Capitol, the Gallery Place Metro stop, and any number of federal buildings, so it was the federal bureaucracy that kept her in business. As a result, it was ten on Tuesday morning before anyone discovered the dead man zip-tied to one of her portable massage tables. The circulation had been cut off to his swollen hands before he died. His wallet had fallen from his back pocket onto the floor. It was only days later that the police, in their genius, would conclude that robbery had not been a motive since no money was taken.

A visit to the family of Wellington E. Chamberlain in Arlington revealed that he had last been seen on Sunday morning, heading to a veteran's event downtown. His wife, Rebecca—Becky —had no further information. His car was parked out in front of the house, ticketed since he was supposed to have moved it for street sweeping. She assumed he'd gotten a ride, but he had left early, so she hadn't seen who picked him up.

Nearly three weeks later, on June nineteenth, the Washington, DC Office of the Chief Medical Examiner delivered a report to the DC Metropolitan Police Department. Sealed in a Tyvek envelope, it went into the inbox of Raymond Hopkins, the lead investigator. But Detective Hopkins had loaded his kids up in the minivan on Saturday the seventeenth to drive nine hundred miles to Disney World and to spend three weeks in Florida with relatives. The OCME report would gather dust in an old-fashioned wooden inbox along with fourteen other murder cases.

When the office finally got around to looking at the case, they deemed the cause of death unusual. This led to a round of discussions among the detectives present. But the case went cold in the face of more pressing matters.

30 May 2000
Falls Church, Fairfax County, Virginia

Memorial Day, May twenty-ninth was also a holiday at Falls Church High School, so, like Loo Chamberlain in Chinatown, Dick Grayson's body had been ripening for a couple of days by the time it was discovered. Nick Kelly was the morning janitor, and he had worked a deal with the coaching staff to use the locker room. Its showers were better than the one in his mobile home, plus it helped him save on his water and electric bill. For eight years he'd maintained the corner locker in the coach's area. The students never had to suffer the indignity of exposing themselves in front of "the help."

Nick had also finagled himself a reserved parking spot next to the rear entrance of the gym. A friend who worked with the City of Falls Church had made an official-looking sign for him: *Reserved for Special Staff.* "Special Staff" was just "Nick Kelley." Nick drove a "classic" 1970 Plymouth Barracuda, and he didn't want it damaged by proximity to the student parking area, even though it was already a rolling heap of junk. It took the coaches some time to catch on to the scam.

On this morning, as Nick unlocked the deadbolt on the rear gym entrance and opened the door, the smell of death hit him immediately. Two years earlier a litter of newborn squirrels had died in the wall behind a row of lockers, and Nick guessed something similar had happened this morning. He soon found out just how wrong he was. Instead of squirrels in the walls, there was a bloated, purple-hued, former white guy duct-taped to one of the padded training tables. There was no blood, but seeping from stains in the man's clothing, bodily fluids dripped to the floor. Nick dropped his nylon duffel and in a single powerful retch he vomited his breakfast —coffee, cheese grits, and three biscuits—to the floor. The eruption puke formed an exclamation point from his feet to a spot under the training table.

So much for protection of the crime scene.

The 911 dispatcher from the Police Emergency Communications Unit matter-of-factly passed on the description of the situation as related by the Falls Church High School janitor. A patrolman from the Falls Church police department, who was nearby at Seven Corners, grabbing a muffin and coffee at a little strip mall shop just off Route 50, was the first responder. The dispatcher directed him to the rear of the gymnasium, where he met a school security guard who had kept arriving students out of the locker room.

Satisfied that the scene was in one piece, the patrolman opened his checklist to ensure he'd properly secured the scene. His only mistake was his failure to recognize that the area outside the locker room was part of the crime scene as well. From the trunk of his patrol car he took out a roll of yellow crime-scene tape and used it to block both the exterior and two interior entrances to the locker room.

A radio follow-up from dispatch let him know that two detectives from the Criminal Investigations Unit were en route, but before they arrived both the chief of police and the operations division lieutenant showed up on scene. They ducked under the tape and entered the locker room holding handkerchiefs to their faces. In under a minute the lieutenant was on the phone to the emergency number for the office of the state medical examiner in Manassas. The patrolman had ordered an ambulance, but the chief put the skids on that request. The ME van would be more appropriate, he reckoned.

Falls Church is a suburb of Washington, DC, a city that's a hot spot for murder on the east coast of the United States. But in this sleepy community, murder was a rare event that attracted attention. Before the chief got off the phone, two patrol cars from the Fairfax County sheriff's office had joined a growing collection in the parking lot. The chief appointed the lieutenant as the on-scene commander. His first task was to organize traffic so that those who needed to be close to the scene were able to get there.

A department photographer from the CIU took countless digital photos. Of particular interest were footprints leading from a pattern of vomit. The photographer didn't realize the "evidence" was an after-the-fact addition to the scene. He had to suppress his own gag reflex while taking shots from every conceivable angle.

An assistant medical examiner showed up seventy-five minutes late claiming to have been stuck in traffic—which was probably true, as backups were a constant challenge for the couple million government workers who made their way each day from Manassas to Washington, DC over two primary gridlocked arteries, Interstate 66 and US Route 50. The ME made his initial assessment, including the official pronouncement of death—as if anyone on the scene could have had even the slightest doubt.

8 June 2000
Falls Church, Fairfax County, Virginia

The Falls Church lead investigator was a seasoned professional, Detective Sergeant Charles "Chas" Conway. He'd just gotten the state medical examiner's report via fax and was looking through it. The ME had called in advance, so there was little surprise, but he knew this was something special. Twenty-three pages, with each stamped "DRAFT," awaiting final approval from the chief ME.

FINAL DIAGNOSIS AND FINDINGS:

Penetrating gunshot wound of the cardiac and peritoneal cavities;

> 1. Fatal trauma to the heart.

> 2. Internal GSW. Bruising and lacerations to upper trachea and esophagus to 23cm from open mouth. Probable rifle barrel.

> 3. 153 spherical machine-produced metallic balls caliper-measured to 1.2mm in diameter (firearms analysis required), potential Rat Shot.

> 4. Path of projectiles: Through trachea, esophageal wall into pericardial sac, though right subclavian artery, aortic arch, through left auricle, left ventricle, and peritoneal cavity. No trauma to lungs or pleural hemorrhage

> 5. Exit: None

Subsequent pages detailed External Examination, Other Identifying Features, Evidence of Injury, Evidence of Recent Medical Treatment, Evidence of Organ Donation, Internal Examination, Body Cavities, Toxicology, Blood Alcohol, Neck and Tongue, and every other anatomical feature. There were hand-drawn diagrams, poor copies of radiographs, a copy of the death report written at the scene, and a ME report from the scene.

Chas flipped to page twelve, the case summary. After

scanning past a recounting of the 911 call, the securing of the crime scene, photos taken, et cetera, Detective Sergeant Conway read: "White male, 54YO, bound with duct tape to a vinyl padded 30" x 80" table in the boys' locker room of Falls Church High School on Jaguar Trail, Falls Church, Virginia. Apparently shot internally by another person. Initial investigation indicates after being secured, the victim was forcibly impaled with a .22 caliber rifle placed into his mouth and implanted in and down the esophagus. GSW fired internally that entered the heart through the esophageal wall causing the heart to stop and the victim to bleed out internally."

Detective Conway had had Grayson's name since the week prior and had notified next of kin. An investigative unit from the Florida State Patrol was assisting his department in interviewing the family, but Dick Grayson had taken a long weekend and the following week to drive his new 1999 Harley-Davidson Road King Classic to the Rolling Thunder POW/MIA Rally in Washington, DC. He had been contacted by Vietnam-era army friends and in conjunction with the rally was attending a reunion of his platoon. His wife, Magan, had seen a letter from an "army buddy," but she was unable to locate it. She assumed that Dick had taken the letter with him. She had no information on who had sent the letter, but she remembered the friend had referred to Dick as "Robin," a nickname she had not heard in over thirty years.

Conway had canvassed the area for witnesses, but came up empty. Vehicles, nothing. Security cameras, zero. Motive, zip.

11 August 2003
Arcadia, DeSoto County, Florida

The man was more tech-savvy than even he would once have thought. He understood that computer searches could be tracked to specific internet protocol addresses and that spending much time on the FindYourFriend website could lead a persistent investigator with a carefully worded court order to a specific computer, a specific user. The online course he'd taken in Wi-Fi cracking helped a lot; it was worth the cost of tuition. Every year hacking was getting harder than the last. Time to try something new.

His experience told him that WPA and WPA2 Wi-Fi encryption protocols employed robust storage regimens and a minimum of eight-character passwords, which slow the speed of automated cracking programs, but he had time. Combining that with the network SSID almost ruled out using pre-computed tables for code-cracking. But by now he knew some tricks from playing around in his own neighborhood.

He stopped his rented panel van on a side street and prepared. Some of his equipment and his capable laptop PC needed more power than the twelve-volt resident system could provide. He'd added a couple of marine batteries and bought a capable inverter from a place called "Car Stuff" in Palm Beach. Leaving the van running in the neighborhood at night would not be smart. It needed to appear dark and parked.

His first step was locating and exploiting the four-way

handshake, the cryptologic process between computers that validated the wireless access points in both directions, to and from. He knew the handshake would take place behind a cryptographic veil that would be all but impossible to tear down. The method that worked for him was to grab transmitted packets during the process and then crack and apply the right password to complete the transaction. At home he had found routine success in under ninety minutes—and even faster when someone was working on the target system. The key was capturing a valid handshake. The portable system in the van was working well.

He targeted Rook's home network, a single Wi-Fi router, with patience while the device was validating itself to the access point. It would be easier if the target connected and then disconnected from the network, but he knew that, short of the neighborhood experiencing a power outage, this was unlikely. Instead he transmitted a de-auth frame—a series of de-authorization packets causing a network blip that would result in an automatic rejoin. If the house was online, it might lose connectivity for a moment.

He adjusted his seating and interior lights a little and turned on his Romin Slipstream wireless hacking tool. It showed a NetWizard192 wireless router with WPA encryption. Standard. With a few mouse clicks he was able to capture a handshake between it and the IOSysGear 266 router in the van by running his Vac-CrackXL software. Vac-Crack sent the requisite de-auth frames.

He waited, invoking slang so common he knew he was becoming Americanized. He muttered to himself, "Come on, you mutha."

The software ran an internal clock. In an anxious seventy-three seconds he had handshakes for the two networks in a packet capture file. His side never lost connectivity with the access points.

"Gotcha!"

He saved the packet captures on his desktop and loaded them into Cirrus-Cracker, a cloud-based website that charged a small fee to run the packet files against almost one billion potential solutions. The return box blinked on his laptop screen for a few seconds. Then the WPA password popped up.

"Something's wrong," he mumbled.

He uploaded the packets again, after another click to his online pay account. Every use required payment. In an instant, the password popped again: "PASSWORD."

He could have saved himself a lot of time and money had he tried that in the first place.

"Idiot. Could have been sixty-three characters. Idiot."

He moved from the back of the van to the front and looked out the windshield to verify that he was not being observed. Around the corner, on the edge of a parking lot for a bulk cigarette shop, he could see down Potilla Avenue. No movement. All was good. He returned to the back, logged on to the FindYourFriend website, and started his searches. Again.

21 July 2006
FBI Computer Forensics Lab

"Sir, his computer didn't have any password protection, so we were able to get some pertinent information. Looks like he uses an unusual internet browser, but we also found Internet Explorer installed. He used that from time to time. We ran a history. Nothing too recent, but Edwards was able to use some trick to dig back further. Seems he has an account on FindAFriend.com and accessed it a few dozen times over the past decade, but we can't tell what he searched for."

"What do you mean, you can't tell what he searched for?"

"The history log tells us *when* he accessed the site—we even got into it—but that's all."

"Who would know?"

"Well, sir, FindAFriend would know, but we would need a CALEA." CALEA was one of those acronyms that's used so much even the experts forget what it stands for. Communications Assistance for Law Enforcement. In short, a warrant.

"Do you think we have enough probable cause to take this to the magistrate?"

"Fuck, even with a warrant, those ass clowns are going to make it hard—trying to protect everyone's privacy and all. Can we crack the account?"

"Sir, we did that. Rook wasn't too smart with computer security. Over half his passwords are the word 'password' in all caps."

"You gotta be shitting me."

"Serious as a heart attack, sir. We signed on to FindAFriend with his email address, but they don't keep records under his profile, at least that we can find, on who he searched for. If we want to know, we're going to have to go to the site with that CALEA warrant."

"Write it up. Document everything you know: dates, times, sites, passwords, all of it. Once we get enough cause, we're gonna have to take it to a judge who handles this kind of shit."

22 September 2006
Arcadia, DeSoto County, Florida

Rook pretended to read the sheaf of papers handed to him, then pulled his glasses off. Except for the title, the print was too small for him to see. And besides, it had been years since he had read much of anything that wasn't associated with internet pornography or the odd email. He liked to tell people he was "out of practice." The papers were headed with the words "SEARCH WARRANT"—that much he could see.

Rook set the papers on the tiny table next to the door and said, "Have at it, dudes, I got nothin' to hide."

"Do you have any firearms on your property?"

"Yep. Quite a few. I keep 'em in a gun safe in the back bedroom."

"Might as well go ahead and open it. A detective will help."

The weapons safe was a huge green steel job, five and a half feet tall, three feet wide, with an electronic keypad lock and a spinning five-spoked brass handle. It must have weighed close to a thousand pounds. The agents were surprised to see something of this quality in such a dilapidated trash-heap of a home.

Rook noticed them looking. "Yeah, picked it up off the internet from that list site where everyone sells stuff. The guy was in a nasty divorce. Hard part was finding help to move it in. Had to beef up the floor from the crawlspace so it wouldn't break through."

They sorted through several handguns on a top shelf and a half dozen rifles standing vertical, but didn't find what they were looking for.

Special Agent Brad Walker had just about called it quits. "When you're looking for ice cream, and it's not in the freezer, you can pretty much hang it up." But he'd had his share of bad experiences missing items not hidden in the obvious places, including, on one occasion, a plastic baggie full of crack hidden in the middle of a bag of frozen peas. So he made one last inspection of the room that was must have once been the guest room, but was now a crazy storage area. It reminded him of that TV show about people who keep everything they've ever owned.

Once he satisfied himself there was nothing of interest in the room that five hundred scurrying palmetto bugs hadn't carried off, he waded his way to the closet, which was situated on an outside wall of the house. He thought of those cartoons where you open the door and everything falls out. This closet was jammed to the top, but nothing fell out since he could hardly get the door open.

"Sorry, dude," Rook said. "I don't go in here much... been

years." Rook's voice was so calm and unconcerned that everyone on the FBI team was convinced that this guy truly had nothing to hide. But they had seen stranger reactions to warrants. Special Agent Tapia had once been welcomed into a home in 2007 and had been complacent in his search, only to find a severed head in the basement chest freezer. He pulled his weapon, but it wasn't needed since the suspect had stepped outside while no one was monitoring him. The suspect drove away and escaped to a nearby interstate, not to be seen again by law enforcement for eight months. With that incident in mind, one agent was left to chat with Rook in the kitchen.

Special Agent Walker squeezed into the closet and pushed the hanging clothes from one end of an old galvanized rod to the other. His hand touched something of interest. From the mess, he extracted a black and gray heavy-gauge nylon gun case. A tiny cloth label showed the image of a bighorn sheep. Two handles like those on a cheap briefcase made it easy to carry. Hanging from a brass D-ring on one of the handles was a set of chrome keys. The zipper was black plastic. Walker unzipped the case and removed a rifle from the fake sheepskin interior. He held it up while calling for his partner.

"Frank, we got a twenty-two over here."

Rook heard them from the kitchen and made the trip down the hallway. "Fuck, officer, I completely forgot about that one. Where'd you find that? Back in the closet? Shit, I haven't even looked at that old thing in ten years. My uncle gave it to me when I was in the army."

"It's Special Agent, not officer."

Lionel pulled an old dusty five-by-seven color framed photo from a narrow shelf in the hall and handed it to Walker. It showed a picture of a young man, and there was no doubt that it was Rook, though with bright red hair, not gray. He stood beside an older adult —Lionel's uncle. Both had rifles at port arms, posing for the photographer. Lionel's uncle was holding two dead opossums by the tails.

Walker wiped the glass so he could see the image better and held it up to the light from the window. "Mind if we take this with us? I'll make sure you get it back."

"Suit yourself," Rook said.

They had Mr. Rook sign for the things they took, shook his hand, and said, "Just procedure. We're pretty sure nothing will come of this."

"What are you guys after anyway? Killin' possums is legal in Florida. Legal everywhere, I gotta hope."

"Like I said, we're just following orders. We'll be in touch."

The trunk of the FBI sedan was blocked from Rook's view by the open lid. The task force lead held a large black plastic garbage bag open. "This is all I have to bag it."

"Be careful," Walker said. "There's old dried-up stuff on the sights and screws."

"Stuff?"

"Yeah, like dead skin or something."

Special Agent Walker was sealing the framed photo in a clear plastic bag. "I'm going to have to write this fellow a thank-you letter.

Why the hell would he hand us irrefutable proof that the rifle is his?" He placed the bag in the trunk. "He could just say he never saw it."

"Maybe he's not our guy," his partner said. "Place is a pit, but if I've ever seen a guy who really thought he had nothing to hide, it was that guy. I thought he was going to invite us for a meal."

"Yeah, right, who'd eat a meal in that shithole?" Walker replied. "He's fucking psycho. This," he said, pointing to the bagged rifle, "is our smoking gun."

2004–2007

On August twelfth, 2004, Michail Grosvenor of Fort Collins, Colorado was found dead in a small abandoned warehouse in the vicinity of East Magnolia and Twelfth Street. He was tied on his back to what the warehouse owner called a "sorting bench," which for all intents and purposes was a long, heavy, hard maple table capable of holding heavy objects. Mickey was well known to the Fort Collins police department, having served for over thirty years as a volunteer in the department's Police Auxiliary Unit where he had, among other jobs, overseen the Explorer Scout Program. He was a community servant of long and distinguished standing, so his death attracted a lot of media attention and personal interest from the police department's Office of Investigations Services.

The Larimer County coroner also took a personal interest in Mickey's death. He and Mickey had served together as scouting commissioners and were friends. The coroner delivered a quick-turn autopsy report to the chief of police. The cause of death appeared to be internal gunshot wound from .22 caliber rat shot. The servicing medical examiner used the word "torture," determining in the course of his investigation that Mickey had spent hours alive on the sorting bench with the barrel of a rifle inserted into his esophagus. His assertion was that this constituted torture by any definition. Later, that conclusion was cited by federal prosecutors, who sought potential federal jurisdiction over the case under Section 2340 of Title 18 of the United States Code. The feds needed something to take over. Torture could be that something.

With the concurrence of the Investigative Services Deputy Chief, the police chief assigned a new homicide detective to the case: Lieutenant Saul Ayala. Saul was one of the few local detectives who had never met Mickey Grosvenor. In the chief's opinion, this would enable him to provide an unbiased, non-emotional look into the case. Saul had been promoted as a condition of employment when he transferred from a county sheriff's office in southern Arizona. He had been a stellar performer there and had then attended the National FBI Academy, where he graduated in July, just three weeks prior to Mickey's murder.

As such, Saul—who made a point of using the Spanish-language pronunciation of his name, *Sah uul* (which of course caused everyone in the department to quite deliberately pronounce his name to rhyme with *Paul*)—was up to speed on state-of-the art investigative techniques and tools. Within two weeks of being handed the case, he concluded that Mickey had been murdered by a serial killer.

Saul suspected Mickey's murder was ritualistic with key indicators and aspects that might be common to other cases. Leveraging new-found contacts in the FBI, he employed the Combined DNA Index System (CODIS), the National Integrated Ballistics Identification Network (NIBIN), and two different automated fingerprint identification systems. The key hit came from NIBIN, where historical records from the Integrated Ballistic Identification System (IBIS) from the Bureau of Alcohol, Tobacco, Firearms, and Explosives retained not only projectile information, but cartridge data and other notes. He found four matches to crimes in which the weapon of choice was .22 caliber rat shot. Three cases had occurred within two days of each other in May 2000. One was in Falls Church, Virginia. A second was in the District of Columbia, and a third was in Maryland. The fourth was in February 2004, when one Peter Mack was found dead by rat shot under similar circumstances in Bradenton, Florida.

Saul provided his data to a second contact at the FBI. A division director there formed a mini serial killer task force, led by Special Agent Frank Mader, to look into the possible connection between the cases. Concurrent jurisdiction is a routine issue to be worked when federal agents begin the process of investigating crimes in individual states. However, in this case there was clear evidence that there was a serial killer on the loose and that the perpetrator had committed crimes in as many as five different states. On the orders of a US district judge, Mader and his task force had authority to reopen relevant cold cases in Virginia, Maryland, and the District of Columbia. The case in Bradenton, Florida was a continuing local investigation, but the sheriff's department there uncharacteristically welcomed assistance; without a single lead, their investigation into the death of Peter Mack had hit a dead end.

Lieutenant Saul Ayala was placed on special assignment to assist the task force. The Fort Collins City Council had to approve additional funding for the months of travel costs he incurred, but in the end it was worth it. Saul became instrumental to the case and was later offered a full-time position in the FBI.

Frank Mader brought in an FBI-trained trace evidence examiner, who spent two and a half weeks poring over the details of the five cases. He concluded without a doubt that the five murders had been carried out by the same person or persons. And once the five cases were tied together, the next step was to find a commonality between them. That quickly emerged from the evidence. All five were members of the same unit in the Vietnam War. Three of the five were together at a veterans' event on the National Mall on the twenty-ninth of May, 2000. Peter Mack had not attended the event, but his wife was in possession of an invitation letter he had received years before from an old army buddy. It matched others.

The first live member of that unit that the task force located was Dr. Clayton Kuykendahl, a college professor in New Jersey. He related the details of a May 2000 threat from one Sergeant Lionel Rook. Over the course of the next few months, the task force accounted for every original member of the Second Rifle Platoon, Bravo Company, Second Battalion, Eighteenth Infantry, Twelfth

Infantry Brigade that had been led by one Lieutenant Darren Bross and Platoon Sergeant Lionel Rook. Of the thirty-three soldiers, eight were killed in action, five were known to have been murdered, and seven more had gone missing under suspicious circumstances since the summer of 2000. Thirteen were in contact with the FBI. Four of the thirty-three had made careers in the army. Three of those four were retired but had continued on as contractors supporting the DOD overseas. They were out of the country during the period the five known deaths had occurred. That may have saved their lives. It also removed them from suspicion.

Corporal Timothy Langman had received a battlefield commission and a Distinguished Service Cross for valor during his second tour in Vietnam. He retired with forty years' service as a major general at Supreme Headquarters Allied Powers Europe (SHAPE) near Mons, Belgium. Nick Nicolletti retired as a command sergeant major. "Beans" Mejia became a US citizen in 1971, re-enlisted in the army, and returned as a hero to Guanajuato, Mexico, where he visited his parents and extended family from time to time. He, too, rose to the highest enlisted rank of sergeant major, improving his English over the years.

Saul Ayala soon became an expert on a seminal event in the history of the platoon: the massacre at Ri'Ga Village. He built a file that included a weekly news magazine from September 1967 devoted to the massacre, original interview transcripts from the original US Army Inspector General investigation, and new speculation that Lionel Rook had, in fact, fragged his platoon commander in a combat environment.

Concurrent jurisdiction raised its head as the case began to get a lot of media attention. Who gets the case? The feds, or the states? Using the many fruits of the task force investigation, the State of Maryland charged Lionel Rook with murder and moved to prosecute rapidly. The states of Colorado, Virginia, Florida, and the District of Columbia negotiated for the chance to prosecute their cases individually. The substantiation was overwhelming. The federal investigators handed near-irrefutable evidence to each state's office of the attorney general.

On the eighteenth of August 2007, Lionel Rook was arrested for murder in Arcadia, Florida. He was extradited before week's end to Maryland. It was a surprise on his seventy-first birthday. He had been sitting on the front porch of his dilapidated home and offered the county sheriff a lemonade. He was completely and utterly surprised to learn that he was being charged with a crime.

By the early afternoon, he understood the charges against him, but he never deviated from the story that he had been framed in an elaborate conspiracy. "I only went to Colorado because Mickey invited me. He always said one day he would." "Why? I told you, he invited me. Sent me a letter and a round-trip bus ticket." "How far is Bradenton? By car? Fuck, I don't know, maybe an hour. What's it to ya, planning a trip? Fuck, I didn't even know Mack. Peter Mack, right? Lived there? Dead? You gotta be fuckin' shittin' me! Don't know nothin' 'bout it. Don't care none for it."

12 June 2003

Southern Georgia, Lowndes County

This one had taken more work than the others. It was the first time he had not met success using the internet. The phone book was not much help either, and the only address he could drum up was a location in Valdosta now occupied by a Piggly Wiggly grocery store. When the man asked if anyone knew George Washington Carver, a typical response was laughter followed by a comment about peanuts. And he knew that asking around too much would forever fix him in the minds of the people residing in this strange slice of America. Even with the year of separation he planned, that would not be wise.

It was only by pure chance that he stopped at a roadside stand on US 41 near Hahira. A sign read "Boiled Peanuts" in large red block letters. The connection between this man and peanuts intrigued him, so he rolled off the asphalt.

An old woman responded to the arrival of a customer by unfolding herself from the front seat of an ancient green pickup. A vanity plate on its front bumper told him the make and age: 56FORD.

He had never tried boiled peanuts, but he liked them immediately. He took them one at a time from a now-wet brown paper bag and got the knack of splitting the soft shells with his teeth to empty the contents into his mouth. The proprietor's accent was difficult to decipher, thick and southern, from deep Georgia stock. He learned the woman was the widow of a long-dead farmer, but she was now too old to help much on the farm and was relegated by her two sons to selling what she could from his truck. "They just want to keep me busy, outta their hair and such."

While fifties country and western music played in the background, delivered from the truck's AM radio, and cars and trucks zoomed by, he talked to this woman, who reaffirmed that looks and accent were often misleading. "What's George Washington Carver got to do with peanuts? Is that what you're asking me? You seem like an intelligent young man, so I'm going to assume you went to school. Didn't they teach you nothin'?"

An old woman. An old woman from Georgia who had worked peanuts her entire life could not comprehend that someone in Georgia, at a peanut stand, had never heard of George Washington Carver. So the woman launched into a history lesson. It immediately reminded the man of a scene from a movie he loved, when Forrest Gump's friend Bubba, with an accent not unlike this old woman's, barraged Forrest with different ways to prepare shrimp. This old woman was like that, but instead of shrimp, she knew peanuts.

And so it was that the man learned about peanuts and their many uses. "Young sir, George Washington Carver put peanuts on the map. Might be the most famous colored man ever lived." She paused, reached into the wet paper bag and, while she pondered what to say next, devoured the legumes like someone who had some experience. "Glad you like 'em, son, but you don't spit the shells. Hell no. You just eat the whole dagnabbed thing. Good stuff's in the shell."

The man tried it, but was not convinced.

"George Washington Carver," the woman repeated. "Ever wonder why some folks is always referred to by their whole name?"

"I never gave it much thought," the man said.

"Famous people mostly. Think about it. There's Tammy Faye Bakker…"

The man had no idea who that was.

"… John Quincy Adams, June Carter Cash, Thomas Alva Edison, James Earl Ray."

At that the man added, "Then I guess you'd have to include Martin Luther King."

"Just right! You gettin' the idea. George Washington Carver. That man put peanuts on the map." The old woman looked up at a passing cloud, just a little too long for comfort, and said, "Ya' know, I know a man with that very same name. Good man. Works a truck stop down south of Valdosta way. Off the highway."

The man feigned a lack of interest. He thanked the woman for the history lesson, bought another bag of peanuts, shook hands, and drove away as the sun peeked through low puffy clouds before it dropped below the horizon. At Exit 11, just north of the Florida line, he left the highway and headed east toward bright lights and neon. It was mealtime in south Georgia. Truckers were taking note. They parked in rows and columns as if there was a convention in progress. There were competing centers on both sides of Georgia Route 31.

For no particular reason, the man pulled off to the right on the south side of the feeder road. He filled his rental up from a self-serve pump while lamenting the endless rise of the price of gasoline. The machine flashed a message that directed him inside to collect a receipt. It gave him an excuse to step in without the need to attract extra attention. He did.

The man had been a young boy when his village was destroyed. Experts on the reliability of witnesses' memories would suggest it would be futile for a witness to recognize a face after so many years. They would say the odds are heavily against the witness. The mind sees what it wants to remember. But this man defied the experts. His reaction was immediate, his recognition certain. In him was the instantaneous flight-or-fight response of the human body. All his senses went on alert at the same time. He tried not to stare, but the face of the man tearing lottery tickets from a stack behind the counter took him back years. It took him back to the cradling of his father, to his father's death, which had replayed in his mind a thousand times.

The man thought, *He has skin the color of water buffalo.* He could not remember where that simile came from. *Water buffalo?* Skin color the same as tens of thousands of African-Americans he'd seen and known since his arrival, but this one was different. And the same. It was him.

Other than the vividness of his father's death, the man hadn't considered other details of the horror in years. Regarding the sounds of that day, his only memory was of screeching, but something in the deep recesses of his mind brought up a voice when he saw the face that must be George Washington Carver. *"All clear here!"* this man had said.

And then his father appeared in an apparition. *"Live, my son. Make a life."*

The man needed no more. He quickly slapped his gas money on the counter, and without waiting for change, he turned on his heel and stepped to the door before a flood of emotion erupted on his face. At his car, he turned back to the store. Through the glass, he could see the man behind the counter.

Tsov raised a hand, a salute, a gesture of thanks. But no one noticed.

CHAPTER 28

18 November 2010

Prince Georges County Circuit Courthouse, Upper Marlboro, Maryland

"Ladies and gentlemen of the jury. Early on the twenty-eighth of May in the year 2000, Andrew Russelvage awoke to a beautiful day in Vienna, Virginia. He slapped off his alarm, showered, dressed, and sat at a small round table in the breakfast nook reading the Sunday morning *Washington Post*.

"His wife, Judy, made him a short stack of buttermilk pancakes, scrambled eggs, and bacon. He washed the meal down with a glass of orange juice and two hot cups of coffee before heading out.

"Russ was proud of his 1997 Honda 800cc Pacific Coast touring bike. It had fewer than ten thousand miles, looked like new, and would stand out at Operation Rolling Thunder on the Washington, DC Mall, where the reflecting pool meets the Lincoln Memorial and showcases the Vietnam War Memorial. He would join thousands of bikers at the annual rally that has a theme of remembering the Vietnam War and especially those still missing in action or suspected to still be prisoners of war. Russ was a veteran of that war. He had received a letter inviting him to a reunion of his platoon near the War Memorial at noon. Police found that letter on his person. We now know the letter was a fake, but Russ didn't know that. He thought it was real.

"The letter was supposedly sent by one Sean MacNulty, another member of Russ's Vietnam platoon, a man Russ had not seen or heard from since serving in Vietnam in 1967. Sean was the platoon medic in Vietnam. They called him Doc. But we now know that Sean died in a hospital in Japan in 1967 from wounds suffered in combat. That letter was not written by Sean MacNulty. It was written by Lionel Rook"— the prosecutor pointed to the defendant —"to lure Russ and several other members of the platoon to Washington, DC. It all seemed real and plausible, but it was not.

"Again, Rolling Thunder is an annual veterans' event that brings tens of thousands of former soldiers, sailors, airmen, and marines together in support of veterans' issues. Lionel Rook typed Russ's invitation to this event, and to the reunion of his old unit, on an electric typewriter. That typewriter was found later in his house. His house in Florida. He worked out a way to mail the letter, and a whole bunch of other letters, from Nevada—to make it appear as if they had come from Sean MacNulty. We know Lionel Rook did this because, in addition to perfectly matching the typewriter to Russ's letter, we found other DNA evidence in the envelope that scientists matched to Mr. Rook and no one else—skin and hair and such."

The prosecutor paused and reached inside his suit coat to get to an itch on his upper left arm. Then he spun around to the jury again and continued.

"So imagine this if you will. Thousands of veterans, as many motorcycles, and in the middle, a group of about half a dozen war buddies who met near the Vietnam Wall and shared old times and war stories. Really. War stories. Did they get letters too? Invitations to the reunion? I can't say, but I *can* say that Russ was one of the group, a war hero, a patriot, a man who loved his country and valued the camaraderie he shared with old friends. He was a man excited to be there."

He turned to Judy and opened his arms like a man expecting someone to jump into them. "Russ's wife Judy is with us here today. She shared with me his excitement about attending that reunion. It's just too bad it was so short-lived.

"Let me back up just a little. The war in Vietnam took place for more than a decade over thirty years ago. You might wonder how Lionel Rook was able to find Andrew Russelvage's address. How was he able to contact this long-lost soldier? This platoon mate. I would love to tell you that Lionel Rook is some sort of computer genius, but he is not. More details will come out in the trial, but in short, FBI experts analyzed his computer and discovered he had an account on one of those services where you can locate old acquaintances. He signed up for a full year of access and paid with his credit card. We have the receipt. The web company that provides this service keeps detailed records of all the searches its clients make. It turns out Lionel had looked for people he'd known as a kid and in Florida reform school."

Rook's defense attorney leapt to his feet. He was only about five foot three, so people in the back of the courtroom might just as well have thought he had remained seated. "Objection, Your Honor. Mr. Rook's time in juvenile detention is not germane to this case."

"Sustained." Turning to the prosecutor, the judge said, "Counsel, I will allow latitude in your opening statement, but limit yourself to facts that have some chance of presenting themselves in evidence."

"Apologies, Your Honor," the prosecutor replied, all the while knowing he'd made his point.

"The FBI located over twenty queries on FindYourFriend.com that could be traced to family and acquaintances going back to Lionel's childhood and time in the army. But there was more than that. In 1967, then-Sergeant Lionel Rook was the platoon sergeant in a unit that had thirty-three members. What I am about to say is important. I don't want to be patronizing, but I need to emphasize this point. *What I am about to say is important.* In the FindYourFriend records, investigators discovered that he had pulled up a dossier on *every single one* of them. All thirty-three. Every last one."

The prosecutor stepped back for a minute to let this sink in. He stepped to the lectern and pretended to be shuffling papers, checking notes and such. He had no need to check anything. He had practiced this opening statement, in the most important case of his career, countless times from start to finish. While riding his stationary bike, while jogging, while sitting in traffic on the DC beltway. Every word had been practiced over and over in his mind.

He wanted to present a compelling but easy-to-comprehend portrayal to the jury. His one chance to make a first impression had to sell.

He organized the lectern and continued. "What's in those dossiers?" He made eye contact with every juror. "I'll tell you: more information than you would want someone to be able to find on you, I assure you. If someone is looking for you as a friend, on FindYourFriend, you are going to want them to be a friend, not Lionel Rook. There were full names, street addresses, phone numbers, and in some cases email addresses. Yes, the site promises privacy. But in the face of criminal activity, they will, they *must* hand over their records when the court orders them to.

"Lionel used this information to send Andrew Russelvage a faked invitation from Sean MacNulty to a platoon reunion on the Mall, near the Vietnam War Memorial, during Operation Rolling Thunder on the twenty-eighth of May in the year 2000. Why pretend the letter came from MacNulty? Because Lionel Rook knew that if the invite came from him, no one would show up. What Lionel didn't know was that Sean MacNulty was dead. Last time anyone from the platoon saw Sean, he was alive. Turns out, he died shortly after being transported to a hospital outside Vietnam.

"Is it a coincidence that May twenty-eighth was the day Andrew Russelvage was murdered? The answer is no. And I will tell you why. It was the day that Judy Russelvage called the Fairfax County Sheriff's Office to report that her husband had not returned from his motorcycle trip to Washington, DC.

"Let's fast-forward just a minute to the Fourth of July. On

July fourth, three boys from Forest Heights, Maryland were playing
in the woods. Forest Heights is just outside the district, sort of over
the hill to the east of Bolling Air Force Base. It was hot, humid,
bugs, thorns, and muck, not a place for human habitation. Perhaps
the place reminded Lionel Rook of his time in Vietnam. But anyway,
these three kids were looking for a place to secretly shoot off
fireworks—fireworks one of them had stolen from an older brother.
But the point is, they were in a spot that few people frequent. They
were there and they will never forget it. Because those boys found
Andrew Russelvage. In a gruesome scene that will stay with them
like a movie in their heads for the rest of their lives, they discovered
Andrew lashed to a fallen tree, on his back—dead. Raccoons and
other vermin had had their way, but identification of the remains by
the Prince George's County medical examiner was straightforward.
Andrew's wallet remained in the back pocket of his blue jeans.
Additional DNA confirmation will come out in the trial.

"The circumstances of how Russ ended up in this remote
location remain unclear to this day. Investigators dragged Oxen
Creek and a tributary called Barnaby Run behind the Eastover
Shopping Center and found Russ's submerged Honda motorcycle
out of sight of shoppers a few hundred feet away, but the fact that
no one saw how it got there is immaterial.

"Okay, now let me take you back to the twenty-eighth of
May, 2000. That's over ten years ago. You may wonder why it took
so many years to solve this case. It's because no one drew the
connection. I cannot tell you all the details of how this crime was
solved, because the law requires me to relate only the details of *this*

crime, even when there were others—"

"Objection, Your Honor."

"Sustained. Last chance, counselor, unless you want me to close for you here and now?" It was not a question. The prosecutor knew he had walked a fine line.

"Got it, Your Honor." He inwardly smiled, then continued. "What I'm saying is, there will be some missing details that led to the arrest of Lionel Rook, but I can assure you that we were able to tie Mr. Rook to this crime in particular. That day on the Mall, there was a scuffle among the old friends. Five witnesses presented nearly identical testimony that Sergeant Lionel Rook, threatened to kill them all.

"Now, back to July and Andrew Russelvage. Russ's death was even more disturbing than previously imagined. Autopsies are required by the state when foul play is suspected. Medical examiners discovered that Russ was shot internally."

One of the jurors gave a quizzical look. The prosecutor picked up on it. "That's right, ladies and gentlemen, internal. While Russ was lying on his back, looking at the sky, tied to a dead tree, probably terrified, Lionel Rook forced a .22 caliber rifle barrel down Russ's throat. No telling how long he took or how he did it. It was with tiny projectiles known as *rat shot*. In case you are not familiar, rat shot is sort of like a tiny shotgun shell full of pellets like grains of sand. It has a short range for a bullet of sorts. My dad grew up in Brooklyn, New York. He used to kill rats in the city with a rifle using rat shot. Anyway, Rook pulled the trigger and emptied the tiny pellets into Russ's heart. Russ bled to death from the inside. The medical examiner speculates that he died in pain."

The prosecutor paused and looked at the ceiling to compose himself. He was affected by this, or so he made it appear to the jury. He took a tissue from his trouser pocket and dabbed the corners of both eyes. Then he uttered a single choked-up word. "Agony."

He paused again.

"While I am on the subject of rat shot, ladies and gentlemen of the jury, let me tell you about one piece of evidence we uncovered. We worked with the judge, who, despite protests from the defense, has declared this evidence admissible in court. That means you might consider it when you find Lionel Rook guilty of murder. We were able to uncover from Lionel's home town of Arcadia, Florida an arrest record that's over fifty years old. Lionel was arrested as a suspect in the murder of a teenage boy. The boy had been drowned, but it turns out the drowning occurred *after* he was shot dead in the chest. And do you have any idea what he might have been shot with? I'll tell you. And you'll see all the evidence. It's incontrovertible. Ladies and gentlemen of the jury, that boy was shot in the chest with rat shot."

The prosecutor strolled around a little without projecting impatience. Again he went to the lectern to check notes. His idea was that the jury would have a little time to ponder the additional evidence and the horrific scene in their minds.

"So in review: Lionel Rook finds Andrew Russelvage through FindYourFriend.com. He sends an invitation to meet in Washington, DC, misrepresenting himself as someone known to both of them who also happens to be dead. They meet as suggested. Rook threatens to kill everyone present. Russ turns up dead that very day."

The prosecutor straightened up and pointed at Lionel Rook, who was seated next to his lawyer behind a long walnut-veneer table. As if to query Rook himself he asked, "What's missing?" Then he turned back to the jury.

"I promise you this is an ironclad case. The state will not keep you long. Should have you out of here by Thanksgiving." He looked down at some notes and spoke to the table for a few seconds. "This is a murder perpetrated by a vicious criminal. But what's missing? I'll tell you. What's missing is the connection between Lionel Rook and Andrew Russelvage after they left Washington, DC and ended just over the district line in Maryland. How do we know Rook had anything to do with this? Could have been anyone, right?" He let his eyes pause just a moment on each of the twelve jurors.

"Wrong. In addition to other incriminating evidence, such as the typewriter he used to write the letters, DNA evidence from dandruff and hair follicles in the envelope, and travel receipts that place Lionel Rook in Washington, DC, there was one other find. The rifle. That's right, the rifle. We have the murder weapon.

"The FBI found an old .22 rifle in Rook's Florida house. Inside a rifle case there was some rat shot that matched the ammunition used to murder Andrew Russelvage. And what's more, it turns out that when you jam a rifle down someone's throat, you leave DNA on the sharp bits of the weapon—the sights, the safety button, stuff like that. You can imagine what I'm talking about.

There was DNA on that rifle from at least five people…"

The defense attorney was not the brightest bulb in the room, but even he understood the requirement to stick to the case at hand. "Objection, Your Honor! Relevance. Five? Really?"

"Sustained. Counselor, keep your remarks to the deceased in question."

Again, the prosecutor had made his point; he could see from the wide eyes of a few of the jurors that he'd achieved his objective. "Just a slip, Your Honor. I am too close to this case."

"Watch yourself," the judge said.

Turning back to the jury, the prosecutor continued. "In short, the weapon that killed Andrew Russelvage was Lionel Rook's .22 caliber rifle, found in his home in Florida, a rifle he had owned since he was a preteen. Heck, we know it's his—the FBI has a photo of him holding it as a kid. That will come out in the trial. That rifle, Rook's rifle, had bits of Andrew Russelvage's DNA on it."

The prosecutor was near the end of his opening statement. He stared blankly around the courtroom in apparent thought and added, "Little pieces of skin." Then he shook his head, sat down, and mumbled to himself, but loud enough to be audible, "Like when you accidentally bite a chunk out of your cheek."

There was a thirty-second period of silence. He'd planned this intentionally to make it appear as if he might have something more to say while leaving an image of a rifle with torn skin-like tissue in the minds of the jurors.

The judge broke the silence. "Counselor, are you through?"

"Yes, Your Honor, for now." Turning to the jury from his

chair behind his table, the prosecutor added, "Thank you. I thank each of you."

With that, the judge lifted his gavel and prepared to hammer it to begin a recess, but the prosecutor stood once more. "Forgot one thing, Your Honor. One thing I wanted to tell the jury."

The judge held back a grimace of annoyance. "Go ahead, counselor, but keep it short."

"It will be short, Your Honor." Turning to the jury, he said, "We don't think you'll find any reasonable doubt of this gruesome crime, so the state will be seeking the death penalty." He saw two, maybe three jurors nod a little in agreement, and then he looked back at the bench. "Thank you, Your Honor."

By the time the trial was over, the Prince George's County Office of the State's Attorney, their Criminal Division, Homicide Unit, and the Principal Deputy State's Attorney himself had pooled their resources to build a compelling case. They had gotten substantial material evidence from an FBI serial killer task force, but they were required by instruction from the judge to limit the evidence and testimony to the murder that had occurred in Maryland.

They did not achieve the prosecutor's goal of wrapping it all up before Thanksgiving. It was a murder trial, after all. But they did have it finished before Christmas. One late holdup was the length of time the jury deliberated on the issue of the death penalty. One of the sequestered jurors was particularly liberal in her political beliefs and categorically refused on principle to find in favor of capital punishment. She told other members of the jury that she had demonstrated twice in vigils in support of individuals on death row. She had kept this fact from the court during jury selection in the secret hope that she could make a difference. She held out for four days. In the end, as a mother of three, she caved in—because she had not done any Christmas shopping. People, it turns out, have priorities.

By the twenty-third of December the case was automatically submitted to the Maryland Court of Appeals. Post-conviction relief was denied by the court and was remanded for action to the US District Court for the District of Maryland. Thus Lionel Bodean Rook entered the federal court system.

Had he ended his appeal with Maryland, he likely would have died of old age. By 2013, Maryland had repealed the death penalty.

6 April 2011
North Branch Correctional Institution
Cresaptown, Allegany County, Maryland

Many involved in the prosecution thought Rook was either telling the truth or was one of the greatest liars they had ever met. They could not hope to know the truth of both points of view. By the eighteenth of November, when his trial for the murder of Andrew Russelvage began, Lionel Rook had already been rotting in a Maryland prison for over three years. To pay legal expenses, he had sold everything he owned, including his pickup truck and the

Florida home and land that had been in his family for more than a hundred years. His younger brother Bobby moved out and found temporary quarters with an old girlfriend. On the twenty-third of December, his Christmas present was to sign an appeal to the state of Maryland, the last official act of his defense attorney, who had been working on a shoestring.

Continuing his mantra of having been framed, Rook hand-wrote letters to more than thirty organizations that represented death row inmates: the ABA Representation Project, Centers for Death Penalty Litigation, the ACLU, the Innocence Project, Justice Denied, and a host of others. Some reviewed his case. One representative even visited him in prison. But do-gooders lean toward those they think are innocent, and not a single one of these organizations took enough interest in Rook to represent him during the appeals process. In the face of four corroborating looming cases from four states, on April 6, 2011, Lionel Rook submitted a request to the Justice Department requesting "removal" of his remaining cases to federal prosecution to "get it over with."

The states in question reluctantly handed over thousands of man-hours of work. The Department of Justice considered the concurrent jurisdictional issues. There had to be clear violation of federal law. They cited 18 US Code § 2340, "Torture," as developed in Colorado; 18 US Code § 844(d), Interstate Commerce; 18 US Code § 1111, First Degree Murder; 18 US Code § 1512, Murder to prevent testimony by a witness; and the fact that the National Mall is a national park and therefore federal property. To further buttress the cases, they piled on use of the US mail to commit a crime. In short order DOJ took the case. After deliberation among three district courts it was handed to the United States District Court for the Middle District of Florida, to be tried at the US Courthouse in Fort Myers.

The US Attorney, under direction from the department, worked to arrive at a plea bargain with Lionel Rook. The government would vacate the death penalty if Rook would divulge the location of the seven members of his platoon who had mysteriously gone missing since the summer of 2000. Rook was afraid to die; he believed to his core that he was headed to hell. He desperately wanted the deal. But once again he bellowed his innocence and recounted his version of the facts. He'd been framed. How could he know where the seven missing guys were? "I didn't kill anyone!" He said it a thousand times over, but few listened.

In point of fact, the seven men were dead, all murdered.

Lionel Bodean Rook was prosecuted for four murders, convicted on all counts, and sentenced to the death penalty. His court-appointed federal defense attorney twice submitted appeals, without luck, to the United States Court of Appeals.

EPILOGUE - THE JOURNEY

Not I, not anyone else can travel that road for you,
You must travel it by yourself.
It is not far, it is within reach,
Perhaps you have been on it since you were born and did not know,
Perhaps it is every where on water and on land.
—Walt Whitman

CHAPTER 29

13 October 1967

WEEKPAST **magazine**

> **GLOBAL SPOT:** Joe Westfall, Saigon--On Assignment—
> Photos copyright: Michael Joseph Westfall. On Labor Day
> a squad of ten soldiers from U.S. Army's Task Force
> Oregon, the Second Rifle Platoon, under Bravo Company
> and the 18th Infantry's second battalion laid waste the tiny
> Montagnard hamlet of Ri'Ga in western Quang Nam
> Province on the Hồ Chí Minh trail near the border between
> Laos and Vietnam. In a professed act of self-defense and
> in the aftermath of the killing of Platoon Leader First
> Lieutenant Darren Bross, of Lufkin, Texas, the soldiers
> dispatched at least three dozen men, women and children.
> Thus far, the response from the Army has been cryptic in
> that this incident is termed an 'act of war,' against the Viet
> Cong. This reporter witnessed the results of the carnage,
> inspected eighteen sets of living quarters, and counted 35
> indigenous dead. Except for spears, machetes, and a few
> knives, there was not a single enemy firearm in sight, only
> those carried by and employed by ten weary U.S. soldiers.
> The single American casualty was Lt Bross.

These words appeared in a boxed inset in bright white font
that overlaid a two-page color collage of gruesome photos of dead
men, women, and children. It was a scoop of giant proportions in

the news trade, in an otherwise black and white news magazine, and the cover photo won a 1968 Pulitzer Prize for News Photography and appeared in countless reprints over decades, accompanying any mention of wartime collateral damage in later conflicts.

In 1911 news editor Arthur Brisbane wrote, "Use a picture. It's worth a thousand words." *WEEKPAST* took the advice to heart. The 12 photos and 166 words were sparks that lit a short-lived public relations blaze against the Department of Defense and the conduct of the war. The momentum might have continued if not for the distraction of the holidays and the Battle of Khe Sanh that consumed Vietnam War news cycles for months. The Army Inspector General investigated the incident, but, "for reasons of national security," produced only a classified report.

14 November 1967

Xa Ruh Village, Quảng Nam Province, South Vietnam

For decades the tiny enclaves of Ri'Ga and Xa Ruh, and a couple of other nearby mountain villages, had divorced themselves from all contact with the outside world. With the exceptions of his great uncle Vak and the grandfather Hlong whom Tsov had never known, the Co-Tu were anomalous in the Central Highlands in that they wanted no contact with the north or the south, the French or the Americans. The mantra, in their language, was, in the simplest terms, *Leave us alone.*

On the "Day of Death," as it would come to be known

among the Co-Tu, Ri'Ga counted sixty-seven residents. The
Americans took a total of forty-four, some dozen of whom were
found face down on trails leading out of the village. They were shot
in the back while on the run. Some fled and made it. Others were
lucky—they were out hunting at the time of the attack. A few, like
Tsov and his cousin Siu, were spared. Tsov's mother, Thia, and his
sister Paj were alive as well—they had been visiting Xa Ruh. But
Uncle Vak was dead. As were H'Blik, Thi, Aunt H'Juel Ya, and so,
so many others.

Against custom that prohibited public displays of sadness,
the few survivors cried—wailed—for weeks. They were
inconsolable. They arranged and attended a separate ceremony for
each of the lost villagers to ensure that every requirement was met
for individual entry into the spirit world. It had taken weeks to
remove all the dead to nearby, shared, aboveground cemeteries.

According to Co-Tu belief those who had died a violent
death faced the possibility, through no fault of their own, of having
their souls wander without peace for eternity—this eternity. The
eldest members of three nearby villages conferred on this point and
came to the common opinion that despite the unfairness of it all,
they could have no influence in the matter. Nevertheless, to enhance
the chance of each to return to the spirit world, they agreed that in
addition to separate ceremonies for each, they would meticulously
prepare individual coffins. Each had to be split and hand-carved
from a fresh pine tree or other soft-wood trunk. Three dozen men
and boys from four nearby villages worked twenty hours per day for
two weeks under the oversight of the Xa Ruh village shaman. His

counterpart in Ri'Ga was among the dead and the first to be placed in the wooden sarcophagus so that he might help lead the others to eternal peace. Placed on crudely constructed wooden stands, the coffins were not buried, but rather exposed to the elements until termites took them back to their elemental state. By then the hope was that the worthy souls of the dead would return to the earth for renewal. The souls of the unworthy would spend eternity above ground traveling in the company of evil spirits. This was not for the DeGa to decide. The spirit gods would know best.

Ri'Ga was abandoned. Just two days after the final service, a local Viet Cong unit visited. They were unaware of the reason for the recent destruction, and made a hasty decision to burn the entire empty village to the ground. So when three US Army armored helicopters arrived on December first with a colonel representing the MACV Inspector General, there was nothing to see but the outlines of former structures scribed in rain-sodden ash.

Of the twenty-three survivors of the attack, seventeen were relocated to Xa Ruh, bringing that village's population to sixty-eight, roughly where Ri'Ga had been before the Day of Death. Xa Ruh carpenters added modules to the longhouse and two rooms to the Guol to accommodate the new members of the village.

The fourteenth of November was Tsov's seventh birthday, but he had no way of knowing this. His people kept time only by counting harvests and the slash-and burn rotation from active to fallow pasture and back. Had Kiep been alive, he might have noticed the angle of the sun, the cessation of the monsoon, or the fact that the village had just completed working pasture number seven.

But on this day, the village held a humble welcome ceremony, complete with the blood sacrifice of four chickens and a goat to commemorate the completion of a new room in the Xa Ruh longhouse made for Thia, Paj, Tsov, and Siu. Now able to move from tight quarters with relatives, Tsov was glad to have a tiny corner in a dark smoky room to call his own. One of the village weavers had worked with an apprentice carpenter to build a box for each of Tsov, Paj, and Siu. Tsov's box was large for a boy, a meter square, so he was able to store some things of his father's: an ax, a knife, two pipes, and some ornate ivory plugs that he would one day use to adorn his earlobes. To those items he added a small package he'd been carrying since the day of death. Wrapped twice in clear plastic material, he had taken the bundle from the pocket of the massive unwieldy jacket worn by the dead green man on the Day of Death. Until this day he had feared looking within it, afraid the plastic contained the man's soul, or perhaps an evil spirit that could take Tsov and his remaining family away.

But today, alone in the room, he inspected the package. He had seen only one book in his life prior to this, a tiny volume that belonged to his father. With a brown cover, it was filled with strange symbols and pictures of men—men with weapons, men kneeling, making fire, holding reflective objects, or sitting in trucks like the ones they were using to widen the road to the west. Tsov's memory of that book was fleeting. He sat for a minute staring at the motes of dust floating in the rays of sun that spilled through the rattan walls of his new room. And he wondered what could have happened to *that* book.

He opened the plastic wrapping. The top had a piece of wire encased in damp, shredded green paper, a twist-tie he had to pull apart. There was a second bag inside the first. It, too, needed separation, one piece of plastic from the other with the thumb and forefinger of each hand. And inside it was a book. It was black with white pages, but when held up to the light, the edges of all the pages converted to gold. Tsov held a single page in the light and looked for the gold, but he could not see it until all the pages were pressed together. "Magic," he said aloud. "This is a magic book." On one side of the book was a cross, also in gold. There were other symbols in gold on one edge of the book. He knew they were symbols of language, but he had no idea what their message was. He opened the book where the pages broke on a strip of black ribbon and found thousands of symbols captured on the pages. "Magic," he said again. *This has power,* he thought to himself.

Tsov heard commotion outside the longhouse in the square. The noise tugged at him, and he felt like he needed to join the group. He stood and was better able to see the book in direct sun from the window, through the mosquito gauze. He held it the light and opened just the cover. There he found more symbols, but these were not as well formed as those inside, those in black on the pages. These symbols were scratched by hand. *In charcoal, perhaps.*

And then he saw it: the symbol of evil he would never forget. Like a hot stone his cousin had lobbed to him from the fire, he threw the book into the box. Surely an evil spirit would take him now. He shuddered, and the memory of the Day of Death came back to him in a flood. His village dead. A dead green man. A green evil man over him.

Slowly, he overcame his nerves and reached into the box. He opened the book once again. In his fear, the thing burned in his hands.

And there it was in the upper corner, unmistakable: the same symbol he had seen on the chest of the evil green man, the man who had taken the life of the other. The devil who had killed his great-uncle. The evil spirit who had murdered his village. He held the book to the beam of sunlight to be certain. A beast was this symbol: two eyes, two ears.

Tsov resealed the book in the double-wrapped plastic, returned it to the box, and left it.

It would be almost nine years before Tsov would touch the book again, and then only because he had to gather his things to avoid a second bout with death at the hands of angry soldiers. But over those nine years his daydreams and nightmares returned often to the face of the green man and the symbol of death on his chest: the two eyes and two ears in black. He remembered the carnage, the massacre of his village, and the man he held responsible. This man. This symbol. This Rook.

Two decades later, when Tsov could read English, he would look through the dog-eared and mildewed *Book of Common Prayer* and know it was a gift straight from his Christian God who had spoken that day to a seven year-old boy—a boy who had become a man and had survived a journey not unlike one described in the Bible. And he would think of his father dying in his arms; he would think of the bodies scattered across Ri'Ga. And he would think of ROOK, wherever that devil was.

The missionary who had taught him to read told him that he and his people had been transported to Thailand like the Israelites who had survived the wilderness journey from Egypt to Canaan. Tsov took this truth inside himself. He knew deep within his heart that his people, those few who survived, were special—they had been spared. He memorized two Bible verses about the journey of Exodus—which was also his and his people's journey. Exodus 21:12, "Whoever strikes a man so that he dies shall be put to death," and Exodus 21:24, "Eye for eye, tooth for tooth, hand for hand, foot for foot."

And he never forgot.

CHAPTER 30

1967–1975

Xa Ruh Village, Quảng Nam Province, South Vietnam

A boy of seven didn't understand how much his life had changed when the war reached his doorstep. The DeGa in other parts of the Central Highlands had been surrounded by near-constant hostilities since the French occupation, but the Co-Tu in the vicinity of Ri'Ga and Xa Ruh had been insulated from contact for years as an accident of geography and because of the tenacious response from their village leaders. After the Day of Death, that time was over. The village leaders were dead, and the custom of maintaining isolation was lost with them. It did not seem to Tsov that the spirits of those dead were guiding his village any longer.

The 1967 monsoon season had not ended before Xa Ruh was visited daily by Viet Cong operatives. The village had little choice but to provide food and shelter to any number of violently angry men who referred to the Co-Tu of Xa Ruh only as *moi*—savages—when it was clear to all the villagers who were the true barbarians. In addition to stealing chickens and goats with impunity, the soldiers would too often hold village men at gunpoint while others would take screaming womenfolk into the Guol, a ritual Tsov did not understand.

On occasion the village would get a respite, thanks to white men who wore green. Those who had crossed the ridge line from Ri'Ga took cover every time they showed. But over time, they came to understand that these white men were friendly and treated the villagers as near-equals. It was the Viet Cong who were to be feared —them and the soldiers who barked at them from under their pith helmets.

It took Tsov longer than anyone else to warm up to the white men in green, but he was transfixed by a symbol all the men wore on their arms: a blue image with a sword cutting through golden lightning bolts. So, timidly, he began approaching the men and touching the cloth of the image. It took a few months, but eventually he came to accept these men.

One of the white men, a man who visited monthly, spoke an understandable form of the village's language. With that man's help, Tsov taught himself some words of the white man's language. He could say, "Hi, GI" and "Good day, Sergeant" and "My name is Tsov" and "I am ten" and "How are you." It was this initial contact at a young age that cemented a lifelong fascination with language. In the back of his mind he remembered that his father, Kiep, like his Uncle Vak, had been able to converse with other *toring*s and even some of the pith helmet soldiers. Even as a young boy, he realized this was key. And over the years, whenever he was confronted with foreigners, even through his innate shyness he made a concerted effort to attempt to learn communication.

Before the next rainy season came, one of the white soldiers put Tsov on his lap and tore the sword and lightning symbol from the arm of his green shirt. He gave it to the boy as a gift. Tsov treasured it and kept it with his book in plastic, and from time to time he took it from his box to admire it. On its edge were scraps of thread in green that contrasted with the lake blue color of the material. He made sure that the threads were never pulled, regarding them as a lifelong connection between him and the white man soldier who had given the powerful symbol to him. Years later he would learn that it was a military patch that designated the men as members of the American army's Special Forces. By 1989, when the patch was grimy with years of contemplation, sweat, and tears, he would remove it from the shredding plastic that encased the book and show it to an old white man in Thailand. Judging by that man's tears, Tsov knew this man had once been a soldier who understood the power of the patch and the bridge it had built between the two of them.

From mid-1968 and through the three years that followed, these kinds of men, whose faces changed with the wind, became Xa Ruh village protectors. They said they were a B-50 team of twelve men. Tsov would greet them every morning with: "Hi Gee Eye, good day bee fifty."

The men set up a camp on a nearby hill. It was surrounded with a wire fence and men with weapons, but the villagers understood that these men were looking out for them. Visits from the Viet Cong became a thing of the past, and the villagers felt a modicum of safety. Some of Tsov's older distant relatives even joined in with the white men. They wore uniforms and carried rifles given to them by the Special Forces. Those who returned home after "missions," as they called them, told fantastical stories about fighting in battle and riding in helicopters like the one that had hovered over Ri'Ga on the Day of Death. Tsov was always in front, wanting to learn of their exploits and everything he could about the worlds beyond the Xa Ruh valley.

Before the fourth rainy season, some four years after their arrival, and with no warning, the Special Forces detachment closed their camp and left the Co-Tu bewildered and alone. They tousled the hair of the children, shook the hands of the village men, and said they would be back. They left orders for the Co-Tu soldiers to continue resisting and to continue fighting the Viet Cong. The Co-Tu rarely saw the white man again, only in an occasional delivery of weapons or ammunition by helicopter. This was 1972. Tsov had reached the age of twelve, but he was old beyond his years—almost a man in the eyes of the village.

After the Day of Death, Xa Ruh and Co-Tu had given up their pledge of neutrality little by little. By 1974 all the men and some of the boys were aligned with what remained of the BAJARAKA Montagnard military contingent fighting against Vietnamese oppressors under FULRO. They shared a common enemy with the Americans, but for a different objective: that of achieving autonomy for all the DeGa.

Everything changed in the spring of 1975. Word spread that the Americans, all their soldiers, and all their Special Forces had been driven out of the county. The Viet Cong soldiers returned in force, and with the help of the People's Army, soldiers in pith helmets from the north crushed all FULRO talk of continued uprising. Those soldiers shot and killed a few of the village elders as a demonstration of superiority, and once again they took screaming women into the huts, the Guol, and the longhouse.

In Xa Ruh, and likewise in other villages, the People's Army cleared out the Guol on the village square and turned it into a school. No one had ever attended a school, but they had heard of them. Tsov brightened up, thinking there might be some benefit to a school—an opportunity to satisfy his curious mind. They were all surprised to learn that everyone was required to attend, from the youngest girls to the oldest men. But the school proved not to be a school by any definition the Co-Tu had learned. Rather, it was an indoctrination center—to break what the soldiers deemed "bad habits" while they mandated adherence to "communist" doctrine and conformity in thinking. It involved a systematic focus on uprooting every trace of native culture.

At gunpoint, the village men and boys were ordered to remove and burn every loincloth in the village. They had a choice of replacing them with either shorts or trousers. The Co-Tu women were ordered to wear shirts to cover their exposed breasts. Shoes, so uncomfortable and ill-fitting as to be implements of torture, were required as well. Any disagreement led to summary beatings.

Tsov was no pushover. He walked a line of disobedience that resulted in severe discipline, but it also more firmly established his credentials as a future village leader and someone to watch. Secretly he tried to see the silver lining in the occupation, and he took the opportunity to learn about the culture and the language of the Vietnamese. He became one of the few Co-Tu who was able to discern the subtle differences between those who were raised in the South compared with those of the North. Gradually, he learned the soldiers' language well, and those few remaining who had known his father were not surprised to see Tsov become an interpreter.

1975–1980
The First Leg of the Exodus:
From Quảng Nam Province to Dak Ben, Vietnam

There was no future, it turned out. The FULRO continued fighting a secret, underground battle against their oppressors, but day by day, it became apparent they could not win. Would never win. Could never hope to win. And so, seven hundred and ninety-one Co-Tu from seventeen villages arranged to migrate. There was no Co-Tu word for "escape," but the oldest woman among them remembered some French, and the group undertook what they termed, by sounding it out, an "evasion." Years after the Americans departed, many of the Co-Tu sustained an inner responsibility to continue the fight as they had pledged. This evasion was a way to fight, so they took it on as a mission.

Among the group, many of the men had been FULRO or soldiers and most had also fought with the American Special Forces. They had traveled far and wide and announced they would lead the group on an interminable wilderness journey hundreds of miles to a promised land known as "Thailand." There they would be safe—according to their leaders.

The elders conferred with the spirit world and made a deliberate decision to take seven hundred men and older boys; fewer than ninety women and older girls were permitted to come along. Families were destroyed in the decision-making process. At a future, better time, the men would return, they promised, for the kinfolk of their individual *toring*s. It was a plan that never came to fruition. Their tiny slice of a mass Central Highlands migration of some eight thousand ended with fewer than five hundred who survived to set foot in Thailand eight years later.

The first leg of their journey consumed the better part of a year. Trudging day and night, they took advantage of the Hồ Chí Minh Trail when possible, but mostly they moved as a slow mass of humanity through mountain jungle following the Annam Cordillera north to south. A journey that, in better times, could have been as short as 250 kilometers was transformed by their circuitous route into a life-and-death marathon of more than twice that distance. But finally, after some 475 kilometers on foot, facing some of the most brutal terrain on earth, they arrived in horrible condition in a small, newly constructed DeGa-like village some fifty kilometers west of Pleiku in the mountains.

When the human body is near starvation, one of the first protections that goes is the ability to ward off disease. A large percentage of the Co-Tu arrived with dysentery, malaria, and a disfiguring skin and cartilage ailment called *yaws*. Of the 791 Co-Tu who began the trip, just 574 stepped into their new surroundings.

Tsov was one. And he made the trip in reasonably good health and disease-free. Now eighteen years old, he had never forgotten the hunting, fishing, and foraging skills his father had passed on to him as a young boy. His talents placed him at a distinct advantage compared to those who could carve totems or weave baskets or harvest rice. Even the village blacksmith had never learned to employ the tools and weapons he had so well created.

The new village reminded Tsov of the Xa Ruh and Ri'Ga he'd left behind, except that it was much larger. And even so, every longhouse was filled to capacity. Instead of families sharing space, the fifty-meter structures were operated more like Guols, filled with men while women shared separate facilities. And here, eight kilometers into Vietnam from the border with Cambodia, the sprawling village of Dak Ben was where Tsov saw the first white woman he'd ever laid eyes on.

Her name was Mary Luther. One of seven Catholic missionaries in Dak Ben, the irony of her appellation would not dawn on Tsov until he was thirty-five years old living in America. During a Bible study class on the history of Christianity and the definition of a Protestant, he would suddenly smile to himself, remembering everything "Miss Mary" and her group had taught him.

Among nearly one thousand residents, Mary took a special liking to Tsov mostly because he took such an interest in her and her mission at Dak Ben. His ulterior motive was to learn her language and culture. He wanted to learn to speak and understand the language of the white man in the hope that he would one day visit what he believed was the real promised land of America. And from 1978 to 1981 he took full advantage of his given situation. Miss Mary took Tsov on as a teacher's aide, and he assisted her in the presentation of mission-focused classes. In the process, he became an interpreter for Miss Mary. In addition to his Co-Tu dialect, he grew impressive skill in English, French, Koho, Rhade, M'Nong, Tha, and Jarai, among perhaps a dozen languages where he could claim at least some proficiency.

Miss Mary took particular interest in how Tsov had managed to come "from who knows where" and all the while maintain an Episcopal prayer book. Over the years Tsov grew tired of telling the story of the book—that he was using the prayer book as an English supplement to learn to read the language. He showed Miss Mary the handwritten notes on the book's flyleaves, and she attempted to explain the concept of street addresses to him. Miss Mary and her fellow missionaries had brought along books and magazines that showed American neighborhoods and houses laid out on tree-lined roads. Each was occupied by a family with a given name. Each home had an associated number. Each house and each number defined a location in America that could be found.

And this is how Tsov came to understand that ROOK was not an actual symbol of evil. He was a person, who lived in a house with a number on a street in America, a far-off land. Tsov grew a renewed sense of hope then, and he built a new dream.

But through it all, he was never convinced that ROOK was not the true name of evil.

1981–1985
The Second Leg of the Exodus:
From Dak Ben, Vietnam, to Cambodia

By 1981 the communist pressure on the DeGa in the area of Dak Ben was too great. Despite protection by elements of the FULRO, Dak Ben and nearby communities were attacked on a near daily basis by a combined and determined enemy in the People's Army. The Montagnard were still considered American sympathizers, which was true, but they also stood in the middle of a conflict that was building between Vietnam and Cambodia. In this conflict, the DeGa had to choose the lesser of two evils, and, siding with the Khmer Rouge against the Vietnamese, they began a new exodus for their original destination: Thailand.

All agreements with the DeGa were informal, but they were sealed by custom and culture in word. The DeGa took the word of the Khmer Rouge that in exchange for fighting the Vietnamese, they would be provided weapons, ammunition, and most importantly, food to cross Cambodia to the west in search of their promised land.

In total, some four thousand began the arduous expedition across a wilderness of Biblical proportions—a wilderness to end them all. For two years they slogged through some of the most inhospitable territory on Earth, all the while losing one after another of their people. It was their own Bataan Death March, with the single advantage of not having overlords beating them on the path. Along the way, on occasion, they had the good fortune to ambush Vietnamese patrols deep in Cambodia—fulfilling their promise to the Khmer Rouge—and from these patrols they stole food and weapons. Still, for the most part they subsisted on an abysmal diet of lizards, porcupine, the occasional weasel or red squirrel, snakes, salamanders and other invertebrates, roots, tree bark, and grass.

After two years of crossing Cambodia from east to west, fewer than seven hundred of the original four thousand had survived. In the classic Darwinian model, Tsov was among the "fittest."

It was now 1983, and to add extreme insult to critical injury, the Khmer Rouge reneged on their promise to permit passage into Thailand, instead rounding up all surviving DeGa into a single internment camp on the Cambodian side of the border, just a stone's throw from Thailand in the Mondulkiri Province. And once again, to a degree that few civilized humans can well understand, misery was their way of life. These few survivors were subjected to starvation, disease, malaria, scurvy, tuberculosis, and all manner of bacteriological infections that could have been cured with the most basic, but unavailable, antibiotics. The deplorable conditions under which they were forced to live helped to cement the Khmer Rouge reputation for brutality. Western observers, particularly Christian missionaries, attempted to visit under a Red Cross rubric, but were turned away. Those who got a glimpse of conditions were reminded of overcrowded Nazi concentration camps with emaciated humans staring out from behind wire fences under constant threat of death by starvation or beating or both. To this day it remains unclear what the Khmer Rouge hoped to gain by imprisoning the mountain people.

Now in his mid-twenties, Tsov became a de facto camp leader. His value as a hunter and gatherer was lost since the Montagnard were never permitted to leave the camp, so he employed himself in the business of keeping people alive. He also learned to speak, but not read, Khmer, and he developed skills as a medic.

Tsov recognized the futility of his people's condition, and he soon came to understand the reality that the 412 persons still alive would die a slow death if he didn't act. So early in 1985, he secretly met with Cambodian sympathizers who told his tiny group that the Thai government was developing a refugee camp on the other side of the border. Getting there would require a forty-kilometer trek through dense jungle, but most of the trip would be conducted in relative safety within Thailand.

Tsov and other leaders chose 361 who were fit for travel. (In truth, many were by no means fit, but they pleaded to not be left behind.) With the assistance and approval of elders, most no older than forty, Tsov helped plan and executed a mass escape.

1985–1991

The Third Leg of the Exodus:

From Cambodia to Thailand

Known simply as "Site II," the DeGa people's new home was just over the Cambodian border in the promised land of Thailand, near the village of Ta Phraya. When the 337 Montagnard who survived the trek arrived at the gates of Site II, they joined a mix of 140,000 wretched civilians from all walks of humanity. The majority were Vietnamese and combined the populations of resistance fighters from a dozen smaller camps, including Nong Samet, Bang Poo, Nong Chan, Nam Yeun, and Sanro. Of the 791 Co-Tu from seventeen villages who began their migration in 1975, a mere 22 arrived at the Promised Land: Thailand. They met together from time to time to mourn the loss of their culture, their way of life, and their relatives, but they thanked the spirits for sparing them at least their lives.

Site II was a sprawling ghetto, but when compared to the concentration camp in Cambodia, there was no question that it was the Promised Land. Tsov reveled in the opportunity to take advantage of basic support services, including the first medical care and sanitation he'd seen in ten years. There was construction and skills training in progress. And above all, there was food—never enough, but it was a daily feast compared with the scraps they'd survived on before the escape. They were given periodic rations of rice and beans, dried fish, eggs, some vegetables when available, oil, salt, and flour. Fresh water was scarce, but Tsov rigged up a mechanism to collect rainfall from the corrugated roof of his barracks. A hundred others copied his ingenuity.

Over and over residents were reminded that their stay was to be temporary. The Thai government never intended any sort of permanency. And that constant refrain of hope delayed the development of community services, including medical services and education. In this "temporary camp" called Site II, Tsov spent eight years, a tenth of his life. In fact, when looking back on his early life, he would remember this place as "home"—blocking out much of what had come before.

Making constant reference to his *Book of Prayer* over the years, Tsov counted himself a devout Christian. Site II was thick with white men and women from a dozen humanitarian relief agencies, and within a few weeks of his arrival, Tsov had visited them all.

A man named Robert Smithson, who represented the American Refugee Committee, spent weeks trying to cajole Tsov to work with them exclusively. The word was out on Tsov's skillsets. He stood out as an anomaly with his unique language skills, and now added Thai to his repertoire. He was courted by the Catholic Office for Emergency Relief, Handicap International, the International Rescue Committee, and Catholic Relief Services. In the end he devoted his most of his efforts to Christian Hands International, for the sole reason that the lead missionary carried and often referenced a prayer book just like Tsov's.

Tsov knew the man only as "Father Tom" and was not surprised to find out years later that he had been the Right Reverend

Thomas Ormes, an Episcopal Bishop Suffragan of the Diocese of North Carolina. Father Tom was a bright spark in the Episcopal hierarchy. In the past, he had assisted former soldiers from his church near Fayetteville with the immigration of their Vietnamese spouses and children. He was childless, and his wife had died tragically on a visit to Chichen Itza on Mexico's Yucatan peninsula. She tripped while descending the pyramid and tumbled to her death. Tom had not been a believer in pagan gods, but he took the tragedy as a personal message that he had not been doing enough to serve God and help the poor. He gave up everything and moved to the Site II camp in Thailand where he felt he could make a difference.

Father Tom declared that Tsov, now twenty-seven years old, would be a teacher, an English teacher. Due in part to Father Tom's pressure, Christian Hands joined with the royal Thai government to initiate a new educational program for elementary school, including curriculum development, the printing of educational materials, teacher training, and the building of schools and classrooms. Although the program was secular, Father Tom nevertheless took this on as his primary mission. Those who might come to the Church as a result, he said, would come of their own accord. And they did.

By the start of the 1989 school year he and Tsov had swung hammers on forty-three elementary schools addressing the requirements of over sixty thousand students. In addition, an emerging need was met with junior high schools, high schools, and vocational education programs serving over ten thousand idle adults. Tsov became the sole DeGa elementary school principal while never giving up his first love of being a platform teacher. And abiding by the adage that there is no better way to learn a subject than to teach it, he became fluent in English.

So when an American television news crew arrived in 1990, Tsov was the natural candidate to sit for an interview. And by then, Tsov's accent was so refined—thanks to Father Tom's help—that at first Wade Rybar, the producer, turned Tsov away.

"Sorry, sir," he told Tsov. "We're looking for someone who is not American, a refugee in the camp."

"But sir, I am a refugee. I'm not American."

"Nice try." Rybar flipped through his notes. "Is it *Tee Sov*?"

"No Tee, just Sov. What do you mean, 'nice try'?" Tsov asked.

"I mean you're American."

"I am not American, sir. I am DeGa. I am Co-Tu. I am Montagnard."

Rybar was taken aback. "Where the heck did you learn to speak English so well?"

"I started as a boy, learning from the Special Forces in my village. Then there was a Christian missionary named Mary Luther, and then—"

Wade stopped him. "I believe you, and I have to say I'm impressed. But the truth is, you really do sound like an American, and I'm trying to do a news story here, with someone who sounds like a refugee. Can you recommend someone else to me?"

It was a seminal moment for Tsov, a short conversation that changed his life. Every bit of his drive and compassion was now focused on getting to America and becoming an American.

1992–1993
The Fourth Leg of the Exodus:
From Thailand to America

In 1992 his dream almost came true. A small group of former soldiers visited Thailand with people from the American Embassy and asked for Tsov's help in rounding up every Montagnard in the camp. This might have been a challenge—sorting through 170,000 persons—but for years the DeGa had worked to maintain their cultural purity, doing what they could to marry within the group, living in a tight-knit community, meeting regularly, and maintaining ties with the varying dialects that had survived. In a few short hours they had filled an elementary school auditorium with almost 250 DeGa men, women, and children. They sat in stunned silence, in complete disbelief, when they were told they would be transported to America. Some had had dreams of this. Others had never considered the possibility. But in October 1992, 221 DeGa boarded buses with all of their belongings. A few went to live with Americans they knew in the vicinity of Sacramento, California. But most went to live near the Special Forces community in North Carolina, men they had never forgotten. Five school buses drove out of the camp main gate. Tsov was not among them.

Father Tom had asked Tsov to stay behind, to continue their work together, and Tsov did. Father Tom promised they would leave

Thailand by 1995. He asked Tsov to scour Site II, to investigate any rumors, and to search for any DeGa he could locate, including the outcast mixed-race DeGa, surviving sons and daughters of American servicemen. Tsov took the task to heart.

The following spring, in April of 1993, Father Tom suffered a heart attack, and he was evacuated by air to Anderson Air Force Base in Guam. Under the direction of the US Ambassador to Thailand, thirty-four surviving DeGa were also permitted on board the C-5 Super Galaxy transport jet. It was the first time any of them had set foot on a flying machine.

This time, Tsov was among those leaving. Finally, his long journey was coming to an end.

At the age of thirty-two, he was on his way to America.

He took with him only a small nylon zippered bag on the plane. It contained a lightweight jacket, a scruffy green beret, an old US Army Special Forces patch, and a tattered *Book of Common Prayer*. At the Anderson Air Force Base Medical Center, he and the other thirty-three DeGa received routine physical examinations and screenings for human immunodeficiency virus, syphilis, tuberculosis, and other conditions. Seven carried malaria in the form of the plasmodium parasite, and would need to stay in Guam for a month to get treatment. A nurse asked Tsov to translate.

"They need to give you drugs for malaria," he told the group. "You'll get better."

On the seventh of June, 1993, he and his brothers and sisters from Vietnam stepped off a US Air Force Lockheed C-141 Starlifter at Pope Air Force Base outside Fayetteville, North

Carolina. Tsov was too far east of the Appalachian Mountains to see those reminders of his boyhood home, but he felt he was home nevertheless. Dozens of old friends from Site II were there to meet them at Base Operations. There were tears and hugs all around. He was home.

The drive to Father Tom's house in Raleigh took under two hours, plus the time they spent stopping for a delicious meal at the Saigon Cafe in Benson. On the way into Father Tom's neighborhood near Lake Johnson Park, Tsov began to notice neighborhood street signs and numbers on houses—addresses. He took the *Book of Common Prayer* from his bag and opened the front cover. In the top left corner of the opening flyleaf, scratched in barely legible pencil was ROOK, Lionel, 1SG 745 Potilla Ave. Arcadia, Fla.

He remembered. He smiled, and then he frowned. He remembered his village. He remembered his father. *Live, son. Make a life.* Tsov felt a village spirit in the car with him. He gazed through the glass at the rain, and he imagined what could be.

———————————————

A WORD ON THE CONCEPT OF FICTION

Many works of fiction, including this one, contain a disclaimer... It's an interesting concept, but there is a lot in this book that is based on reality. Any work of fiction comes from the mind of the person who writes it, and will reflect their experiences and what they know. So, much of this story comes from what I experienced and remember, combined liberally with my imagination.

At various times in my life I lived in Falls Church, Virginia; Fort Collins, Colorado; Belleville, Illinois; Montgomery, Alabama; and many of the other locations I mention in this story. While I have never been to West Point, I attended my brother's graduation from OCS at Fort Benning, Georgia in 1967. My dad was a career army officer who was stationed on Clark Air Force Base in the early '60s. As a kid I visited Base Operations in Guam. I was once a military unit commander, though in the air force, not the army.

All that being said, there was no Second Platoon from any service in the Central Highlands that did what this platoon did. The platoon, company, battalion, and brigade depicted in this book are fictitious. There was no Lieutenant Bross, nor is he based on any person in particular. In fact, with the exception of Ben King and a handful of famous names I mentioned, if you're wondering whether any particular character is based on any particular person, my answer is an unequivocal "no."

A final note: For those who might see similarities between television-based criminal methods and those depicted in This Eternity, *please note that I wrote a version of the Prologue in 1998 after visiting a Georgetown bar. The first episode of the HBO series* Dexter *aired on 1 October 2006.*

APOLOGIES TO THE DEGA ON VILLAGER NAMES AND CO-TU CULTURE

The Montagnard, the DeGa, or often the Degar, are real people who for over a thousand years occupied the mountainous regions of Indo-China. Their anthropology is complex, but experts largely agree, both through archeology and DNA testing, that the genome of the DeGa most closely aligns with Malayo-Polynesian ancestry. Therefore, in the most simplistic terms they arrived in waves, by boat or on foot from Polynesia or Malaysia over the millennia. They sustained a largely coastal livelihood until, over time, they were forced to migrate to escape persecution into the central highlands as ethnic Chinese expanded into Indo-China, claiming the territory as theirs. By the 1950s there were thousands of villages spread over the highlands and foothills, representing dozens of tribes, each with their own language and dialect.

Some researchers conclude that the DeGa spoken word is divided into two basic linguistic families: Mon-Khmer and Malayo-Polynesian language groupings. If the villages of Ri'Ga and Xa Ruh existed (and they did not), the Co-Tu in this story would have spoken a Malayo-Polynesian dialect. As depicted, in the 1960s hardly any of the villagers would have spoken or understood Vietnamese.

Villager names used in this book are only loosely correct. I attempted to choose reasonable male and female names, but though they may be foreign-sounding to the reader, they will not resonate well in the minds of surviving DeGa people. I apologize to the DeGa for this methodology. I arrived at name choices based on the ability of a native English speaker to be able to pronounce the names while also being able track an individual character over time. (Most sophisticated readers recall a book or two in which the names of the characters were so hard to grasp and remember that they stumbled every time they were encountered.) Additionally, depending on the tribe, women's names might all begin phonetically with Ka or H, a female pronoun of sorts, while all male names might begin with Y or K. I felt it would be even more difficult to separate characters if every name began with the same letter. Ultimately, the names were chosen in order to minimize reader confusion.

I studied DeGa culture and the Co-Tu (a people who existed and survive as a distinct culture today) through many written sources. While this story is fiction, my desire was to help the reader to understand that the DeGa in general and the Co-Tu in particular are human beings with every human need and desire felt by any race, creed, or culture of humans the world over. Many DeGa experienced horror during the Vietnam War. The Montagnard journey from 1970s Vietnam to 1990s America was real and harrowing, though I describe it with poetic license. I have never run across a novel that attempted to depict either the DeGa or the Co-Tu as people. I will bet that you, the reader, have never even heard of them.

To surviving members of the Co-Tu: My attempts to create family-centered, loving villages fail on many levels. I regret what I did not get right. You deserve better.

THESE SOULS

Villagers described according to their relationship to Kiep:

Baap'Can—Pronounced "bop con." Kiep's first cousin and Uncle Vak's only living son. He is two years older than Kiep. The two are like brothers.

Giang—the spirit who, when treated with reverence, protects the villages of both Ri'Ga and Xah Ru

H'Juel Ya—Pronounced "hee jewel ya." Kiep's aunt by marriage, and Y'Nen's wife. She is the village tobacconist and supplies several villages in the immediate area of Ri'Ga.

Hlong—Pronounced "long," but with a forced exhalation on the letter "L". Kiep's father and Tsov's grandfather. Fought on the side of the French in their Indo-China war. Kiep last saw his father when he was nine years old.

Kiep Dool—Pronounced "keep dool." The central figure in Ri'Ga village. He is a member of the Brui Thi *toring*, roughly equivalent to a tribe. He courts and marries Thia Pholoong. Kiep and Thia raise three children: Mai, a daughter, is the oldest; Paj, a daughter, is number two; and Tsov is their third child and only son.

Mai—Pronounced "my." The first child and daughter of Kiep and Thia.

Mr. Pholoong—Pronounced "fo-lung." Kiep's father-in-law and Thia's father. He is the Xa Ruh village elder and a peer of Hlong. A member of the Riah Thi *toring*. Mr. Pholoong is tall by Co-Tu standards and is an imposing figure.

Mrs. Pholoong—Pronounced "fo-lung." Kiep's mother-in-law and Thia's mother. She is wife to the Xa Ruh village elder and a peer of Kiep's mother.

Mrs. Dool—Pronounced "duel." Kiep's mother and Thia's mother-in-law. She is a widower, having been married to Kiep's father Hlong. She is accorded due respect as the wife of a former Ri'Ga village elder and is therefore a peer of Thia's mother.

Paj—Pronounced "page." The second child and second daughter of Kiep and Thia.

Siu—Pronounced "sue." Kiep's second cousin, Baap'Can's son, and Vak's grandson. Also Tsov's friend. The two are inseparable and stand side by side at a critical juncture in the story. No, Shel Silverstein did not write about, nor did Johnny Cash perform a song about, this boy named Siu.

Thi—Pronounced "tea." Thia's uncle and Mr. Pholoong's brother.

Thia Pholoong—Pronounced "tia fo-lung." Kiep's wife and mother to Mai, Paj, and Tsov.

Tsov—Pronounced "sov." The third child and only son of Kiep and Thia. In the Co-Tu dialect, "tsov" is the word for "tiger." Though numbers are dwindling, there were and are tigers in the wilds of Indo-China.

Vak—Rhymes with "talk." Kiep's uncle and Hlong's twin brother. Hlong has been gone so long, and his visage is so like Vak's, that many have forgotten Hlong altogether. Vak was like a father to Kiep.

Y'Nen—Pronounced "yee nen." Kiep's mother's brother. He is the village distiller and wine maker.

THOSE OTHERS

*I never meet a ragged boy in the street without feeling that I may owe him a
salute,*
for I know not what possibilities may be buttoned up under his coat.
—*James A. Garfield*

Armstrong, James—Truancy Officer, DeSoto County, Florida

Ayala, Saul—Detective Lieutenant, Fort Collins Police
Department, Colorado

Belford, Nathan—Former resident of Perry, Florida. Lionel's
friend at the Florida Industrial School for Boys. Nickname "Curtin."

Bidwell, Mr.—Old teacher and owner of "The White House" at
the Florida Industrial School for Boys

Bitsy—Arlene Humphries's dog

Bross, Alex—Alexander Newman Bross. Darren Bross's father, Lex
Bross's grandfather, and Ren Bross's great-grandfather.

Bross, Christy Mudd—Darren Bross's wife and Lex Bross's
mother. Captain of the cheerleaders, Lufkin, Texas.

Bross, Darren—Darren Alexander Bross, Sr. Graduate of US
Military Academy, West Point, New York, Class of 1966. First
Lieutenant, US Army.

Bross, Lex—Darren Alexander Bross, Jr. Civil servant, US government, Las Vegas, NV.

Bross, Lindy Warren—Married Lex Bross in 2015.

Bross, Margaret—Margaret Olive Hopkins Bross. Darren Bross's mother, Lex Bross's grandmother, and Ren Bross's great-grandmother.

Bross, Ren—Darren Alexander Bross, III. Graduate of US Air Force Academy.

Byers, Martin—"Marty," PFC Rifleman, Montgomery, AL. Knew Mrs. Rosa Parks.

Byung, Dung Yu—Corporal in the Army, Republic of Korea

Carver, George Washington—"Peanut," CPL, Rifleman, Valdosta, Georgia

Caudle, Jerry—Lionel's sadistic friend at the Florida Industrial School for Boys

Chamberlain, Hunter Stone—Loo's son, born 1973

Chamberlain, Rebecca "Becky"—Wellington Chamberlain's wife

Chamberlain, Wellington—"Loo," PFC, Rifleman, Arlington, Virginia. Nicknamed by his drill sergeant in Basic Training after the Battle of Waterloo.

Cole, Gary—CPL, Bearer and Rifleman, Chico, California

Conway, Charles "Chas"—Homicide detective. Falls Church Police Department lead investigator.

Davis, Roy—Captain (USAR). Chaplain at LZ Regulator.

Presbyterian by ordination, nondenominational by US military custom. Boise, Idaho.

Đinh Quang Tý—"Ty," a VC officer until he found out the VC had tortured and murdered his parents and burned his village. He defected to the US and South Vietnamese side as a Tiger Scout.

Elphick, Kimball—"Elf," SGT, Squad Leader, College Station, Texas

Emma—Kook's aunt who would send him letters from time to time.

Evans, Mark—Captain, Bravo Company Commander. Darren Bross's commander and direct supervisor. West Point Class of 1962.

Father Louis—Witz's childhood priest

Gibson, Paul—Lieutenant Colonel, Retired. West Point Class of 1966.

Grayson, Dick—"Robin," SGT, Rifleman Team Leader, Gainesville, Florida. Nicknamed after Batman's sidekick.

Grayson, Gabe—Richard Grayson's uncle

Grayson, Magan—Richard "Dick" "Robin" Grayson's wife

Grosvenor, Michail—"Mickey," CPL, Rifleman and Backup Medic, Fort Collins, Colorado

Guzman, Ramie—Foreign National Filipina maid, Clark Air Force Base, Philippines

Hagen, Robert "Bob"—Attorney, DeSoto County, Florida

Haines, Ralph—General. Actual person in the US Army in the 60s.

Hartsdale, William—"Willy," CPL Machine Gunner, Gifford, Florida

Hernandez, Francisco—"Paco," PFC, Grenadier, Zapata, Texas

Hill, Daniel—Major, XO Ninth ASA Field Station, Clark AFB, Philippines

Hopkins, Katherine—"Auntie Katherine." Darren Bross's aunt on his mother's side. Margaret Bross's sister.

Hopkins, Raymond—District of Columbia lead detective investigator

Humphries, Arlene—Lionel Rook's cousin, Vero Beach, Florida

Hyland, Brian—released hit pop song "Itsy Bitsy Teenie Weenie Yellow Polkadot Bikini" in June 1960, and hit pop song "Sealed with a Kiss" in June 1962

Jacobs, Robert "Bobby"—Lieutenant, Second Platoon leader prior to Darren

Jensen, Dave—Classmate of Bobby Rook in Arcadia, Florida

JoEllen—Court Reporter, DeSoto County, Florida

Johnson, Harold—General, actual person. US Army Chief of Staff in 1966.

Johnson, Scott "Scotty"—SSG Squad Leader, Gulfport, Mississippi

Johnson, Willie—Classmate of Bobby Rook in Arcadia, Florida

Kelly, Nick—Falls Church High School Chief of Sanitation, janitor

King, Ben—Ben King is a living person. He gave the author permission to use his name in *This Eternity*. Ben King earned his Bachelor of Science Degree in Biology from Loyola University of Los Angeles in 1959. Following graduation he served three years in the US Navy. Early on he chose to be an ornithologist and specialized in the birds of Southeast Asia. Before the age of thirty he was named Chief of the Migratory Animals Pathological Survey in Thailand. A project sponsored by the US Army's Far East Research and Development Group, this bird migration study aimed to find links between migratory birds and human disease. He accepted all the help he could get.

Kingery, Gary—Lieutenant General, US Army Deputy Chief of Staff for Operations. Bought a guayabera shirt in Panama.

Kisa, Tracy—CW4, Chief Warrant Officer, Air Cav, UH-1 senior pilot

Kuykendahl, Clayton Andrew "Kook"—Platoon Radio Telephone Operator. From Franklin Park, New Jersey. PhD in History from Princeton University prior to serving in the US Army during the Vietnam War.

Kuykendahl, Donna—Kook's wife. Married a decade after Kook returned from Vietnam.

Langman, Timothy—"Lassie," CPL Rifleman Team Leader, Beavercreek, Ohio

Lee, Park Hee—Private Army Republic of Korea

Long, James—Lieutenant Colonel, US Army. Battalion Commander

Luther, Mary—A Catholic missionary in Dak Ben who took a liking to Tsov

Mack, Peter "The Knife"— PFC Rifleman, St. Petersburg, Florida

MacNulty, Sean "Doc"—CPL Medic, Las Vegas, Nevada. Dog lover.

Mader, Frank—FBI Special Agent, Florida

Maples, Carter—"Maple" SGT, Rifleman Team Leader, Sacramento, California

Master Sergeant Stargardt—An army master sergeant is an E-8, one step from the top of the enlisted corps, which is E-9. Stargardt is a Green Beret member of the SOG.

Masterson, James "Bat"—SSG Squad Leader, Chillicothe, Ohio

McCloskey, John "Jack"— PFC Machine Gunner, Nederland, Colorado

Mejia, Vicente "Beans"—PFC, Rifleman, Guanajuato, Mexico. Enlisted in exchange for a green card.

Mesner, Scott—KIA in Vietnam. SGT, served with Rook on Rook's first Vietnam tour.

Message, Craig—SGT, Rifleman Team Leader, Birdwatcher, Belleville, Illinois

Miller, Andrew—"Andy," Juvenile Court Judge, DeSoto County, Florida

Mudd, Allison—Christy Mudd Bross's mother, Darren Bross's mother-in-law

Mudd, Gary—Christy Mudd Bross's father, Darren Bross's father-in-law

Mudd, Ted—Christy Mudd Bross's brother, Darren Bross's brother-in-law

Nguyễn Hữu Thảo—Captain, People's Army of North Vietnam. Commander of a logistics and engineering company under Group 559.

Nguyễn Văn Trà—Captain. Viet Cong Commander of an infantry company charged with helping supply and protect NVA Group 559 in October 1966. Nickname "Nhung."

Nicolletti, Norman "Nick"—SGT, Rifleman Team Leader, Bellevue, Nebraska

Nutsy—Sean "Doc" MacNulty's Frisbee dog. Shot and killed by Sergeant Rook.

O'Neill, Lorne "Chip"—Lieutenant Colonel, Battalion Commander

Ormes, Thomas—Right Reverend of the Episcopal Church. Missionary for Christian Hands International at Site II.

Owens, Mark Swingle—Corporal and Rifleman, St. George, UT. After the war, Mark served a career as a police officer in St. George.

Park, Hun Sae—Captain, Army, Republic of Korea

Peers, General—Two Corps Commander, Operation Greeley

Peterson, Chad—Resident of Arcadia, Florida. Died in reform school.

Pixton, Kennan "Pixie"—PFC, Rifleman, San Antonio, Texas. Yahtzee fanatic.

Polk, Walter—Congressman, Texas Seventh Congressional District

Ramirez—FBI Special Agent, Florida

Rattray, Jim—Guidance counselor at Arcadia High School, Florida

Rook, Bobby—Lionel Rook's younger brother

Rook, Lionel Bodean—A troubled boy and man from Arcadia, Florida

Rook, Sylvan Bodean—Lionel's uncle

Russelvage, Andrew—"Russ," CPL, Rifleman, Blue Ridge, Georgia

Russelvage, Judy—Andrew Russelvage's wife

Rybar, Wade—Member of an American news crew at Site II

Sadler, Mildred—Resident, Arcadia, Florida

Salisbury, Ernest "Ernie"—PFC, Bearer and Rifleman, Portland, Maine

Sanchez, Dave—Major, Fort Gulik, Panama

Schmidt, Daniel "Jiggles"—Rifleman, Falls Church, Virginia

Sherman, Mr.—Principal of the Florida Industrial School for Boys

Smith, Mitchell "Smitty"—PFC Rifleman, Peyton, Colorado

Smithson, Robert—Represented the American Refugee Committee at Site II

Snedeker, Eric—Attended West Point at some time prior to Darren. From Lufkin, Texas.

Staubach, Roger—Actual person. Graduate of US Naval Academy and Heisman Trophy winner. Naval Officer when his role in the book takes place.

Stockman, Blue—SFC. Rook's fellow squad leader when he was stationed near Darlac, South Vietnam.

Tapia—FBI Special Agent, Florida

Torrens, Cesar "Switch"—PFC, Grenadier and Rifleman, San Juan, Puerto Rico

Peckham, Stanley "Stan"—PFC, Grenadier, Alamogordo, New Mexico

VRT—Initials of the weather forecaster from Detachment 19, 30th Weather Squadron who prepared a forecast discussion on 6 June 1966, the day Tsov went canyon fishing with his father, two uncles, and a cousin

Walker, Brad—FBI Special Agent, Florida

Warren, Charles "Chuck"—SGT, Rifleman Team Leader, Cocoa Beach, Florida

Weeks, Harold—Captain, HHQ Company Adjutant, Hohenfels,

Germany

Westfall, Michael Joseph—Freelance photojournalist

Whitsun, Carper "Witz"—SSG Squad Leader, Marblehead, Massachusetts

Wilding, Mr.—Young "teacher" at the Florida Industrial School for Boys

Williams, Gary—Corrections officer, Federal Corrections Institute, Terre Haute, Indiana

Wilson—General. No further information.

Wolusky, Bill "Mister Ski"—Weekend manager, Francisco's Drive-In, Lufkin, Texas

Wright, Van—PFC Assistant Machine Gunner, Olympia, Washington

Young, Chuck—Car mechanic, Fort Morgan, New York

THESE WORDS—GLOSSARY

Silence is better than unmeaning words.
—Pythagoras

105mm howitzer—Large cannon on wheels that can be towed behind a truck or jeep

11B—Military Occupational Specialty code for Infantry Rifleman. "Are you eleven bravo?" "Yep, how about you?"

1LT—First Lieutenant

1SG—First Sergeant

2LT—Second Lieutenant

4.2 mortars—Korean War-era old stock. A rifled 4.2-inch (107 mm) mortar. By Nam standards the rounds were huge bullets. They could not be moved easily and were used primarily to defend the fire base or for longer-range fire support.

60mm mortar—Lighter weight mortar used for company fire support

762 round—a 7.62mm bullet. Essentially a .30-caliber round used in the US M-14 rifle and the M-60 machine gun.

81mm mortar—Medium-weight, smooth bore mortar. Too heavy to take off the LZ, but used for company and battalion fire support.

81s—See *81mm mortar*

Air cav—Air cavalry

AK-47—Soviet assault rifle

Americal Division—23d Infantry Division. Took over Task Force Oregon. Contraction of *American, New Caledonian Division.*

AN/PRC 25—See *Prick 25.*

AN/PRC-6—See *Prick 6.*

AP—Air Police. US Air Force Military Police. MP equivalent. Derided as "apes" by army soldiers.

APO—Air Post Office

Article 15—Non-judicial punishment whereby a commander with authority under the Uniform Code of Military Justice can take stripes, money, and/or liberty from a military member under his/her command

Autovon—Department of Defense telephone system. Employs commercial lines, but uses government switching systems. Under large contracts with telecommunications providers, enabled DOD to bypass high long-distance rates.

BAJARAKA—A DeGa resistance group formed in the early 1960s with the express intent of sustaining DeGa culture by keeping out all foreign influence. An acronym formed by the first two letters of four major DeGa tribes. The FULRO was a subset of this group and advocated armed resistance. See *FULRO.*

Bakelite—Early molded plastic. For example, 1950s-era telephones were made of Bakelite.

Bandolier—Cross-body belt with pockets or slots to hold bullets and equipment

BFE—Bum Fuck Egypt, slang for the middle of nowhere

BG—Brigadier General, one-star general

Big iron bird— The airplane that would fly you out of Vietnam. Also called *silver bird* and *silver freedom bird.*

Bitch box—Slang for a speaker put on the exterior of radio-telephones enabling those close by the radio to hear without using headphones.

Blooper—M-79 grenade launcher. Single shot, shoulder-fired break action launcher. Fires 40mm grenades.

BN—Battalion

BOQ—Bachelor's Officer Quarters. Think apartments for unmarried officers.

Bouncing Betty—Slang for a bounding mine. One that launches an explosive into the air for detonation at around chest level. Also called a *bounder mine.*

Bounding or bounder mine—See *Bouncing Betty*

Bravo 6—Radio call sign for the Bravo Company Commander. The person talking always says the call sign of the person they are calling first, then theirs. So "Bravo 6, Bravo 6-2" is Lieutenant Bross calling Captain Evans on the radio-telephone.

Bravo 6-2—Radio call sign for the 2d Platoon Leader, Bravo

Company

Bravo 6-2-3—Radio call sign for the 3d squad leader, 2d Platoon, Bravo Company. 6-2-1 is First Squad, and so on.

Bravo 6-2-5—Radio call sign for the platoon sergeant, 2d Platoon, Bravo Company. There is no Fifth Squad.

British MI-6—British Secret Intelligence Service… where James Bond served

Butter bar—Slang for the rank insignia of a Second Lieutenant, a single gold bar

Ca nuong—Mountain trout in Co-Tu language

CALEA—Communications Assistance for Law Enforcement

Care package—Any mailed box containing items from The World

Casual status—When soldiers are drawing a paycheck but do not have any well-defined job. Often soldiers are assigned to casual status when they have completed one assignment, or school, and are waiting for the next assignment or school (on a strict schedule) to begin.

CG—Commanding General

Charlie— The enemy in Vietnam. South Vietnamese rebels. Also Mr. Charles, Charley, Chuck, and VC.

Chi-Com grenade—A grenade, often manufactured in China, that was used extensively by the North Vietnamese Army and the Viet Cong

Chiêu Hồi—See *Kit Carson Scout*

Chink—a highly derogatory slang term to describe Chinese people

CIB—Combat Infantryman's Badge. The badge of honor awarded to infantrymen and Special Forces, and Rangers in the rank of colonel and below, who are engaged in active ground combat. In Vietnam, the requirement was thirty days. Earning a CIB is a big deal in the US Army. Those who serve in the infantry corps and fail to earn a CIB during wartime are viewed with suspicion at best and derision at worst. Wearing a CIB that is not earned is an offense punishable under the Uniform Code of Military Justice.

CID—The US Army Criminal Investigation Division

CIU—Criminal Investigations Unit

Clacker—A "clacker" comes with each claymore mine to electrically activate the blasting cap

Claymore—Used by the US military and its allies since 1960, the M18 claymore mine is packaged in a convex green plastic case to ensure an optimum distribution of internal fragments and ball bearings at fifty meters. Embossed on the case are the words "Front Toward Enemy." It is aimed by use of an open sight on the top surface and includes metal scissor legs. The mine is constructed with C-4 explosive behind a matrix of seven hundred 3.2mm steel balls encased in resin. The weapon and all its accessories are carried in a bandolier. There are a variety of methods to detonate the mine by manual and electrical means. Ingenious soldiers invented new ways never intended by weapons developers. An M57 "clacker" comes with each mine to electrically activate the blasting cap.

CO—Commanding Officer at any level in the army

CODIS—Combined DNA Index System

COL—Colonel

Combat Journalist—Civilian war correspondent. Lives war with engaged units to "get the story."

Cordite—Smokeless propellant that was designed to replace gunpowder. Leaves behind a recognizable smell after firefights.

Cow—West Point Second Classman. Junior year at West Point is called "Cow Year."

CPL—Corporal

CPT—Captain

CSA—Confederate States of America

CSM—Command Sergeant Major

Defilades—Combat term to refer to objects that can be used to deflect fire from the enemy

DeGa—Indo-Chinese Mountain People. "First People." The DeGa were called "Montagnard" by the French during their occupation of Indo-China.

DEROS—Date of Estimated Return from Overseas. The date soldiers tracked. The day they were scheduled to return home.

Dinks—Highly derogatory term for just about any Asian, but especially those engaged in combat against US forces.

Dust Off—Nickname for a UH-1, a Huey slick that was marked with a Red Cross. Dust Off carried medical professionals who flew into dangerous battlefield situations to extract the wounded.

LT—Slang for Lieutenant. Some officers prohibited troops from using the contraction. They thought it was disrespectful.

FAC—See *Forward Air Controller*

Fast mover—Fighter jet, US Air Force, US Marines, US Navy

FB—See *Fire base*

Fire base—A central location where long-range artillery was located to provide artillery support for infantry operations. The idea was to always have a fire base within range, but that was not always possible.

Five by—"I read you loud and clear."

Flip—Highly derogatory slang characterization of a Filipino

FNG—Fucking New Guy. Also called *greenhorn* or *cherry*.

FOIA—Freedom of Information Act

Forward Air Controller—US Air Force pilot and aircraft who assist in directing fires

Four deuce mortar—See *4.2 mortar*

Fuckin' Chuckin'—See *Charlie*

Full bird—A full colonel. Wears an eagle as rank insignia, therefore "bird."

FULRO—The United Front for the Liberation of Repressed

Races. A BAJARAKA armed effort that attempted to force autonomy for all DeGa tribes. Under FULRO the Montagnard first aligned military support with the US armed forces, chiefly the US Army Special Forces.

G4—Division Logistics, Supply, and Engineering

GEN—General, four-star general

GI—Government Issue. Slang for any member of the US armed forces.

Gook—Highly derogatory term for just about any Asian, but especially those engaged in combat against US forces

GP—General Purpose

GP-medium—A general purpose, medium-sized tent

Group 559—A unit of North Vietnamese Army and Viet Cong who were charged with building and maintaining the Hồ Chí Minh trail

Gs—The level of effective gravity a fighter pilot is experiencing. Five Gs is five times normal gravity, so that a two-hundred-pound man effectively weighs one thousand pounds.

GS-13—A civil service rank roughly equivalent to a major in the military

GSW—Gunshot wound

Guard—A common radio frequency that anyone with a US-made radio should be able to tune in to and monitor. US military pilots always monitor "Guard" so that anyone can contact them for any reason, chiefly an emergency. For example, if an F-4 Phantom jet was on approach to land at an airfield and did not have its landing gear deployed, someone on the ground would call them on "Guard" and scream, "Go around! Your gear is up!"

Gui—A DeGa grass woven basket carried on the back with back straps

Guol—An ornate, common-use building in many DeGa villages. In this story the Co-Tu used the Guol as quarters for village bachelors.

Hand frags—Fragmentary grenades that are thrown by hand. Also called *hand grenades.*

HHQ—Higher Headquarters. The staff that supports the commander at any level.

Hooch—Slang for soldier's living quarters at the LZ, or just about anywhere else in Vietnam

Howitzers—Large cannons on wheels that can be towed behind a truck or jeep

HQ—Headquarters

Huey—UH-1 single-engine helicopter. A "slick" was unarmed and unarmored.

Humping—Carrying. "He had to hump his ruck twenty miles."

IBIS—Integrated Ballistic Identification System

ID—Infantry Division

IG—Inspector General

Indian Country—Anywhere there is the possibility of encountering the enemy, particularly when you are not close to support

JP-4—Common-use jet fuel. Essentially treated kerosene.

KIA—Killed in Action

Kit Carson Scout— Any of a variety of Viet Cong defectors who worked for US forces. Also called *Tiger Scout* or *Chiêu Hồi*.

Klick—Kilometer

KP duty—Kitchen patrol, i.e. washing dishes and peeling potatoes

Lay down a field—Lay down a field of fire. That is, shoot whatever is "that way."

Lima Charlie—In radio transmissions, this indicates you hear a transmission "loud and clear"

Longhouse—The largest building in a DeGa village. Some can extend to fifty meters long. They are shared living facilities.

LRFB—Little rubber fucking boat, the kind Special Forces use

LRRP—Long Range Reconnaissance Patrol. Pronounced "lurp."

LTC—Lieutenant Colonel, normally referred to in speech as simply Colonel

LTG—Lieutenant General, three-star general

Lurp—See *LRRP*

LZ—Literally the Landing Zone, but also the remote base often co-located with a fire base

M-14—Toe popper mine

M-14 rifle—A Korean War-era combat rifle, used widely in Vietnam, particularly by allies. Was replaced by the M-16.

M-16—The US soldier's rifle. Caliber 5.56mm.

M-18—See *Claymore*

M-203—Grenade launcher

M-406 grenade—Low-velocity grenade designed for use in the M-203

M-57—See *Clacker*

M-576 buckshot grenade—Low-velocity grenade designed for use in grenade launchers filled with twenty large encased metal pellets

M-60—a .30 caliber or 7.62mm machine gun. Also called *The Pig*.

M-7—A bandolier to hold claymore mines

M-79 grenade launcher—Single-shot, shoulder-fired break action launcher. Fires 40mm grenades. Also called *Thumper* and *Blooper*.

MA—See *Mechanical ambush*

MACV—Military Assistance Command Vietnam. Higher Headquarters during the Vietnam War.

MAJ—Major

Manioc—wine made from the cassava plant

MARS—Military Affiliate Radio System. DOD sponsored network of volunteer amateur radio operators to extend and enhance defense communications. Employed by soldiers to make exceedingly poor-quality phone calls back home.

Marsden matting—Heavy corrugated steel sheets, 120 x 15 inches. Used by combat engineers to create flat ground for everything from runways to camp enclosures.

ME—Medical examiner

Mechanical ambush—A booby trap which can actuate without any local assistance from armed forces. In a perfect world, once set, it works against the enemy. In practice it can kill and/or maim friendlies and non-combatants.

MEPS—Military Entrance Processing Station. Where soldiers first take the oath of office and enlist in the military.

MG—Major General, two-star general

Mimeograph machine—Sometimes called a stencil duplicator or inaccurately a "ditto machine," the mimeograph was a low-cost duplicator that worked by forcing ink through a stencil. The resulting copy came out blue and had a unique smell that to this day recalls elementary school to many people worldwide.

Moi—A highly derogatory Vietnamese word, literally meaning "savage." It was often used by Vietnamese soldiers against the DeGa.

MOS—Military Occupational Specialty code

Mouse duty—Slang for walking point. The first soldier in the formation. The position is notoriously dangerous due to the potential for ambush and/or tripping mines, i.e. finding "mouse traps." See *Point.*

MP—US Army Military Police

Mr. Charles—See *Charlie*

MSG—Master Sergeant

Nap of the earth—In tactical flying parlance, this meant flying just high enough, particularly in a helicopter, to miss the tops of the trees. It had the benefit of keeping the enemy from seeing you until it was too late to react, but the disadvantage of placing you in range of small arms fire.

NCO—Non-Commissioned Officer. Enlisted soldier in the rank of E-5 or above. NCOs are accorded additional leadership and supervisory responsibility.

NDP—Night Defensive Position

NIBIN—National Integrated Ballistics Identification Network

No joy—Radio terminology indicating, "I don't see it."

Nón lá—Conical grass hat worn by field workers and countless others in Vietnam

NVA regulars—Members of the North Vietnamese Army or Air Force

O-1 Bird Dog—A Cessna, high-wing, slow-moving light airplane for use in forward air control, that is, directing fast movers on where they should drop their bombs

OCME—Office of Chief Medical Examiner

OCS—US Army Officer Candidate School. Provides training to become a second lieutenant.

OD—Olive drab, the military shade of green

OJT—On-the-job training

P-38—A tiny folding can opener. A few came with each pack of C-rations so that soldiers could open the cans. The extras ended up as litter everywhere.

PA—Public address system; loudspeakers

PFC—Private First Class

PJs—Pajamas

Pluto Platter—Before Frisbees were Frisbees, they were called Pluto Platters

Point—The position of the first man in any sized unit on patrol. It can be dangerous since that man is the first to encounter booby traps or ambushes. It can be punishment, or it can be a spot of honor for the soldier with the best sense of what's going on. An attentive man walking point can save the platoon or the squad more than once. See also *Mouse duty*.

Popping smoke—Actuating a smoke grenade so that friendly forces can locate you. Different color smokes can send different messages. Also army slang for getting started or moving out, e.g., "The boss told us to pop smoke on your plan."

Prick 25— AN/PRC 25 portable radio-telephone transceiver. Contains vacuum tube technology and is heavy.

Prick 6—AN/PRC-6, a walkie-talkie-style portable radio

Purple Heart—A medal all military members get if they are wounded or killed in combat

PX—Post Exchange. Think small Walmart where they don't charge tax. The Army and Air Force Exchange Service is required by Congress to provide consumables to US armed forces worldwide, so even in the most remote locations there could be a tiny PX set up where soldiers could purchase a variety of amenities from shaving cream to chewing gum to a letter-writing kit.

R&R—Rest and Recuperation. Sometimes *Rest and Rehabilitation* or *Rest and Recovery*.

Ranger Joe's—An actual institution. Now a US Army and Law Enforcement supply superstore, Ranger Joe's began as a soldier supply establishment in Columbus, Georgia in 1963, off-post (outside Fort Benning) on Broadway (the central Columbus strip). The store proprietors were Paul Voorhees and his father, Jack. This was *the* location to purchase all the combat gear that the army didn't issue and that the Military Clothing Sales Store on Post did not sell.

Ranger tab—The Ranger tab is a US Army service school uniform decoration that signifies completion of US Army Ranger School, a course in small-unit combat tactics. Ranger School is considered a difficult rite of passage in the army. Graduates get a Ranger tab, which is worn on the upper shoulder of the left sleeve of all army uniform combinations. Rangers wear the tab for life.

Recondo School— Reconnaissance and Commando School. In

Vietnam, the LRRP finishing school, used to train soldiers who will engage deep in enemy-held territory.

Red Horse—US Air Force combat civil engineers

REMF—Rear Echelon Motherfucker. All combat support people in Nam were derided as REMFs by the small percentage of soldiers that were actually engaged in combat.

Ribbon rack—Rows of ribbons that military members wear on dressier uniforms. Some signify medals won, while others are awarded for mundane accomplishments like being a member of the Department of Defense.

ROK—Republic of Korea

ROTC—Reserve Officer Training Corps

RS bird—Resupply helicopter

R-T—Radio-telephone

RTO—Radio-telephone operator

Ruck (also rucksack)—Military backpack

S2—Company Intelligence Section

SACTO State—California State University at Sacramento

SFC—Sergeant First Class

SGM—Sergeant Major

Silver bird—The airplane that would fly you out of Vietnam. Also *big iron bird* and *silver freedom bird*.

SITREP—Situation Report

Slope—Highly derogatory term for just about any Asian, but especially those engaged in combat against US forces

SNAFU—Situation Normal, All Fouled Up. Soldiers often substitute an alternate word for the "F".

Snake-eaters—Special Operations troops

SOG—Special Operations Group

SP4—Specialist 4, also "Spec Four"

SPC—Specialist

SSG—Staff Sergeant

SSID—The Service Set Identifier in a computer network

Ta vak—coconut wine

TA-50—Table of Allowance #50. Refers to the web gear, belts, suspenders, vests, pouches, etc. that enable a soldier to carry a load of ammunition, water, rucksack, canteen, etc. Also called *load-bearing web gear*.

Tactical Operations Center—Central Command Post for the division, battalion, and company

Tally-ho—Radio terminology indicating, "I see it"

Task Force Oregon—A provisional, division-sized headquarters and organization. Replaced by elements of the Americal Division by 1968.

The World—The States. Home. Where the big iron bird would take you when your tour was over.

Thumper—See *M-79 grenade launcher*

***Tian* basket**—A fishing trap. Imagine a large wineglass shape woven from sticks and reeds that can be quickly placed over fish in shallow water. A hole in the small end of the trap enables easy capture.

Tiger Scout—See *Kit Carson Scout*

TOC—See *Tactical Operations Center*

Toe popper—See *M-14 mine*

Toring—A Co-Tu tribe or clan, normally bound by common locality in the same village

Tracers—Think lighted bullets; often set as every tenth round from a machine gun to assist the gunner in aiming. The downside of tracers is they give the enemy the location of the shooter. Also called *tracer rounds*.

Triple key—On the radio-telephone mic is a button you press to transmit. When you do so it creates a distinctive static noise on the receiving end. Soldiers would often pre-arrange to send a signal without voice. A single key of the mic might mean, "Got it," while a double key might mean, "What?" A triple key often signaled, "Ready," as in we are ready.

Tu es un vrai ami, comme un member de la famille. Nous ne t'oublierons jamas.—French for "You are a true friend, like a member of the family. We will never forget you."

Tung'tung—A Co-Tu tribal dance

UCMJ—Uniform Code of Military Justice. Penal code unique to the US Armed Forces in all services.

VC—Viet Cong. Việt cộng is a contraction of Việt Nam Cộng-sản, essentially, Viet communist; the National Liberation Front for South Vietnam.

Ville—The local village outside every US military installation anywhere in Asia

Warrant—Warrant Officer, often referred to as *the Warrant*.

WIA—Wounded in Action

Wilco—Radio talk meaning "Will comply"

Willy-Pete—White phosphorous. Burns hot with a white light. Used in illumination rounds.

WPA—Wi-Fi protected access, a computer encryption protocol

XO—In the army, the #2 behind the commander in all units company level and higher. ("Major Jones is the Battalion XO. He's the boss when the old man isn't around.") The XO has authority, but he/she does not have command authority under the UCMJ.

Yards—A US soldier slang term for Montagnards

THESE THANKS

The essence of all beautiful art, all great art, is gratitude.
—Friedrich Nietzsche

The basis for this story has been rattling around in my head since 1981. I was jogging from the Pentagon around the Washington, DC Mall. The Vietnam War Memorial was under construction. This was a time when you could walk right up to the site and talk to the workers. Veterans were already camping nearby and more than willing to talk. One of the guys seemed to have lost his marbles. I began imagining what his experience must have been. When I got back to work, I took a few notes. In 1985, while on a flight back to my home in Las Vegas, I jotted down the first outline of a concept for the story. I still have that scrap of paper.

Appreciation goes to my wife, Mary, for the time she spent helping me with my early drafts after wondering what I was doing in my office all the time. Mary was the first to read the draft manuscript from front to back. She helped me make the next version much better. She was last to read it before it went to editing and found mistakes when there were no more mistakes to be found.

Thanks to my son, Mark, for getting me started. I told him the basis of my idea in 2012. By early 2013 he effectively used guilt to remind me how I could divert time from other hobbies to writing. He was right. To the prospective writers out there, it's amazing how fast it rolls from your mind to your hands when you take the critical step of making a start. Telling Mark turned out to be one of the smartest moves I made. Without his nudge, I might never have started this journey.

Special thanks to my brother Chris who served in Vietnam as a lieutenant. He doesn't even know the value he added over more than a decade when I would ask him about this or that, then would add his perspectives on scraps of paper to a growing file. I called him to ask questions about what it was like on the ground. "Tell me about flak jackets." And when I was having problems with developing Rook's character, I asked, "How did you get along with your platoon sergeant?" Reply: "He was Hitler Youth." That simple response gave me a flood of ideas.

Thanks to Chris's son and my nephew, Christopher, who gave me so many excellent suggestions to make the work better that I'm sure a publisher could hire him as a copyeditor with no additional training.

I appreciate the time my brothers John and Mark and sister-in-law Pam put into providing me exceptional input. They found major and minor mistakes that everyone else missed.

Thank you Cody Kuehl. Cody is an amazing Denver-based artist. He was commissioned to provide original artwork for the cover. I loved what he did, but it did not resonate with my beta test readers. In the end, I went a different direction, but his beautiful painting of the boys is included inside the book in black and white.

Jenn Ervin-Stafford gets singular mention. The better half of the couple that includes my nephew Patrick, Jenn applied her master's degree in English Education to my work and found a thousand items needing attention.

Gary Miller was my college roommate many years ago. He not only graduated from the Naval Academy, and so had insight to some service academy rituals, but also served in the Marine Corps. Gary spent a career as an attorney. He found countless inconsistencies and helped me with creative ways to move the story along.

Thank you to Mary Jones. Mary is married to my nephew Regan who was a lieutenant and Marine Corps platoon commander in Iraq. Mary played the role of Christy as a spouse who has lived it. She read the story, then wrote the letter to Darren embedded in the text.

For structure, flow, and ideas to restructure, my hat is off to my old friend Ted Ferriter. A retired naval officer, Ted is one of those *constant readers* who knows it when he sees it. He was able to tell me where to put it so that others would see it as well.

One scene came from the mind of Brigadier General (USAF, retired) Joe Mudd. Joe is a direct descendant of Dr. Samuel Mudd, who was wrongly convicted of aiding John Wilkes Booth in the assassination of President Lincoln. As a teenager, Joe stood at the front door of his home when a military officer and chaplain arrived to tell the family their father had been killed in a helicopter crash. A long-time friend, Joe relived the experience as he related the details to me over the phone. It was not pretty. I hope I didn't drag up something better left forgotten. The essence of Joe's experience that day is captured in the pages of this book.

In no particular order, I offer my thanks to Saul Herrera

(Class of '91), Andy MacLean (Class of '95), and Tom Westfall (Class of '82), three West Point graduates who were able to describe traditions that I hoped hadn't changed any faster than the rest of the army. Sara Russ immigrated to the US from the Republic of Korea at the age of 12 speaking little English and is now a Colonel in the US Air Force. Thank you Sara for your expertise on Hangul, the written language of Koreans. Appreciation goes also to Steve Olivares, who is an expert military investigator. He helped me take ridiculous ideas about the processes of committing, investigating, and solving a crime, and spin them with enough realism to, hopefully, pull the wool over the eyes of all but seasoned readers. We'll see. Final wrap-up thanks goes to Deb Wolusky. When everything was finished and every mistake was corrected, Deb read through it and found dozens more. You need *readers* to do this for you. Deb is one.

Appreciation goes to Ben F. King. Ben is not a fictional character. In 1975 he published *A Field Guide to the Birds of South-East Asia, Covering Burma, Malaya, Thailand, Cambodia, Vietnam, Laos, and Hong Kong*. From 1966 to 1967 Ben lived in Bangkok, Thailand where he was conducting research on his forthcoming book. He met countless US servicemen who were visiting Bangkok on rest and recuperation (R&R). Ben graciously answered my initial contact. He had some poignant suggestions to make the narrative more real. Yes, there were soldiers who had their screws loose enough to observe nature while fighting for their lives.

It turns out that when your grandfather's sister marries, she starts a new branch of your family tree. My grandfather was Oliver

Sheldrick Howe. His sister Ethel Sarah married Harold Ernest Victor Burgess on 27 March 1913. Ethel is the great-grandmother of bestselling author—and my second cousin once removed—S. F. Burgess. I'd like to thank Sara and her talented husband John Richards of Jojosala Publishing for all the guidance they provided me on how to bring my novel to life. Perhaps their success will rub off.

Thanks to my editor, David Gatewood. As this is my debut novel I anguished over whether or not to employ a professional in this effort. I will never look back. Genius is a word I don't use lightly. David is a genius. He made a thousand suggestions. Every one made this story better.

Finally, my deepest gratitude goes to Elizabeth "Betty Gene" Bradford Hensick. Mrs. Hensick was my eleventh-grade English teacher at Vero Beach Senior High School. Sadly, she passed away, so she will never know the impact she had on me with a single statement after I'd turned in an assignment: "Richard, you can write." Teachers matter.

THIS AUTHOR

After serving a career in the United States Air Force, Richard Wilks Taylor and his high school sweetheart, Mary Lou Compton settled in Colorado Springs before finally relocating to Austin. The two keep busy tossing a Frisbee to the family border collie Bean, reading, putting miles on a tandem bicycle, walking, hiking, and traveling. Richard is an avid birder and geocacher.

Made in the USA
Coppell, TX
15 January 2021

48282597R00343